# *Royal Harlot*

## A NOVEL OF THE COUNTESS OF CASTLEMAINE AND KING CHARLES II

## SUSAN HOLLOWAY SCOTT

NAL NEW AMERICAN LIBRARY

New American Library
Published by New American Library, a division of
Penguin Group (USA) Inc., 375 Hudson Street,
New York, New York 10014, USA
Penguin Group (Canada), 90 Eglinton Avenue East, Suite 700, Toronto,
Ontario M4P 2Y3, Canada (a division of Pearson Penguin Canada Inc.)
Penguin Books Ltd., 80 Strand, London WC2R 0RL, England
Penguin Ireland, 25 St. Stephen's Green, Dublin 2,
Ireland (a division of Penguin Books Ltd.)
Penguin Group (Australia), 250 Camberwell Road, Camberwell, Victoria 3124,
Australia (a division of Pearson Australia Group Pty. Ltd.)
Penguin Books India Pvt. Ltd., 11 Community Centre, Panchsheel Park,
New Delhi – 110 017, India
Penguin Group (NZ), 67 Apollo Drive, Rosedale, North Shore 0745,
Auckland, New Zealand (a division of Pearson New Zealand Ltd.)
Penguin Books (South Africa) (Pty.) Ltd., 24 Sturdee Avenue,
Rosebank, Johannesburg 2196, South Africa

Penguin Books Ltd., Registered Offices:
80 Strand, London WC2R 0RL, England

First published by New American Library,
a division of Penguin Group (USA) Inc.

First Printing, July 2007
10  9  8  7  6  5  4  3  2  1

Copyright © Susan Holloway Scott, 2007
Readers Guide copyright © Penguin Group (USA) Inc., 2007
All rights reserved

 REGISTERED TRADEMARK—MARCA REGISTRADA

LIBRARY OF CONGRESS CATALOGING-IN-PUBLICATION DATA:

Scott, Susan Holloway.
   Royal harlot: a novel of the Countess of Castlemaine and King Charles II/Susan Holloway Scott.
   p. cm.
   ISBN: 978-0-451-22134-6
   1. Cleveland, Barbara Villiers Palmer, Duchess of, 1641–1709—Fiction.   2. Charles II,
King of England, 1630–1685—Fiction.   3. Mistresses—Great Britain—Fiction.   4. Great
Britain—Kings and rulers—Paramours—Fiction.   I. Title.
PS3560.A549R69 2007
813'.6—dc22          2006102816

Set in Minion
Designed by Elke Sigal

Printed in the United States of America

# Prologue

I was, I think, a gambler born.

I don't mean a few pennies at whist or ombre, a piddling hand of pasteboard cards. I speak of grander games, where the stakes are power, titles, great fortunes, even the heart of the King of England. Mark you, I'm no coward. I wouldn't have survived so long if I were. I know how to take my risks, and my vengeance, too, on those who dare to cross me. But how I did parlay my beauty and wit to rise so high: *that* was the game I chose, the game that became my life.

A gambler, yes. Yet as I sat in the hired carriage not far from the beach and the sea, I was not half so sure of my courage. I was only nineteen then, and I'd never yet strayed from England. The moonless sky was black and wet as pitch, the sea below it clipped with white-caps. The little sloop that was to take me across to Holland bobbed and tugged at her moorings, her crew scrambling about her narrow deck with their heads bent against the wind and spray as they made their last preparations to sail. It seemed a woeful vessel to trust with my life, as well as with the hopes of so many others.

"There's the signal, Barbara." Beside me in the carriage, my husband, Roger, pointed at the lantern held aloft by a sailor. "You must go to them now."

"I know." I retied the ribbons of my hood beneath my chin, not because they'd come loose, but to give my anxious fingers some occupation. My maidservant Wilson had already climbed down from the carriage, and was waiting for me in the rain outside. "Though I wish the sailors could wait until dawn."

"Oh, yes, so all the Commonwealth's navy can be sure to come and bid you a happy farewell." He sighed with exasperation. "You knew this wouldn't be a pleasure boat when you agreed to go, Barbara. It's too late now for you to change your mind."

"I've not changed my mind, Roger," I said, wishing he'd show a bit of concern for my welfare. "I only hoped the weather were less fierce, that is all."

"It's better this way." His pale face was serious in the carriage's half-light. "I've told you before that if you're caught, no one will come to your rescue, especially if you've no time to destroy the letters. You're far safer on a night such as this."

I nodded, smoothing my hand along the front of my bodice with a flutter of excitement. I *was* courting danger, no mistake. Hidden between my whalebone stays and my smock were letters of great importance to the Royalist cause, letters of support and promises of money for King Charles in exile. Sewn into my quilted petticoats were gold coins, too, destined for the royal pockets. Not once in my short life had there been a king upon the empty English throne. As Lord Protector, Cromwell, aided by his sour-faced followers, had seen to that with a long and hateful civil war, and had hidden away all the country's natural merriment beneath a gray pall of restrictive laws and false piety.

But now Cromwell was dead, and the government he'd created was falling in crumbling disarray. There were more and more of us around the country working for the restoration of the monarchy. Roger was thick in the middle of the plotting and planning, and well trusted by the Royalist leaders, which was why, as his wife, I'd been chosen as a courier. Yet the old laws were still in place, and if I were captured and the papers I carried discovered, I'd be damned as a spy and sent to the Tower until I was tried for treason. If convicted, I'd be executed, for there was little mercy to be found among the parliamentary judges for Royalists.

"You're the only one of us who could go, Barbara," Roger continued. "There's no one else who could be spared from our work in London."

"You mean there was no one else who was willing to sail to Flanders and risk the smallpox." I'd had the disease the year before, one of the rare folk to survive, and with my face left clear and unpocked, too. I could travel with impunity into any outbreak, such as the one now ravaging the city of Brussels.

"Your immunity is a consideration, of course," Roger admitted. "But that's only part of the reason you are being sent, Barbara. I shouldn't have to remind you of how important His Majesty's return is to my family's fortunes. I've personally given over a thousand pounds I could ill afford to support the king."

I'd grown vastly tired of hearing of this famous contribution, trotted out whenever Roger wished to puff his own importance. "You wish such praise for your precious thousand pounds, while you think nothing that I'm to risk my life for the same cause. A pretty balance, that."

His voice turned sharp, the way it often did when he criticized me. "You've been quite willing to enjoy the benefits of being Mistress Palmer. It's high time you returned the favor to my father and me, and prove for once you can be an obedient wife."

I looked away at the spray-dappled glass, refusing to let him open this old quarrel again. We'd so many of them between us for less than a year of marriage, most centered on what he perceived to be my excessive frivolity. Yet I was no better nor worse than the others among our Royalist friends. With so much unhappiness in our war-ravaged pasts and only uncertainty to our futures, we all took our pleasure wherever we found it, and gave no more thought when it was done. Roger had known when we wed that he hadn't been my first lover, any more than I had been his, and if he continued this harshness with me, I vowed he wouldn't be my last, either. Was it any wonder that I now lamented the grievous mistake I'd made, letting my mother push me from her house into such a marriage?

As if to prove it, Roger's lecture was continuing still. "I expect you to present my family's case to His Majesty, how much we've sacrificed by supporting him, and how we hope to be rewarded for our loyalty. Be agreeable to the king, Barbara, and make good use of every minute you have in his company."

"But I will, Roger," I said, and I meant it far more than my husband, so full of smug conceit, would realize. Even in impoverished exile, Charles Stuart was reputed to be everything a monarch should: tall, virile, intelligent, and charming. How could I not wish to break free of my husband's overbearing shadow to meet such a man?

"Obey me in this, Barbara," Roger warned, his misguided idea of a farewell between husband and wife. "I'll hear of it if you don't."

"Perhaps you'll hear of it sooner if I do." I opened the carriage door, my cloak whipping around me, driven as if from my own anticipation as by the wind. "Good-bye, Roger."

Four days of hard travel later, first by sea to Antwerp and then by poor Dutch roads, I was in Brussels, in the Spanish Netherlands. I recall little of this city beyond that the stone houses had strange false fronts and jagged roofs and that there were many Romish churches and statues, with golden crosses glinting high into the sky.

I sent my maidservant ahead, and repaired at once to His Majesty's lodgings. These were my orders, true, but I'd imagined our meeting so often, and in so many ways, that I was all afever to see him at last. Because I'd neither time nor opportunity to change my gown or dress my hair, as I would have wished, I prayed the king would interpret my disarray as proof of my urgency and loyalty to the crown. Besides, I was still of the winsome age where beauty needs little artifice or improvement, and I counted on the brisk glow that the sea air had given to my cheeks and how my dark chestnut hair had been whipped into curl.

And when I saw the meanness of the royal exile, I realized, too, how wrong it would have been to present myself in finery. I'd heard His Majesty was poor, but I'd no notion of how sadly reduced and impecunious his situation truly was. I was greeted by Sir Edward Hyde, the king's closest advisor and his lord chancellor, an older gentleman with a ruddy, veined face and watery pale eyes. While Hyde went to fetch the king, he put me to wait in a tiny chamber too humble for a country post inn in England.

Behind my hidden cache of letters, my heart thumped with anticipation. I'd scarce time to bite my lips to make them redder and to untie my cloak before I heard the door open behind me. I turned, and there, at last, was His Majesty.

*His Majesty.* Those two words couldn't begin to convey the impression he made upon me. He was standing before the fireplace, the tallest man I'd ever met, dark and handsome as a gypsy, with thick black hair to his shoulders and a curling mustache to match. Hardship and suffering made him look older than his twenty-nine years, as did his somber dress of a plain black doublet and breeches, worn and frayed along the hems. Yet there was a regal presence to him that withstood mere clothes or poverty, and if I'd seen him among ten score of other men, I would have known him at once as their king.

"Your Majesty, Mistress Palmer," Sir Edward was saying, though I scarce heard him, I was so dazzled by his sovereign master. "Mistress Palmer has come as an agent from your friends at home, sir."

I bowed my head and swept my curtsey, low and elegant. I had been born a Villiers, after all, and knew how such things were done.

"I trust you will be my friend, too, Mistress Palmer, as well as my agent," the king said, his smile warm and welcoming. "How generous of Palmer to share his wife with me!"

I smiled up at him, delighted that he'd say such a wicked, teasing thing to me. He was still a bachelor king, and it showed. "I am your friend and your agent, Your Majesty, and whatever else it pleases you for me to be."

"Whatever, Mistress Palmer?" he asked, chuckling at my boldness. He glanced down from my face to my tight-laced bodice as I rose, and his open interest made his black eyes bright as jet. "Would that all my subjects were so obliging."

"Forgive me, sir," Sir Edward interrupted with doleful resignation. "But might the lady be asked to present the letters?"

"Of course, Sir Edward," I murmured. "Of course."

I raised my chin and tipped my head to one side, so my eyes would be shaded by my lashes. If the king would wish to play the teasing game, then I would as well. "They've not left my person since clearing England, nor have the gold pieces."

I turned away for only a moment to pull the letters from beneath my stays, a show of modesty for Roger's sake. But it was the king who was smiling when I placed the letters into his hand, and I remembered with droll amusement how my husband had ordered me to be agreeable to His Majesty.

"They carry your heat," he observed, then passed the letters beneath his nose to discover my scent, too, upon them. "What fortunate letters."

Sir Edward cleared his throat. "You've brought gold for the cause as well, Mistress Palmer?"

"Oh, yes," I answered, not looking away from the king. "I've great sums sewn into my skirts."

That made the king laugh aloud. "We've never had such a resourceful agent, Sir Edward, have we?"

But Sir Edward looked more pained than amused. Clearly he'd been down this path with his royal charge before. For all that the king was reputed to be a man of sober habits, not given to excesses of drink or intemperate speech, he had a great fondness for beautiful women—a vice that seemed no vice at all for such a well-made, manly sovereign.

"I must urge caution, sir," he warned. "Pray be mindful of your precious health, and the risk of the smallpox so much in the city."

"But I've had the smallpox, Sir Edward," I said cheerfully, never so pleased to have survived that oft-fatal disease. "His Majesty won't take it from me."

"And so, Sir Edward, have I, as you must recall, and so there's no danger at all." The king handed the older gentleman the letters, as much as dismissing him. "Perhaps you should begin reading these, while I tend to the gold."

Yet once we were alone, the king's mood turned more serious.

"I thank you, Mistress Palmer," he said softly as he came to stand closer before me. "By coming here, you've risked much danger for my cause."

I smiled up at him. "You've risked more for England."

"For England." His dark eyes filled with melancholy pride. "Did your family follow mine?"

I should have spoken of the Palmers then, as Roger had bidden, but instead it seemed more natural to speak of my own family's sorrows.

"My father was Lord Grandison, sir," I said, "and in your father's service he was killed during the assault on General Prior's fort at Bristol. I was not two years old, and never knew him. My mother's fortune was soon after confiscated, and she and I together were left paupers, to manage as we could."

"I am sorry," he said, sharing my sadness. There was no need to mention his own losses to Cromwell's evil war. The awful litany was well known to his followers: his father, Charles I, tried and beheaded, his mother in penniless exile in France, his brothers and sisters scattered throughout the courts of Europe, his home and property destroyed, his rightful kingdom torn from him.

Strange to think how much alike we were, this king and I, each of us without fathers or homes or anything of value beyond what we carried inside ourselves. Strange to think, too, how such suffering could be shared, just as desire could become a remedy for easing that same pain.

Even for a gambler born.

He cradled my face in his hand, his fingers warm against my cheek and jaw. "So you're a Villiers. That makes us distant relations, doesn't it?"

"Cousins, sir," I whispered, and dared to touch my hand to the royal person. In every way, so great a prize would be worth every risk. "Though far removed, cousins still."

"Then kiss me, sweet cousin," he said, his dark face coming close over mine. "Kiss me now."

# Chapter One

"This is the house, miss," called the driver of the hackney carriage as he climbed from his box. "Was they expecting you?"

"Oh, yes." Eager as only a fifteen-year-old can be, I didn't wait for his help but hopped down boldly to the dusty street on my own, still clutching the crumpled paper with my mother's address.

Here was London, London at last! I gazed about at the close-packed houses and the tall square tower of St. Paul's, my eyes as wide as tea dishes and my mouth gaping like a fish's. What else could I do, truly? I'd spent all of my short life tucked away in Suffolk for safekeeping, first with a nursemaid, then with a country woman my mother had paid to keep me from trouble, and little else. I was plump and sleek as a young wood-pigeon, and with as little cleverness as that bird, too. Though most who knew me later would never credit it, I came to London as innocent as any other country lass who's plucked up from the tavern stage by a cunning bawd to break and school for brothel work.

But on Ludgate Hill that sunny afternoon, there was no waiting bawd to sell me into the fleshly trade for profit. My own mother would do well enough for that.

Eagerly I presented myself at the doorway, shaking the dust of the road from my best stuff petticoat. My mother's infrequent letters always lamented her constant lack of funds, and how far down in the world she had tumbled since the poor king had been beheaded by

Oliver Cromwell's followers and the Protectorate had taken to perse-cuting all good Royalists like us.

I'd understood, or thought I had. No extra money for ribbons or sweets ever came with those letters. I was assured of her distant love, but never felt or saw the proof. Even deep in Suffolk, I'd spent my childhood alone beneath the pall of Cromwell's Eastern Association, those misguided dour folk who had first raised the parliamentary army against the crown. England had been torn by civil war for most of my short life; I knew no other way. I'd been taught to loathe this parliamentary army, the ones who'd killed my father when I'd been scarce more than a babe, and caused my mother to leave me behind when she'd wed again.

Yet while I'd heard how the bulk of my mother's great wealth and lands had long since been seized by the government, she and my stepfather—who was also by blood my uncle, having been my father's cousin—were still the second Earl and Countess of Anglesea. To my wide country eyes, their London home seemed large and handsome, with white stone steps and more window glass than I'd ever seen in any house. The maidservant who finally opened their glossy painted door was dressed far better than I, her skirts smartly pinned back from her petticoat to display green thread stockings.

"Please tell Lady Anglesea that I am arrived," I said, smiling wide and squinting in the sun.

The maid kept the door half-closed, looking down her nose at my untrimmed kerchief and flat chip hat. "What name?"

"Miss Barbara Villiers," I said proudly. "Her Ladyship's only daughter."

With reluctance the maidservant finally opened the door wide enough to admit me and the driver with my traveling trunk. I paid him with my last shillings and tucked my empty purse away into my pocket while the maidservant went to fetch my mother. I was left alone in the hall, my heart thumping with anticipation. I'd not seen my mother in four years, the last time she'd come to visit me in Suf-folk, and this lack of welcome worried me.

"This way, miss," the maidservant said as she returned and bid me follow her up the stairs. "The footman shall see to your trunk."

Uncertainly I stood in the doorway to my mother's chamber. Though it was afternoon, she was still abed, sitting up against the bolsters with a peeled orange in a blue-and-white porcelain dish in her hand and a small black spaniel curled asleep on the coverlet beside her. The bed's embroidered hangings had been turned up into swags for the day, and the two tall-backed chairs beside the bed showed that my mother was in the habit of receiving guests in this fashion. Her fair hair was arranged in stiffened curls, spilling from a small lace cap, and her blue satin jacket, fastened before with three pink bows, was banded at the sleeves and throat with rich brown fur. Even here in bed, pearls like fat dewdrops glistened at her ears, with more pearls around her pale throat.

"Come, Barbara, and greet me properly," she said, setting the dish beside her on the coverlet as she offered her cheek for me to kiss. "There's nothing to be gained by being shy, especially with your own mother."

"Good day, madam," I said as I curtseyed prettily, the way I'd been taught. I then stepped forward to the bed to kiss her dutifully, noticing how she smelled of the orange, and how the pink of her cheek seemed to sit on the surface of her skin.

"You're much larger than I recall," she said, taking my hand to hold me near so she could study me. "Like a dairymaid. I suppose that comes of so much cream and eggs. At least you've all your teeth."

I pulled my hand away. "I'd always judged it better to have them than not."

"Now, miss, don't be pert," she warned. "You're strong and lusty in the country manner, true, but gentlemen will see that as a promising sign for breeding. We must put more boning and a wider busk into your corsets to narrow you, and then I'll have my maid lace you more tightly to give you a suitable waist. Take down your hair, so I might see it."

I loosened the ribbons of my hat, unpinned the high knot of my braid, and with my fingers pulled the plait apart and shook my hair over my shoulders and to my waist. Surely she'd find no fault here: my hair was deep shining chestnut, thick and curling.

"It was much lighter when you were a babe." She reached out and captured a lock, rubbing it gently between her fingers. Her father—my grandfather—had been a famous merchant in the City of London, trading silks and spices to great profit, and surely the method of my mother's considered appraisal of my hair must have come from his mercer's touch. "This is Villiers hair, like your father's, and your eyes—turn toward the window, child, so I might judge the color."

Obediently I turned my face toward the leaded glass casement. My eyes were often remarked, so dark a blue that they were mistook for black, and framed with thickets of dark lashes unlike my hair.

"As I thought," she pronounced as she reached once again for the dish with the orange. "That's more of your Villiers legacy, Barbara, and precious little Bayning. The first duke had those same rare eyes, and look how far they carried him."

Sheltered as I'd been, even I knew of that first duke: my notorious great-uncle, George Villiers, the first Duke of Buckingham. A most beautiful youth at the court of King James I, he'd used his charm and grace to win the favor of the slobbery old pederast king. I'd overheard tales of my uncle and his scandalous actions when my elders thought I wasn't listening, and learned how much he'd been hated yet envied in his time, and how even now, thirty years after he'd been killed, he was still so reviled that his murderer was lauded a hero. But I also knew that through his beauty, my uncle had raised himself to a dukedom, and his family—*my* family—to power and influence that continued now with the second duke, in exile on the Continent with his friend, the young King Charles II.

Yet no one before had dared tell me that I favored this fantastical uncle so, and the notion startled me both with its possibilities and its hazards.

"Do not look so shocked, Barbara," my mother said, her voice brittle. "I cannot provide you with a suitable fortune with which to attract a husband. No one will care for the Villiers name now, not when the most desired brides are the daughters of Cromwell's ill-born generals. You must pray that your beauty makes some suitable gentleman desire you in spite of your poverty. Why else do you think I've brought you here to town?"

"I—I thought you wished to see me," I stammered through my disappointment. "I thought you wished my company."

"Your *company*?" repeated my mother with scathing incredulity as she bit into another slice of the orange. "You're fifteen, Barbara. When I was your age, your father had already fought a duel with Lord Newark for the right to my hand, and I was wed to him before my next birthday."

Her smugness, and my own dismay, made me speak more frankly than was perhaps wise. "You were worth twenty thousand pounds a year. You've told me that yourself. That's why you'd gentlemen fighting over you."

Her pale eyes sparked. "You would fault me for having no fortune left to lavish on you? Foolish child! Have you any notion where that money has gone?"

"Any *child* knows that." I flipped my loose hair over my shoulders. "Because we've followed the rightful cause of the king and Father died fighting for it, we've been treated like traitors, and all our estates confiscated by the low villains of Cromwell's Parliament."

"What a tidy explanation." She took another slice of the orange, plucking the white membrane from the tender fruit with vengeful precision. "But only half the tale, you see. What you, *child,* do not know is that the slow rapine of my estate was begun by your own father, long before Cromwell's war. Your father made loans to his highblown friends, secured by their property. Ten thousand to the Earl of Cleveland! Another eighteen thousand to the Duke of Lennox! It was nothing to your father, yet less than nothing to those fine friends. For years I've tried to sue for repayment, but where do I take my case when there's no longer a House of Lords? Where's my recourse when the estates that were my security have been sequestered by another pack of thieves?"

She bit into the orange as if the fruit itself were those negligent lords, heedless of the sweet juice that sprayed and stained the silk of her jacket.

"But that is not all, Barbara," she said. "Consider all the money I've tossed away upon those drabs who raised you in the country. I can get nothing from those others, but you—you owe it to me, yes, to make as favorable a match as you can."

I'm certain she intended this speech to make me feel suitably contrite and docile. I hadn't known that my father had made such loans against her dowry, reason enough, I thought, not to let my fortunes depend entirely upon my husband. Perhaps if she'd seen fit to offer me so much as a slice of her orange and a smidgen of kindness, I might have gone that way with her. But instead the obligation she wished to instill in me turned against her, and made me feel not filial duty but rebellion.

"Perhaps I do not wish to wed so soon, madam," I said tartly. "Perhaps I'd rather enjoy the pleasures of the city before I am saddled with some tedious husband."

"The pleasures of the city are vastly overrated, Barbara," she said with acid on her tongue. "If you do not take care, you will find those 'pleasures' will bring you nothing but sorrow and pox."

I turned away without her permission, and in unhappy petulance went to stand before the grate. There was no fire, it being a warm day, but over the mantel hung a framed engraving that at once caught my interest.

A melancholy portrait of the martyred King Charles I was flanked by smaller ovals with his two elder sons, James, the Duke of York, and Charles, now King Charles II; pictures such as Royalists would keep in secret, for such shows of loyalty were banned by parliamentary law.

James was comely enough, with a winning smile and fair, flowing hair, but it was his brother the king who both fascinated and attracted me. Charles was a young man not so much older than myself, with coal-black hair and dark, heavy-lidded eyes that were more Italianate than English. I had yet to kiss a man, or have a kiss bestowed upon me, yet still I intuited the sensuality in this young king's full lips, and the warmth that Nature must have granted with his regal blood.

"I wish there were still a royal court in London," I said wistfully, more to the engraved king than to my mother.

"I suspect you'll find mischief enough here, Barbara, without courtiers to lead your way." My mother sighed crossly behind me, and I heard the clatter of her setting her now-empty dish on the table beside the bed, as if she wished to discard me, too. "I'll see that you're properly dressed as fits your rank, and taught the skills that seem so sadly lacking in you. Then Lord Anglesea and I will introduce you into company, with the hope that you will attract a suitable attachment, a gentleman with not only the proper political connections to help us but a fortune as well."

"I am ready, madam," I said, turning to face her. I was so eager, so confident, to start this new life, I was almost giddy with it. Not even my mother's ill humor could tamp my spirits. "For whatever London may offer, I'm ready."

As summer progressed, I began to take my place in this new world, as boldly and as bravely as any voyager exploring new countries to stake beneath his own flag. To anyone who recalled the old London, before the war, this new version under Cromwell's rule must have seemed but a withered, empty shell. My mother and my uncle complained of it often, as if all the deprivations and changes had been ordered specifically for their torment.

The playhouses were long since shuttered, puppet shows and traveling acrobats banned, and the gardens made for pleasure empty. Music was forbidden, from the orchestras and singers who had entertained the court to the great choirs in the churches. Most celebrations and holidays—May Day, Christmas, Twelfth Night, St. Valentine's Day—were deemed either pagan or papist, and likewise forbidden. Books and papers were strictly censored, and nothing could be printed without a special government license. The grand houses that had belonged to the noblest families of the country had been confiscated and given to Cromwell's generals instead.

Even the great cathedral of St. Paul's on Ludgate Hill, near to where we lived, had been sadly ravaged, its colored glass windows smashed, its hangings and high altar destroyed, and its long nave converted to a stable for use by the parliamentary cavalry.

But to me, with nothing but the tedium of Suffolk for comparison, London seemed an endless string of diversions and amusing company. We Royalists lived beneath the surface of Protectorate London, like clever foxes tunneling our burrows beneath the fields, and so long as we kept to ourselves and drank to His Sacred Majesty's health and return to the throne out of their hearing, we escaped the government's reprobation. This wasn't so very hard. At that time London had nearly 300,000 citizens, behind only Paris and Constantinople in size, and as many before me had discovered, it's always easier to keep from notice in a crowded city than in a country village.

If the playhouses were closed, then the players now gave their performances in the great chambers of private houses, for a smaller, select audience. Musicians who had once performed at royal masques and other palace entertainments now gave their concerts for us. We attended fine suppers or visited the more genteel dining houses. We rode through the parks in carriages or along the river in boats. We played every manner of card game: whist, ombre, bassett. We even attended church, and flirted shamelessly with one another over our pews, ignoring the fact that even our Anglican prayer books had been banned by the Commonwealth.

There was, of course, a tattered melancholy to our pleasures. The world seemed changed forever for people of our rank, with little hope of it changing back in our favor. Even the slightest attempts at rebellion had been instantly quelled by the Commonwealth's forces—most recently the sad small uprising at Salisbury led by Colonel Penruddock—and were followed by such punitive measures as the Decimation Tax, a 10 percent levy against the income of anyone with Royalist leanings.

Yet our despair also bound us together. I quickly made friends among the young Royalists of noble families, many of whom, like me, had lost both fathers and fortunes in defense of the king.

Over that first summer, my mother concentrated on improving me and polishing away my country manners. I was taught to dance to develop my grace, which I enjoyed, and given lessons upon the virginals, which I did not. We spoke French at meals so I would learn that language. My plain stuff gowns were replaced with lutestrings and satins, and my hair was cropped shorter around my face, the better to curl into tendrils and lovelocks against my cheeks. I grew in height and in slenderness, while my breasts blossomed to a more womanly fullness.

And by early autumn, when Philip Stanhope, Earl of Chesterfield, returned to London from France, I was ripe to fall headlong into love for the first time.

"Who is that gentleman, Anne?" I whispered behind my fan. "He is most splendidly handsome, don't you think?"

Beside me, Lady Anne Hamilton's green eyes widened with delicious interest. Lady Anne was one of the four daughters of the Duke of Hamilton, but more important, the dearest of my new London friends, one whose wicked laughter alone could cheer me from the deepest doldrums. She had a frizz of blond curls and wide-set eyes, and together we made an eye-catching pair on account of being so opposite. Though we were close in age, she had been in the town much longer than I, and I learned of many things in her company that doubtless my mother would wish I hadn't.

Now Anne leaned close to whisper in my ear. "Why, that is Lord Philip Stanhope, the Earl of Chesterfield. And yes, yes, by all that's holy, he *is* the most handsome gentleman in this room."

I nodded in agreement, watching this same young gentleman as he stood chatting with a group of other men. We had gathered here at Lady Walthrop's house for the eventual purpose of dancing, but for now, while the musicians readied their instruments in the next chamber, we were all occupied by observing one another. I knew most everyone else in the room save this Chesterfield, and I forgot them all while studying him.

He was beautifully dressed in the French fashion, with many elegant ribbons and love knots strewn across his doublet and sleeves, and a fawn-colored satin cape tossed over one shoulder with disarming carelessness. His auburn hair flowed over his shoulders in a profusion of curls, and his dark eyes showed both wit and spirit.

"He's already been widowed once, and only twenty-three," Anne continued in my ear. "And he tried to wed General Fairfax's daughter Mary—a plain, sorry creature, but vastly well placed—and though the banns had been cried twice for them, she finally ran off and married the Duke of Buckingham instead."

"My cousin George Villiers?" I whispered with surprise. I'd heard of this before, of course, for abandoned bridegrooms made too good a tale to forget, but I'd imagined the jilted fellow to be some homely scarecrow, not this lovely fellow, and my estimation of my cousin's political audacity—as well as his amatory skills, to win the heart of such an influential lady—rose even higher. "She chose George instead?"

"She did," Anne said soundly. "I've heard poor Chesterfield's now come to London to find diversion from his broken heart."

"To lose both a wife and a bride must be most grievous to a gentleman," I murmured. "No wonder he needs diversion and consolation."

"Take care, Barbara," my friend warned. "Lord Chesterfield is charming, yes, but also rash and reckless. He drinks and plays and games and swears dreadful oaths. They say he's killed at least five men through dueling, and claimed a wreath of ladies' hearts. Why, he boasts of making love to six or seven at once!"

"In the same bed?" I asked archly. "He's every right to boast of that, if he's able to please so many ladies like a heathen sultan with his harem."

"Hush." Anne giggled. "You shouldn't speak so, Barbara. You know not even the most debauched gentleman could manage *that*."

"I know nothing of the sort," I said, pretending worldliness. "And neither do you, Anne."

I grinned behind my fan. In the time since I'd come to town, I'd caught the eyes of several gentlemen, and permitted a few trifling favors, more from youthful curiosity than anything else. In turn none had captured my lasting interest as a possible husband, least of all the somber young men proposed by my mother. Yet still Anne and I prattled endlessly to one another of love and longing and gentlemen, and of how much we wished to have charming lovers of our own rather than to be bound by the demands of a single grumpy husband.

This was brash talk for green virgins of a scant fifteen years, I know, but common enough in our Royalist society. We all had too much time with too little to occupy us, our shabby futures stretching endlessly before us without purpose. England's leader was the Lord Protector, a man we'd been taught to hate as our enemy and regard as our inferior. To mock Cromwell's Puritan ways was perceived as a way of supporting our exiled king, a kind of perverse loyalty, as well as a ready excuse for the most outrageous behavior. How could any mother's warnings counter that?

Now I glanced back at my friend. "Tell me true, Anne. Is Lord Chesterfield so dangerous that you yourself would turn away if he smiled upon you?"

But Anne only sighed, then laughed behind her fingers, as if this were the most preposterous question imaginable. "If Lord Chesterfield would smile upon me, Barbara, then I would melt like warm butter at his feet."

"Warm butter, hah," I scoffed, knowing our game. "If he but smiled at *me,* why, I'd freeze him with an icy glance, and make him come beg me for more."

"You would not." Anne's eyes fair popped from her head. "Not with him, you wouldn't."

"Watch me, then," I said, and furled my fan against my palm. I'd heard it said once that my cousin George could draw every eye in a room toward him, simply by the power of the Villiers charm alone. Since then I'd aspired to the same effect, and practiced before the looking-glass whenever I was alone. Now this would be my test, and with a formidable foe, too.

I raised my chin and let my shoulders soften, and composed my features into an expression that I hoped was mysterious yet seductive. Contriving some errand in the next room, I set my course across the chamber near the cluster of men, giving my skirts an extra twitch as I glided past Lord Chesterfield.

"What goddess is this, to venture so near to mortal earth?" He turned to face me, his expression one of frank admiration. "Tell me your name, fair one, so I might worship you properly."

"If I were to make my name so common, then how should I remain a deity?" I paused, and parried, striving to mimic the same elegant banter of the older ladies. "How could I keep from being sullied by that same mortal soil?"

"What if I were to kneel before the altar of your beauty?" he countered, sweeping his hand before him to indicate where he'd kneel, right there on the well-swept mortal soil of Lady Walthrop's parlor floor. "Would that be worshipful enough to earn the honor of my goddess's name?"

Behind him one of the other men sniggered. "It's Barbara Villiers, Chesterfield."

"Miss Villiers, then." Recognition lit his eyes, as almost always happened when others heard my family's name. "I'm honored, dear Goddess Villiers."

I tipped my head a fraction in cool acknowledgment, though my cheeks grew hot against my will. No doubt he'd lay the fault for his jilt at my cousin's door; what if he shared me in that blame?

"What, so chill a greeting, my sweet deity?" he asked, taking a step closer to me. "No warmth to spare for me, your humble supplicant?"

I granted him the hint of a smile, though in truth I found him even more pleasing at this range than from afar. How much more manly he was than the callow youths who'd tried to court me!

"No more acknowledgment for my devotions, my goddess?" he asked, and pressed his hand over his heart, a practiced gesture, but one that in my youth still thrilled me.

"Worship should be its own reward, my lord," I said with what I hoped was airy disdain. "A faithful follower expects nothing more."

"But the most faithful of worshippers expects to be rewarded." Before I'd realized it, he'd hooked his arm into mine with the audacity of a privateer with a new-captured prize, and was leading me away to his port. "Come with me, Goddess Villiers, and let me sing a paean or two to your ears alone."

His boldness startled me. It was one thing to play this game before others, but I worried that my novice's skills would not be equal to his if we were alone. Yet I was likewise too flattered by his attentions to refuse him entirely, and thus I made myself smile, as if such suggestions were commonplace to me.

"To Lady Walthrop's gallery, then," I said, pointing with my fan. "There, and no farther."

He didn't wait, but swept me away, and my last glimpse of my friend Anne's face showed amazement, and envy, too, that I'd succeeded in beguiling such a gentleman on her challenge.

The gallery ran across the front of the house, with windows full of moonlight down one side and along the other old portraits of grim-faced ancestors deemed too ugly and out of fashion to display anywhere else in the house. These, then, would be my guardians, such as they were, and yet as I gazed up at Lord Chesterfield beside me, I did not doubt or falter.

"You're new to London, aren't you, my goddess?" he asked, stopping beneath one of the portraits, a cross-eyed fellow with a beard as pointed as a Jesuit's. "I would have known you otherwise."

"I'm not so new as that," I said, unwilling to paint my youth quite so openly. Most gentlemen believed me older than my years, and I hoped Lord Chesterfield did as well. "Rather it's you who's new returned to England."

"Ah, a clairvoyant goddess," he said, and laughed, displaying his fine, even teeth by the moonlight. "Yes, my affairs did take me away from England for a time, but then I was also able to meet with His Majesty in Brussels, and reassure him of my loyalty."

"His Majesty!" I exclaimed, recalling at once the engraving of the handsome young sovereign that hung in my mother's bedchamber. "What is he like? How does he fare so far from home?"

Chesterfield's face turned solemn. "His situation is very grave, and most reduced, and enough to break the hearts of those still loyal to the crown. His Majesty's clothes are shabby and lacking, as are those of his attendants, and he is entirely dependent on the gifts and kindness of others for his very food. They say he's so low that he can dine each noon upon but a single dish, and only one of meat every seven-day at that."

"How dreadful!" I cried, and quickly looked down at His Lordship's fine dress. "Were you able to give him comfort, my lord, a gift, however slight, to ease his distress?"

"Alas, my pockets were near as empty as his," he said with a fine show of sorrow. "I'd hoped, of course, that I'd soon be able to make a better offering, but those prospects were dashed."

"Your wedding," I said, assuming a measure of remorse for my cousin's theft of his bride. "I'm most sorry for that, my lord. To lose your beloved to another so close to the wedding—"

"What was beloved was not the lady but her estate," he said with surprising frankness. "Because her father's General Fairfax, Cromwell's hero at Naseby, she would bring connections beyond measure, as well as having my lands restored to me. For that I was willing to take her plain muffin of a face, but she tossed me over for your cousin."

"I'm sorry, my lord," I said again, for lack of anything else. "I'm sorry."

"Why should you be, my goddess, when it's scarce your fault?" He looped one arm familiarly around my waist, taking no notice of how I stiffened in return. "No, the same did happen to me with old Nolly's daughter, too. She was as good as promised to me, with a dowry of twenty thousand pounds and a plum military appointment, but at the last I decided I couldn't stomach the lady. She wanted Warwick's grandson, anyway. It's trade, sweet, not love. You should know that as well as I."

I nodded, thinking of the dour young men my mother had tried to steer my way. "There's no love in any of it. My mother wishes to marry me to some ugly old general or his son to repair *her* fortunes."

"Exactly so," he murmured, idly reaching out to stroke his finger across my cheek. "And precisely why we poor noble folk must steal love where we may. Which branch of that rotten old Villiers tree had the good fortune to drop you, my goddess?"

"My father was Lord Grandison," I said, breathless from that tiny caress. "My mother is now wed to Lord Anglesea. She wishes I weren't so old, and scarce wishes to admit me, for she prefers people to believe she's still too young to have me for a daughter. But she *is* old, my lord. She paints her face. She thinks I don't realize it, but I've seen her maid mixing the Venetian ceruse beside the ground cochineal in the morning."

"My, my, but that's damning," he whispered, deftly turning me a fraction so that we were standing to one side of a tall, japanned cabinet, hidden from the sight of the others. With his fingertips, he turned my face upward, so all I could see was his handsome face with the moonlight behind it. "Ceruse and cochineal! May you never be so old as that, sweet."

He kissed me then, which I'd been expecting, and thrust his tongue into my mouth, which I had not. Nor did I anticipate how swiftly he managed to disengage my breasts from my bodice for his handling, the air cool on my suddenly bare skin.

I should have done what I'd been taught and pushed him away. I was a noblewoman, a lady by birth. I was a *Villiers*. But as soon as my first shock passed at being so used by him, I realized I liked what he was doing. His tongue, his touch, gave me a startling pleasure, and the more I answered him back in kind, the more pleasure I felt.

"Ah, what a little minx you are," he whispered roughly, now lavishing kisses on my throat and lower, to my breasts. "You're a Villiers, aye, with sin bred into your blood."

"What—what do you mean, my lord?" I stammered as I writhed against him, not really caring if he answered me or not, so long as he did not stop this rare delight.

"I mean that you're made for love," he said in a low, wicked whisper that delighted me as much as any caress. "You were made for me, goddess."

In the room behind us, one of the men laughed with raucous, drunken enthusiasm. The sound was enough to remind me of the danger of what I was doing. It was not so much the act itself that worried me, but that I'd be caught and sent back to the country before I could meet Lord Chesterfield again.

I slipped free of him, as hard for him to grasp as a spring eel.

"No more, my lord," I said, my words torn to a breathy whisper by my desire. "Not here."

"Then tell me where, goddess," he demanded. "Don't leave me like this, perishing from want of your love and regard."

His words came so earnest and fervent that I felt a heady rush of power, knowing I'd inspired such feelings in such a gentleman. I'd yet to cover my breasts, still shamelessly bare above my disheveled bodice, for I delighted in how he could not look away. He scarce knew me, yet already he loved me, and my own heart swelled in instant response.

Ah, ah, is there anything more foolish, or more eager to be broken, than the heart of a young maid?

"You must prove yourself to me, my lord," I said breathlessly as I put my bodice back to rights. "Then—oh, then!—I'll grant what you desire most."

He pursued me with rare ardor for the rest of that year, with great protestations of devotion and loyalty whenever we met. He sent me posies tied with ribbons, and letters filled with fine poetry of his own device. Even when he was far away from London, tending to his estates in Derbyshire, he would make certain that he remained in my constant thoughts.

I forgot the wreath of other ladies' hearts that he freely wore like some ancient victor, and blinded myself to any sense of calculation in how expertly he stirred my passions. I refused to consider that he might have selected me as a tool of vengeance upon my family, and against my cousin who had stolen his prize of Fairfax's daughter. All I chose to comprehend was that the Earl of Chesterfield loved me, and I him, and because love had been a most rare commodity in my life, I believed him.

Before long I'd slipped my mother's traces for an afternoon, and made the fateful journey across the town to his lodgings in Lincoln's Inn Fields.

"Almost there, my goddess." Philip hurried me up the stairs to his lodgings, past the baleful watch of his landlady. I was beside myself

with wine and excitement, and so stirred from the caresses he'd lavished upon me in the carriage that I was as tame as a hen who lays her
own neck upon the chopping block.

As it was, I scarce waited for him to latch the door before I threw
my arms around his shoulders, pressing my yearning young body
against his.

"My dearest, dearest Philip," I sighed, raining kisses across his
face. "I would follow you anywhere, from farthest India to Africa's
burning sands!"

"All that I care is that you've followed me here, my fair goddess,"
he said, his arms curling round my waist. "My own Barbara."

He kissed me with such purposeful passion that it stole my breath,
and he drew me close to his body so I could feel the steely length of his
cock within his breeches. That should have been enough to warn me
away—oh, most fearsome instrument of my ruin!—but he'd brought
me along so well in his seduction over the last weeks that instead it
only served to feed my desire. He pushed me back onto the bed and
climbed atop me, giving me only a moment to accustom myself to the
feel of a man's weight and force.

There were no honey'd words now, no tender caresses. I'd let him
come too far to retreat, even if I'd wished it. Instead he swiftly freed
his cock from his breeches and shoved aside my petticoats, baring me
to his attack. I'd a blurry awareness of the rough woolen of his breeches
rubbing against the inside of my thighs and his fingers parting my
quivering virgin flesh.

Mind you, I was but fifteen, and not nearly so worldly as I'd pretended to be. With no knowledge of a man's strength or urgency at
such times, I panicked and tried to wriggle backward across the bed.
But he'd pinned me fairly with his knees on my skirts, and with three
quick thrusts the thing was done, and he was buried deep within my
poor little nest.

"So tight you are, my goddess," he muttered, and groaned as he
moved within me. "Fuck me now, Barbara, hard."

I squeezed my eyes shut as if to hide away, so overwhelmed was
I by my plight. I now possessed what I'd craved for so long, yet I'd no

notion what to make of it, or how to do what Philip ordered of me. What had become of the sweet blessing he'd promised, the joy he'd sworn would be greater than that which he'd given me with his fingers and tongue?

"What is it?" He pushed himself up on his arms to look down at me. "Does it pain you?"

I shook my head. I couldn't answer more from fear I'd weep and seem the sorriest fool. Besides, it wasn't the bodily pain of my ravished virginity—to be honest, we'd dallied so much before that I doubted there'd been much of that left—but the dull ache of disappointment, and that would be far too hard to explain.

Yet still he guessed, either from tenderness for me or more likely from experience with all the other maids he'd undone.

"The worst is over, I vow," he said, huffing and puffing as if he'd just run a league uphill. "Now look, Barbara. Look, and see what you've done to me."

Slowly I opened my eyes. Driven by the same curiosity that had brought me this far, I slipped my hand between us to touch the place we were joined. I was soft and slick where I stretched around him, while he was hard, and sticky with my juices, in the most wondrous contrast imaginable. Pleasure shot through me as I touched myself, taking me so by surprise that I gasped and rose up with it, twisting like a cat.

"Ah, there, there, you hot little jade," Philip said, gasping as well. "I knew you were born for this."

And so, it would seem, I was. Whether from my own inclinations or because of my wanton Villiers blood, I found my rapture that first time with Philip, and ever after. With the destruction of my maiden's gate, any shred of reserve vanished, and my wanton desires spilled out in a feverish rush. The more times I lay with him, the more I craved. I was delighted with my new knowledge, and why not? I now had a lover, a handsome, daring gentleman for my first prize, and to me that was worth a dozen virginities.

I likewise displayed a gift for the more adventurous amatory arts. Philip—for since I shared his bed, he now granted me leave to call him by his Christian name—meant it as a shining compliment, which I accepted as readily as the lessons he took care to teach me. In addition to instructing me in how best to please him, he showed me how to please myself as well, a skill few ladies ever do acquire. He showed me lewd books, Aretino's *Postures* and *L'escholle des Filles,* and explained the use of lovers' toys, like false phalluses that he'd bought in his travels in France and Italy. He taught me other practical things useful to a budding female libertine, too, such as to drink deeply of wine before I retired with my lover, so that I'd be sure to make a freshet of water in the chamber pot immediately afterward, and thereby safely purge myself of his seed. He also taught me the French pleasure, by which I took him in my mouth, and safely spat away his essences afterward.

Thus many ingenious hours were stolen and passed in this fashion, from that year into the next. I relished Philip's company, and that of his friends as well, enjoying a leading role in their merry, wine-laden escapades. Scandal floated about me like a fine-wrought veil, enhancing without touching me. If my name was now often included among those gentlemen and ladies infamous for their exceeding wildness, I did not care. My wantonness only served to burnish my beauty further, and while I was content with one serious lover, so many other gentlemen clamored for my attentions as well that I did on occasion indulge with them. Philip pretended not to notice, nor did I think he really cared, as we were all cut from the same bolt of promiscuous cloth at that time. To my considerable amazement, my mother neither heard nor suspected any of this, or perhaps simply preferred not to. Thus I soon achieved my sixteenth birthday, as pleased with myself as any lady of that tender age ever born.

But being pleased, like pleasure itself, is a fleeting state, and before long the clouds of discord did gather around my love for Philip. While I was mostly constant to him, he would not so much as pretend faithfulness. He claimed it was man's base nature to prefer variety, and made no apologies. His name was tied with other ladies, low and high, as well as with servants, milliners' girls, and the penny-slatterns who let themselves be worked each night against the walls in Drury Lane.

I could not contain my jealousy, and both railed and wept my bitterness to him, even though I feared such scenes would do more to drive him from me than otherwise. I labored hard to contrive new fancies and games to amuse him and keep his love.

And in the summer of 1657, it was one such contrivance for Philip's beguilement that did change my life, and send me on another path, from which there'd be neither recourse nor return.

# Chapter Two

The afternoon sun was warm, and Anne and I had thrown open the windows of her bedchamber to catch whatever breeze might waft past. Fat bumblebees drifted in and out, determined to taste the nectar of the blossoms—sweet William and gillyflowers—that Anne kept in pots on her sill to remind her of her family's confiscated home and gardens in Scotland. The scent of the flowers was honey-sweet and heady with the warmth of the sun upon them, and the drone of bees made the afternoon drowsy and languid.

Because of the warmth, and to be more at our ease, Anne and I had shed all our clothes save our cambric smocks, the fine linen our only vestige of modesty as we lay tumbled beside one another on her rumpled bedsheets. It was too hot to bother with more between such dear friends as we, and our conversation was not inclined to cool our passions, either.

"You let him love you in a boat upon the *river*?" Anne squealed at the thought. "Didn't the waterman take notice?"

I shrugged, my shoulder bare where my smock had slipped, and sipped the sweetened lemon-water from my tumbler. "What should I care if he did? It was dark, far past midnight, and the light from the boat's fore lantern wasn't much. Besides, I'd taken care to spread my skirts over my thighs as I sat astride Philip, so there was little enough to view, save the delight in dear Philip's face as I rode him to the rhythm of the waves around us."

"Oh, Barbara, how wicked of you." Anne laughed, and with both hands smoothed her unbound hair behind her ears, her way, I knew, of hiding her excitement. She'd had a lover or two and shed her own virgin-skin, though no gentlemen had lasted in her favor. Because her own adventures had been so pallid thus far, she did enjoy to hear me speak frankly of my own.

"But tell me, dear," she continued now, "what would you have done if you'd capsized the boat?"

"What would we have done?" Absently I poked my finger at the lemon slices in my tumbler, making them bob and dance much as we'd done to the small hired boat. "Why, I would venture that Philip would have had to float and swim upon his back, while I rode upon him, until we reached the shore."

"Or until you spent, and sank, done in by the waves of your passion." She giggled and clapped her hands together, imagining the scene, I suppose, and applauding our inventiveness. "Oh, Barbara, how you will oblige His Lordship's every letch!"

I leaned close, as if to confess a great secret, and lowered my voice. "It wasn't his letch to have me in the boat, Anne," I whispered with mock solemnity. " 'Twas mine."

Anne bubbled over with laughter and flopped back against the piled bolsters, her bare freckled legs sprawled before her.

"You are *so* fortunate," she said with a sigh of longing, hugging her arms beneath her breasts. "To have a lover like His Lordship who is so willing to play at amusement."

I twisted around to gaze upon her. She was a lovely lady, there in the sunlight, and I couldn't help but think of how Philip himself would have delighted in such an intimate view of my dearest friend.

"He's a most agreeable gentleman, you know," I said, thinking.

"To you, he is," she said with a sigh that rippled through her rounded breasts, scarce covered by fine linen and the long locks of her golden hair.

"He'd be so to you, too, if you weren't so shy around him." I sat up, cross-legged on the bed, and from my tumbler plucked a lemon slice, now dripping sweet. "He finds you charming, you know."

"He does?" She propped her head upon her arm. "He's said that to you?"

"Oh, often." I took the lemon slice and trailed it lightly along my friend's bare calf, leaving a sugary trail along her skin from her ankle to her plump, rosy knee. "Does that tickle?"

"Not at all," she said, going very still as she watched me. "Then why hasn't he ever said so to me?"

"Because he knows you're my friend and would not wish to come between us." On a whim, I bent and ran my tongue along the glistening trail, tasting the sugar and the lemon and Anne's skin before I looked back up at her. "Of course, if you joined me one day, then that would be different."

"Joined you?" Anne asked, though I knew she understood. "You and His Lordship?"

I nodded. "You could come with me when I visit him in Lincoln's Inn Fields, or we could arrange another place. That is, if you wished to."

Her eyes widened. "Have you ever done that with him before?" she asked. "Invited another lady, that is?"

"Not another lady, no," I said, and wrinkled my nose to show my distaste. "Philip did suggest an acquaintance of his, a lowborn, common woman, and I refused, fearing she'd be poxed. But with you to share, it would be . . . wondrous."

I saw the desire in her eyes, the green color shading darker. "You would share His Lordship with me?"

"I would," I said, and slipped the lemon slice into my mouth, tart and sweet upon my tongue. "Dear Anne! How much I'd like to watch him take you, too, and fetch you with the greatest joy imaginable."

"Then let us do it," Anne said, giggling with anticipation. She rolled from the bed and scurried barefoot across the floor to her writing desk, and set a fresh sheet of paper beneath her pen. "We must invite him properly, Barbara. Tell me the words, and I'll write them down."

"Oh, yes, that's very true," I said eagerly. "He says there's nothing that heightens pleasure like honest anticipation."

"Then we must tempt him, Barbara, tempt him royally." Inspired, Anne dipped her pen into the pot of ink. "How should we begin?"

"Let me consider," I said, thinking what would intrigue Philip the most. "Write this, Anne: 'My friend and I are just now abed together a-contriving how to have your company tomorrow afternoon.'"

"Perfection," Anne said, her pen scratching swiftly over the page. "Gentlemen do love to picture ladies abed, as if we never do repair there every night to sleep."

"No ladies *sleep* in Philip's bed," I said archly. "Here, write this next. 'If you deserve this favor, then you will come and seek us at Ludgate Hill about three o'clock at Butler's shop, where we will expect you.' Mr. Butler won't mind if we linger there a bit, and we can make our plans forward from there."

"No one will suspect us, either," Anne said. "We'll look thoroughly innocent."

"Hah, so long as they never know," I said, laughing. "Now, here's the last bit, to tease him. 'But lest we should give you too much satisfaction at once, we will say no more. Expect the rest when you see—'"

"See what?" Anne asked, swinging her legs in the chair.

"Why, us, of course," I said, and grinned, delighted with the notion of pleasing both my friend and my lover. "We'll sign our names there, to tempt him more. Barbara Villiers and Lady Anne Hamilton. Hurry now, and we can send it directly by one of your servants. And if that won't tempt and please Philip, then nothing will."

Such a wonderful plan did keep me awake all that night. How could it not?

But when I arrived at the Duchess of Hamilton's house the following afternoon to collect Anne, as we'd agreed, I was shown not to my friend's chamber, as was usual, but to the front room. There in a black oak chair sat Anne's mother, Her Grace, the most fearsome Dowager Duchess of Hamilton, a Gorgon waiting more to waylay me than to offer any hospitable greeting. She curled one hand like a griffin's claw around the head of an ebony walking stick, and her gown, though of the first quality, was in the style of twenty years before. Her graying hair was likewise curled after the fashion of Henrietta Marie, the dead king's queen, and her mouth set with immovable loathing against me.

"Miss Villiers," she said as soon as I'd made my greeting. "It is my duty to tell you that you are no longer welcome in this house."

I'd no answer to this, and so tried to begin afresh. "Please, Your Grace, if Lady Anne—"

"My daughter the Lady Anne is no longer in residence here, Miss Villiers," she said, clipping her words with the northern accent that Anne had relentlessly worked to forget. "She has gone to Windsor, with no plans to return to London."

I couldn't keep from frowning at this; Anne had said nothing to me of going to Windsor. "You surprise me, Your Grace," I said. "Lady Anne and I had arrangements together for this day, and I—"

"Oh, I know of your debauched *arrangements*, miss," the duchess said, fair spitting at me like an angry old cat. "The footman my daughter entrusted with that foul missive recalled that he is employed by me, not her, and rightly brought it to me instead."

I gasped with dismay, and forced my wits to scramble in retreat. "But that letter was never intended for your eyes, Your Grace. It was a thing of sport, a fantastical creation meant only for our amusement and nothing more, and I—"

"Silence!" The duchess struck her ebony walking stick against the floor to quiet me. "It was a despicable letter of assignation, Miss Villiers, in which you contrived to deliver my daughter into the hands of your pimp."

"Lord Chesterfield is no pimp, Your Grace, nor—"

"He is your pimp, Miss Villiers," the duchess repeated succinctly, "just as you are his whore. Good day, Miss Villiers, and rest assured that this door will never be opened to you again."

I parted my lips to protest, and she stopped me short again, shaking her walking stick like a bludgeon toward me. "Go, Miss Villiers, away with you, before I have the footmen turn you out in the street like the vilest whore that you are."

Seeing no reason for lingering, I departed in sorrow for my

mother's house. I was sick over the loss of my dear friend, for having Anne banished to Windsor made her as remote and unapproachable to me as if she'd been sent to a prison in Rome. Moreover, I'd much anticipated our dalliance with Philip, now never to occur, and the praise I'd receive from him for the novelty. It seemed most unkind to me that Anne should be made to suffer so grievously for the simple misfortune of being my friend and Philip's acquaintance.

But while I'd been happy to avoid Her Grace's walking stick, my welcome at home was no less menacing. I'd but stepped into the hall when my own lady mother confronted me with a poker from the hearth in her hand, brandishing it over her head while sparks fair flew from her eyes at the sight of me.

"You shame me, daughter, how you shame me!" She shoved me into the parlor, closing the door after us so the servants would not hear. "I've just this hour had word from the Duchess of Hamilton of the filthy tricks you tried to play with her daughter."

"The letter was meant as a jest, madam," I said, trying my tactic with a different foe. "It was never intended for other eyes than our own."

"Surely you take me for a pretty fool, Barbara, if you think I should believe that rubbish." She tossed the poker clattering beside the hearth with obvious disgust. "I have tried to look away, and hoped that your untrammeled behavior would in time settle itself. I prayed that some decent gentleman would offer for your hand, and make you his wife, and guide you safely through these troubled times of ours. But now you have openly ruined yourself and your prospects with a wastrel like Chesterfield, and I can neither hope nor pray any longer. And with *Chesterfield*, Barbara! Chesterfield, bah."

"He's the *Earl* of Chesterfield!"

"He's a libertine, a drunkard, a gambler, and a duelist," she continued in relentless litany. "He'll never marry you."

"He *loves* me!"

"Chesterfield loves no one but his own pleasures," she said scornfully. "One day His Majesty will return to claim his throne, and where will you be when he does? Will you be ready to take your place as a jewel in his court, a respected lady, or will you be no more than a pox-riddled slattern, of use to no one?"

"Her Grace cursed me as a whore, too," I said, my voice rising to match hers. "Yet you would bid me do the same, to barter my body to a man for the sake of a fortune. At least I have pleased myself with His Lordship's company, which is far more than I could ever do with the sorry males you would thrust upon me!"

She regarded me so coldly that, even in my temper, I feared she might turn me out-of-doors forever. "You're not a whore, Barbara, for a good whore would demand fair payment for what you give for free."

I tried to answer her heartlessness with a stony look of my own, my hands squared upon my hips. "Do you speak from experience, madam? Is that why you settled upon my uncle, that he gave fair payment for what little comfort you could offer him?"

She struck me hard across my cheek with the flat of her hand, so hard that I saw wheeling stars before my eyes, and her furious face did seem to spin before me. But I didn't stumble, or cry out, no matter that the tears smarted behind my lids. I would not give her that satisfaction.

"Because you are my daughter, I'll not treat you as you deserve," she said, her breath coming in rapid puffs of rage. "Because you are your father's dear child, I will give you another chance to save yourself, and your Christian soul. But, Barbara, I vow by all that's sacred, if you continue in this manner your life will be marked with nothing but wildness and infamy."

I knew better than to answer her and have my ears boxed for my trouble, but in my heart I countered her boldly. Somehow, I vowed, I would find my place on the world's bright stage. I would have love, and pleasure, and have all the pretty baubles of wealth and position: a house grander than hers, a richer title, jewels and gowns and carriages.

Such a prediction from her, and such a promise to myself: and yet how strange to think that, in time, both would come true.

. . .

I never learned if that thwarted frolic disappointed Philip (for of course I told him of it, fool that I was) so much that he drew back from me, or if, more likely, he acted simply in the pattern of such gentlemen and his fading interest with me was as natural to him as the changing of the seasons. For though I tried every amorous fancy I knew to keep him bound to me, his letters and poesies became less frequent, and worse, he began to invent a score of petty reasons for us not to meet.

He first removed himself to Tunbridge Wells, away from London and from me, and then retreated farther to his estate of Bretby, in the Peak District. I seldom knew exactly where he was, let alone in whose arms he chose to dally. To my misery, I heard his name linked with many others, including Lady Elizabeth Howard, the daughter of the Earl of Berkshire, a lady far my superior in rank and fortune, if not beauty. Yet my poor heart was so wounded that my pride swallowed that indignity, too, for the sake of but hearing his dear name.

When at last he returned to London, matters were no more improved between us. On the few occasions when he would summon me, I would fain run to his faithless embrace, and forgive him every other transgression. His skill at lovemaking could still make me so weak with trembling delight that it clouded every other thought and common sense. Again and again I suffered these humiliations for what I perceived was his love, with no lasting proof to show for it other than a handful of empty words—a hard lesson for any woman, most especially for one of my still-tender years, yet one I would not forget.

I've often considered what would have become of me if Cromwell's war had not claimed my father, and I'd been blessed with his love, and that of my mother, as she must have been then, before she'd been hardened and drained by misfortune. If as a child I'd seen around me real love, lasting love as warm as a chimney corner, then would I have been better able to recognize the falseness in Philip's protestations, and tell true love from feigned? If my heart had not been so parched and needy for love of any kind, would I have lapped so desperately at the well-practiced affection he offered?

Is it any wonder, then, that I also missed my friend Anne, whose mother had kept fast her promise to withhold my company from her daughter. I'd not seen Anne since that last summer afternoon, nor did I receive letters from her. Her banishment had been complete. Further, I'd heard she was soon to be married to Lord Carnegie, and would be as good as buried to me forever in the cold Scottish country.

In this sorry fashion, my days did pass until the autumn of 1657, and a fresh scandal for my inconstant lover brought him more trouble than even he could dodge. Having drawn a new lady's name for a Valentine, he amused himself by sending her a specially made gift, a chamber pot fitted with a looking-glass in the bottom, and a lewd verse to her private charms that would thus be revealed, painted along the rim in French.

But the lady was neither entertained nor seduced—as, alas, I surely would have been—by such a witty token. She soon found a champion in Captain John Whaley, the member of Parliament for Nottingham and Shoreham, and a staunch friend to Cromwell himself. The duel was short, with Philip dispatching Whaley with brisk efficiency and leaving him with a grievous wound. This news roused Cromwell's vengeful temper, and he sent Philip to imprisonment in the Tower, vowing that if Whaley died, then Philip's own life would be forfeited.

Even resourceful Philip could discover no way to conduct his affairs of passion while imprisoned in a guarded tower of stone and iron, and while I worried over his eventual fate, I was also spared imagining him with his other loves. This was no small relief. I found jealousy difficult to bear, and had let it gnaw away at me like a plague.

Besides, there were other matters to draw the attention of even the most halfhearted Royalists in London. Groveling Parliament had offered Cromwell the crown, but to the relief and surprise of the true king's supporters, Cromwell had declined it. While some viewed this as a sign of the Lord Protector's humility, among my friends it was seen as proof that not even Cromwell or his Puritan God dared interfere with Charles II's right to the English throne, and there was much giddy talk about a joyful future.

Perhaps because I'd never known England with a king instead

of a protector, I was more skeptical than this. Every breath of rebellion that the Royalists had mustered in my lifetime had been quickly smothered, and I couldn't see that this would be any different. The young Royalist gentlemen of my acquaintance were charming and amusing, yes, but more given to sitting about with their drink and boasting vaguely of what they wished to do against Cromwell's army than actually accomplishing anything. It was only brave talk, and little more. As quick as Philip's sword might be in a duel, I'd no wish to see his skill pitted against the grim, somber soldiers who paraded and drilled each day in St. James's Park.

Oh, it would be pleasing to have that handsome young king to rule us in Whitehall Palace—I still would study the picture of him in my mother's chamber, fascinated by his regal mien—but in my head I thought of his triumphant return to London as no more than an idle fancy, like wishing for a songbird's feathered wings so I might fly high and soar over the spire of St. Paul's.

Yet one evening that autumn, while Philip was still held in the Tower, I was made to realize that such dreams could yet become real.

I had gone to a gathering at Lady Sillsbury's house on the Strand. It was an old pile of a place, two hundred years old or so, a reminder of the last time that government and religion had warred and claimed each other's property, in the reign of the eighth King Henry. I'd heard the house had first been built for a flock of papist nuns who haunted it still, reason enough for Cromwell to let the equally ancient Lady Sillsbury keep it. More likely the house was merely too worn and out of fashion for Cromwell's ambitious generals to bother with, but its rambling wings and black-timbered walls reminded me of the country of my childhood.

I soon wearied of the music we'd been invited to hear, an Italian singer with a quivering belly and a rumbling voice, and the merriment of the company did not suit my loneliness without Philip to leaven it first. Instead I left the singing and found my way to a rambling balcony off the parlor. The house's green lawns spilled down to a private landing on the Thames, where the boats that had brought guests were tied up and waiting, the clay pipes of the watermen tiny glowing pinpricks in the dusk. Mists rose in gauzy tangles from the river's surface, as they do in that season of the year, yet the slivered new moon still hung fresh and bright in the darkening sky.

Heedless of the cooling evening air, I stood and gazed upon this pretty scene, finding some small, rare peace in its tranquility. When I heard another's footfalls behind me, I didn't turn, I was so loath for interruption.

"A beautiful evening, is it not?" the gentleman asked.

I'd no choice now but to answer, else seem ill-mannered. "It's the river that makes it so. Without the Thames, London would be a drab and cheerless place."

"That will never happen, Miss Villiers," he said, "so long as you are in London."

There was an awkward earnestness to this unimaginative compliment that caught my ear and at last made me turn to face its giver.

"Prettily said, if untrue," I said, deflecting the compliment neatly back to him. "Mr. Palmer, isn't it?"

"Roger Palmer, your servant." He swept me a courteous bow, but not before I glimpsed the uneasiness that was close to real fear in his face.

"Miss Villiers, yours." Was I really so very daunting? I wondered with amusement. He gave the appearance of a man with little to fear, a gentleman by his dress and manner. He was pleasant enough, if not handsome, with a slash of dark brows that sat atop his long nose, dark eyes, and a thin, thoughtful mouth.

"I know who you are," he said. "Everyone knows you."

This was true, if bluntly stated, and I smiled to put him at his ease. I felt I should know him, too, for he was close to my own age and did seem familiar, but among the dashing male peacocks in our circle, he'd slipped to the back, unnoticed.

"You didn't care for the music either, Mr. Palmer?" I asked, languidly opening my fan. Regardless of whether he was handsome or no, an unfamiliar face always meant a new audience. "Did you find that plump Italian rascal as tedious as I?"

"I confess my thoughts were elsewhere," he said. "I don't often attend such entertainments as this, you see."

I raised one brow in play, considering him over the curve of my fan. "You're not one of Cromwell's dour men in disguise, are you, sir?"

"Don't slander me like that, madam!" he exclaimed, with real fire in his dark eyes. "I've dedicated my life toward the return of the rightful king to his throne. My father served the last two kings until their deaths, and though old in years, he lives still and burns with the hope that he can serve their son and grandson as well. I will do my best to make that happen, Miss Villiers, no matter the risks or cost. To see Charles crowned here in London—ah, I'd die content."

"Hush, hush, sir, and be calm," I said softly. "I spoke but in jest. How could you follow Cromwell yet be among these people as well? We're all Royalists, sir, else we'd not be here."

"Perhaps not," he said, looking away from me and off to the river, though I doubt that was what he saw in his mind's eye. "But there are degrees of loyalty, Miss Villiers. To listen to the trills of some Roman popinjay and sigh over the lack of a court is not the same as risking one's very life for the king's cause."

"How do you mean, Mr. Palmer?" I asked, intrigued, for this was not the sort of talk I was accustomed to hearing from gentlemen. "Are you party to planning another uprising?"

"What, those ill-conceived ventures?" he asked, clearly offended I'd suggest such a thing of him. "No, no, there's other, quieter ways to work to greater effect."

"Indeed," I said. "And how precisely do you prepare for these ways?"

"I feel first what is in my heart, and be guided by that," he said, answering my question in perfect seriousness. "But I also read much of history and political government while at Eton College, and at King's, Cambridge, and I'm at present a student of the law in the Inner Temple."

"You are a clever fellow, aren't you?" Yet I was impressed. For most gentlemen of our generation, education had become but one more casualty of the war, and I couldn't recall meeting another who could claim such scholarly achievement.

"The king needs educated men as well as soldiers," he said. "Support must be cultivated with care and diplomacy among the greater populace as well as across the Continent in other courts, not just with a few hotheaded malcontents."

"You have done this, Mr. Palmer?" I thought of how when Philip traveled through France, all he'd accomplished was to bring back more wicked books and pictures for his own pleasure. "You've sought support for the cause abroad?"

He tipped his head to one side with becoming modesty. "I do not work alone, of course. I'm but a link in a greater chain."

I looked at him in a new light. His earlier shyness had dissipated as surely as those mists upon the water. Instead he seemed decisive, a man of action and importance, bravely risking everything for his monarch. I took a step closer to him, lowering my voice so others—if there'd been others—couldn't hear.

"Who are these other links?" I asked with excitement, eager to learn more. "Does this courageous chain of yours have a name?"

"To tell the others' names would be to break a most solemn oath," he said with genuine regret. "Even though I would do whatever I could to earn your favor, Miss Villiers, I cannot do that. There are too many others who would wish to stop us to make that possible."

I nodded, intrigued by his loyalty and reticence. "Have you ever met His Majesty? Surely you can tell me that."

"I've had that considerable honor, yes," he said. "I've brought him both assurances from his country and the funds necessary to help him maintain his household and his hopes. My father remains His Majesty's Chancellor of the Order of the Garter, and as his son, I am welcomed in the royal presence. Charles Stuart is truly the first gentleman of his realm, a thorough king no matter how reduced his circumstances."

"How pleased His Majesty must be to have such a loyal servant in you, Mr. Palmer," I said softly, smiling as I did. I was surprised that he'd yet to attempt a kiss; by now most other gentlemen would have done so, and the fact that Mr. Palmer hadn't was another way he set himself apart in my mind.

He bowed again, a courtly man without a court. "I know of no other way to behave," he confessed. "Loyalty to my king has been bred into my very blood and bone, and nothing Cromwell or his minions can do will change that."

In the chamber behind us, the last strains of music had faded away, replaced by applause.

"You'll want to return to the others, Miss Villiers," he said, glancing wistfully over his shoulder. "I thank you for your company."

"Perhaps I'm not ready to return to the others," I said, slipping my hand into his arm. "Perhaps I should like to walk along the lawn to the river instead."

He cleared his throat, and I vow that if there'd been more light, I should have seen a blush to his cheeks. "Miss Villiers, I must tell you," he blurted, "you must be the most beautiful lady I've ever seen."

"I know," I said, smiling as I curled my arm more closely into his. "Everyone tells me that. Now come, walk with me, and tell me instead more of what you do for King Charles."

"Is it true you've been keeping company with that dull ass Roger Palmer?" Philip asked. He lay sprawled across his bed with his hands linked behind his head, splendidly naked, while he watched me dress. Once again he'd been freed from the Tower, spared of further prosecution by the earnest pleas of his friends. "Or is that only more ridiculous gossip meant to destroy your reputation?"

"I've kept Mr. Palmer's company, yes," I said, seeing no reason to deny it. "He is a gentleman of great intelligence."

"Oh, aye, a scholar," he scoffed. "How long has he been tutoring you, sweet?"

I drew my blackthorn comb through my hair, pulling apart the knots that our passion had tangled into it, and conscious, too, of how my raised arms would flatter my still-bared breasts to his eye. It was warm here in his bedchamber, the afternoon sun heating the shingled roof overhead, and I was in no hurry to dress.

"I met Roger last autumn," I said. "I've seen him since then, here and there."

"That's eight months," he calculated shrewdly. "And a considerable amount of here and there."

I looked at him from beneath the arc of my raised arm. It was true, I had seen much of Roger this last year. I was seventeen now, and eager for different amusements, and Roger had been one of them. "Are you jealous, my darling?"

"What, of Palmer?" He tipped his head back against the pillow-bier, his rich auburn curls falling over the white linen, and laughed derisively. "We're well beyond jealousy, Barbara, you and I."

That stung: not so much that he denied being jealous of me, but that he so readily expected me to feel the same of him, and let him graze wherever he pleased without risk of reprobation.

"I like his company." I glanced back at my reflection in Philip's looking-glass, putting from my mind the thought of how many other women had gazed into that same glass. "Roger shares his thoughts with me."

"His *thoughts*, Barbara?" asked Philip with mocking emphasis, stretching his muscular, unclad body across the bed in case I somehow missed his meaning, or the sight of his cock against his thigh. "Is that all the sustenance he offers you? And here I'd always believed you'd more a taste for meat."

A year before, and I would have blushed, but he'd so thoroughly broken me to his ways that I felt more regret for honest Roger to be so abused than for myself.

"Roger sees me as a fit companion for his conversation," I said, testy. "It is a pleasant change."

"Oh, Barbara, Barbara," he said, reaching for more wine from the table beside the bed. "Let him whisper whatever he will into your pretty ear, but his goal's the same as any other man's, to lecture his way between your legs and up your cunt."

"Don't judge every man by yourself, my lord," I said tartly. "Roger speaks to me of important matters. He tells me of the growing efforts to overthrow Cromwell and his part in the plans to return King Charles to the throne."

Philip groaned with mock dismay. "There you are, sweet, exactly as I said. He paints himself to be a glorious hero in your eyes, the better to dazzle you onto your back."

"If that were true, then why has he told me of your doings as well?" I snapped, resentment making me use the secrets that Roger had sworn me not to share. "He's informed me of the time you've spent in the Derby gaol for Royalist plotting, and how you're likewise with him a member of the Sealed Knot, a group sworn to restore the king."

Philip went very still with the goblet before his lips. "He speaks to you of that?"

"He does," I said, realizing my sudden advantage. "Because he trusts me, and regards me as clever enough to understand such important matters. He has not only confided to me many of the activities of the Knot, but the names of members."

His eyes narrowed. "What makes you believe him?"

"Because of his loyalty to his sovereign," I answered. "And because unlike you, Roger has no reason to lie to me."

"Or to lie with you, either? Is that where all these confidences are made? In Palmer's bed?"

"You know none of that." I pulled my smock over my head, determined to leave. In truth Roger was either so shy or so respectful that he'd yet to press his suit beyond a handful of dutiful kisses. It was pleasing to be treated with such reverence, yes, but also puzzling, and I did wonder what it was about me that could make all other men desire me in an instant, yet seemingly failed to inspire the same in Roger. "Nor is it any of your affair."

"It is when Palmer tells tales of me." He lunged across the bed and caught the hem of my smock, holding me fast. "He'd no right to do that, Barbara."

"Why not?" I demanded, looking down at him. "Do you fear I'll carry your name to Cromwell himself? Do you have so little use for my loyalty as that?"

"Because you're a woman, Barbara," he said, as if needing no further explanation. "It's against your nature to be loyal, or to keep a sworn secret. As a lot, you're not to be trusted, especially not with secrets of such importance to the well-being of the country."

I tried to pull my hem free of his grasp without tearing the linen. "And I say that with a woman, a man will spill his secrets with his seed, and betray his dearest friend in the process."

"Because that is your magic, Barbara, your lure," he said. He slipped his hand inside my smock to reach my bare knee, his fingers teasing along my thigh. "I acknowledge your power, sweet, just as I swear my complete allegiance to it."

I stopped my struggles, intent instead upon his caress. Such a fool from love, I think now, such a fool, and yet I could not refuse him.

"You should trust me, my lord," I said, even as I realized my point would be lost. "I would never betray you, or the king."

"Then forget whatever Palmer has told you of me." His cunning fingers crept higher along my thigh, and with unthinking obedience I shifted my legs apart to ease his path. "Forget plotting and the king and any other dangerous notions that may have found their way into your head."

"But I don't wish to forget the king, or the plans to bring him back to England," I whispered, swaying toward him. "I wish to—to be of use to the cause, and to—to be a part of it."

"Better to wish for this, Barbara," he said, his voice as seductive as the serpent in the Garden. "Better to take pleasure in what you have than to crave what will never be yours. Better to be my Barbara, and love me as no other woman can."

I was still too young to see the hollow core to such reasoning, or to look beyond the giddy pleasures he was even then stirring within me. He'd said he loved me as none other, and because I wanted so much to believe him, I did. Instead of rebuffing him as I would have been wisest to do, I accepted both his argument and his caresses, and let him tumble and swive and delight me yet again on his wide pillowed bed.

# Chapter Three

I stood beside the gate to James's Park—which the low creatures of the Commonwealth, ever vigilant against Anglicans and popery, had deprived of the appellation of St. James, and given over to the honor of every ordinary Jemmy instead—shielding my eyes against the slanting sun of late afternoon while I waited for Roger. I wondered at his delay. Roger was never late to our meetings, and more often was kept waiting by me.

It was the first week of September, still more summer than autumn, with the Spanish broom in riotous flower behind me. The night before, a great wind had blown through London, almost a *hurricano*, as the Spaniards call it, tearing trees up by their roots and bricks from the chimney tops. The streets and lawns were still littered with leaves and papers and other rubbish, and I wondered at how few persons were to be seen about. My mother's servants, a superstitious lot, had whispered darkly this morning that such a wind could only bring misfortune and death, but I'd paid their prattle little heed, glad only that the sun had returned so that I could come to the park.

Just enough breeze remained to toss my artful side curls against my cheeks and into my eyes in a most annoying fashion, so that while I looked for Roger I was compelled again and again to brush them back from my face until, finally, I lost all patience, and stuffed them unbecomingly inside the crown of my wide-brimmed hat. Wrapped in a handkerchief inside my white satin muff, I'd hidden a pair of ruddy apples as a special treat for Roger.

It sounds odd, I know, to recall so much in such detail, but because of the great news to be heard that day—September 3, 1658—every petty detail of the morning became gilded and crystallized, preserved along with that single event.

When Roger finally came, his long face was somber, though his eyes seemed bright with excitement. He seized my hand and drew me close so no others would overhear.

"Have you heard the news, Barbara?" he demanded, with no apology for his tardiness. "Most awful news. Most wondrous, blessed news!"

I looked at him askance, unsure what could have disordered him from his customary composure. "What news is this, Roger? I've heard none of it."

"Cromwell is dead!" he whispered. "Think of it, Barbara! The Lord Protector is dead. Can his unlawful Commonwealth not follow soon after?"

"Dead?" I repeated, stunned. I couldn't recall a time when that grim, wart-covered general had not ruled over England. "How? When?"

"This very day," he answered, his voice fair trembling with emotion. "You know he had been ill this past fortnight, and we've all been ordered to say our prayers for him, but there was no hint nor suspicion of impending death. And now—now he is gone."

"But what will happen now?" I asked, his excitement contagious. "Surely His Majesty can—"

"Not so soon, not so soon," Roger cautioned. "They say the Council of State has already confirmed the son's appointment to the Protectorate, and as his father's dying wish."

"Fah," I scoffed with a little sweep of my hand. "As if we're to believe that! The old man himself turned down the crown, fearing what would happen if his weakling of a son came to power."

"Take care of your words, Barbara, I beg you," cautioned Roger swiftly. "The Commonwealth still holds sway, and their laws with it."

"But the army won't follow Richard Cromwell." I'd well learned the complicated lessons in politics that Roger had taught me. I understood that the true leaders within parliamentary England were not those members themselves, but the old Protector's generals, Monck and Lambert and Fleetwood, taciturn men of action who were as chary with their allegiances as they were with their men's lives. "They believed in the father, but distrust the son. If Richard had, say, General Monck in his pocket, then that would be another matter, but without the army's support, then Parliament's grip on the country surely must collapse."

"In time, Barbara, in time," Roger cautioned. "These things never run swiftly. There'll be official mourning, of course, and a state funeral, but after that is done, confusion is sure to follow in Parliament and across the country. And you are correct about Richard Cromwell. He hasn't the stomach for leadership."

"And then the king shall return!" I'd heard so much of Roger's plotting and scheming, eagerly following his allies' successes and failures, that I couldn't keep from crowing now. "Oh, what a joyful day for England!"

Roger nodded solemnly, though his joy beamed from his eyes there in the slanting sunlight. "And for us, Barbara. An auspicious day for change and transformation of every kind."

"Of course," I said, not quite understanding, but not caring, either. "If England is joyful, than we shall be, too."

Belatedly I drew one of the apples from my muff, and handed it to him like a golden prize.

"Here you are, Mr. Palmer," I said playfully. "I offer you the bravest of worlds, if you'll but claim it for your own!"

He took it slowly, briefly clasping his hand over mine with the fruit inside. "I could have all the world in my hand, yet still not be happy were you not a part of it."

I tipped my head to look up at him from beneath my lashes, still unsure as to where this serious gambit of his might lead, and studied the curves of my own apple for the choicest place to bite. "How vastly kind of you to say, Roger."

He nodded again and looked down at the apple in his hand while the wide brim of his hat shadowed his face. "It is bold of me, I know, but might I ask the state of your, ah, your connection to the Earl of Chesterfield?"

I felt my smile turn dry and brittle, like the leaves in the trees overhead soon would with the coming season. Once again Philip had chosen to absent himself, though whether for an amorous intrigue or a political one, he'd not vouchsafed to me. His absence and neglect both pained me, and I'd no wish to be reminded of it like this.

"It is bold of you to ask that of me, Roger, unconscionably bold," I said. "I do not see how my *connection* with His Lordship is any worry of yours, Roger."

"It's not," he said, clearly so miserable that I almost—almost— pitied him. "That is, my father is concerned."

"Concerned about me?" I asked, that brittleness still in my voice. "Why should Sir James Palmer concern himself about me, when we've never so much as bowed to one another across a street?"

"Barbara, please," Roger pleaded. "My father is old, and in weakening health. It's natural for him to show concern for me as his son."

"So this concern of his is for you, and not for me?" I bit into the apple, my teeth piercing the skin and digging deep into the sweet flesh.

"Father no longer lives in our house in London, you see, but at Dorney Court, near Windsor, in the country and away from the noise of the city, in the care of my mother, a most pious lady," Roger explained in so much anxious, unwanted detail I could easily guess what was coming next. "He has heard rumors that have, ah, put your name with mine, and he—"

"He is *concerned.*" I bit again into the apple, heedless of the sweet juice and flecks of bright skin that sprayed and beaded on my lips. "Sir James is *concerned* because his only son has been seen with a Villiers. A *Villiers.* And what, pray, is your country nest of pious Palmers compared to that?"

Roger began again. "I'm sure the rumors were false, Barbara, yet—"

"Are you so sure?" I demanded. He was foundering like a man thrown out of his depth in a stormy sea, but I was too angry to offer him any succor or relief. "I thought you knew me well enough,

Mr. Palmer, but perhaps you don't, if you would dare ask me such a question."

"I do not ask for myself, Barbara," he said, humbly bowing his head again, "but for my father's sake."

"You are a man grown, Roger," I said, biting each word with the same savageness with which I'd bitten the apple. "At least you should be, if you wish to address me. I've made my own choices of friends and actions, my decisions, and whether they've been wise or not, I'll make neither apologies nor explanations. Accept me as you find me, Roger, else you'll not see me again."

He looked back down at his own apple, the very picture of dejection. I'd not intended to be so harsh, but his father's question inflamed me because of what lay behind it. Clearly the old man judged me to be a whore and a slattern because I was Philip's lover. I'd never hidden that, nor felt shame for it. None of us in our circle who were similarly engaged did. Roger himself had dallied with other ladies, and I'd wager that even this sanctimonious father of his had had his sport when he'd been young, in the days of the old court.

"Which is it, Roger?" I asked. "If I don't suit you as I am, then I'll take myself away from you, and not sully you further."

"You'd never sully me, Barbara," he exclaimed, wounded. "Not a lady so beautiful and delightful as you."

"Is that your answer, then?"

He paused, clearly at war with himself, for which in a small, vengeful way, I was glad. His gaze dipped lower, from my face to my bosom, and I knew at once his decision.

"Yes," he said, puffing out his cheeks with the single word. "No more questions."

"I am glad." I slipped my hand into the crook of his arm and smiled, willing to be gracious now that I'd gotten my way. "You will, I think, never regret it."

For as long as the dreary Protectorate had been in power, it seemed his heirs took longer still to bury the Lord Protector himself. The first day allotted for the funeral, over a month after the death, was deemed insufficient, and it was postponed again until the end of November. Roger had cautioned me that these things seldom run swiftly, and how right he'd been.

Burdened with irony that his followers refused to see, Cromwell was buried with all the pomp and costly ceremony usually reserved for true kings. Those spectators who could recall the funeral of James I saw remarkable similarities; to younger folk such as I, the whole affair seemed no more than a mockery of beliefs both Puritan and Royalist, with everything jumbled together in an unholy mess of symbolism.

Though it was commonly understood that Cromwell's body had been buried by his family soon after his death, a cunningly wrought effigy now took the place of his rotting corpse. Crowned and dressed in royal robes with an orb and scepter tucked alongside, this effigy was borne through the streets on a bier drawn by six horses with plumes atop their heads. A lengthy procession of distinguished mourners followed, from diplomats in the elegant mourning of foreign courts, to great lords, country mayors, and generals, to a cluster of nicely wailing common women.

I stood on one side of the Strand beside Roger, watching the procession from behind the special draped railings as it passed us by with excruciating slowness. Of course we hadn't been among those to receive tickets to participate, and a good thing, for they'd had to gather at Somerset House by eight in the morning. Huddling in the blustery cold as long as we did was more than enough for me, and more than enough, too, to see the gaudy show of plumed horses, drummers, banners, and trumpeters on its way to the abbey.

True, we were not sympathetic mourners, but there to ogle from curiosity more than anything else. But it did seem to me that the mood of the crowd in general was closer to ours than to the wooden-faced folk in the procession—a splendid omen for the king's return. Few wept, and more than a handful made disrespectful jests as whispered asides. Even the infantrymen guarding the railings in their new black-banded crimson coats drank strong spirits and smoked and spat at will, and winked slyly at me when Roger's head was turned.

"Let's leave, Roger," I said at last, though the procession still stretched into the distance in each direction, farther than we could see toward Charing Cross and Whitehall. "I'm so cold you'll have to bury me soon, too."

He nodded with no argument, and we began to make our way through the hoards. We had no choice but to walk, for the streets had been ordered closed, and besides, they were so full of people that no carriages or hackneys could have passed. Finally we found a small cookshop that had remained open, and though nearly every bench inside was taken, we squeezed our way to a place in the back, mercifully close to the fireplace. There was more merriment than somber mourning here, too, with voices happily raised in convivial good cheer.

A harried maid brought us ale in pewter tankards and set a steaming dish of sausages before us. I'd never smelled anything so deliciously fragrant, the scent of the ground mace together with the browned chopped meat and suet cooked in butter, and set in a pool of mustard sauce.

"Here you go, Barbara," Roger said, tipping several of the glistening sausages onto my plate. "Is there any finer dish on a chill day than Oxford Kate's sausages?"

I pushed back the hood of my cloak and drank deep of the ale. "And who, pray, is Oxford Kate?"

"You shouldn't ask that of a Cambridge man," he said, laughing, "but I've always heard she was the first cook to concoct these little sausages for the students there. Go on, try one."

I speared one of the small sausages with my fork, holding it up before my face to consider it: no larger than the size of my middle finger, yet delectably greasy, with juice oozing around the fork's twin tines. "Poor Kate! Is this the best-sized prick she can expect, surrounded by so many randy young scholars?"

Roger gulped and snorted his ale, and glanced about to see if any others had heard me. "You're a wicked lass, Barbara."

"Not wicked, Mr. Palmer, but honest," I said, running my tongue the squat length of the sausage. "Fie, fie on your puny Oxford men, if they expect to please the ladies with only so much meat as this."

I slipped the sausage daintily between my lips and into my mouth. Because it was so small, it was no great trick to take the entirety into my mouth, and a tasty morsel it was, too, after so long and cold a day. My cheeks must have bulged with it, and my lips glistened with the fatty juice.

Ah, but all gentlemen are alike in their carnal thoughts, and how easy this makes it for women to play them however they please! From the dumbstruck look upon Roger's long face, I knew he'd watched me devour that sausage with his own share of simmering lubricity, just as I knew he was imagining another essence of his own manufacture glistening on my sated lips.

All of which, of course, was exactly how I'd hoped to stir Roger on this day of national mourning. I was honest, yes, but I *was* wicked, too. The more ale and sausages I consumed amidst the cheerful clatter of the cookhouse, the more delectable Roger looked to me. I'm not sure what else could have made me choose that day, except that I'd neither seen nor heard from Philip for over two months, and Roger was here and being extraordinarily pleasant to me, and that I wished to send the most priggish man in all England to his next reward with a tribute more fitting than all drums and trumpets.

But then Roger did something that reduced all these wicked inclinations of mine to a sentimental pudding. He reached inside his coat, drew out a small leather box, and slid it across the pockmarked table to me.

"I had this made for you, Barbara." He cleared his throat with a sawmill's scraping rumble, so unsure was he of how to give a token to a lady. "Because, ah, you share my devotion to His Majesty, and my belief in his right to the throne of this country. It seems especially proper for today."

I set down my fork and opened the little hinged box. Nestled inside was a chain and pendant framed in herringbone silver gilt, a faceted glass heart. Buried deep within the heart for safekeeping was a cypher wrought of twisted golden wire, so finely made that it might have been the work of dainty fairy fingers rather than mortal man's.

"It's a *C* and an *R*, of course," Roger explained. "For Carolus Regnum. Charles the King. They first were made to honor our martyred sovereign, but now the followers of his royal son wear them as well. You've shown yourself to me to be worthy of our party, and with this around your throat, others will recognize your loyalty as well."

"Oh, Roger," I whispered, tracing the cypher's delicate outline with my fingertip. The significance of his gift was not lost on me. This was no ordinary bauble, such as a man gives to his sweetheart, but a symbol of far greater meaning. "That you would grant such a pendant to me!"

He was watching the glinting gold and glass in my hand, and I'd no notion of which mattered more to him. "I've spoken of you to the leaders of our group, and they agree that a lady of impeccable loyalty could be of use. There would be risks. There would be danger. I can't deny that."

"Do you mean I could carry messages for you?" I asked with excitement. My teasing play with the sausage now seemed shameful bawdry. No one had ever expected more of me than that I be amusing and beautiful, and this—this was a heady expectation indeed. "You would trust me that much?"

"In the right circumstances, yes," he said, and the admiration with which he regarded me made me shiver. "Put the chain around your neck, Barbara. I wish to see it there."

Obediently I unhooked my cloak and let it fall back from my shoulders, and unwrapped the fine wool kerchief I'd needed against the cold. The neck of my bodice was cut low and wide and banded with a velvet ribbon, as was the fashion, with only a narrow ruffle of my white smock beneath for an edging. The pendant's glass was cool against my skin, and once I fastened the chain at my nape, the heart lay at the top of the cleft between my breasts.

"There," I said. "This way the king shall forever be near my heart."

"As is right." Yet Roger's gaze was not as focused upon the pendant as upon the swell of my breasts below it. "Ah, Barbara, if you could but see yourself now! You are as beautiful, as serene, as any saint."

I'd heard that compliment often before, and it had perplexed me until I'd seen the old Italian paintings and drawings of Romish saints that still hung defiantly in many Royalist homes. I had the oval face so favored by those painters, the delicate chin and fair skin, and my deep blue eyes—that most lasting legacy of my Villiers blood—had the same heavy-lidded cast to them. I'd always thought they made me look as if I'd slept ill the night before, but Philip had told me they were the sort of eyes that made a man believe I was inclined toward lascivious amusement.

Lightly I stroked the pendant's smooth surface. When Roger gazed upon me, did he see only the saintly face, or the one more happily familiar with sin as well?

"Thank you, Roger," I said softly, reaching across the table to lay my hand over his. "You cannot know how much this pendant and the faith it represents mean to me."

"I'd dared to hope I'd please you, Barbara," he said. "That is my constant goal. That, and to have you with me forever."

"Is it?" I asked, and idly slipped my fingers higher along the back of his hand and into the cuff of his shirt to find his wrist. I always liked the strength to be discovered in a man's wrist, the way the bones were so different from my own.

"It is." His Adam's apple bobbed upward as he swallowed, poor man. "You know I've countered my father's objections to you, Barbara, my desire to see you is so vast."

"Objections, hah," I murmured, unperturbed. "Your father loathes me outright, though I mean to outlive him."

Roger smiled weakly. "I'm not a peer like His Lordship, Barbara, but I—"

"Hush," I said softly, making tiny circles along his wrist to distract him from swearing vows he'd no intention on obliging. "We needn't speak of him now."

"Then I'll speak of you," he said. "You bewitch me, Barbara. I've never met another lady like you."

"Nor I a gentleman like you." I smiled. Even my honorable Roger had found his way from sainthood to bewitching sin. "You keep your lodgings not far from here, don't you?"

He emptied his tankard and thumped it down hard on the table, then rose and boldly offered me his hand.

"Madam," he said. "I shall be most honored."

While Roger knew full well that I was not a maid, on that first night I thought it kindest to hide my experience. Most gentlemen prefer it that way, to believe they are the omniscient mighty conqueror in the bedchamber, and ready to crow like a very rooster at the break of day.

It was not a difficult role to play with Roger, either, because I did like him and appreciate the respect and regard he accorded me. Likewise, he was lean and pleasingly made, and as eager a lover as any woman could wish. Since many weeks had passed since I'd last been with Philip, I found my satisfaction swiftly and with ease, but took such care to lavish every praise on him that he insisted on repeating his performance twice more before dawn.

And yet that morning as I lay in his arms, clothed in nothing more than the cypher heart around my neck, I felt not joy but a kind of melancholy. Was this, I wondered miserably, how Philip regarded me? That I was a pleasant diversion, yet no more? That when I spoke of a shared future he saw only as far as that night? That my heartfelt protestations of eternal love, which Roger was even now echoing so fervently in my ear, sounded as flat and unmagical to Philip as Roger's did now to me?

When the footman brought us a morning tray, I drank a morning draft with Roger, while he ate his hearty servings of toasted biscuits, quince conserve, and red kippers, doubtless to restore the strength he fancied he'd exhausted in the course of the night. Then to his regret, I made my farewell, contriving some excuse or another for repairing home to my mother's house. I'd much to consider as I rode alone in the Palmers' carriage to Ludgate Hill, and wonder, too, at this next step I'd taken on my life's journey.

Yet if I'd hoped to find peace at home, I was sadly disappointed. I'd scarce stepped through the door when my mother came rushing from the parlor as if the very walls around her were ablaze, her small spaniel in her arms.

"Barbara, Barbara, you are safe!" she cried, setting the dog down to embrace me. "Oh, daughter, you've no notion of how I'd feared you'd come to some terrible end. Why, I was almost ready to send for the watch, to have them search for your ravaged body in the parks."

"You've no reason to worry, madam," I said wearily, tossing my cloak and muff to the footman. "I went to view the funeral procession, as I'd told you, and then was among friends."

"Friends!" she exclaimed, following close behind me into the front room. "Why shouldn't I worry when you're with your *friends,* given how you consort until all hours with only the lowest rascals and scoundrels?"

I pressed my fingers to my temples, wishing she'd not begun this same sorry tune again. "You keep your friends, and I'll keep mine," I began. "You don't need to tell me again how much you despise Chesterfield."

"Chesterfield," she said, and puckered her lips dismissively. "I only wish you were with His Lordship, because at least I'd know the name of the man whose bed you shared last night, like any other whoring gypsy."

"Madam, please, I'd rather not—"

"Don't lie to me again, Barbara, for I know you weren't with His Lordship." She waved a small salver with a letter on it beneath my nose.

I recognized Philip's seal pressed into the wax, as well as his hand. Eagerly I reached for the letter, but my mother swept it from my hand.

"Not yet, daughter, not yet," she said, holding the salver from my reach while her little dog jumped and yipped below. "I know you were not with His Lordship last night, for his servant brought this late, searching for you. Tell me where you were, Barbara. Tell me whose bed you shared."

With Philip's letter my golden prize, I didn't hesitate. "Mr. Palmer,"

I said. "I was with him and no other from the beginning of yesterday until now, when his carriage brought me home."

My mother was so startled by this that she let me seize Philip's letter at once.

"Mr. Roger Palmer?" she demanded. "The youngest son of Sir James Palmer, of Dorney Court?"

"You know he is." I cracked the wax seal with my thumb, my heart racing with anticipation. "Just as you've known I've been a friend to Roger for months and months. There is nothing new whatsoever."

Swiftly I scanned Philip's letter, or rather, the three sentences of nothing.

He addressed me as "His Dearest Life," the way he always did, yet he was still vaguely away from London. He thanked me cordially for the many letters I'd sent to him, but could offer no confirmed date for his return to London. He trusted I was well, and would keep my love constant until he could hold me in his arms once again.

He wrote nothing of love for me.

"What is new is that you've clearly beguiled Mr. Palmer with your company," my mother was saying. "Though the Palmers suffered certain reverses during the war like the rest of us, Sir James has managed to keep a good estate at Dorney Court. He and his sons are situated to do well when the king returns."

"When?" I asked dully, refolding Philip's letter without reading it again. "You said 'when the king returns,' not 'if.' "

"I choose my words with intention, Barbara, not accident," she said. "With Cromwell finally buried, it's only a matter of time before the king is set properly back upon his throne. Everyone says so."

"That is true." I touched the heart pendant, thinking of what it meant to King Charles, and to me as well. If Roger kept the promise that this heart signified, then I could have a part in bringing Charles back to his kingdom. Hadn't he said that I could be of use to the cause? And hadn't that possibility meant so much more to me than all his other compliments to my grace and beauty?

"Surely you must have noticed the quality of his belongings when you were there," my mother prompted. "His furnishings, his goods. Sir James has always been clever about guarding his fortune."

"Roger says his father raised an entire troop of horses for the king's cause during the war. By his reckoning, Sir James spent at least seven thousand pounds of his own estate to support His Majesty." I'd heard often of this seven thousand pounds, perhaps too often; not only was Roger proud of his family's generosity, but at the same time he lamented the gift with a miser's unsavory grief.

"Seven thousand pounds?" My mother sniffed to show she was duly impressed. "That's a fine luxury, to have seven thousand pounds to share with the king. But that is what I mean, Barbara. His Majesty has marked such loyalty, and will reward it when he returns. You'll see. The Palmers will have that seven thousand pounds back tenfold in offices and land. Whenever Sir James drops his bread, you can be sure it will land with the butter upward."

"Likely it will," I said, turning away. "I'm going to bed now."

"Don't you leave before I'm done speaking," she said, hurrying to block my path to the staircase. "Mark what I say, Barbara. Without a fortune, you won't have many chances as choice as this one. Mr. Palmer would make a splendid match for you, and a useful alliance for your uncle and me. True, he is only a second son, and by a second wife, so the Palmer estates won't come to him, but Sir James will look after him handsomely nonetheless. And if you have already pleased Mr. Palmer as you seem, why, then—"

"Of course I pleased him, madam," I said, my voice stony. "Three times last night."

Embarrassment stained my mother's cheeks through her paint, as I knew it would. "I need no unsavory details, Barbara. I'll trust you to, ah, do what is necessary to secure the gentleman's attachment."

"I'm too young to wed," I protested, as I always did. What was it that Philip had told me so long ago—that we poor noble folk must trade away ourselves in marriage, and steal love instead wherever we might? "I'm scarce seventeen."

"Too old is more the truth," my mother said tartly. "You'll be eighteen next week. Once the king returns and there's a proper court around him, then London will be full of girls of good family, far prettier than you, Barbara, and far younger, too. And they'll be virgin ladies, not the Earl of Chesterfield's soiled leavings."

"I've no desire to hear this from you again, madam." I moved to squeeze past her, but she seized me by the arm to keep me there.

"Chesterfield will never marry you," she said bluntly. "You know that as well as I."

I didn't answer. How could I, when she was right, and I'd Philip's charming, faithless nothing of a letter still in my hand?

Yet my silence only made my mother more relentless, her fingers pressing into my arm. "Mr. Palmer can marry where he pleases, Barbara. You know that, too, else you should. Men can be coaxed into love."

"I don't love Mr. Palmer," I declared, "and never shall."

"What, you would lift your petticoats and spread your legs for Mr. Palmer without love, but you wouldn't accept him as your husband?"

"But I don't *wish* to marry Roger!"

*We poor noble folk must trade away ourselves in marriage. . . .*

"Your wishes are not the only thing that matters," she said sharply. "Your uncle and I will not keep our home open to you forever, not when you refuse to help your own situation. Given your scandalous behavior, no one would fault me if I sent you back to the country and left you there to rot."

I pulled my arm free. "I'm your daughter. You wouldn't do that to me. I wouldn't let you."

"Don't test me, Barbara," my mother warned. "Better to consider well the consequences of your licentious behavior, and then consider Mr. Palmer."

With her argument done, she turned and left me, her petticoats briskly sweeping the floorboards and her flop-eared little dog trotting at her heels. She'd always kept her word before. I'd no reason to doubt that she would again, not in this.

I thought of Philip, and I thought of Roger, but most of all I thought of myself, and whether I truly wished to spend the rest of my life stealing love wherever I might find it.

. . .

Five months later, on a day when the April skies wept with gray rain, I married Roger Palmer in the church of St. Gregory, in the shadow of St. Paul's. Pointedly none of Roger's family attended, leaving my mother and my uncle as the only witnesses to this folly, and the only ones to sign the register in the vestry afterwards.

Hand in hand, Roger and I ducked beneath the dripping portico to kiss as newly minted husband and wife. When the raindrops splattered into my hair and eyes, he laughed at my misfortune, and I crossly turned my cheek against his lips.

Less than an hour into our marriage, then, and already it was hard to say which of us had been dealt the more sorrowful hand.

# Chapter Four

Winter had given way to spring, and spring to early summer, and yet none of our hopes for the Commonwealth's collapse and King Charles's return had come true. As everyone had predicted, the new Lord Protector Richard Cromwell couldn't become half the leader his father had been. He was soft-spoken, hesitant, and unprepossessing, and when he reviewed the troops that had made his father so proud, he sat astride his mount so awkwardly that the men labored hard not to laugh. In London he'd become commonly known as Tumbledown Dick, while the army was more blunt about his deficiencies, and called him Queen Dick. As one of the Royalist wits sourly proclaimed, it was as if the old vulture had died, and from his ashes had risen a titmouse.

It could not last, and it didn't. When Richard refused to consider a separate commander in chief and tried to keep all the power to himself, as his father had done, then the army council began to meet in secret. In April, two of the most prominent officers—and those who'd been most loyal to the elder Cromwell—General John Desborough and Major General Charles Fleetwood, led a coup that removed Richard as Lord Protector and dissolved the Parliament that he'd called.

The country was now ruled by a Council of State, a republican mask donned by the army. Also brought back to office were the remnants of the Parliament that Oliver Cromwell had long ago dissolved, now ingloriously called the Rump—a name that always made me snort and laugh, no matter how solemnly it was invoked. This Rump was full of supporters for the restoration of the monarchy, and it truly seemed the time was ripening for Charles's return.

Even so, the Royalists seemed incapable of assembling a suitable force to bring the king back to power. Though other countries—Holland, Spain, Portugal—had sworn to help Charles regain his throne, none of them was offering the armies and funds to make such idle promises real. Since so many other attempts to retake England had ended in disastrous losses, the king's advisors refused to let him return without this show of force, or any real willingness of the people to welcome and support him.

For this, really, was the greater problem. While most of England had long grumbled into their ale about the weakness of Richard Cromwell and the oppression of life under the Commonwealth, few were willing to give life to those grumbles with real action. Even the noblemen among my friends, men whose families had lost the most in the wars, and who in turn sought to gain the most were the monarchy restored, seemed incapable of so much as raising a regiment from the people on their own lands. Roger's father had told him long ago that this was not so much from lazy torpidity or disinterest, but because these fatherless young gentlemen simply did not know how such things were done, having grown to manhood deprived of the examples of their elders.

I cannot say whether this was true or not. All I knew was that for whatever reason, Charles remained mired in Brussels with only his Lord Chancellor Sir Edward Hyde and a handful of tattered courtiers for company, while the Royalist cause did little more than plot and plan and send coded letters back and forth among themselves, like harmless schoolboys playing at spies in the attic.

My heady dreams of taking part in the king's return likewise lay fallow. Roger always had an excuse or reason why my services were not needed, and instead expected me to limit my activities to those of any drudging wife. As unpleasant as my life had been under my mother's roof, at least there I'd not been expected to attend tediously to the keeping of the house and staff, or to plan dinners for my husband with the cook, or to advise the laundry maid on how he liked the sleeves of his shirts pleated, exactly so. I saw little of the reputed Palmer fortune, either, and when I begged Roger for a new gown or petticoat to cheer my spirits, he'd tell me there was no money to spare on my fripperies, and I was forced to make do with the shabby leavings that I'd brought from my mother's house. Further, Roger wished me to be content with his company and no other, which only added to my growing unhappiness as his wife. It was as if he'd married me as one woman, and then as soon as we'd wed expected me to change into another.

Little wonder, then, that I was resentful and rebellious, unfortunate qualities in any new bride. When Philip returned to London and wrote to me, I returned his letters with the same fervor as before, and met him, too, as eagerly as if I'd no husband. I *was* the same woman after all; I hadn't changed a bit.

And though I continued to wear the glass cypher heart that Roger had given me around my neck, I thought of it as a sign of my loyalty to the king, and not to Roger. In a way the crystal heart was a perfect symbol for his love for me: hard, transparent, and without vibrancy or life.

But as is always the case whenever one believes life is cruel or unfair, worse was to come.

In the first week of June, I felt out of sorts and faintly ill, feverish one day and chilled the next. I said nothing to Roger, attributing my malaise to my general unhappiness and little more. Vague distempers and agues were common in London every summer, a part of the place and season. Still, my head and limbs ached and I'd lost the stomach for food, and one morning I felt so weary I could scarce crawl from our bed. When at last I finally did rise and sat at my looking-glass for my maid to dress my hair, she was the one who discovered what ailed me.

"What is this, madam?" she said, frowning down at my shoulder. "A scrape, yes?"

I twisted my head to look down to where she meant, pulling the gathered edge of my smock to one side to bare more of my shoulder.

This was no scrape, nor scratch, but an angry red rash spreading beyond my shoulders to my arms and back. The maid drew back, for she knew as well as I what such a rash did signify:

Smallpox.

The maid fled to fetch others, and I staggered back to the bed on my own, weeping into my pillow with suffering, grief, and fear. A sentence of death for a prisoner in the Tower could at least be revoked, but smallpox was never so generous. Nearly all its victims perished, and the few who by miracle survived seldom escaped without faces pitted and ravaged with scars. I was only eighteen, and I knew not which would be worse: to die outright, or to live, yet with my Villiers beauty forever destroyed.

By the next dawn, I was past caring either way. Fever racked my head, and I tossed and whimpered with the pain of it. Afterward I learned that Roger had ordered all the proper curatives. The bedchamber was draped in red cloth to draw out my fever, the windows sealed shut against any breath of draft or chill, the fire kept burning high. He summoned the best physician to my side, who bled and cupped me, and Dr. Harris of our church, who prayed over my delirious self to ease my way from this life to the next.

The first redness blossomed into pimples all over my face and body, which next turned to pustules that oozed and crusted as the first fever relaxed its grip. I saw the long faces of the physicians and understood what was not said in my hearing. They'd abandoned hope. I was going to die. I did not notice when my looking-glass was taken away from the room. When I finally did see its absence, I wept again, realizing how hideously flawed my poor face must have become.

As soon as Roger left me that day, I asked a servant for paper and pen, and wrote as best I could to Philip, begging for him to come to me one last time before I died. I knew he'd had smallpox himself, and thus would be in no risk from visiting me, and I was past caring if his last glimpse of me was one of ugly deformity. All I wished was to see him one final time in this life. I vowed that my last words would be a prayer for his happiness, and that I meant to die as I'd lived, loving him above all other things. I gave this over to the servant to deliver, and prayed for the strength to survive long enough for him to join me.

I would have done better simply to pray for myself, and left Philip from my plea. His message was as faithless as always: he was sorry to learn of the illness of His Dearest Life, and wished for my complete and unscathed recovery, but he regretted that circumstance made it impossible for him to fly to my bedside. I shrieked, wondering what the pretty name and face of this circumstance could be, and hurriedly penned another note, humbling myself further miserably. What did I have to lose, facing death? I swore that if only he'd come to me, I was sure to recover, and further, that I'd then leave Roger and run off with him whenever and wherever he pleased.

To this I received no reply from Philip, and my poor heart ached at such abandonment. I longed for death, to put an end to the torment he inflicted upon me. Yet Fate had determined me for greater things, or perhaps my plain country upbringing had simply made me too strong and willful to succumb. Whatever the reason, my health began slowly to improve. My fever subsided and my strength and appetite returned, and I watched as one by one the scabs fell from my skin.

Best of all came the day that Roger himself brought my breakfast tray as I sat in the bed, propped up by pillows.

"Good day, Barbara," he said, setting the tray onto my lap. "You look as bright as the morning."

"You flatter me," I said, peeking beneath the napkin to see what the cook had sent up for my breakfast. "You're kind to bring this yourself, Roger."

He *had* been kind to me in my illness, more kind than I either expected or deserved. I'd freely grant him that, and thank him for it, too.

"It's no flattery at all," he said. "You're my wife. You'll always be beautiful in my eyes. But likely the rest of the world will agree with me, too."

He pulled my small tortoise-framed looking-glass from inside his doublet and handed it to me. I seized it, and with shaking hands held it up to my face while Roger drew back the window curtains and let the morning sun fall full upon me.

"It's clear," I whispered, stunned. "My face is clear, Roger, without a single pockmark!"

"I told you, you're as beautiful as ever," he said softly. "No one will ever know you were afflicted."

"Not a mark," I whispered, tears of joy in my eyes as I ran my fingers across my smooth cheeks. I know it must sound as if I were the vainest creature in the world, concerned with my own face and no more. Yet like many women, I was known only by my beauty, even famous for it, and to have that taken from me at so young an age would have left me bereft and lost as to whom I might truly be.

Roger smiled, watching me, and I smiled in return, believing he understood my joy, and shared it.

He understood me, yes, but not the way I'd thought.

"At least my prayers were answered, Barbara," he said slowly, "if not your own."

Still giddy with relief, I looked at him over the glass in my hand. "Oh, Roger, you make no sense! Of course I prayed for my deliverance, just as now I'll make my prayers of thanks for having been restored."

"So many prayers, Barbara," he said, reaching into his pocket. "It's a wonder you can recall them all."

He pulled out a folded sheet, and to my dismay I recognized it as the second letter I'd written to Philip when I'd been so ill.

The seal was broken, and I could be sure that he'd read the contents. Yet even then my first thought was not of my sworn husband, Roger, but of my lover Philip, and how he'd not come to me because he'd never received my letter. Ah, how willingly I made excuses for Philip, no matter how unworthy he was of my love, and how little in turn I'd spare for Roger!

Now I stared at the letter in his hand, my cheeks no longer flushed with smallpox, but guilt. "How did you come by that letter?"

"Your servants were mine first, and still answer to me," he said, not so much angry as sad. "So you do recall writing to Lord Chesterfield? You don't deny it, or blame it on a feverish delirium?"

"Of course I don't deny it, Roger," I said uneasily. "How can I, when you're holding the proof in your hand?"

He tossed the letter onto the bed beside me, as if he didn't want to touch it any longer. "I suppose I must grant you credit for honesty, if for nothing else."

I glanced down at the letter without gathering it up. Why should I, when I recalled every fervent word I'd written?

"You knew me before we wed," I said defensively. "You knew what manner of woman I was."

"I did," he said. "But that was before you swore before God to be my wife, and all that entailed. Or have you forgotten that in your lust for Chesterfield's bed?"

"I didn't forget." The letter on the bed now seemed doubly damning, yet still I was too foolishly enraptured of Philip to throw myself on Roger's mercy, as I should. "How could I, with you to remind me?"

Roger's lips pressed tightly together, and too late I realized my tart words had cost me whatever tender kindness my illness had inspired in him.

"That is good," he said. "I'll see that you'll have sufficient time to act upon those vows in the coming months."

I frowned, not liking the sound of that. "What are you saying, Roger?"

"That you are still my wife, Barbara. Not even the drivel you write to Chesterfield will change that." He bowed curtly. "I'll send your maid to pack your things. We leave London for Dorney Court in the morning."

As long as I'd known Roger, he'd praised his family's home at Dorney Court, in Berkshire near Windsor: how felicitous its air, how sweet its flowers, the elegance of the ancient timbers and bricks and the boundless warmth of the hospitality to be found therein. Anyone who heard his rhapsodies would believe it was a woman that inspired him, certainly not a creaking pile of plaster and wood, and I soon realized that I could never hold a candle to the sentimental brilliance of Dorney Court.

I had put off visiting this inanimate rival as long as I could. It was not only the estate itself that I dreaded, so far from my beloved

London, but Roger's mother, who'd continued to live there after Sir James's death at the end of 1658. She was a papist, given overmuch to dogged prayer. I'd known the old man had despised me and had pleaded with Roger to break with me, but his mother's hatred ran even deeper. Roger was her only child, and she defended him like a mother lioness does her cub. Through Roger, I learned she blamed me somehow not only for beguiling her son but also as the cause of her husband's death. No matter what the reputation might be for hospitality at Dorney Court, I'd guessed there'd be none for me, and I was right.

Roger and I came by the river, the best way, he claimed, to see the house the first time. I saw, and I was unimpressed: a rambling, old-fashioned pile from the time of Queen Elizabeth, brick and timbers and plaster and greenery all jumbled together in the mists. Roger often lamented how badly the house had been ravaged by the parliamentary army in the war, and how his father's collection of rare miniatures and medals had been plundered, but I suspected the estate still looked much as it had for the last century or two.

We were given chambers far from the others on account of our near-newlywed status, certain proof that Roger hadn't confided much to his family. The main chamber had floors that dipped and chairs that creaked, and a high, water-stained ceiling that I stared at whenever I lay in bed, turned away from Roger.

I'd been a guest there for three days before Roger finally introduced me to his mother, a weary, faded woman who mercifully kept her dislike for me locked inside her black woolen mourning, along with most of her conversation. The only question she asked was whether I was with child yet. I told her no, and she then ceased to have any further to do with me, which was perfectly agreeable by my lights as well as hers.

That night, I felt Roger's hand upon my hip.

"You needn't have looked so shocked when my mother addressed you, Barbara," he said in the dark, his fingers spreading as they journeyed along my hip to my thigh and back again. "A child would be a great blessing to us."

I curled my fingers into a ball, trying not to tense beneath his touch. By law I belonged to him, as every wife did to her husband, and though I could withhold my own pleasure from spite if I chose, I could not refuse him the use of my body. "I was no such blessing to my mother."

"Your mother had no choice because of the war," he said. "You know that. She sent you into the country, where you'd be safe during the war. If you had a child of your own—of our own—you'd understand."

"I cannot say if I would or not." Unlike most young women, I'd been raised without any siblings, in a household of two childless women who had always made it clear they kept me for my mother's payment alone. I'd never seen children and babies as other than noisy, demanding, untidy, and costly—a plague more to be avoided than desired. Surely this impression was my own mother's legacy to me as well; the only time when my presence had given her any pleasure was when she'd successfully pushed me into wedding Roger.

"I think you would, dearest," he said softly, shifting closer to me on the lumpy mattress, so I could feel his thighs pressing against mine. "I've heard that a woman doesn't know true contentment until she holds her firstborn in her arms."

"Did your mother tell you that, too?" I asked, unable to contain my bitterness. I didn't want a child now, not his or any other man's. Childbirth was as great a fatal peril to women as war to men, and even those who survived the pain and suffering likewise bore the scars—lost teeth, withered breasts, fat stomachs—to prove it. "That you must breed your wild filly to tame the spirit from her, and make her your broodmare?"

"My mother would never say that." He'd worked my smock over my hip, his hand insistent and slightly moist upon my bare skin. "But tell me, Barbara. Where's the sin in me desiring my beautiful wife?"

I sighed, not knowing how to explain my unhappiness. I'd try as many of the little tricks Philip had taught me to keep myself safe, but if Roger was determined to sire a child, then as my husband, he would have his way.

Yet still Roger sensed my resignation. "What is ill, Barbara?" he said, his reproach unmistakable even as he slipped his hand between my legs. "I know by nature you've a warm temperament. In London, you were always ardent for love."

I squeezed my eyes shut, trying to will myself to keep still. I'd not lain with a man, Roger or Philip, since before I'd sickened with the smallpox, and no matter how miserable my heart might be or how artless Roger's caress, I feared my body's longing would betray me.

"In London I wasn't buried among the rushes and the conies, the way I am here," I whispered, my breath coming faster. "In London, I wasn't fit to perish of boredom."

"Then I must do my best to see that you are better entertained, dearest." He rolled me onto my back and settled between my legs. It seemed he was done in less than a blink, long before he'd come near to fetching me in return. He did not seem to notice, either, kissing me afterward as if he were granting me the greatest gift imaginable, and not the other way round.

For a long time I lay in the dark and listened to Roger's soft, satisfied huffs as he slept beside me. His seed still lay sticky upon me, yet my body and my heart together ached from unfulfillment.

I would not die of boredom at Dorney Court, no matter how much I longed to. Even I knew such a death was the purlieu of poets, not true life. But to expire from a lack of pleasure, from the joy to be found with love—now that, *that* seemed a hazard genuine enough.

Within the week, my life at Dorney Court did in fact become more interesting, though not in the way that Roger had meant.

I was coming back from my early walk through the gardens when I saw the carriage being led into the stable yard. I'd not heard we were expecting visitors—the house was still officially in mourning for Sir James—nor did I recognize the carriage. The horses looked weary from hard driving, as if they'd journeyed the night long on some urgent business. All the servants could tell me was that the newcomers were two gentlemen, friends of Mr. Palmer's, and that the three of them were now closeted in the library, not to be disturbed.

By the time that Roger came upstairs to dress for dinner, I was in a froth of curiosity, demanding to know who these mysterious gentlemen could be.

"I'm surprised you haven't guessed, Barbara." He pulled a fresh shirt over his head, playing my suspense like a fisherman with his catch. "One gentleman should be well known to you by reputation, I believe. Sir Alan Broderick."

"Sir Alan here!" I gasped with delighted surprise. Though I'd never met Sir Alan, I'd certainly heard enough of him from Roger. Sir Alan was the leader of the Sealed Knot, and was reputed to have been chosen by the king himself to further his cause in England. "Is the other gentleman party to the Knot as well?"

"He is," Roger said, lifting his chin to tie the collar strings of his shirt in a tidy bow. "Lord Thomas Mulberry. It's natural for Sir Alan to come to visit. He's distant kin of yours, you know."

"Everyone is distant kin to the Villiers," I said, scarce able to contain my excitement. "That's not why he's here. Are you making fresh plans? Are you gathering forces to support the king's return? Oh, Roger, tell me all!"

He smiled smugly, pleased he could make me beg for even something as petty as this. "In time, my dear, in time. Sir Alan and Lord Thomas will be with us for a few days. They find this house an agreeable refuge, considering the army's ban against papists and Royalists within twenty miles of London."

"Oh, pish, Roger, no one heeds that. Why, even here we're but five miles from London."

"We're as good as a hundred, for all the army cares."

"We're as good as two hundred to me." I gave his arm a little shove. "If you won't tell me now, Roger, then you must let me stay when you gentlemen begin to speak in earnest. You must let me hear and judge for myself."

He frowned and shook his head. "I do not know, Barbara. My mother will expect you to retire with her. It's not customary for ladies to remain at the table with the gentlemen and be present for such serious discussions."

"Once you wished me to know of such things, the things that mattered to you." I touched the cypher heart I still wore around my throat, then idly trailed my fingers lower, over the plump curves of my breasts, to remind him of other things as well. Though my gown was at least six months behind the French fashion, it still became me: pale pink satin that made me look like a glowing, tender blossom waiting to be plucked. The bodice was cut low and snug, with a falling lace collar that somehow revealed more of both my breasts and creamy shoulders by veiling them than displaying them outright.

"You recall, Roger," I coaxed gently. "Before we were wed—when you claimed I was more . . . ardent—you kept nothing from me."

"That's Sir Alan's decision to make, Barbara." His gaze followed my hand, and I knew I'd have my way from the manner in which he swallowed, his lips pressing together as if to keep his lust from bubbling from his mouth. "I cannot promise anything."

But in his way he already had.

"I see you wear the cypher of our martyred king, Mistress Palmer." Across the table, Sir Alan raised his wine toward me with approval. "An admirable ornament."

"Thank you, Sir Alan," I murmured, smiling in return at this distant kinsman. "It was a gift from my husband."

Sir Alan nodded, and held his goblet up for the servant to refill. He'd no share of the Villiers beauty, that was certain, being short and stout, with a sandy mustache draped over his mouth. I'd already learned he was a man full of unseen prickles, quick to take offense where no slights were intended: an unfortunate quality, I thought, for a leader of so delicate and important an organization. "It's always wise for a gentleman to brand what belongs to him, eh, Palmer?"

Roger and Lord Thomas laughed, yet while a dozen quick retorts came to mind, I said nothing. Honey-sweet words always fared better with men than tart ones, no matter how much that sticky sweetness would sometimes choke and clog my throat. It was worth it. At least now at the beginning, the price of being permitted to remain here among the gentlemen was that I present myself as a beautiful, obliging decoration, and nothing more taxing—a role I could play to perfection even while I slept.

Now I leaned forward, turned a bit in my chair, just enough to prettily display both my arms and bosom, and slowly drew through my fingers one of the long, glossy curls clustered by my cheek.

"I'll gladly wear my husband's mark, Sir Alan, just as I wear his ring," I said, "but my loyal heart and duty must always bow first to my sovereign lord, His Majesty King Charles."

"Well said, Mistress Palmer." Sir Alan shoved back his chair and raised his goblet, forcing the others to join him. "To His Sacred Majesty, and his return to his rightful throne."

"To the king," all echoed, but only Sir Alan emptied his goblet again, holding it out impatiently for another filling. I'd heard King Charles detested drunkenness, and could not tolerate company that toppled headfirst into the grape. Clearly he'd never dined with Sir Alan, else there'd be another leader for the Sealed Knot.

"There now, Sir Alan, I told you my wife was to be trusted," Roger said with unbecoming eagerness. "No questioning her loyalty, eh?"

"No, indeed." Sir Alan's face was flushed as he studied me, and I knew it wasn't from wine alone. "His Majesty can always count on the beautiful women to support him."

"Have you met His Majesty, Sir Alan?" I asked.

"Oh, scores of times," he answered, likely expanding those times for my benefit. "Every inch the monarch, and a good many inches at that. He's half a head taller than most men, you know."

"How fascinating," I said, and I meant it. I'd not realized the king stood so far above his subjects, and I wondered wickedly if the rest of him were to a royal scale as well. How else could he truly be the first gentleman of his kingdom?

"I can assure you, Mistress Palmer," Sir Alan continued, warming to his subject, "that there's never been another English monarch like him. Intelligent, virile, thoughtful, benevolent, even in his current reduced circumstances. He's very dark, on account of that foreign Italian blood from his Medici grandmother, but still the ladies do sigh and judge him most handsome."

"The ladies should not be discounted, Sir Alan," Roger said cheerfully. "They will constitute a sizable part of his kingdom, and if my wife is any indication, their loyalty will never be questioned."

I smiled. Ah, Roger had no notion of what I thought when I imagined our tall, handsome king in exile, and it had nothing to do with loyal duty, either.

"Your wife, Palmer, and your sister as well," Sir Alan said. "Or more properly, your sister's husband, and his brother beyond that. What a fortuitous connection that has proven to be for us!"

I turned to Roger, my smile now not quite as charming. I'd yet to meet his sister Catherine, nor had I much desire to do so, yet it irritated me that she might know more of my husband's activities than did I. "What connection is this, Roger?"

"Through the Darrells, my dear," he said, his smile sickly with an earnestness that pleaded wordlessly for my cooperation before these other gentlemen. "You recall that Catherine is wed to Marmaduke Darrell. His brother Henry has recently secured the place of principal clerk to the Council of State and is privy to their most secret debates and correspondence—all of which he is now copying, and forwarding to Sir Alan. We've never before had such access to the most privileged information."

I cared not a fig for either Marmaduke or Henry themselves, but this connection between the Darrells and the Palmers could prove most profitable to Roger in the future, and to me as well. No wonder he'd not wanted his mother to overhear such a conversation, considering how he'd led his sister's husband into this treasonous activity.

"This is your doing, Roger?" I asked, pleasingly surprised he'd show such daring. "To arrange such service to the king?"

"Don't let your husband be modest, Mistress Palmer," Sir Alan said heartily. "This must all be held in the greatest secrecy, of course, but I've made sure His Majesty is aware of every one of your husband's contributions. And with this last gift of a thousand pounds—"

"A thousand pounds!" There was nothing feigned about my astonishment. I'd been forced to follow endless grating economies while he'd been keeping a secret worth a thousand pounds?

"Such generosity is sure to be rewarded when the king returns to London, my dear," Roger said hurriedly. "I consider it not only an investment for the crown but for ourselves in the future."

Sir Alan leaned back in his chair, his smile showing how thoroughly pleased he was with himself, and with our wine, too. "Make no mistake, His Sacred Majesty will recognize his true friends and glean the gold from the base pretenders like Mordaunt."

"Mordaunt?" I asked, still painfully focused on that lost thousand pounds. "Pray, who might be Mordaunt?"

"A rogue and a rascal, Mistress Palmer," Sir Alan said disdainfully. "A dissembling fellow quite unworthy of your notice."

I looked to Roger for more explanation. The name niggled at my memory, something I couldn't quite grasp.

"John Mordaunt, Barbara," he said with that now-familiar pained look to his face. "A low sort of man who has beguiled the king into granting permission to form another group of supporters, a group with the audacity to call themselves the Trust."

"Your rivals, you mean," I said, rapping my knuckles lightly on the table before me for emphasis. I did this partly to make my words ring with truth, but also to distract Roger's attention from whatever guilt might have flashed across my own face. For now I recalled where I'd heard of Mordaunt, and of the Trust: my own dear Chesterfield had been one of the group's earliest members, and a close associate of John Mordaunt's.

"To call Mordaunt a rival is to make him our equal for the king's attention," Sir Alan said peevishly. "Let me assure you, Mistress Palmer, that he is far from that."

Lord Thomas leaned across the table, his mouth an earnest pucker. "I've heard that Mordaunt is in Brussels even now with His Majesty. I've heard he sailed last week, and was well received. I've heard—"

"Mordaunt means nothing," Sir Alan said curtly. "We must act as if he does not exist."

I frowned, too irritated by their sniping not to speak my mind. "Wouldn't it serve the king better, Sir Alan, if you ceased bickering among yourselves and presented a common unity?"

"Barbara, please," Roger cautioned. "In time, in time."

"Pray, Roger, what time will that be?" I scoffed. "His Sacred Majesty has become no more than a mirage on a hot summer's day, his promise glittering bright in the distance, only to dissolve and vanish and reform again with his return ever farther away."

"Oh, he's real enough, Mistress Palmer," Lord Thomas promised. "There are plans being made even now for a concerted uprising that could bring him here as soon as this summer. I've heard that this time His Majesty has twenty-five hundred troops ready to help carry him to victory. I've heard that—"

"No more of that, now," Sir Alan said, tapping his forefinger to his nose—a foolish gesture that I always associated with drunkards who believed they were being cunning and sly, and were neither. "We needn't overburden Mistress Palmer's pretty head with our machinations."

"True, true, Barbara," Roger said, striving to soothe me, I knew. "You can be sure that the king's interests are being addressed in the best manner, and with the greatest alacrity. It's no easy thing to send word to him or to Hyde in Brussels."

With my chin tucked low, I slanted my eyes at him, an expression that generally succeeded in my having my own way. "If it's so very difficult, then perhaps a different messenger should be sent."

Roger swung back as sharply as if I'd struck him with the flat of my hand. He knew full well what I was suggesting—that I'd happily serve as a courier—and his response proved to me he'd never so much as suggested the notion to the others, no matter what he'd vowed to me.

Not that Sir Alan noticed anything amiss between Roger and me. "With so much at stake, we're always cautious with our messengers, Mistress Palmer, relying upon only the most trustworthy of—"

"What of me?" I asked swiftly. "Would I be sufficiently trustworthy for your purpose?"

Sir Alan glanced at Roger with anxious surprise. Why is it all men are conspirators with one another against our sex?

"It's not so much a matter of trust, Mistress Palmer, as, ah, as the ability to evade enemies, and—"

"Who is better at evasion than a pretty woman?" I smiled, and the way his ruddy cheeks turned redder still only served my argument. "I doubt there's an enemy from here to Brussels who wouldn't let me pass."

"That *is* true, Barbara," Roger said slowly. I couldn't tell if he were trying to make up for being caught in falsehoods by agreeing with me, or if he actually believed I could serve the king's cause in this way. "But there would be risks. Your life and freedom could be in peril."

"The parliamentary men are not the only danger, Mistress Palmer," Sir Alan said. "Why, this summer there's been such an outbreak of the smallpox in the Hague and in Belgium, we've been loath to send anyone."

I smiled again. Everyone in the room knew that the real danger was not so much smallpox but the king himself. Our bachelor monarch was reputed to be an infamous gallant with the ladies, a man who'd sired his first bastard while scarce more than a boy himself. Many would argue that no reasonable husband would even dream of sending his beautiful young wife on such an errand, to such a monarch, that to do so was the same as touching flame to pitch.

Not, of course, that I chose to remind the gentlemen of this now.

"There again I can be of use to you, Sir Alan," I said cheerfully, "for I have only this summer had the same pox, and now shall never fear it again."

"Nothing frightens my dear wife," Roger said, looking down into his goblet. "She's unlike any other lady you'll ever know."

Everyone at the table realized that was no compliment, yet still I smiled.

"The Palmers have a long and honorable history of service to the crown, Roger," I said, putting a silver edge to my own words. "If these gentlemen choose to send me on an errand to His Majesty, then I'll only be adding more glory to your family's name."

"I should hope so, my dear." Roger set his goblet down, squaring it to the edge of the table with one finger against the stem. "I expect you to use the opportunity to remind His Majesty of exactly how much the Palmers have already sacrificed for his cause, and recommend our loyalty to his favor in the future."

"Of course, Roger." I motioned for the servant to refill my husband's goblet. "That thousand pounds is a debt that should be repaid, and with interest, yes?"

"Yes." That was all, and that was enough. My husband's expression when he finally looked up was so composed that it shocked me for its levelness. So that thousand pounds was of far more value to him than his wife, I thought with no small bitterness. The best role I could serve him in was to shepherd his gold.

And he believed a child would solve all the trials of our marriage!

Sir Alan leaned forward, his eagerness so unmistakable that I realized to my delight how welcome my offer was.

"So if I were to employ your wife on an errand to Brussels, you would consent?" he asked. "You would not try to stop her, no matter the risk?"

"I would only ask that she not be put into unreasonable danger," Roger said, and gave a small humorless laugh. "She is my wife, you understand. Like all my property, I'd want her returned to me undamaged. But as for her wishing to serve the Royalist cause with the same fervor and courage as the others in my family—why, I can hardly forbid her such a brave show of loyalty to both the Stuarts and the Palmers, can I?"

No, he could not. And if my smile mingled triumph with that much-vaunted fervor and courage, then so be it. Once again I'd gotten my way, and I meant to make the most of it however I could.

Not for Roger, or the rest of his loathsome clan, or for that poisoned thousand pounds. Instead I meant to strive for the betterment of the one person I could truly trust in the entirety of England: Barbara Villiers Palmer.

# Chapter Five

It is the peculiar way of this life that whenever we mortals prepare some fine scheme for ourselves, an event or occurrence we could never have foreseen suddenly pops up to twist and toss our tidy plans to the winds. That was what became of my great hope to become a courier to the king, in that last summer we were ruled by Parliament.

First of all, the Sealed Knot itself began to unravel, with ugly accusations of deceit everywhere. On the very eve that His Majesty was set to sail back to England, a fresh scandal broke in London that made him cancel his embarkation, and likely save his royal life. One of the founders of the Knot, Sir Richard Willys, was publicly accused of being a double agent and feeding news from the king's supporters to the army and back again. Willys and several of his nearest conspirators were imprisoned in the Tower for treason. Such betrayal shook the faith of Sir Alan, and my husband as well. Like nervous mice they raced for cover in the wainscoting, forgetting their loyalties to the king in their haste to save themselves and sulk afterward.

Worse followed in August. The uprising organized by Mordaunt was set for the first of the month, and was rumored to feature not only a military show of strength but also a concerted demonstration by the common people for His Majesty. The king had even gone to Calais, certain that at last he'd be able to cross the Channel to reclaim his kingdom.

But like every other uprising, this one collapsed as well beneath the weight of expectations and confusion. Disappointed, the king left Calais and returned to Brussels once again. Only the forces led by Sir George Booth at Chester made any sort of showing, but even that was soon put down by the army, the leaders marched to the Tower.

Among them, to my sorrow but not my surprise, was the Earl of Chesterfield. Although Philip had been in and out of the Tower so many times that he jested about how it should be his permanent lodgings in London, this time the accusations would not be so easily dismissed. He was charged with high treason, and all his estates were confiscated.

This I learned from others, from friends we had in common in the old days before my marriage. I'd no letter from Philip himself, nor had I tried to write to him. I hadn't received any word from him since I'd been at Dorney Court. Still, I made excuses for Philip's silence, telling myself that Roger would have intercepted any letters that had come for me, which was, in truth, possible enough. I was as much a prisoner there in the country as Philip himself was within those bleak stone walls over the Thames.

Yet when at last I heard of Philip's release, the news came from the most unlikely of sources: my husband.

He came rushing into our bedchamber one morning in January, bringing with him a great gust of chilly wind from the hall that made me burrow deeper beneath the coverlets. Dorney Court was such an old and rickety place that the fireplaces had little effect no matter how much wood was piled in the hearth, and I was almost always cold there. Though it was nearly noon, I was still abed and keeping warm with a new French novel, for really, what reason had I to rise?

"Barbara, have you heard this?" he declared, waving a newssheet in the air. "What have you to say of it?"

"I can't say a word until you tell me what you mean, Roger," I said, yawning. " 'Have you heard this, have you heard this!' You might as well be the watch, roaring out the hour."

"It's your old acquaintance Chesterfield," he said, tipping the paper toward the window to read. "He can never keep his name clear of speculation and gossip, can he?"

That made me sit upright. "What has happened to him?" I demanded anxiously. "Is he hurt? Have they harmed him in the Tower?"

"Oh, no, nothing of that kind." Roger was clearly enjoying tormenting me this way, even as he scowled down at the paper with righteous disapproval. "Chesterfield's long since been released from the Tower, anyway."

"He has? When? Why didn't you tell me before?"

His glance was as cold as the snow on the sill of the windows. "Because it's not seemly for you to know of that gentleman's activities, Barbara, much less to care."

"But you can't just tell me half, Roger," I cried. "That's barbarously unfair of you."

He gave a great heaving sigh, as if this were the hardest demand ever put upon him. "Very well. Because there are so many others crowded into the Tower these days, the courts released Chesterfield on his own surety. He had to pledge ten thousand pounds and swear that he'd not engage in further treasonous activities."

"At least he's free," I said with no small relief. "It's very hard for him to be locked away like some vile criminal."

Despite Roger's best efforts to stay stern as a judge, he couldn't help but smirk. "But you see, that's exactly what he's become. He's wanted for murder."

"Murder?" I repeated, shocked afresh. "Philip a murderer?"

"Oh, come, Barbara, you know the man far better than that. He'd scarce given his pledge before he'd found trouble again. He challenged some poor young fellow—a Francis Wooley, it says here—to a duel over the sale of a horse. They met at dawn in some field in Kensington."

But I knew exactly which field, behind the house of a certain tolerant Mr. Colby, who accepted a few coins from Philip in exchange for taking no notice of dueling on his land. Oh, I knew: just as I knew how Philip could no more refuse a chance to clash swords on a misty dawn morning than he could turn his cheek away from the kiss of a pretty lady. I'd long ago lost count of the number of challenges he'd fought, just as I had of his dalliances.

"And Philip killed the other man?" I asked, sickened, though I already knew the answer.

"He did," Roger said with inappropriate relish. "This Wooley was an inexperienced, pious young gentleman, no match at all for a practiced duelist. Chesterfield wounded him first in the hand, then took further advantage to run his blade clean through Wooley's heart. Wooley's father—a reverend doctor and a court preacher, mind you, and the old king's chaplain as well—was stricken to discover his son's body facedown in the grass, his prayer book still in the pocket of his coat."

"And Philip?" I asked faintly.

"Fled to France, they say, as good as banished," Roger said. "If he sets foot once again on English soil, Reverend Dr. Wooley has vowed to have him seized, tried, and hanged for murder. Chesterfield's ruined now. Not even his connections to the king will be able to gain him a pardon, not given those circumstances. Besides, you know how the king hates dueling."

"Such a waste," I murmured unhappily. "Such a waste of a life."

"I'll choose to believe you're lamenting young Wooley, Barbara, and not His Lordship." He tossed the newssheet and it fluttered onto the bed. "You can read it for yourself, if you please."

Numbed by such grievous news, I stared at the paper and left it untouched, drawing the coverlet higher over my shoulders instead. "I see no reason to read it, no."

"That's the wisest thing you've said in months." He began to leave, then paused at the door, as if the notion had only then struck him. "Have your maidservant pack your belongings, Barbara. So long as the river stays free of ice, we'll return to London the day after tomorrow."

He shut the door with a self-pleased thump, leaving me to sink down against the pillows. I closed my eyes, too stricken now even to weep. It is one thing to be a young fool in love, and quite another to be forgotten and left behind simply for being a young fool. There was no other way for me to consider this last careless action of Philip's, and both my heart and my pride felt the pain of it. France would be full of beautiful, obliging ladies. I would soon enough be but a fading memory to Philip, if I wasn't already.

At least my imprisonment at Dorney Court was done, and I'd finally return to London. There was some solace to be found in that, if in nothing else.

And though I'd no way of knowing it then, within the week my fortunes would shift again, and I'd soon embark on the single greatest adventure—and the most passionate love—of my life.

I was nineteen years old, and I was ready.

Philip's hasty departure from England was not the only reason for Roger and me to return to London. A new election was pending to mark the dissolution of the much-despised Rump Parliament, and Roger was in the forefront of those toiling earnestly to secure a new Parliament favoring the king. He was even planning to run for a seat himself, representing the borough of New Windsor, near Dorney Court. To win such an election, he needed to become better known in political circles in London.

Thus, as soon as we'd settled back into our lodgings, we began to host a series of small gatherings in the evenings for gentlemen that Roger wished to impress, as well as their ladies on occasion. I won't so much as call these evenings entertainments, as they were for the most part deadly dull, with solemn gentlemen in deep conversation with one another, while the few ladies only wished to speak of their children. We often served a cold supper for these hard talkers to nibble upon, a light collation of meats and fowl, and though we offered wine, too, no one ever dared drink to excess, or even to amusement. Like jockeys on a racecourse, they were jostling with one another to improve their place and rank for the ribbon at the finish, that glorious moment when Charles would return to power.

I tried my best to leaven these evenings with my own natural merriment, but to little avail, nor did Roger wish me to be too spirited. Somberness was the order of these days, and the evenings, too, and in small rebellion I began to call Roger *Monsieur,* after the French, because it vexed him so. And if I dallied once or thrice with old friends from my days with Philip, well, so be it. For the short time they took, I could feel wanted and forget my troubles in an amiable if fleeting embrace. I was lonely and forlorn, and such encounters meant little to me of lasting significance or value.

The best I could say about this time was that Roger loosened the strings on his purse and let me have a new blue quilted petticoat, and a French lace collar to freshen the neck of my best bodice. God knows this was little enough, and scarce worthy of a lady's maid, let alone the Palais Royal, but still I presented a pleasing enough figure to make the somber gentlemen ogle me when they thought I wouldn't notice.

Into one of these dull evenings came Sir Alan Broderick. I'd not seen him since Dorney Court, and welcomed him at the door as cousins should, with a kiss. This time his face was ruddy with the winter night, not drink, the skin of his cheek cold and tight beneath my lips and his breath frozen into a rim of frost along the edges of his gingery mustache.

"How good of you to join us, Sir Alan," I said, making sure the servant took his cloak and hat. "Come by the fire where it's warm. My husband will be glad to see you after so—"

"I've come to see you, madam, not your husband." He looked past me into the front room, gauging who else might be within. "Is there some chamber where we might speak unheard?"

"Of course," I said without hesitation, and led him into the small closet that I used for writing letters and reading. There was no fireplace—when I sat at the desk in the winter months, I often brought a tin box of coals to set beneath my feet, under my petticoat—and scarce room to turn about, but no one would think to disturb us here. I lit the candlesticks while he stamped and flapped his arms to warm himself, more like a stocky small horse than a man. I motioned for him to take the armchair, and sat myself on the small stool before the window.

"I'm glad I've found you home," he said as he dropped heavily into the chair, his sword's scabbard thumping against the carved wooden arm. "Do you recall when we last met, madam? When you offered to serve the king's cause however you could?"

I nodded eagerly. "I do recall it, yes," I said, "and my offer still stands, a hundred times over."

"I am glad to hear it." He leaned forward, his voice dropping to a confidential whisper. "We need you at once, Mistress Palmer, as soon as you can be spared by your husband."

Briskly I waved my hand, dismissing any objections that Roger would dare to have. "I give myself entirely over to you, Sir Alan, and I'm sure *Monsieur* will likewise agree."

"*Monsieur*?" he asked uncertainly.

"My husband, Mr. Palmer," I said, unable quite to keep the scorn from my voice. "It is a small endearment I keep for him."

I caught the hint of hesitation in his expression, or perhaps it was only a trick of the shifting candlelight. "As you say, madam. His generosity and your bravery are to be much applauded."

I clapped my hands together before my face. "There now. That's all the applauding I require. Tell me the nature of my task, Sir Alan. Pray tell me at once."

He smiled, pleased, I think, by my boldness. "I've a small number of letters of the most urgent variety that need to be taken to Brussels, and a parcel of specie as well."

"To Brussels? To His Majesty?"

"Hush, hush, not so loudly, I beg you," cautioned Sir Alan, glancing nervously over his shoulder. "But yes, to His Majesty, and to the lord chancellor."

I sat back in my chair, stunned by such a fortunate opportunity. I would be able to leave this dull world of parliamentary politicking. I would instead have adventure and excitement such as I'd sorely missed.

I would finally be in the company of His Majesty King Charles II, and my thoughts flashed back once again to that first image I'd seen of him, the engraved portrait that likely still hung in my mother's bedchamber.

But Sir Alan misread my anticipation. "Forgive me, Mistress Palmer," he said, rising to rest a calming hand upon my arm. "I didn't mean to upset you."

"You didn't, Sir Alan, not at all," I exclaimed, excitement making me breathless. "In truth, I cannot wait to leave, and begin—"

Without warning the door flew open, Roger's hand still upon the latch. Clearly from the fierceness in his expression he'd intended to catch me in some manner of misadventure with a gentleman, and the swiftness with which he was forced to change that face when he realized it was Sir Alan almost made me laugh aloud.

"Good day, Palmer." Sir Alan straightened, jerking his hand from my arm with the kind of haste that showed he'd felt guilt where no guilt was necessary. "I was just, ah, addressing your lady."

How amusing that Sir Alan's conscience should be so lacking in ease, while mine was completely at peace.

"Sir Alan has come with an urgent request, Roger," I said. "He needs a courier to take letters and gold to His Majesty in Brussels, and he has asked me to go."

"He has?" Roger asked uncertainly, his gaze shifting from Sir Alan to me and back again.

I smiled up at him as pleasingly as I could. "Sir Alan has honored me, yes. Of course I'm sure he would have asked you to go first, except that you're far too occupied with the coming election."

Sir Alan nodded vigorously. "I remembered that Mistress Palmer had offered last summer. We were at Dorney Court, and it was hot as blazes. You were there, too, Palmer. You had no objections then."

Sir Alan still sounded like a boy who'd been caught filching meat pies from the cook, when all he'd done was touch my arm. Ah, what fools men can be!

"Quite true, Sir Alan. You do recall that, too, don't you, Roger?" I prompted, coaxing his ruffled male plumage to smooth. "We all agreed that a lady wouldn't be suspected, that I could pass more freely than any gentleman, and that because I've already had the smallpox, I'd not be at risk again from the outbreak in Brussels."

"I recall," Roger said slowly—too slowly for my tastes. I couldn't bear it if he now forbid me outright to go, not when I was this close. It was not that I wouldn't dare disobey him, for I had before, and would again. But if he refused to let me go, then Sir Alan would respect his wishes and find another courier.

"It's for the sake of His Majesty, Roger," I said, and finally played the trump card that he'd so often waved before me. "And recall, too, that I'll be able to remind His Majesty directly of all the sacrifices that you and your family have made for the Royalist cause."

He lowered his chin into the white linen wings of his collar and puffed out his cheeks, letting the air escape slowly through his lips. It was the face he always made when he was considering deeply, and one that reminded me of the Four Winds that are often drawn in the corner of maps and charts.

Finally he glanced back at Sir Alan. "Tell me, Sir Alan," he said, "have you already arranged Mistress Palmer's passage to Antwerp, or shall I?"

The next two days passed in a frenzy of preparation. I quizzed Sir Alan for as many details as he'd confide of the journey and the people I might meet while abroad. I spent little time in packing my belongings: I was only to stay in Brussels long enough to deliver my packages to the king and lord chancellor and then return home to London, and besides, I would do better not to be burdened with excessive trunks and traveling boxes.

Yet the bodice, jacket, and petticoat that I was to wear needed to be altered to conceal my contraband. We couldn't turn to a tailor or seamstress, because no one beyond our small household could know of my plans. Instead my maidservant Wilson—who was accomplished with her needle, whilst I was not, neither by talent nor inclination—and I contrived a thin linen pocket between my stays and my smock for safekeeping the letters. Then Wilson opened the hems of my quilted petticoat and one by one stuffed inside the gold coins that Sir Alan had brought, taking care to keep them flat within the narrow quilted channels. She stitched the hems closed again with waxed linen thread for extra strength, for it would hardly do to have those stitches snap beneath the weight of the gold and scatter coins with every step I took. For the same reason, Wilson also added stouter tapes to tie the petticoat around my waist to help keep the skirts in place.

When she was finally done, the petticoat had become such a weighty garment that I hoped I'd not have to walk far while wearing it. I was glad that Wilson was traveling with me, not only for her companionship, but for her assistance in dressing in this formidable attire. As for what might happen if I were by accident to topple over the side of the boat carrying me across the Channel—ah, surely I'd plummet straight to the bottom of the sea and stay there, with only the fishes for company.

It was decided by Sir Alan that I'd not risk sailing directly from London, but would be met by a small boat on the coast that would carry me directly to Antwerp. Roger insisted upon taking me himself to this lonely beach near the mouth of the Thames, not far from Southend, giving us a long day's ride in a hired coach for dismal conversation. Wilson, of course, rode outside beside the driver, and despite the foul weather, I envied her.

"No matter what happens, Barbara," Roger said for what seemed like the hundredth time, "you must keep to the tale that Sir Alan's fashioned for you. Your very life could depend upon it."

I sighed, propping my feet upon the opposite seat beside Roger. The day had been cold and windy enough to rattle the coach's windows, and though I'd refilled my foot warmer with fresh coals when we'd last stopped to change horses, the heat had long ago faded away to nothingness.

"I should hate to think that my life depended upon that sorry concoction of Sir Alan's," I said as I crossed my ankles, the weight of the coins in my petticoats heavy across my shins. "I doubt that even the dullest port officiary would believe that long-winded blather."

"Sir Alan has far more experience in these matters than do you, Barbara," Roger said sternly. "The explanations he has provided for you to give if questioned make perfect sense to me."

"But not to me," I said, idly spinning my fur-lined muff around my wrists, "and I'm the one expected to say them. To pose as another lady whose husband's too ill to travel as I must rush to Antwerp to attend my dying aunt—oh, pish, Roger, that's far too complicated for anyone to believe. The best lies are always the most simple. Even you must realize that."

"I don't lie as a habit, Barbara, so no, I didn't realize it," he said, as tediously righteous as any Puritan preacher. "I believe that being prepared with good reasons if you're stopped only makes reasonable sense."

"Only to *Monsieur*," I said rebelliously.

"Barbara, enough," he said sharply. "You know how that displeases me."

I sighed. "Very well, then. Such storytelling makes sense only to a man."

I recrossed my ankles again so that my skirts slipped farther up my legs, and lightly prodded my husband's thigh with the toe of my shoe, the better to make my point. "The truth is, Roger, that for a young woman, reasonable beauty always trumps reasonable sense. So long as I go about my journey as if I've every right to be wherever I am, no guard, watchman, or soldier will question me, except to prolong the chance to have my attention to himself."

Roger grunted, not really conceding, and looked down at my foot resting against his leg. "Are you wearing scarlet stockings?"

"Yes," I said. "They caught my eye at the mercer's last week. They're very merry, aren't they?"

From the look on his face, I knew I'd won my argument, though I was clever enough not to gloat. I pointed my toe and made little circles in the air to better display not only my red thread stockings but also the plump yellow ribbon rosettes I'd added over the tongues of my shoes. And if Roger—or any other gentleman—took notice of my ankles, too, well, wasn't that the real reason for bright stockings and ribboned shoes?

"They're merry indeed, Barbara." He captured my twirling foot and rested it on his leg. Lightly he ran his fingertips back and forth along my shin, almost as if he were seeing it for the first time.

"You've as pretty a leg as I've ever seen, Barbara," he said, his voice gruff. "Very pretty."

I chuckled, and with my hands still tucked within my muff, I raised it to cover the lower half of my face to peek beguilingly over the fur at him. I wondered if the scarlet stockings were lure enough for him to be more impulsive and take me here in the rocking carriage on the open road.

At once the fancy seized me: such a posture was not the fastest way to find release, to be sure, but a pleasurable enough way to pass the time. It would be only a moment's work for me to untie his breeches and coax his cock to rampant life for me to sit astride. What better way for us both to forget the dull, dutiful effort he'd put forth in bed last night, and provide a more luscious reminder of one another while we were apart?

I lowered my eyes and puckered my lips, and blew a kiss to him over the muff, gently ruffling the fur. As I did, I slid lower on the carriage seat, so that I could rub my leg against the inside of his thigh. I thought that would be invitation enough, even for Roger.

I'd thought wrong.

His hand stilled on my leg. "Why wear those stockings today, Barbara? Do you hope to inflame the good sailors who'll carry you on this errand? Is that your scheme to amuse yourself on this journey?"

"I don't have a *scheme*, Roger." I pulled my leg away from his hand, dropping my skirts. I was not accustomed to being refused, and I did not like it. "I'm risking my life for the sake of carrying letters to the *king*."

He grunted with contempt and crossed his arms over his chest. "I know you too well for protests like that, wife. You'll rise from your coffin to beguile the gravedigger who's come to bury you."

"Better that than to be so consumed by jealousy that I'm incapable of enjoying the pleasures that life offers!" I could not venture which offended me the more: that he'd thought I'd nothing to offer to the Royalist cause, or that I'd worn my new stockings only for the sake of amusing a crew of common sailors.

"Listen to me, Barbara," he said sharply. "This journey is not for your pleasure. The sole reason I am permitting it is so that you might further the Palmer interests with the king."

"Oh, yes, the *Palmers*," I said, as scathing as Roger deserved. "How should I ever forget the importance of your family, great and good above everyone else, even the Stuarts?"

"You are one of us through marriage, Barbara," he said sharply, "whether you care for it or not."

I didn't bother to answer, but turned away to stare unseeing from the window. There was no use quarreling with him when he was like this. Besides, what did I stand to win, anyway? He cared more for that wretched nest of Palmers and all their imagined slights and sufferings than he ever would for me. I don't believe he truly cared for His Majesty, either, except for what could be gained for the Palmers with the king returned.

All that truly mattered to my husband was his retribution. I meant to see that he received it, too, exactly as we both deserved.

# Chapter Six

"Hurry, Wilson, make haste, make haste!" I hooked my garnet ear-bobs in place while my maidservant finished lacing the back of my bodice. "Make it as tight as you can now. I must look my best for His Majesty."

"As you wish, madam." Obediently Wilson gave the lace an extra-hard tug, jerking me backward a step with the force of it, but I was satisfied. I hadn't had room to bring another petticoat with me other than the one in which I'd traveled here, but I had made certain to bring this bodice: dark blue velvet that heightened the color of my eyes, piped with pale green silk cording and embroidered with swirling vines across the full sleeves. Wearing this atop, no one would notice if below I wore a petticoat of sailcloth.

The bodice was well boned and snugly cut, and set to sit below my shoulders. The puffed sleeves reached only to my elbows, leaving the lace edging along the neckline and cuffs of my smock to offer a veiled enticement to my breasts and my forearms. Roger disliked this bodice, damning the cut as too French for his wife's modesty, but it had always been Philip's favorite.

Now I hoped it would please the king as well.

"Your shoes, madam." Wilson knelt down to slip my shoes with the rosettes onto my feet, clad once again in the scarlet stockings that had caused such trouble for me with Roger.

I gave my skirts a sweeping flourish and took three small steps, as if in a dance without music, and laughed gaily. "I'm ready, Wilson. Come, fetch your cloak, and you shall walk me to His Majesty's lodgings."

Sir Alan's arrangements had placed me in an inn run by an Englishman and his Dutch wife. This had been chosen for both the convenience of my native tongue and for its proximity to the king, so I might deliver my letters and gold with ease and speed, and without the bother of hiring a carriage. Courier or not, my situation remained an uneasy one, an English lady alone, save for my maid, in a foreign country. But now that I'd been specially invited to return this night to His Majesty's lodgings and join him and his company, I praised Sir Alan's careful arrangements with fresh appreciation.

From my mother, I'd heard tales of the old king's court at Whitehall Palace before the wars and Cromwell: handsome lords with their beautiful ladies, all lavishly dressed and bejeweled as they attended to King Charles and his queen, Henrietta Marie. There'd been much drink and rich food served on porcelain and plate, elegant paintings by the greatest master artists upon the walls, witty conversation and elaborate masques and music composed by Italian *maestros* expressly for a single night or occasion. I'd no knowledge of my own of this long-lost world of the court, of course, but I was eager to experience it now, even if on a reduced and exiled scale.

But the sad little gathering I found when I returned that night to His Majesty's lodgings bore no resemblance to the bright and glorious company my mother had described. Instead I was shown into the same small, plain parlor where I'd first met the king earlier in the day.

Now on a stool in one corner sat an Irish fiddler, bowing a mournful tune that seemed fit to echo every detail of the chamber. The white plaster walls were marked with sooty black patches behind the sconces, and the close-set, unpainted beams overhead had likewise been cured dark by countless fires and pipes. The furnishings were common, too: well-kicked benches against one wall, a trio of dark wood chairs with inhospitably low backs arranged around a small table cleared for playing cards. Another table was covered with a threadbare carpet, overlaid with a diaper cloth, and set with a humble supper centered by a half-carved roast fowl, its bare-picked breastbone jutting awkwardly from the plate like Lazarus halfway from the grave.

"Mistress Palmer." Sir Edward Hyde was the first to greet me, which was fortunate, since I knew no other in the room besides him. His Majesty had yet to appear, else I would have noticed him at once. So this, then, was the English royal court in exile: a dozen or so gentlemen standing in conversation about the tiny fire, shabbily garbed in outmoded clothes. There were also two tired-looking ladies, whom I surpassed so thoroughly in both beauty and youth, the coin of women's power, that I took no further notice of them. My real interest lay with the gentlemen. Ill dressed they might be now, but when the king came back to London and to the throne, these would be the men whose loyalty in desperate exile would be rewarded first, and most lavishly—the men who'd likely have the most power in a new government, and not the likes of Roger, who remained safe and snug in our home in London.

"Mistress Palmer," Sir Edward said again to recollect my attention. He cleared his throat, sending his fleshy chins aquiver, clearly peeved that I'd been looking past him to the others. I guessed he must be nearly sixty years of age, though he still clung to the inflexible and priggish manner of the barrister he'd long ago trained to be. "Mistress Palmer, His Majesty will be pleased that you were able to attend."

I smiled, for his meaning was clear enough. "And you are not, Hyde?"

His watery blue eyes were cold toward me. "I knew your father, madam, and was honored to call him friend. He was an excellent, pious gentleman of great bravery and rectitude."

I put an edge to my words. "None of which you believe me to be, sir, do you?"

"His Lordship your father was an exemplary gentleman, madam," he said, dancing away from my question with a courtier's finesse, "and I am led to believe that your husband, Mr. Palmer, is as well. But I cannot say the same of Lord Chesterfield."

"Then you must never have had the pleasure of Lord Chesterfield's personal acquaintance, Sir Edward," I said, "else you'd hold a different opinion entirely."

I continued to smile, opening my fan blade by blade. It was not that I needed the breeze the fan could provide, not this far from the fire, but because I wished to reinforce the barrier between me and this odious fat man.

Sir Edward smiled in return, but with challenge, not amusement. "I fear you're mistaken, Mistress Palmer. I am thoroughly familiar with Lord Chesterfield, and stand by my assessment of his character."

"Indeed, sir," I said over the curve of my fan. "Then I must conclude you've likewise judged me."

He'd stopped bothering with even that cursory smile. "His Majesty is not Lord Chesterfield."

"Nor am I you, Sir Edward."

He made a snuffle of disgust. "His Majesty is more than clever enough to discern the difference between us, Mistress Palmer."

"Oh, I quite venture he already has," I said, recalling how His Majesty had kissed me—and kissed me well—before I'd left him earlier. "But tell me, Sir Edward. Am I so . . . daunting that for the sake of your king you must treat me with this show of ill manners? Do I threaten you so much as that?"

His face turned a florid purple, answer enough, his lips compressing so tightly that I doubted he could make them bring forth a reply even if he'd wished to. Instead, he abruptly turned away, abandoning me to make my own way in the company.

I watched him go, his broad bottom waggling beneath the skirts of his doublet like a goose's backside. I didn't care that Sir Edward had known my father, or that he had the ear of the king. If he was so determined to dislike me, why, I was happy to oblige him, and return his disregard.

I looked back to the gentlemen at the fireplace. Some were watching me in turn with bold interest, while the rest were pretending not to do so, while doing exactly that, being guided by Sir Edward's rudeness toward me. The fiddler's music would have masked our words, but even a child could have seen the inhospitable manner in which I'd been treated.

I could remain here in the door, keeping forlornly apart until one of these gentlemen deigned to come forward and rescue me. That, I suppose, would be what Roger's ideal, modest lady-wife would do. But I'd never before been afraid of gentlemen, in number or alone, and in all my days I'd yet to be either modest or ideal.

Instead I gave my fan a languid pass across my breasts to make certain the gentlemen had not overlooked my splendid blue velvet bodice, and approached the fireplace as if I'd every right to join them—which, of course, I did. I held my head high and smiled not with invitation but with confidence, and as I walked I took care to place my beribboned feet in time to the fiddler's tune, as much to amuse myself as to beguile them. I'd make certain they wouldn't forget either me or my name.

"Good day, my lords and gentlemen," I said. "I am Mistress Palmer."

Knowing that there's less sin to be found in giving too much respect than too little, I decided to treat them all like lords until I learned otherwise, and swept a pretty curtsey. I lowered my eyes and bowed my head the precise amount necessary to make my bright chestnut hair tumble over my shoulder, and smiled as I rose, confident that I'd made near conquests of them all. The ring of widened eyes and gaping mouths and pipes clutched forgotten in frozen fingers before me only proved it.

Hah, I thought merrily, how long these gentlemen must have been banished from their native soil, if the presence of one fair English lady could reduce them to such unthinking simpletons!

Yet before I could press home my point and claim every one of their hearts, I heard a rough sort of scuffling across the floor behind me. I turned and discovered two small dogs, brown-and-white-spotted spaniels with long ears and feathered legs and tails, scurrying toward me with their tongues hanging from their mouths. The fiddler recognized these dogs for the harbingers they were and immediately stopped playing, then slipped from his stool. The others around me, too, began to bow low as a young equerry hurried into the room after the two dogs.

"His Majesty the King!" the equerry announced breathlessly, only an instant before the king himself came striding into the room, his long legs easily outpacing both the equerry and the dogs.

At once I, too, sank down, dropping into another curtsey, though this for the sole benefit of His Majesty. This might be only a ragtag excuse for a court, but still I knew that reverence must receive its due. The kiss we'd shared earlier in private meant nothing before that. My heart was racing with anticipation and delight to be again in His Majesty's presence, and only with the greatest effort could I keep my gaze suitably averted, I longed so much to look upon his handsome royal face again.

"No ceremony, no ceremony," the king said with the easy cordiality that I would come to recognize was his by nature. I began to rise as he'd permitted, and as I did I realized he'd stopped directly before me, his little dogs panting at his feet.

"Why, Mistress Palmer," he said. "Our newest friend. How happy we are to see you've returned to us so soon."

"Thank you, Your Majesty," I said, more starry-eyed than I wished to admit. "But how could I ever think to keep away?"

He chuckled and held his hand out to help me rise. He was dressed in a plain black doublet, breeches, and stockings that made the white of his linen all the more stark. Scattered with dog hair, the black cloth was worn and shiny at the seaming, the hems frayed and feathered in a sorry way that no monarch should be forced to suffer. Even here among his courtiers, there was nothing in his dress—no special ribbons, or medals, or other signs—to mark him as their king; I'd learn later this was from necessity, not choice, for he'd had to pawn every one of his orders and ornaments to support himself and the royal cause.

"You're kind, madam," he said wryly. "I assure you, there's been plenty who have thought far worse than that of me."

I took his hand, relishing the strength and size of his fingers around my own, and stood. I still had to bend my neck to meet his eyes, he was that much larger, and I tall for a woman, too.

"Then far worse are those who'd dare think such thoughts, sir," I said, making my smile as warm as I could for him. He was much darker than any other English gentleman I'd known, not only in complexion but in the blackness of his eyes and hair. Doubtless he was vain about the luxuriance of his hair—a weakness for so many gentlemen above youth—for he wore it long and curling over his shoulders, and he wore a mustache, too, after the style of his cousin the French king. Though his hair was touched with silver here and there before his years—he was twenty-nine, hardly a graybeard—it only served to add distinction and a touch of gravity to his face. "In fact, sir, I should call it disloyal to the point of treason."

He laughed, not so much at what I said as with pleasure in my company. "How thankful I am not to be forced to plead my innocence before such a righteous judge!"

"Only righteous, sir?" I asked, tipping my head to one side so my eyes were veiled by my lashes. "Am I so stern as that?"

"Righteous, stern, just, and beautiful, Mistress Palmer," he said without hesitation, and raised my hand briefly to his lips. The whiskers of his mustache tickled the backs of my fingers, making me imagine how that mustache could taste and torment me in other, more intimate places upon my body.

"Now you are the kind one, sir," I said, chuckling at my bawdy thoughts. "And you've quite convinced me of your boundless innocence as well."

He laughed again, both understanding and appreciating the jest I'd dared to make. In perfect honesty, I doubted he'd ever been innocent of anything, not with those worldly black eyes. None of us who'd been born at that time were ever truly innocent, I think, innocence being the rarest luxury in childhoods torn by war, death, and loss.

"I thank the merciful wisdom of the bench, madam." He nodded to the fiddler to resume his tune, and as if likewise prompted, the others once again returned to their conversations. I'd almost forgotten they'd been there, a silent audience watching me with the king, and I blushed, shamed by my own foolishness.

But the king misread my pink'd cheeks, and leaned closer.

"There now, madam, you're innocent, too," he whispered as he led me away from the others to stand beside the chamber's lone window.

I could feel the cold evening air through the single pane of glass, and glimpse the wavering light from the fires and candles from the house close next door. "We can pardon you of any sin or crime, you know."

"You have such power, sir?"

His dark eyes seemed to darken further with cynicism or bitterness—likely both—and too late I realized I'd misstepped.

"I know it would seem that I'm a ruler without a country, madam," he said, "but God willing, that will not always be so. Are you hungry? Will you have wine? It's the gold you brought with you that's paid for this small collation."

I shook my head. "Forgive me, sir," I said, resting my hand upon his forearm. "I spoke without thought, a grievous error."

"And I should not have taken offense where none was offered." He glanced at my hand on his sleeve, and with an obvious effort smiled. "With such supporters as you to cheer me, Mistress Palmer, I should find only comfort, not fault."

"Then pray let me cheer you more properly." I spread my fan again, and fluttered it before my face. He was the King of England, true, but beneath his crown he was only a mortal man, and how fortunate for me! "What amusements does your court enjoy here in Brussels, sir? What diversions?"

"Amusements?" He raised his brows, as if pondering a difficult question. "We are much as you see us, Mistress Palmer. We compose letters to those dear to us. We read new books from Paris or Rome. We listen to music and converse with friends. We walk, we ride, we hunt. And if a suitable partner of beauty and grace can be found for us, why, then . . ."

He paused, his dark eyes hinting at such great lascivious promise that I couldn't help but smile knowingly in return.

"And if such a partner is found, sir?" I asked. "How then will you amuse yourself, and her?"

"Why, with a game of whist, madam," he said with studied blandness. "Why else would one wish such a rare partner?"

I tipped back my head and laughed aloud. He laughed with me, his teeth white and even beneath his black mustache. I do not know if it was the shared strain between his Stuart blood and my Villiers, but there was a rare understanding between us two already. I can explain it no better than that, except to venture that whatever their station in life, whether by moonlight or sun, true rogues will always know one another.

I walked to the small table that had been set for card play and took my place beside the farther chair. I reached down and with one hand fanned the deck of cards into a neat half circle across the cloth.

"Will it please you to play now, sir?" I asked, still leaning forward to offer him a splendid view of my breasts, if he so chose to take it. "That is, if I am suitable to serve as your partner."

"Oh, most suitable," he said, coming to take the other chair. "But I prefer piquet to whist for its quickness and suitability for wagers. Piquet being a game best played by two hands, I'll choose to be your opponent, not your partner."

"Piquet it shall be." I sat gracefully, sweeping my skirts to one side, while he took the other chair, his long-eared dogs settling around his feet. Although gaming with cards had long been outlawed by Parliament as an idle, wasteful pastime, it had proved an impossible prohibition to enforce, and my friends and I were all devoted gamesters. I was blessed with an apt head for ciphering points and stakes, and I loved the whim of fate, the heady joy that came when the cards fell right. I, too, liked piquet best, for it pitted one player against the other directly, without the tedium of waiting for a turn.

I gathered up the cards—already sorted and prepared for piquet, with only the sixes through aces and the other cards drawn—shuffled them into a stack and set them in the center of the table. "Shall you deal, sir, or shall I?"

"I'll be the younger," he said, using the name for a dealer in piquet. He claimed the stack of cards, shuffled them again, and began counting out our separate hands.

"Then I shall be the elder, to your younger," I said playfully, for of course I was nineteen years to his twenty-nine.

"I will master you regardless, Madame Elder," he said, studying his own cards. "Shall we set a wager?"

I looked at him over the cards in my hand, wondering if he'd set my honor at stake. Even now I could feel his knee pressing against mine as if by accident beneath the shield of the table.

I ran my fingertip lightly over the edge of the cards, the flat-faced queens and jacks staring up at me like doleful flounders. "But I've no money for wagering, sir."

"Neither do I," he said. "But there are other sorts of wagers."

"A wager for the sake of amusement?"

"Amusement, yes, and sport," he said, resting his elbows on the table to lean closer to me. "A stake gives urgency to the game. A purpose."

Oh, I'd already guessed his purpose, just as I'd already decided I'd not grant it tonight. Even kings would do better to show a modicum of patience and realize how anticipation only served to heighten pleasure.

"A purpose, sir?" I asked, feigning innocence. "I thought that winning was purpose enough."

He shrugged, but his knee against mine was more insistent. "For some, perhaps."

"But not for you?"

"Oh, Mistress Palmer," he said softly, "how can I say otherwise, when my entire life is a gamble?"

As he spoke, his smile turned charmingly rapacious, like a great dark wolf. I knew then he would indeed play to win, just as I realized in that moment that he *would* return to his throne and rule England as he'd been born to do. No one would keep him from seizing what was his by right and by blood. Nothing would stop him, except for his own death.

A great dark Stuart wolf, then, to my small fair Villiers vixen. I could sense the power that came not only from his royal title but from the man himself. Was it any wonder, then, that as he pressed his knee into mine under the table, I did not move away, but let my legs slip suggestively apart for him beneath my skirts?

"Very well, sir," I said, making my voice low and velvety. "Then let us play not for points or money, but for a kiss."

He glanced up, newly intrigued. "Your kiss, freely given?"

"Your kiss against mine, sir," I said. "With such stakes, we both win."

He laughed. "Then play away, madam, play away."

Play we did, through blanks and discards, ruffs, and sequences, sets and tricks, pique and repique—all the pretty steps of the game, over and over. The king was as quick at the tallies as I, and I had to concentrate to keep my pace ahead of his, anticipating his next plays so I could plot my own.

The footmen came to stoke the fire with a fresh log, and when the candles burned low and guttered in the twin-armed sconces, other servants came to replace those as well. I'd lost any sense of time, or of how long the king and I sat there at our play, and I was nigh feverish from the heat of the play and the proximity of the king, with the flush of competition and excitement in his company upon my cheeks and bosom. So intent was I that I scarce noticed when the others gathered around the table to watch, praising a particular trick or groaning in unison when the cards fell amiss.

I did glance up once to see Sir Edward standing behind the king's broad shoulder, his droopy-cheeked face glowering with disapproval for the sake of his royal charge. Likely what old Hyde saw he judged wicked enough, but if he'd only known what was happening beneath the table's cloth, why, he might have perished from an apoplexy on the spot, and spared me much trouble later.

For while our hands were occupied with our cards above the table, below we blindly pursued another kind of sport. Before the king as the younger could deal the hands a second time, I'd already slipped my foot from my shoe, and dared to trail it across the king's foot. He'd smiled at me, letting the others believe it was the cards that pleased him, though I'd known otherwise. As the evening progressed, my foot in its scarlet stocking had grown bolder, teasing against his shin, his calf, his knee, and thigh.

Yet unlike most men, the king believed that sauce for the goose served the gander as well, and before long his own stocking'd foot had worked its way beneath my skirts and smock, high above my garters to the bare, blushing skin atop my legs. Over our cards, we laughed and chuckled merrily, sharing the extent of our secret dallying between ourselves.

"There," the king said as at last he tossed his final cards to the center of the table. "I've over a thousand points by now. If that doesn't mark me as the winner, then by God, I don't know what else will."

"You are clearly the winner, sir," a tall, ginger-haired gentleman beside me said with annoying eagerness. "I've counted every point myself, and yours far outnumber the lady's."

"Now, now, Conwell, you know better than to shame a lady like that," the king scolded mildly, his gaze never leaving me. "Especially a lady as fair and generous as Mistress Palmer."

Nodding my acknowledgment of his compliment, I sat back in my chair, taking surreptitious care to tuck my errant toes back into my shoe. By my own reckoning, I was certain I'd won the game, but I'd freely concede that to claim the far greater prize.

But the king, being a king, wished for more from me. He thumped the table with his open palm to claim my attention—as though he'd lost it, even for a moment.

"Come, madam," he said. "You know a gamester's duty. Surrender your forfeit."

Around us the other gentlemen whooped and hooted like wild savages in a forest. The other two women had long ago vanished, doubtless from either boredom or indignant propriety. True, if I'd been the proper Mistress Palmer my husband wished, I would have been offended as well, even scandalized. But because I was my own self, I only smiled, and stood, shaking down my skirts so none would be the wiser.

"Am I to surrender my forfeit, sir?" I asked, holding my head high. "Or are you to claim it?"

Now he rose, too, coming to stand before me, while the other gentlemen around us continued their raucous encouragement.

"In the Christian spirit of compromise and diplomacy, Mistress Palmer," he announced, "we shall meet in the middle."

Before I could answer, he'd taken the last step necessary to close the space between us, circled his arm around my waist, and pulled me close to kiss me. He meant to startle me, I know, and to demonstrate that he was still my king and master no matter how I'd amused him beneath the table's cloth. Doubtless he expected me to sputter and squirm, and try to shove him away, for the entertainment of his friends. Men were always alike in such matters, wanting to make a great show of their manhood whether highborn or low.

But among ladies, I was different. Instead of fighting him like a half-drowned cat—and losing, too, for he was vastly larger and stronger—I slipped my arms about his neck and kissed him as boldly as he was kissing me. Perhaps more boldly, truth to tell, for female passion is sorely undervalued.

And he *was* surprised. I could taste it in his mouth. Surprise, yet excitement, too, as his grasp upon me tightened. So he'd not been left unaffected by our play, nor by me. Oh, most delicious thought! He wanted me, and because he was king he now expected me to remain with him this night, and warm his bachelor bed.

How unfortunate for His Majesty that he'd not get his wish!

I was at last the one to break the kiss, and slip free. While the gentlemen applauded, I curtseyed, and bowed my head in a pretty gesture of acquiescence. "Your winner's spoils, sir."

He smiled down upon me with anticipation. "A fair beginning, yes," he said. "But surely not all. I won far more games than that, Mistress Palmer."

"I am sorry, sir," I said with a sigh, "but our wager was for a single kiss, and no more."

He frowned, the black brows drawing sharply over blacker eyes. "Surely not, madam."

"Surely yes, *mon sire*," I said, adding the melting softness of French regret to my voice. "As loyal a subject as I am to you, I fear I must remain more loyal still to my absent husband, and beg leave to retreat to my lodgings for this night."

With that one sentence, I doused the jollity from the room. Nothing will spoil rollicking male pleasure faster than the protestations of a faithful wife, or at least the pretense of one.

"I mean no insult to Mr. Palmer, of course," the king murmured, watching me closely and hoping, I suppose, for a change of heart. "But can you not be persuaded to linger in our company?"

I shook my head and demurely lowered my gaze to the floor.

The king grunted with disappointment. As much as he wanted me, I knew he wouldn't toss me over his shoulder and carry me off, like the pagan kings of old, or at least he wouldn't before so many witnesses.

"You are certain in your decision, madam?" he asked gruffly. "You will not change?"

"A thousand apologies, sir, but my refusal must stand," I said softly, my head still bowed, my tender white nape displayed before him. I'd only a view of his large square-toed shoes with the worn red heels and the trailing ribbon lace that he'd neglected to retie in his earlier haste. "I must remember my husband."

"Your husband is a most fortunate man," he said and sighed. "As you wish, Mistress Palmer. You have my leave to go."

"Thank you, sir." I rose gracefully and began to back from his presence and from the room, as was proper. At the last moment, I looked at him once again, to offer him one final glimpse of my longing and regret.

Surrounded by the others, his face was composed, his expression even and regally distant. Yet in his eyes I discovered such rare merriment that I nearly laughed in return, surprising proof that he'd seen through my demure protests as easily as if they'd been fashioned from the clearest water. And further: he was not angered by my ruse, but entertained no end.

"Sleep well, madam," he said softly, his eyes bright with amusement and fresh regard. "We shall want you refreshed for tomorrow."

Tomorrow: ah, I could not wait, nor, I suspected, could the king.

I called my maidservant Wilson to my room as soon as I returned to my lodgings, to learn what she'd culled from the servants who waited on the king. Wilson was good that way, most useful to me. She was a clever-witted woman, the spinster daughter of a Chester squire who'd lost both his life and his estates to the war. Roger paid Wilson's wages, but she'd been quick to realize that the wind would blow in my favor long before it graced Roger, and she trusted me to carry her with me. I trusted her, too, because she was so plain of face: and thus are the best alliances made between women.

"So come, come, tell me all," I said eagerly, sitting before her so she could tend to my hair while she spoke. Though it was close to dawn, I was not weary. How could I be? I was far too enraptured with the memory of what had occurred between the king and me, and the anticipation of seeing him again. "What are the secrets of His Majesty's household?"

"His Majesty's household, madam?" Wilson dug her fingers into the thick tangle of my hair, searching for the few last pins that might be buried within the chestnut waves. "Or the secrets of his bedchamber?"

"Don't be pert, Wilson," I said sharply, in no humor to be teased. "Tell me what you heard from his footmen or the others in the kitchen."

"Yes, madam." Carefully she began to comb out the knots and curls, beginning at the ends where she wouldn't pull. "They say that though His Majesty enjoys the company of ladies, and they him, he is not nearly the libertine that the gossips say."

"Parliamentary tattle, that's what that is," I said with a contemptuous sniff. "Cromwell's men would link Saint Andrew himself to the queen bawd of a Moorfields brothel if they thought their masters would profit from it."

"Yes, madam, too true," Wilson said. "Which is not to say His Majesty has abstained from sowing the royal seed while in his exile. He has acknowledged several bastards, as well as their mothers."

"Tell me of the mothers, not the bastards," I demanded, wincing as the tortoiseshell comb caught my hair. I needed to hear these facts now, like a bucket of deep well water tossed in my face, to keep my thoughts clear and sharp. "What are their names, their ranks? Has he kept to Englishwomen, or taken these whey-faced Dutch creatures to his bed?"

"Mostly His Majesty has preferred English ladies, madam," Wilson said, "those who have followed him into exile for one reason or another. He chooses ladies who have experience in worldly matters, whether with husbands or not. They say his tastes for pleasure were honed here on the Continent, madam, and that he relishes a spirited lady who will not be shocked, and likewise enjoys exploring the French and Italian manners."

I nodded, my anticipation quickening to hear my intuitions about the king thus confirmed, and I thought too of the size and strength and imagination that he'd surely bring to any bout of lovemaking. It had been many months now since I'd last been with Philip, and I'd sorely missed his adventurous inventions whilst in bed with my tediously straightforward Roger. I was, in short, as ready for diversion as I was to advance my future.

"They say the king has no interest in callow virgins," Wilson continued, "and will scarce remark a too-young lass, no matter how fair. He's not like some gentlemen for whom chasing maidenhead's the greatest sport imaginable."

"Not like some, indeed," I said, trying not to think of Philip and his unfortunate taste for ever-younger maids. Better to think of what my future could bring than the hard lessons that had come with past pleasures.

"No, madam," Wilson said, pointedly saying nothing to echo my own thoughts any further. "The first lady in his exile was quite some time ago, an older woman named Betty Killigrew, and sister to the chaplain of His Royal Highness the Duke of York. She gave him a daughter for his efforts."

"Hah, sing a psalm to that," I said, amused by the image of a gentleman in orders struggling to reconcile his loyalty to his king with his holy teachings. "Who else, then?"

"In Bruges, there was a Derbyshire lady named Catharine who bore him two more children," Wilson continued, beginning to draw the brush through my hair in long, sweeping strokes, "and in Paris, the twice-widowed daughter of Viscount Kilmorey. They say she was too old, beautiful but past fecundity, else she would have borne His Majesty a bastard, too."

I tipped the mirror in my hand so I could see Wilson's face over my shoulder, as plain as a common pudding wrapped round with her white linen coif. "Why should I care for his nameless brats?"

"Because if you lie with him, madam," Wilson said, "then you must consider the possibility of bearing a nameless brat of your own."

"Don't be impudent," I said tartly. "I know how to keep myself safe and my belly empty."

"Whores' tricks, madam, and not to be trusted," she said succinctly. "Leastways not with a man so potent as the king."

I'll admit that this litany of royal bastards did give me pause, and I did not question its veracity, having met His Majesty and felt for myself the blatant force of his virility. I hadn't factored a misbegotten child into any of my happy, hazy schemes and plans, though I'd seen how other women had bound their lovers more closely to them by bearing children. And a royal bastard was not like the spawn of a Covent Garden whore. A child carrying half the king's blood could be legitimized, favored, and granted titles and estates, advantages that no child I might conceive with Roger could ever claim.

Not that I'd confess such thoughts to Wilson. "I've never said I intended to lie with His Majesty, have I?"

"No, madam," Wilson said dutifully, but the extra sniff she added said far more.

"Do not presume to know my mind, Wilson," I warned. "Tell me instead more of the king's past lovers."

"Yes, madam," she said, unperturbed by my chiding as she separated my hair into sections for braiding for the night. "I've told you all who were mentioned by name below stairs. There have been others, too, that were of no lasting note beyond a night or two. Yet they say, madam, that at present no single lady holds the king's attention."

I smiled slyly at my reflection in the glass in my hand. *That* would change.

"And of course they've all followed after the king's first mistress, madam," Wilson continued, "when he was still a prince. You recall her, madam: that Welsh creature Lucy Walters. She died last year in Paris, they say of drink and the French pox."

"Lucy Walters," I said, reflecting upon poor foolish Lucy's fate.

I'd heard the king had been her great love, yet she'd sadly neglected to make certain he felt the same for her. I'd not make the same mistake. "Once everyone knew of Lucy Walters, just as everyone's forgotten her now."

"You're the one they're speaking of tonight, madam," Wilson said as she plaited my hair. "Even as I sat among them, they whispered of nothing else but your beauty, your grace, and how you'd fascinated the king on so short an acquaintance."

I smiled with satisfaction, stroking the long braid between my fingers. I'd only another day before I must return to England, but when I recalled how the king had already shown his interest in me, I knew that would be enough to make a good beginning between us.

"Let them whisper, Wilson," I said with fresh resolve. "I mean to give them plenty more to say, and soon."

# *Chapter Seven*

The letter was brought the following morning, before I'd risen from my bed. I'd been expecting such a missive, yet when Wilson drew back the bed-curtains to put it into my sleepy hand, I still felt a shiver of amazement when I recognized the king's seal pressed into the wax that held the sheet closed. The message within was brief, more a command than any sweet-worded wooing.

> *Come to me tonight,*
> *Carolus R.*

Carolus R., Carolus Rex, Charles the King, King of England, Ireland, and Scotland: what woman wouldn't tremble to be summoned by so mighty a person?

"Ha, Wilson, he's asked me," I said with a small huzzah of triumph. "The king's invited me for tonight!"

"Congratulations, madam," Wilson said. "That was your wish, wasn't it?"

"Of course it was, you foolish creature, as you knew perfectly well." I sank back against the pillow-bier, all thought of sleep now gone. "Ah, sweet tonight!"

Wilson sniffed and began to loop the bedstead's curtains up for the day. "You would not stay with him last night, madam. How was I to guess that this night would be so very different?"

"Because you and I must leave Brussels for home tomorrow," I explained, though any woman who understood the habits of licentious men would have found it most obvious. "This way, His Majesty can have my company for the single night and no more, and I'll leave him with the wanting so keen he'll not be able to put me from his mind."

Wilson bent down, stuffing the mattress and trundle in which she'd slept at my feet beneath my taller bed.

"That's a prideful bit of confidence," she muttered into the bed-clothes, "to think she'd so beguile a man such as the king."

"I heard that, Wilson," I said swiftly, rolling over in the bed to swat at her arm. "And if I weren't so certain I would beguile His Majesty, as you said, I'd have you thrashed for it."

Primly she folded her hands across her apron, as if she'd said nothing wrong. "What if the king never does come back to London, madam? What if Parliament refuses to bow down and send for him to rule again, and all your confidence and cunning come to naught?"

"Then I will have gambled and lost," I said, stretching my hands over my head. "It won't be the first time, nor the last. But if I am not willing to stake such a risk for the sake of my future, why, then I truly deserve to be no more than *Monsieur's* drab. Did you bring chocolate with the letter?"

"Yes, madam." Wilson went to the tray she'd set near the door and returned with my cup of chocolate.

"You'll see, Wilson," I said, stirring the milky skin from the chocolate's surface. "As soon as the king returns, he'll ask for me to come to him at Whitehall Palace, and again after that. And he will, Wilson. He *will*."

Wilson considered this briefly. "Forgive me for speaking plain, madam, but if you wish that to be so, you must also consider Sir Edward."

"That wretched old breakwind?" I fanned my hand back and forth over the steaming chocolate. "Hyde's made it clear enough that he despises me. I'll make short work of him."

"Yes, madam." Wilson's mouth was set and stern, the way it always was when she meant to say something I'd no wish to hear. "I saw to it that the footman who brought this message was given a pot of ale and a slice of bread and ham in the kitchen."

"How clever of you, my own Wilson," I said with new admiration for her wiles. "What did this thirsty fellow tell you?"

"He said that Hyde heartily wishes you back in London, if not to Hell itself," she answered. "He believes you could be an unfortunate influence upon the king."

I sipped the chocolate. "Is that the worst he can say of me?"

"No, madam," she said. "He called you an 'evil low jade,' too."

" 'Evil low jade,' is it?" I chuckled with amusement. "Hah, I've been called worse, and by my own mother at that. All that matters to me is what His Majesty thinks, not that querulous old rascal, puffed up like a pig's bladder with his own importance."

"Forgive me, madam, but you must be wary of him," Wilson said with rare urgency. "They say Sir Edward's like another father to His Majesty, having been at his side since he was still a prince. They say he's the only one the king will ever turn to for counsel and guidance. If you test His Majesty by forcing him to choose between you, madam, he'll choose Hyde."

"Then I must make certain he'll never have to choose." I set my cup on the chair beside the bed with a clatter of porcelain against wood. Filled with fresh determination, I shoved back the covers, swung my legs over the side, and hopped down from the high bed-stead. My smock fluttering around me, I went to the chair and bench that we'd contrived as a dressing table here in the inn, and began holding different earrings beside my cheek as I peered into my tiny glass, trying to decide which flattered me the more. I always took care with choosing my jewels, humble though they might be; often, at day's end and in bed, they were the only part of my dress that remained upon my person.

"The garnets, Wilson, or the amethyst bobs?" I asked, frowning critically at my reflection. "The amethysts do flatter the color of my eyes, yet the garnets are the finer stones."

"The amethysts, madam, if they please you," Wilson said, coming forward to settle a woolen shawl over my bare shoulders against the chill of the room. "Madam, I must beg you, in regards to Sir Edward—"

"I know precisely what I must do in regards to Sir Edward, Wilson." I turned on the chair to confront her, an earring in either hand. "Before I left London, Sir Alan warned me that Hyde was the king's most trusted advisor, a dangerous man to cross, and thus one I've taken pains to understand. I learned that Sir Edward's as great a friend to the Anglican faith as he is an enemy to the Romish one. He wishes the king restored to the throne through diplomacy rather than by force, so that he'll not be indebted to his Catholic cousins for the show of an invading army. And I saw for myself last night that he links me still to Chesterfield, another he loathes, and fears somehow we'll both waylay the king from his true path back to the throne."

"Forgive me, madam," Wilson said contritely, adding a small curtsey for good measure. "I should not have presumed."

But I refused to be easily mollified. It was not so much Wilson's anxious warning but how her words seemed an unpleasant echoing of Roger, and Philip, and my mother, together a derisive chorus of everything I shouldn't or couldn't do.

"What you *presumed,* Wilson," I said, "was that I was a blathering, empty-headed idiot, fit for swiving and correction and nothing else, and I assure you that I am not. I know how carefully I must tread between Sir Edward and the king. I *know.* But I've also learned his weaknesses. He is proud and stubborn to a fault, and would rather falter than admit his errors. He is rigid in his beliefs, and won't listen to any others. He longs for a magnificent match for his fat daughter, the one with popping eyes like an overfed dog. *Those* are the weaknesses of Sir Edward Hyde, Wilson, and if he dares cross me, I'll prick every one."

"As you wish, madam," Wilson said, her eyes wide after such a tirade from me. "As you wish."

"Aye, as I *wish,*" I said firmly, turning back to my glass. "For I'll not do anything further in my life that I don't."

That night I was shown not into the parlor but directly to the king's bedchamber. Once again I was struck by how small and mean his quarters were, half the size of the room Wilson and I shared in our own lodgings. It seemed neither fair nor proper, and shameful, too, that our country showed such little respect for our ruler, and I thought proudly of the gold I'd brought to him to help ease his situation.

When I entered, he was sitting alone at a table before the fire, writing letters, his pen scratching furiously across the paper. His dogs were asleep on the bed, curled up against one another for warmth. The page announced my name, and the king grunted in reply, but because he didn't turn toward the door, I doubted he'd realized I stood behind him.

Yet I wasn't offended. Such trust had an intimacy of its own. I'd a long moment to study him while he completed whatever thought he'd been wrestling; he wore a loose, dark red dressing gown over his shirt and breeches, the sleeves of his shirt rolled back from his wrists to spare his cuffs from the ink, his feet thrust into comfortably worn slippers that showed the darned heels of his stockings. His broad back and shoulders faced me, his black hair spilling over the red dressing gown, and just that much was sufficient to send a small frisson of excitement coursing through my blood.

"A moment, a moment," he said absently, absorbed still by his composition. "Nearly done."

"No haste on my account, Your Majesty," I said softly, drawing off my gloves. "I shall wait."

Swiftly he turned toward me, his hand with the pen resting across the spindled back of the chair. "Mistress Palmer!"

"The only lady by that name." I sank low in my curtsey, never breaking my gaze from his. "Good evening, sir. Pray, finish your letter."

"It's nothing that cannot wait until morning." He tossed down his pen and rose, then came toward me, capturing my hands in his to lift me up. "Come now, I told you. Let there be no ceremony between us. Now sit here with me and share my wine."

I did as I was told, sitting in the only other chair, and I turned it so it was close enough beside his that my skirts trailed across his foot as if by accident. By the wavering light of the fire behind us, his face was planed with deep shadows to match his black hair and eyes. His shirt was open at the throat, carelessly, as men do after riding or hunting, and permitted me a glimpse of his chest beneath and the first tuft of black curls to be found there.

"I can write a fair hand, you know," I said, glancing down at the unfinished letter while he filled the second goblet on the table—proof that he hadn't entirely forgotten I'd been invited. "I'll play your secretary if it will help your cause and bring you back to London the sooner."

"I told you, sweeting, there's nothing that can't be put aside until tomorrow." He raised his own goblet toward me in salute. "But I will drink to London, and a glorious future."

"To London, and the future." I drank deeply of the sweet wine, the kind favored in Brussels, and when I lowered the goblet, I left a little of the wine to glisten provocatively upon my lips as I smiled.

The king noticed, his gaze first lowering to my mouth, and then to my breasts. I'd worn the same blue velvet bodice—the only suitable one I'd brought, anyway—as the night before, though I'd asked Wilson to be sure the knot at the back was not so tight that it couldn't be undone with ease. Given the king's history, I doubted he'd be thwarted by any feature of a woman's wardrobe, but there were few obstacles more frustrating to passion than a tangle of unyielding clothing.

I leaned my elbow on the arm of my chair, gracefully turning more toward him as I touched my fingers to the crystal heart around my throat. The cypher inside had been intended to honor his father, true, but the initials would be the same for this Charles as well. And the fact that the necklace had been my first lover's gift from Roger— ah, that I put from my mind entirely.

"London will be much changed when you return, sir," I said. "I've never known it other than under parliamentary rule, not in my life, but I've heard so many tales of the old days that paint it as the most magical place on earth."

"For some it was, yes," he said, and sadness darkened his face. None of us of our generation could escape that melancholy, I suppose. Everyone I knew had lost fathers, brothers, and uncles, great fortunes and long-held estates. The king was no different, having his father murdered by the executioner's axe, his kingdom and crown stolen away, and his mother and brothers and sisters scattered like poor relations about the rest of Europe. Nine years he'd been wandering in exile himself, nearly a third of his life. But the greatest loss of all to us, I think, was how we'd been robbed not only of our place in this life but of our purpose. It would fall upon the broad shoulders of the man beside me to restore that to us.

I'd no doubt he could do it, too, and lah, how fervently I wished to be at his side when he did!

"I've been away from London so long I can recall only certain things with any clarity," he said at last. "The sound of the church bells rolling across the city on a cold winter morning. Visiting the wild beasts at the Tower with my father and brother as a treat; the old lion was my favorite, even though he was so ancient he'd lost his teeth and most of his mane. The soldiers parading behind the palace, the drums and the pipes, people cheering and the dogs all barking. Foolish things, really, the stuff boys remember."

"Not foolish, sir," I said, laying my hand on his arm as a comfort. To hear so grand a gentleman as the king confess such humble delights touched me in a way I'd not anticipated possible. "Sometimes the memories are all we have until happier times come around again."

He smiled wearily. "Jolly company I am for a beautiful lady."

"My life's not been lilies and roses, either, sir," I said softly. "But I always try to place my hopes in the future, and not dwell upon the sorrows of the past."

He took my hand in his, and raised it to his lips. "Spoken like a true angel."

I chuckled, turning my hand in his to trace my finger lightly across his lips, below his mustache. "No ethereal angel, sir. Only a mortal woman of flesh and blood and bone."

"A Villiers angel, then," he said, his smile unfurling beneath my fingers. "Divine flesh and blood, coupled with a pragmatic heart."

"Too true, sir." It was easy enough to leave my chair to sit upon his lap. "Is it any wonder, then, that among the seraphim the Villiers sit so close to the Stuarts?"

"Clever seraphim." He curled one arm around my waist to steady me and draw me closer, while with his other hand he turned my face toward his. "Kiss me, fair angel, and prove to me that we belong in the same celestial choir."

"I'll be the most obedient of seraphim for you, sir," I whispered, chuckling to hear this wry rubbish from him even as I lowered my mouth to his. "All you must do is claim what I offer."

By way of an answer he kissed me: not the public kisses he'd made to me before, kisses before witnesses for show, but to please himself, and me. Unlike many larger men for whom kissing is but one more way to overpower a poor lady by force and slobber, the king kissed without haste, yet with coaxing skill, and so artfully that my heart quickened and my desires stirred eagerly for more.

I slid my hand inside his dressing gown, inside his shirt. I'd heard he delighted in a vigorous life, enjoying the French game of tennis as well as riding to the hunt and swimming in both the river and the sea, and the proof showed in the hard muscles of his chest and arms. He pulled me closer, letting his hand stray to dip into my bodice. I arched into his caress with a happy sigh, and as his thigh shifted beneath my bottom, I could feel his interested cock rising strong against my hip.

"Will you stay, madam?" he asked, his eyes heavy-lidded, his embrace more possessive. He'd stopped smiling now, just as the bantering tone had left his voice. I'm not sure he'd have let me go even if I wished it—which in a wicked way only made me want him the more.

By way of answer, I slipped free and stood before him, reaching up to unpin my hair. My raised arms lifted my breasts higher, too, so with each pin I drew from my hair they threatened to bob free of my bodice. He watched me hungrily, and when at last my hair fell free, I shook the chestnut waves loose over my shoulders, clear to my waist in a rich curtain that was my glory. I next began to reach around my back, meaning to unlace my bodice, but I'd misjudged the intensity of his ardor.

"Enough, madam," he said gruffly. "We're weary of waiting."

Before I could answer, he'd seized me in his arms as if I were but a featherweight and swung me onto the bed. He did not bother with

the niceties of lovemaking, but threw up my skirts and opened his
breeches in seemingly the same motion. He entered me at once, and
though I gasped at first with surprise at the size of him—surely contrived upon a royal scale beyond the more ordinary gentlemen of my
experience—I quickly made my accommodation, and welcomed him
warmly with my legs wrapped tight around his waist and cries of delight torn from my throat.

With the edge taken from our hunger by that first encounter, we
took our pleasure for the rest of the night with more leisure, and more
invention. To my amusement, his dogs remained on the bed with us as
panting witnesses, though they'd thoughtfully shifted to the farthest
corner of the bed to be away from our sport. We rattled the bedstead
against the wall, and afterward laughed into the pillows as we imagined what the other guests lodged around us must have thought of
our noisy racketing.

We were both of the perfect age for such amusement, with our
eyes unclouded by protestations of love and our souls unbound by the
shackling obligations of marriage vows. Instead our tenuous attachment was born of common attraction and little more, and for us, that
was sufficient. I matched his every suggestion and desire with another
more daring of my own, pleasing him, I know, far beyond his expectations. And so, I will admit, did he do equally for me.

I woke first in the morning. Untended, the fire had long since
burned down to gray ash, and the small chamber was so cold that my
breath showed as a cloud when I peeked from the warm snuggery of
the bed. A dovecote on the roof across from the room's single window
had come to life with the dawn, and fat maiden doves fluttered and
cooed beyond the frost-etched glass. Within the lodging house I could
hear servants and others on the stairs and in the hallway, laughing or
shouting or quarreling. The house, and the city, had begun the day,
and it was past time I began mine as well.

I pushed myself upright, shoved my hair from my face, and looked
down at the sleeping king beside me. He lay flat upon his back, one
large arm thrown over his head to show the whorl of hair beneath. He
did not snore, most rare in a large man, and I smiled fondly at him.

He'd a right to sleep as long as he wished, for he'd pleased me well. My body ached wonderfully from all the contortions I'd asked it to assume, my hair was a magpie's nest of knots and snarls, and I smelled as rank as any brothel on a Sunday morning.

My dear royal majesty! I'd not felt so enchanted with a lover since my earliest days with Philip.

Taking care not to make the rope springs of the bedstead creak and wake him, I slipped from the warm cocoon we'd created of coverlet and sheets and into the chilly room. I scurried shivering about the room, naked save for my earrings, to gather up my clothes from where they'd been dropped—always the most humbling conclusion to a night of passion.

"Barbara?" His voice was muffled, thick with sleep. "Where are you, sweet lady?"

"Not far." I pulled my smock over my head and drew my hair free. "Forgive me, sir, but I must go."

"You can't." He propped himself up on one elbow to watch me. His jaw was darkened with a night's growth of beard, wicked as a Caribbean pirate. "I won't permit it."

"In this, sir, I fear you have no choice," I said, combing my hair as best I could with my fingers. "I must begin my journey home to England."

"Why today?" he asked. "Why not tomorrow, or the day past that?"

"Because Sir Alan Broderick was forced to make the most complicated arrangements imaginable to convey me here and to take me back," I said as I separated my hair into thirds for braiding. "There are drivers waiting for me at every step, and a boat to carry me across the Channel to England, all planned by Sir Alan."

"Sir Alan Broderick," the king said, musing, as a brown-and-white spaniel pressed against his shoulder to be petted. "What do you make of him?"

"I?" I paused in my braiding, surprised he'd ask my opinion, but determined to be honest. "I believe Sir Alan cares much for your cause, sir, and has a gift for complicated plans such as the ones that brought me here. But as a man, he drinks too deeply, and grows quarrelsome from it, which in the end would make him not to be trusted."

He nodded in agreement, gently stroking the dog's long, silky ears. "That was my unfortunate experience with Sir Alan as well. Yet you will trust his plans to take you home?"

"God willing, yes." I realized now I'd just passed judgment on Sir Alan's careful hopes for the future, and I realized with a start that this was a taste of the rare power I'd have from sharing the king's bed. "But if I don't go as I should, then I'll vex Sir Alan, and inconvenience a great many others besides."

"If you leave, Barbara," he said, "you'll inconvenience me more than all these great many others combined."

"Oh, pish," I protested, even as I hopped back into the bed, pushing him back onto the pillow as I lay across his chest. "You may be the king, but you cannot say such tenderling things to me. It's not fair."

He chuckled, shoving aside my smock to cup my bottom with his hand and make certain I couldn't wriggle free again. "*This* is not fair, madam. Sir Alan sends me the rarest beauty in my entire kingdom, and now he wants to steal you back."

"To my husband," I said softly. To be sure, I was in no haste to return to Roger, but to my surprise I found I'd grown to like the king so quickly and so well that I'd no wish to leave him, either. I'd caught myself in my own snare, and my regret was for once genuine. "Mr. Palmer will be expecting me to return."

The king's brows rose with wry skepticism. "Is Mr. Palmer that much of a fool, or so very trusting?"

I wrinkled my nose, deciding how best to answer, while the crystal heart around my neck seemed to grow heavier. I'd keep my word to Roger, whether he deserved it or not.

"He is, I think, ambitious to serve the crown," I said with care, "as his father did your father before him."

His hand spread across my nether cheek, appreciatively encompassing more of my soft flesh. "We like Mr. Palmer's ambition. He'll be remembered when we come back to power."

I smiled smugly, thinking of how my ass had accomplished so

much more than *Monsieur's* wretched thousand pounds. "Mr. Palmer will be honored to have their loyalty rewarded, sir."

"I cannot scoff at any loyal subjects," he said, sharing my amusement. "Especially when this one's been so obliging with his wife."

I said no more, contenting myself with only a smile. I doubted that Roger would indeed be so obliging about being openly crowned with his cuckold's horns, even for the sake of the Palmers of Dorney Court, and I foresaw much unpleasantness before this all was settled.

"There will be a place for you in my court, too, madam," he continued. "Whitehall Palace will need your beauty and grace after so much dreariness."

My heart leapt with joy, to have such a prize dangled before me. "I will be waiting for you in London, sir," I said breathlessly. "Never doubt my loyalty."

"Soon, then," he said. "Very soon."

"Truly?" I asked, startled by his confidence. It was not that I doubted him, but it seemed I'd been hearing of the king's imminent return to power for all my life. Now to be told by His Majesty himself that those longed-for hopes would be answered, and soon—why, it seemed too grand to believe. "How? Is there an army ready, a force gathering to carry you to victory?"

He smiled. "It will be a quieter victory than that, I think, more the work of diplomats than soldiers."

"But how?" I asked again, my excitement growing. This *was* news. "How can such a feat be arranged?"

He touched his finger to my nose. "I cannot tell you, my fair, demanding imp, not yet. Suffice to say that I believe that Cromwell's death, combined with the incompetence of the Rump Parliament, has at last made the London climate warm toward me."

"Oh, yes, the Rump is done," I said. "Do you know that boys in the London street will taunt one another to 'kiss my Rump,' as if it were the same as their very asses!"

"They do?" He laughed, and I laughed with him. "Then let me hope those same boys will cheer my return."

"I think they'd cheer anyone who'd promise to keep the country from more war," I said, and then my laughter fell away. "The whole city's on edge with discontent, sir, not knowing what may come next. The price of food is very dear, for farmers don't wish the risk of coming to market, and some shops stay closed tight as drums. We hear rumors, of course, that General Monck's army will come down from Scotland, or that the Common Council of the City is demanding a newly elected Parliament to take the Rump's place. Doubtless you've heard it all from others with more knowledge than I, but that is what I see."

"I've heard it all, yes," he said, shaking his head. "But that's no reason not to hear it again. Londoners have suffered enough, and God willing, I mean to end their troubles soon. I cannot share more than that, sweet, but it will be common knowledge once Hyde has finished all the proper negotiations."

"Sir Edward?" I asked, my heart sinking at the name. "He is behind your return?"

"One of many," he answered solemnly. "There's no man more devoted to me, or to the throne, nor is there another better able to cope with these foreign ministers than a barrister brought up at the Middle Temple."

I sighed, my breasts pressing against his chest. "You know he does not care for me."

"He'll like you less after last night," he said evenly. "His chamber lies directly below this one. I doubt we gave him a moment's peace for sleep."

My eyes widened with surprise, even embarrassment. Then I pictured Sir Edward sputtering and shaking his fist impotently at the ceiling as our bedstead had creaked and thumped over his head, and I laughed, and again the king laughed with me.

"Ah, Barbara, you're a bold, wicked creature behind that beautiful face," he said, laughing still. "Is it any wonder I don't wish to let you go?"

I smiled, easing myself more completely over him, my legs splayed over his hips. He was already hard; he'd need little encouragement from me for a final flourish before I had to leave.

"Then bid me a proper farewell, sir," I whispered, my voice husky with promise as I reached down to guide him home. "Give me more to remember and keep dear, until you can return to London, and to me."

The journey back to London with Wilson seemed at once tediously long and unfairly short, with only Roger waiting for me at the end of it. I'd too much time alone with my thoughts and the memories of the king's handsome dark face, how we'd made one another laugh, and how we'd delighted in the bold, lascivious play I'd shared with him. Truth to tell, I missed him, not just as a Royalist misses her king but as any woman longs for a man.

I'd likewise too much time to recall that lengthy list of the royal bastards he'd already sired. Too late I lamented how careless I'd been with myself in that regard, and knew from the looks that Wilson gave me that she was thinking of that, too. On the night I returned home, I made sure to lie with Roger, taking his seed deep within me. That way if I were in fact with child, I could fairly say it was my husband's, and not the king's.

Four days later, my flowers came to prove I'd nothing to fear. Yet for the first time in my womanly life, I was mournful and sad. I shut myself away in my little closet and wept, and grieved for what had never been.

# Chapter Eight

London
*May 1660*

For those of us who suffered through the time of wars and of Cromwell's rule, England had seemed a somber, unhappy place, as if the endless dark days of winter would never give way to the cheery hope of spring. Yet just as it seems that every April all at once green shoots will thrust through the cold ground and the sun's warmth will come again, so it felt that the king's return happened overnight.

While I'd been away in Brussels, General George Monck had finally decided the country could bear no more chaos and indecision, not if it wished to be spared another civil war. As governor of Scotland, he'd kept his army from the old days, and marched at their head to London. Parliamentary resistance melted away before this show of well-trained force, and as soon as he'd entered the city, he demanded that the tattered remnants of the Rump Parliament dissolve themselves, setting the way for new elections. This we'd been expecting—and was the reason that Roger had been so busily organizing his own campaign for a seat—but it still came as both a relief and a joy to most Londoners. Bells pealed from every steeple and tower at the news, and dozens of bonfires lit the winter night skies around the city. Blessings were called after the general in the street, and the joyous crowds pressed drink and money into the hands of his soldiers.

Roger won his seat handily. In celebration, buckets of ale were drunk by his supporters at Dorney Court, and Roger himself seemed to glow from within from his new title and prestige. I congratulated him, as was his due, but remained unimpressed by my new status as the wife of the member for New Windsor. I aspired to higher titles, and honors won by my own wit.

But first more wonders were to come. As we all learned much later, Monck had decided privately that England's only true salvation was to restore the monarchy and welcome back Charles Stuart as king. The most secret negotiations flew back and forth between the king and Monck, acting on behalf of the state. I pictured His Majesty sitting with his little spaniels in his humble lodgings in Brussels, sorting through these momentous letters in his darned thread stockings as he weighed not only the future of his monarchy but of England as well.

By late March, at Monck's delicate suggestion, the king shifted from the Spanish Netherlands—now an inappropriate perch for a possible English sovereign, considering how England and Spain were officially still at war—to the politically neutral town of Breda.

In early April, the king wrote formally to the new Speaker of the House of Commons, and likewise sent forth the Declaration of Breda for the rest of his countrymen. Both promised that the king would be merciful, intent upon healing the breaches of every sort within the country, and would stand fast in the Protestant faith.

But in the declaration, the king outlined his plans for the future in more detail. He offered indemnity to all who'd taken part in the wars against him and his father save those excluded by Parliament, freedom of conscience and tolerance for worship, land settlements, and reparation of long-overdue pay to the army—all, of course, dependent not on the king himself, but on a vote by Parliament. Except for those directly responsible for his father's death, the king was willing to pardon anyone who was willing to ask his forgiveness.

As soon as I read the public copy of the declaration for myself, I understood at once the king's confidence in Sir Edward's abilities as a barrister and a diplomat. Never was there another legal document more judiciously worded to achieve desired goals, nor to make the king appear the true patron of peace, grace, and righteousness. Grudgingly even I had to praise the genius in it, and agree that in this the fat old breakwind had earned his salt.

Both the letter and the declaration were read aloud in the House of Commons on the first of May. On that same day, the House passed a resolution inviting their king to return and lead the government and the country. The members had not left the House before the plans for the coronation had begun. Not one further drop of blood had been spilled to achieve this wondrous revolution, and if that was not in itself a miracle, then I know not what else could be.

The rejoicing in London and across the country was universal. Suddenly it was a good thing—no, a great thing!—to be a Royalist. Even my cousin Buckingham, a weathercock if ever there was one, had stopped flaunting his parliamentary wife and had taken to sporting his Garter instead, brave upon his chest for the world to see. All the gaiety that the Puritan rule had ground down came bubbling back to the surface. People danced and sang and drank freely in the streets, and much more in the spirit of the old May Days occurred between men and women in the parks that night, as open in their coupling as dogs—a celebration of the new freedom that disgusted Roger but made me laugh with amusement, and with sympathy. I understood their fever.

The hand of Providence had reached down to the king, and he'd happily accepted every blessing that now came spilling his way. Everything was changing in London. Nothing would ever be the same for any of us. Soon the king would be restored to his rightful place and have his throne, his crown, his country, his cheering subjects.

And me.

A little less than a month later, I sat on the bench with the woven-cane seat in Roger's chamber, watching his servant dress him for his role in the great procession to welcome the king back to London. This procession had begun the moment the king had landed at Dover, greeted on the beach by General Monck himself, and now, after having passed through Canterbury, Rochester, Blackheath, Deptford, and every other little town or village in its path, it was at last set to reach its glorious conclusion today in London.

"I don't see why I can't watch like everyone else in London, Roger,"

I said, waving my fan before my face. It was still morning, but the day was already warm for May. "To miss the first chance in my entire life to see an English king in London!"

"I've given you my reasons before, Barbara," Roger said, pretending to be the very soul of patience. "But foremost among them is that it's not proper for my wife to display herself so publicly."

He looked not at me but studied his own reflection in the glass as the servant fastened the long row of tiny pewter buttons on his doublet. Every tailor in London had spent this last month working long by candlelight, for every gentleman wished a new suit of clothes in which to honor the king. Roger's doublet and breeches were a soft buff color, with pale blue ribbon points all around and a matching short cloak. His stockings had deep cuffs of knitted lace that flared over the tops of his boots, and his tall-crowned beaver hat carried a curling white plume. Yet such finery looked more like a costume than gentleman's dress on Roger, his pale face sitting atop his shirt's collar like a disembodied mask.

"Oh, pish, Roger, no one will be looking at me," I said. "Every eye will be upon the king, and nowhere else."

"The king could be naked on his horse, Barbara," he said, "yet more would gaze at you. Should I wear my ribbon and sword over the cloak, or beneath?"

"Over the doublet, under the cloak," I said, thinking how Roger himself seemed perfectly capable of not gazing at me, even though I wore nothing beneath my pink dressing gown. "I could take Wilson with me, and a footman, too, if that would appease you, and I—"

"No, Barbara," he said sharply. "That's my last answer. It's not safe for you to be among the crowds on the street."

I sighed my unhappiness. "Do you remember when we went to view the procession for Cromwell's funeral? We stood along the Strand for hours, and no one disturbed us then."

"How can you consider that the same at all?" he asked incredulously. "Besides, I was there to watch after you. If you stand at the open window, you should be able to hear the trumpets and the cheering. That's the convenience of this house being so nicely located."

I crossed to the open window, looking down into the Privy Garden of Whitehall Palace that lay beyond our farther fence. As soon as he'd been returned to Parliament, Roger had begun to hunt for a house more appropriate to our new station than our own lodgings, though he'd found none that had suited. Then this one had been offered to him—quite magically, he thought. Belonging formerly to Cromwell's cousin Edward Whalley, who'd fled to New England when he'd received no pardon from the king, the house in King Street—oh, what delicious irony!—was large and fine, and situated between the palace and Parliament House, with Admiral the Earl of Sandwich and his lady as our closest neighbors. Roger believed the house had come to him as the first of his rewards for his loyalty and that loathsome thousand pounds.

I, however, knew otherwise. This fine house and its clever location so near to the palace had been granted not for Roger's convenience, but the king's.

"I'll remember everything to tell you, Barbara," he said, lifting his arms so his servant could buckle the wide belt with his scabbard. "It won't be the same, I know, but you won't be the only lady left at home today. This is the most important day for England in our lifetimes, and the procession and the ceremonies afterward—it's how we gentlemen will demonstrate our fealty to the king. What is it, Wilson?"

"Forgive me, Master Palmer," Wilson said, standing in the doorway. "I came to ask if Mistress Palmer was ready to dress."

"She's with me now, Wilson," Roger said, more crossly than was necessary. "She'll come to you once I leave."

"Yes, sir." Wilson curtseyed again. Yet as soon as Roger turned away, she held up a small letter for me to see. I knew what that letter would say, just as I knew Wilson was showing great wisdom in keeping its arrival secret from my husband. My heart racing with excitement, I nodded quickly before Roger could notice, and Wilson ducked away.

"I still wish I could watch today, Roger," I said, hoping my voice didn't betray me. "He's to be my king, too."

"I'm sorry, Barbara, but for your own safety, I must insist." He kissed me with dutiful regard on the cheek, not embracing me so as to keep from mussing his finery. "There will be plenty of parties and dances at the palace to come, I'm sure of it. From what I know of the king, he'll insist upon it. You won't be neglected."

"Oh, I know that," I said, and smiled. "When will you be home?"

"Late, very late," he said, full of his own importance. "Perhaps not even until tomorrow. You know how these ceremonial events can be. You go to bed whenever you please. Don't wait for me."

"I won't." Oh, that was so wicked of me, agreeing to all those things that Roger was saying with another meaning in my thoughts! "Good day, then."

"Good day to you, too," he said, and from the door he solemnly touched the brim of his plumed hat in salute. "And God save the king!"

As soon as I heard the front door of the house close after him, I hurried to find Wilson, who was in turn hurrying up the stairs to me with the letter outstretched in her hand. I caught her on the landing and pulled her and the letter into the nearest room, shutting the door tight after us so none of the other servants might hear us.

"The king?" I asked, even as I tore the letter from her hand. "Oh, please, please, say it's so!"

"It is, madam," Wilson said, nearly as excited as I. "But oh, Mistress Palmer, if Mr. Palmer had seen the page that brought it! Dressed in crimson and gold, he was, the Whitehall livery. What would he have said then?"

"My husband would have simply assumed the page was delivering some message of importance to him, though God would needs have preserved me if the page had given Mr. Palmer this." Swiftly I scanned the letter, and I pressed my hand to my cheek. "Oh, Wilson, he wants me to join him—to be waiting for him this very night!"

"Here, madam?" she exclaimed in an awestruck whisper. "His Majesty wishes to visit you here?"

"No, no," I said, the awe in my voice as well. "He wants me to come to his rooms in the palace. He wants to spend his first night in London with me—with *me*."

·   ·   ·

Everyone who was in London that glorious day—and a great many who weren't, but pretend to have been—has their own recollection of how warmly the city and people welcomed the return of the king, "this miraculous prince," as the Dutch did call him. For those who admitted to having been denied such a memory, there were plenty of paintings by artists there to document the ceremonies, and before the end of the summer it seemed that prints of the procession were pinned to the wall of every tavern and rum shop from Portsmouth to Glasgow.

As for me, I saw none of the king's triumphant entry with his two younger brothers, James, Duke of York, and Henry, Duke of Gloucester, across London Bridge, riding bareheaded in the sun to display his humility and trust of his subjects. In this I obeyed my husband's edict, not so much that I was the demure wife he wished me to be, but because I feared I'd be spied by one of his friends, and sent home under a more fearsome guard that would prevent me from stirring from the house later.

So yes, I missed the tapestries that hung from the windows and balconies of the great houses along the Strand, and the silken banners that drifted in the breeze from every pole. I only heard later of the girls who'd ridden in wagons from the country long before dawn to strew the path of the king ankle-deep with flowers. I never saw the ranks of cavalry, bright in crimson and gold, as they cantered through the streets, or the stalwart Life Guards. The endless assemblies of dignitaries grand and small—the members of both Houses, the mayor of the City and his aldermen, the ambassadors from every court in Europe—marched in dignified phalanxes or rode their steeds without my notice.

Instead I joined the celebration in my own way, my memories singular to me. For given my circumstances, how, really, could they be otherwise?

It was shortly after nightfall when the plain carriage came to our door for me. Though Whitehall Palace was close by, near enough for me to have walked with ease if I'd chosen, the celebrations caused the driver to take a longer, more circuitous route.

I didn't care. That night London was exactly as Roger had pre-

dicted, full of drunkards and wastrels, but it was also filled with rejoicing, and merriment, and purest joy. Laughter and cheer bounced
from one close-set house to the next as crowds streamed through the
ancient streets. Every corner had its bonfire, with shadowy figures
dancing and singing before it, and every wine shop and tavern poured
freely, so that all might drink to the health of the king.

I grinned as well, giddy to be part of such an adventure. With
reckless joy, I shoved my velvet hood back from my face and leaned
from the carriage window to drink in the night like a heady draught.

"Here, my beauty!" A ruddy-cheeked man saluted me from the
street as my carriage lumbered by. I waved in return, and he tossed
a sprig of white primroses to me, doubtless torn from some nearby
garden. Laughing, I caught the flowers and tucked them into the deep
neckline of my silk bodice, the stems snug between my breasts.

At last my carriage drew up before a side door of Whitehall Palace.
I should explain that at that time, Whitehall was not a single building in
the style of most royal palaces, but a rambling assortment of intercon-
nected houses and halls strung along the river's bank and wandering
back toward St. James's Park. This "palace" had been built over many
years, by many different architects and undertakers, and while parts
were exceptionally beautiful, such as the last king's Banqueting House,
other portions were shabby, dark, and worn. It was in short more fit for
a nest of conies than for the court of the King of England.

Yet Whitehall's meandering also granted its inhabitants a measure
of privacy. With so many entrances and doorways, it was surprisingly
easy to slip inside or out without much notice by the palace guards, or
anyone else. With all the excitement of the celebration that night, no
one saw the equerry meet my carriage and lead me inside and along
the maze of ill-lit hallways. Quite suddenly we stopped and entered
through one unassuming door, climbed a narrow staircase, and found
ourselves in a large, sparsely furnished bedchamber.

The bedstead was old, with bulbous posts carved of some dark,
heavy wood, and of a size nearer to a tennis court than an ordinary
furnishing for repose—which, of course, amused me, imagining as I did
what other sport could take place within such ample boundaries. The

hangings had been replaced, new red velvet with golden embroideries and fringes, and the bed linens were likewise new and fresh and pressed. But beyond the bedstead, the chamber was scarcely better than that humble room in Brussels, and sadly I recalled hearing how Cromwell's vile creatures had carried away most of the art and rich furnishings from Whitehall, like vultures picking a fresh carcass clean.

"Is there anything you require, madam?" the equerry asked, his expression studiously dispassionate.

I glanced again around the room. On a sideboard, there was wine and other drink and the makings of a light cold supper. Because the evening was warm, the windows were open still, and I could hear the rush of the river's current far below, and see the glow of bonfires all over the city.

"Thank you, no," I said. "I've all I need."

*Except the king* . . .

"Very well, madam." The equerry bowed, hesitating as he sought the proper words. It had been so long since a king had lived within these walls that we'd all forgotten the correct rules for court ceremony, if we'd ever known them in the first place. "You will, ah, be joined shortly."

"Thank you," I said again, though I knew my eyes betrayed my amusement at his inadvert choice of words. He flushed, realizing too late what he'd said, and scuttled away.

I went to stand by the window, relishing the coolness of the evening breeze from the water. After today, I'd guessed the king would be feeling a surfeit of gold thread and luxury, and thus had dressed myself simply, in a jacket of green embroidered silk and a darker green petticoat beneath. The primrose tossed to me still lay tucked between my breasts. My hair was loosely knotted high on my head, with shorter pieces in front cropped to curl about my cheeks, and I wore neither paint nor powder on my face, and only tiny garnets in my ears.

I leaned from the window, listening. Even now the sounds of revelry and high spirits could be heard—a new beginning for us all. I wondered wryly how many women would wake tomorrow with an aching head and a new-filled belly as a result of this celebration. For how many babes would this night truly be a new beginning?

"Barbara."

I turned swiftly, for I'd not heard the door open or shut. He was exactly as I'd remembered, or perhaps as I'd not let myself forget: dark and regal, the most charming man I'd ever met, and without doubt the one I most desired. With him were the same two small dogs I remembered from Brussels, plus two more, trotting importantly after him like flop-eared attendants.

He'd come directly to me, without pause, and without changing. While the others around him had strived to outdo themselves in tinseled splendor, he'd chosen to dress in black twilled woolen stuff—though of the highest quality—as a way to let his own innate glory shine through. As he came toward me, I could see the exhaustion carved into his face after so many hours in the adoring gaze of his subjects. Yet the care fell away as he smiled at me, and almost too late I remembered to curtsey.

"Your Majesty," I said. "What a magnificent day!"

"Barbara, Barbara," he said as he raised me up. "A glorious day indeed. And after such a day, what good it does me to have you here."

"You honor me," I said simply, and it was no empty praise. Although I was no innocent, I was in many ways still very young. As much as I saw and knew him as a man, he was now indisputably the *king,* and I couldn't help but be a little awed.

Not that he'd let me remain so for long. How much he must have smiled today, yet still he could smile so warmly for me! "You honor me as well, sweet, by being here."

"I am only another loyal subject, sir, and your servant," I said, remembering Brussels. "Your most *obedient* servant."

He laughed, deep and rich, and as he plucked the primrose from between my breasts, his fingers trailed as if by accident across the warm valley between. "I doubt you'd obey any man, Barbara, not even me."

"Then for now, sir, I'll remain simply your servant and no more." I looked up into his face so far above mine, keeping my eyes heavy-lidded and full of promise. "We'll leave the pleasure of testing my obedience for another night."

"Oh, I'll test you, Barbara," Charles said, laughing at my flippancy. He tucked the flower into my hair and slipped his arms around my waist. "Just as I did on that other night, I'll test you and try you, and mark it, I'll win."

"Then come, rest yourself," I urged, leading him to sit on the enormous bed. I crouched down and unlaced his shoes, easing them from his feet.

He groaned aloud from the simple pleasure, and let himself topple backward across the bed. The dogs jumped up beside him, settling there as if they'd every right.

"I've been fifteen hours in the saddle this day, Barbara, fair worshipped like some pagan's gilded idol," he said, lying flat on his back as he idly ruffled the fur of the nearest dog. "I've had every last member of Parliament kiss my hand and the most venerable lords of the land kneel before me."

I tried not to think of Roger, unwittingly bending with reverence to kiss the hand of the man who'd cheerfully lain with his wife.

"I've heard more praise than is wise for any man," he continued, "so much that I feared I'd shame myself and tumble face-first to the ground, like a boy who gluttonously eats too many sweets. I had to make my apologies for the service at the abbey. I'd reached my fill, and could bear no more."

"You left early?" I asked, surprised and gladdened. Hah, he'd traded the service of the abbey with scores of clerics and bishops to come here to me. To *me*.

"I couldn't bear it any longer," he said. "Yet it *was* glorious, Barbara, beyond all dreams. I cannot tell it any other way."

I climbed onto the bed to sit beside him, my skirts rustling around me. "It was only what you deserved. You'd been away too long."

"Would that I'd never had to leave." He sighed, linking his hands behind his head as he stared upward, unseeing, at the velvet-covered canopy. "My greatest wish was that my sainted father could have felt the same true love and gratitude of the people."

"I'm sure he did, watching down upon you from his place in heaven," I said gently. I understood how he could feel melancholy today, even amidst so much splendor and acclaim. Anyone who'd lost and suffered as he had must have no heart to feel otherwise. "Can I bring you wine, a biscuit or an apple?"

He shook his head back and forth, his long hair tousled across the coverlet.

"No, my dear, you're everything I need." He smiled at me, and reached his hand up to cradle my cheek against his palm. "Ten thousand men in procession for me today, Barbara. Ten thousand men, and not a single woman."

"That hardly seems fair." I turned my face to press my lips against his palm, giving it a languid swipe of my tongue for good measure.

"Oh, but it is," he said, pulling my face down so he could kiss me, "since the single woman waiting for me here is you."

He kissed me with leisure, as if he'd the whole night to enjoy me, which, of course, he did.

"Ah," he said, his smile happy and his face already beginning to lose its earlier sorrow. "That kiss alone was worth a thousand sermons from a thousand preachers. There we are, wise as Solomon."

"You are wicked." I laughed, tucking my forward curls behind my ears as I still leaned over him. "You can't let the canting Presbyterians hear you speak such scandal."

The Presbyterians were the strictest of any British sect, near as close-minded as the Puritans had been, but much easier to mock, being largely Scots.

"The Presbyterians will never know," he said, "unless you tell them. Now I'll play the papist, my dear lady, and make my confession to you. I'm so confounded weary from this day that I can scarce move my limbs. You must toil for us both. Go now, undress yourself, and I'll watch to make certain you tend to the task properly."

I laughed again as I hopped from the bed. "Very well, sir. That's an easy enough task, even for this obedient servant."

"Obey, then," he said, chuckling with me. "Go on."

I stood before him, making sure the candlestick's light would wash across my flesh in the most flattering fashion, while he rolled to his side, supporting his head with his bent arm the better to watch me.

It is no easy trick for a lady to disrobe without another's assistance, but Wilson had cleverly anticipated this dilemma for me and suggested not only the jacket, which tied before with bows of ribbons, but my easier pair of stays, the lighter ones I wore for summer. Covered in cherry pink linen, these likewise unlaced down the front, without the busk or extra boning that a more formal bodice would require. Yet still I took my time with each ribbon and lace, knowing how to keep and build the king's interest until at last I wore only green thread stockings with striped garters, red silk mules with high yellow heels, and a fine Holland smock so sheer as to hide nothing beneath.

"The smock, too," he ordered. "But keep the stockings."

"As you wish, sir." I whisked away the last veil of my smock. I had no false shame or modesty about my body, for I knew it was as perfectly made as my face, and I found as much pleasure in revealing it to him as he so clearly took in viewing it. "You see, I can be most obedient."

"Yes, you can," he said, his gaze devouring me with undisguised intent. "Now come, you must tend to me as well."

"What, and play your manservant?" Laughing afresh, I clambered onto the bed without further beseeching. I pushed aside the dogs and began to unbutton and unlace his clothes, too.

But quickly I learned he'd not the patience I'd demonstrated, and before I'd stripped him fairly, he'd tumbled me backward onto the bed. For a man who'd claimed to be so exhausted, he made a fine, lusty accounting of himself that left us both blest and sated.

"Now that was at least another ten thousand sermons in the balance," he said as we lay together afterward, my limbs white and round against his. "Likely my very soul, too."

I laughed wickedly. "Only to the sternest of those Presbyterians. Though if you wish it, I can venture a different pleasure with my lips and tongue that will earn you their ire more thoroughly."

"You would, too," he said, laughing with me. "But let me relish what you've just granted me before we begin again."

"Well enough," I said, and lifted my head so our faces were close. Gently I traced his mustache with my fingertip, smoothing the bristling hairs. "You know as much as I wish it, I cannot stay the night, or be found here."

"I know it as well as you do, sweet, no matter how it would please me," he said, running his hand along my spine. "Though it's no real sin for a bachelor king to have a lady in his bed, I should let my people grow more accustomed to me before they must realize it."

"What they would see first is that I am another man's wife," I said carefully. I knew he'd well earned his cynicism, having been born to an overbearing French Catholic mother, raised as an Anglican by a raft of conscientious bishops, and made fatherless by an army of self-righteous Puritans. But though I was no more rigorous than he in my faith, I did know that with his restored crown he'd also accepted his role as the defender of the Anglican church. "They won't like that."

"They wouldn't like it if I roamed the countryside pillaging virgins, either," he scoffed.

"You must be serious in this, sir," I urged. "To most folk, adultery *is* a sin, whether among Presbyterians, Romans, or Anglicans. It was my mistake to marry Roger, not yours. I've made peace with myself in this matter, yes, but I won't have your subjects cry out against you because of me. You need their loyalty, else you'll never accomplish all you wish to do as their king."

He grunted, that catchall utterance that men employ when they've no wish to face a hard truth.

"Very well, then," he said. "Wake in your own bed in the morning, beside that dry stick of a husband. My days will belong to Sir Edward and the others for a good while to come, but once they've folded their letter-books for the night, I want you at my side, to grace my court. Come to me each evening, Barbara, however you needs contrive it."

"However I can, however I shall," I agreed softly. "No matter how Roger tries to keep me back, I will come to you."

"Your husband likes his new house and his new place in the government, doesn't he?" he asked. "We'll see that he's persuaded to be accommodating. What would he wish?"

"From you?" I paused, wondering exactly how greedy Roger might become for the sake of soothing his pride. Of course, in time, as

my acquaintance with His Majesty deepened, I'd expected such gifts
and honors would come my way. Hadn't I volunteered to go to Brussels with exactly that chance of betterment in mind? The king was
known to be a most giving gentleman. Even when his pockets had
held nothing but holes and darns, he'd managed to be generous to
his mistresses and support his bastards. But this offer came far sooner
than I'd any right to expect.

"Come now, Barbara," he urged me. "I needn't tell you how this
game will be played. All of England will come begging to me in the
next weeks, all believing themselves completely entitled to have whatever they wish that I can grant. At least Roger will have a better reason
than most."

"That is true," I admitted. "A government post or office, fit for the
new member from Windsor. A title, of course."

"A title," he said. "I'll speak to Sir Edward tomorrow."

"That's a great deal of trouble for you, sir," I said, strangely
touched by his generosity. "You scarce know me at all."

"I know enough," he said. "You please me vastly more than other
women, Barbara."

"Hah," I said bluntly. "You like my quim, not me."

"A good thing, too, because you like my cock." He grinned. "We're
much alike, you see, two apples dropped from the same gnarled tree."

I raised my hands over his chest, plopping them down twice to
mimic the effect of those two apples falling side by side.

"Stuart and Villiers," I announced gleefully. "Not so very far apart
at all."

Yet when I looked back at him, I was startled by the depth of the
expression in his eyes.

"I missed you, Barbara," he said, his voice rough, as if the words
were hard for him to admit. "I want you to stay close to me, so I won't
have to miss you again."

I leaned forward and kissed him: a kind of thanks, yes, but a
pledge as well, such as I'd never made to any other man.

"As you wish, sir," I whispered. "Exactly as you wish."

# Chapter Nine

If any had asked me, I would have said that I'd more than my share of happiness in my young life, especially once I'd traded the tedium of the country for the amusements of London. But that first summer of King Charles's reign—ah, there never could be a more magical time than that! It seemed the sun always shone and the air was always sweet and warm those months. In the near-constant company of England's brave new king, my life was full of gaiety and merriness. We danced and played, dined and drank and laughed. We watched the fireworks over the city, we glided along the river in a gilded barge, and we loved—oh, how we loved! *That* is what I remember the most, and what I shall never forget.

"Set those flowers there, by the wall," I said one night early in July, pointing the way as the two hired men trooped down the alley with buckets of roses and daisies from the market. Roger and I had moved into this house too late in the planting season for a gardener to have much effect, so I was forced to rely on potted flowers to make our small yard sufficiently engaging for guests. "Higher, if you please, to give us privacy. I don't want strangers peeping at us, you know."

"Mistress Palmer!" Tom, our household's single footman, came trotting toward me. "The boy from th' cookshop's come with the venison pies."

"Already?" I sighed, perplexed. Though our house was equipped with the luxury of its own bake oven, neither I nor our kitchen maid had the experience necessary to utilize it for more than warming food purchased elsewhere. Besides, the evening was already warm enough without adding more heat from the oven, jutting out from the kitchen as it did. To my joy, I'd found a nearby baker who made most excellent pies of fowl, venison, and eels, when he could get them fresh from the river, and I'd placed a large order with him for tonight. They'd be the centerpiece of my small collation—gentlemen always do love a savory pie—though I hadn't counted on the pasties arriving so soon.

"Very well, then," I said, striving to sound as if I was hostess to such gatherings every day. "Have the pies set on the long table in the kitchen, and mind that Deborah covers them with fresh cloths to keep the flies away."

"Flies away from what?" Roger asked, appearing in the garden seemingly from nowhere. At this hour, he should have been engaged in his parliamentary affairs, and not here vexing me. "Barbara, who are these persons in our garden?"

"Beg pardon, Mistress Palmer," Tom said, hurrying back from the kitchen. "But Deborah says the man's here with th' sillery, and she would know whether to put it in th' cellar to keep it cool, or above stairs, for convenience."

"Sillery!" Roger cried. "Since when do we keep French wines in this house, either in the cellar or otherwise?"

"Hush, Roger, please," I said. "Tom, have the man put the wine in the cellar for now."

But Roger refused to be hushed. "Roses in pots, lanterns hung from the trees, new cushions on the benches and chairs! Barbara, what is all this?"

"It's for tonight, Roger, as you know well, or you would if you did but listen to me," I said, retying my apron tapes more closely about my waist. "We're expecting a small group for music, and because the weather's been so fair I thought to have it here."

"A small group, Barbara? Here?" He scowled and shook his head, his flat-brimmed gray hat bobbing back and forth. "Forgive me, but I do not recall hearing of this at all. Who are these guests of yours?"

"They're *our* guests, Roger." I took him by the arm to lead him away from the flower-men to the far end of the yard, and lowered my voice, too, so they would not overhear. "His Majesty the King, Their Graces the Duke of York and the Duke of Gloucester, and perhaps several other acquaintances I've made at court. I know I've told you."

Roger drew back. "The king and the princes in my house?"

"In *our* house," I answered firmly, though an excellent case could be made for the house being more properly mine by rights. "It will be a considerable honor, you know, and if you could make yourself pleasant and agreeable in company, I'm sure it will go far to helping your place in the government."

"What will help me advance is hard work," he grumbled, "which is far more than this court seems to do. Every night while I must toil, you're among them at Whitehall, drinking and gaming and dancing and—"

"Do you deny that His Majesty works as hard as his ministers?" I demanded, defending the king instead of myself. "Does he ever shirk his meetings with them, or excuse himself from the call of a foreign diplomat? Hasn't he listened to every single petitioner seeking reparation from him, listened with gravity and consideration?"

"That is true," Roger admitted grudgingly. "His Majesty has demonstrated a most prodigious gift for the work of his position, and is always among the first to begin at Whitehall, no matter how late he retired to his bed the night before."

"*Completely* true," I said, perhaps more frankly than I should have volunteered. I'd seen for myself how little sleep Charles—for so I now thought of him in my head; I'd never dare presume to address him so informally, of course, no matter how intimate our connection, and never would—seemed to require. Not only did he devote long hours to the work of sorting his country's affairs, but he also continued his regimen of long, fast walks through St. James's Park, riding as fast as any jockey, swimming in the river, and vigorous games of tennis.

Yet each night he was still ready for a long evening of dancing and gaming, in addition to the frequent retreats to his private quarters with me, sometimes as often as three diverse times in a single evening, if he was in the proper humor. "So why, then, do you begrudge him his diversions at the end of the day?"

"It's not His Majesty I begrudge his diversions, Barbara, but you," he said. "There's no question that His Majesty is the first gentleman of the realm, but the same cannot be said about those he chooses for his courtiers. Why you must spend so much time at the palace among those drunkards and whoremongers—"

"Because that is where preferment begins, Roger," I said vehemently. "Toiling away with your pen in your hand in a dark closet at the Parliament House will never bring you to favor, but each time I am seen by the king marks another time he recalls your name as well. Were you not among the first to be repaid for what you'd loaned to the royal cause?"

"Yes," he admitted heavily. "Yes, I was."

"Well, then, you understand." Mollified, I drew a small paper fan from my apron's pocket to fan my face. I'd found this summer deucedly warm, or maybe it was simply the effect of keeping pace with Charles. I was young, of rosy health, but still I found I needed to crawl back to my bed here in King Street to sleep whenever I could. "Now, I must go see if Deborah has—"

"I don't see why York must be included tonight." Roger's face was flushed an angry red. "He has no influence over our station."

"His Highness?" I asked, unsure of what he meant. The Duke of York was the middle Stuart brother, full-lipped and fair where the other two were dark, and stolid to a fault. He was said to have fought valiantly during the wars, but I found him so dull and dogged as to seem slow-witted. "Why shouldn't the duke be invited? To be sure, I'd hear more conversation from one of those pots of flowers than from him, but that—"

"Don't dissemble, Barbara," he said sharply. "I've heard what's being said, how his name is often linked to yours."

"Mine with the duke's?" I tipped back my head and laughed, not only with relief but with true merriment. To confound the gossips, Charles would often be sure to have one or the other of his brothers about him when he was with me, but I'd never thought such a ruse would fool anyone, let alone my husband. "Oh, Roger, please."

"If it's so ludicrous, then swear to me that you've never encouraged him," Roger ordered. "Will you swear it?"

"I'll gladly swear on any holy book you please," I said, laughing still. "I shall never, never, never be tempted by the Duke of York."

"No?" he asked again, his gaze fair scrubbing my face for the truth. "You are sure?"

"I told you I'd swear, didn't I?" I rolled my gaze toward the heavens. "Besides, if you'd paid heed to gossip and scandal, then you'd know that His Highness is already so far in the muck with the lord chancellor's daughter that he'd have no time to squander upon me."

"The lord chancellor's daughter? Anne Hyde?"

"Oh, yes," I said, positively licking my lips to be able to repeat such a juicy tale, bringing shame as it did upon my old nemesis Sir Edward Hyde. "They say she first caught the duke's eye at the Hague, where Anne was maid of honor to the Princess Mary of Orange—his eye, and his cock, for they say now her belly's swelled large as a hayrick with the duke's brat."

Roger looked pained. "Barbara, please. Such vulgar talk belongs in the mouth of some foul doxy, not a lady of the court."

"Why not speak plain, when what Anne and the duke have done is plain enough?" I laughed again, unperturbed by his criticism. No one minced or parsed their words at Whitehall; to be overnice in one's speech was to be a toss-back to the prudish days of the Protectorate. "No one can fathom why the duke would choose such a woeful, pasty creature as Anne, either. She favors her father the lord chancellor, you know, and is every bit as disagreeable and gouty as he. It's a marvel anyone's been able to tell she's with child, she's that dreadfully fat. And as for her face, why—"

"You are certain York has no interest in you?"

"Yes." I smiled with confidence, for this was the truth and easy to face without any bluster. I could not tell if Roger yet knew of my dalliance with the king, or if he'd even suspected it. For all I could tell, he might be perfectly aware of his cuckold's horns, yet had decided the rewards of compliance were worth the effort of looking away and feigning ignorance. Yet though I much preferred Charles's attentions to my husband's—what woman wouldn't choose a king, I ask you?—I didn't neglect my duty toward Roger, either, and he had my attention whenever he wished it. By my lights, he'd no reason whatsoever for complaint.

I furled my fan and tapped him lightly on the arm with it. "If you still have your doubts, then be sure to attend this night," I said, smiling winningly. "You'll see for yourself you've nothing to fear regarding me and His Highness."

"Perhaps later, Barbara," he said gruffly and cleared his throat, shifting from one foot to the other. "I'm set to dine with two gentlemen down from Windsor. You can tell me all tomorrow."

His glance had strayed from my face to my breasts, for I'd left off a kerchief on account of the heat, leaving nearly all exposed to his view. He cleared his throat again, a sound I could read as clearly as mariners read the stars in the sky. Aha, so he'd be expecting to conclude his night carousing about the town with the gentlemen from Windsor, and I'd do well to be there waiting when he finally came home.

Or perhaps not, if I eased him now.

"Might you linger for a bit, Roger?" I asked in a honey'd whisper, standing close to him so the servants wouldn't be able to see me slip my hand inside the front of his breeches to dandle his cods. "I'm done with the preparations here, and His Majesty and the others won't arrive for some hours. Surely those fine gentlemen from Windsor could wait as well."

He groaned and moved against my hand, and I knew I had him when he kissed me with the hunger of a famished man.

"You're the very devil, Barbara," he muttered, not bothering to hide his despair. "How could I ever refuse you, eh? How could I ever refuse?"

As the two fiddlers and the flute player finished the jig, I gave one final turn on my toes, and with my skirts held wide I sank to the ground in a deep curtsey, the king's dogs yipping and prancing around me with excitement. The three brothers applauded and cheered, and Henry, His Highness the Duke of Gloucester, came bounding up to raise me back to my exhausted feet.

"Well done, madam, well done," he said, giving me a heartfelt embrace to show he'd appreciated my little dance. By then the hour was well past midnight, and we'd all drunk so freely of the sillery and other wines that the boundaries between our ranks had faded quite away.

Besides, it was easy to be familiar with Henry. He was much like Charles, with dark hair and eyes, and a dashing, gallant manner born of his years at the French court with his mother. He was my age, too, within a year of twenty, and with him I felt at liberty to act with the freedom of our youth.

While the fiddlers continued to play, I now looped my arm around his waist and he did the same to me as we stumbled and laughed across the grass toward where the king and the Duke of York still sat. In the guise of supporting me, I felt Henry's hand slide purposely lower than it should across my rump, but all I did was laugh, and shove him gently away. As pleasing as Henry was to me, I knew my place was with his older brother, and as lightly as I could, I perched upon the king's waiting knee.

"Oh, come now, Barbara, don't be shy with me," Charles said, laughing himself as he pulled me against him. I yelped with surprise, but quickly settled against his chest, a place that gave me special delight. Sitting there, I felt small and protected, like a tiny girl upon her father's lap, a memory I sadly could never claim for myself. But I also liked the womanly intimacy of such a posture, too, sprawled across my lover's long, well-muscled legs and knowing his cock lay beneath me. He nuzzled against the side of my throat, his mustache bristling against my skin, and I turned my face to kiss him even as he slipped his hand down into my bodice to fill his palm with my breast.

"You've an audience, Charles," James said, watching us critically over his goblet. When we looked up, he raised the wine toward the next house, as if in a silent salute. I could just make out the shadowy form of my neighbor, his long face pressed to the window glass to gawk at us.

"That's my own private audience," I said with a shrug. "My neighbor Admiral Lord Sandwich and likely his secretary Mr. Pepys beside him, pretending that they're toiling late upon the business of His Majesty's navy. It doesn't signify to me. Let them look their fill, if it pleases them so mightily."

Henry climbed up onto a bench the better to peer back, cleverly cocking his hand over his eyes like a foretopman on one of the admiral's ships. "Aren't you afraid they'll tattle to your husband?"

"No," I said, and emboldened by the sillery, I wasn't. "My husband already knows I'm entertaining you here this night."

"Hah," James said scornfully, reaching for the bottle on the grass beside him to refill his goblet. "That's a more forgiving husband than I'd ever be."

Charles laughed softly. "Mark those words, Jamie, for you'll be testing their truth as a bridegroom soon enough."

"You're to marry?" I asked, sitting upright with disbelief. "Not that fat cow Anne Hyde, I hope."

"Have you heard the latest verse about her, Barbara, likening her arse to the footman's box on a coach?" Gleefully Henry hopped down from the bench, ready to make his recitation before us. " 'With Chanc'lor's belly, and so large a rump / That there, not behind the coach, her pages jump.' Ah, James, what a lovely bride she'll make, waddling at your side."

I clapped my hands in wicked appreciation both of his speech and the verse itself. I'd met Anne Hyde in passing and had dismissed her as being as plain, as jowly, and as irritating as her father, and completely unworthy of my acquaintance.

"Enough of your rubbish, Henry!" James barked sourly, leaning out to strike his younger brother before Henry danced back out of reach. "No one said I was to wed her."

"*I* said it," Charles said mildly. "You see, Barbara, it appears my brother here was so cunt-struck with Mistress Anne that he made a secret contract vowing to wed her. Now that the lady's carrying his child for all the world to see, I say he must honor the contract, and her. There's some who even say you wed her already in Brussels."

Furiously James shook his head, his long blond curls tossing against his shoulders. "That's all Hyde's doing."

"No, it's not," Charles said, and I could hear the steel beneath his words. "Sir Edward's so shocked and shamed he's telling anyone who'll listen that his daughter belongs in a dungeon at the Tower for treason, with an Act of Parliament passed to order her beheaded. He swears he'll be the one who'll propose it, too, he's that furious with her."

I tried very hard not to laugh at such a droll scandal, even as James thrashed about in agony and denial.

"What of *my* honor, Charles?" James sputtered. "What of *my* name and future? It's not as if you've married any of the wenches you've gotten with your bastards."

"I never made promises to them that I'd no intention of keeping," Charles said. "This sorry affair is a mistake of your own making, James, and now you must make it right. Soon, too. I hear Anne's expected to drop your brat in the straw any day now."

"Poor, poor James," Henry taunted. "If only you'd waited to pick a beautiful princess for yourself."

Now Charles laughed, too. "Don't be so quick, Henry. Wait until you see the highborn ladies paraded before you. You'll discover soon enough that 'beautiful' and 'princess' are words seldom used together."

"Pity you can't find a crown for Barbara," Henry said. "She'd make as beautiful a queen as any."

I smiled, for he'd meant it as only a compliment, yet I couldn't entirely swallow my own bitterness at the hard unfairness of Fate. I *would* have made a splendid queen, especially Charles's queen, but even I knew better than to dream so high a dream as that.

"You forget, sir, that I cannot be a queen since I'm already a wife," I said as lightly as I could. "Though queens can have whatever they please, even they aren't permitted a harem full of husbands."

"Though it would be amusing to see the look on the archbishop's face if I proposed it," Charles said. "Ah, well. I suppose I'll have to settle on one princess soon enough."

I twisted around on his lap to face him. "Why must you marry, too?"

"Because I'm a king, my dear," he said ruefully. "I'm not so young that I can wait. Kings need heirs to secure their successions."

I swept my hand toward his brothers. "What of these fine fellows? Aren't they your heirs?"

"Can you imagine the outcry if I left England in the care of James?" he asked, a teasing question, but one that masked a serious doubt. Not only was James stubborn, dull, and overbearing—there'd been plenty of English kings with such liabilities—but he also made little effort to disguise his entanglement in the Romish church, and no good Anglican Englishman would tolerate that. "I take great comfort in having James behind me. With him waiting there, no Parliament will dare cut off my head like our father's."

Horrified, I swatted his chest. "Don't even make jests like that."

"She's right, Charles," Henry said, his good humor abruptly turned somber and serious. "Recall what I swore to Father on the morning he was murdered, that I'd not let them make me king if it meant they cut the heads from my brothers to do it."

"No one would hold you to such an oath, Henry," Charles said lightly. "You were only eight when you made it."

"Old enough to understand," Henry said grimly. "Old enough to understand it all."

No one said anything to that, and from respect, even the fiddlers stopped their songs. Henry had been the one brother of the three left in England to say farewell to their father on that fateful January morning, the only one shown the headless corpse by his captors, as proof of the wrongness of kings. Our merriment gone, only the mournful song of the nightingales in the trees overhead filled the silence.

"Well, now, that's a pretty way I've ended our party for the night," Charles said at last. He kissed me again and set me on my feet before him. "Will you stay here, madam, or come with us to Whitehall?"

It seemed suddenly impossible to remain here by myself, or worse, for him to be alone, either.

"I'll come with you," I said, slipping my hand tightly into his. "With you, my dearest sir."

Later that same month, I lay in my bed in the King Street house, trying to guess the hour of the day without opening my eyes. I'd not stayed out particularly late the night before, but I'd drunk more than was wise. Now my head ached abominably and my stomach was so uneasy that I'd not tried to launch so much as tea or toasted biscuits onto its rocky waves.

My darling Wilson had seen my plight, and without comment had covered my eyes with a chilled cloth soaked in lavender water, left the curtains drawn against the too-bright sun—which, in my situation, most any sun would have been—and thoughtfully set the chamber pot on a chair beside the bed. I lay as still as I could and marveled at how much work it could be not to move.

My only solace came from the knowledge that time would bring relief to the sorrowful results of my self-indulgence, and that by the time the case clock in Roger's study sounded twelve times for noon I was sure to feel better. I'd gained much experience in such matters this merry summer. Indeed, it seemed that ever since Charles had returned I'd suffered through every morning like this—and how glad I was that Roger went to his offices so early, and never saw me thus, to scold me for it.

I could hear wagons and carriages in the street, enough that it must be broad day. I'd have to listen for the clock's chime and count the hours to be sure, but if I could—

"Mistress Palmer?" The hinges to the door of my bedchamber squeaked open.

Without moving more than a flinch at the terrible racket of the hinges or raising the cloth from my eyes, I knew it was Wilson.

"What is it?" I asked, my voice hoarse and tremulous. "Must you disturb me now when I feel so ill?"

"Forgive me, madam, but I have only your interest at heart," Wilson whispered, coming closer to my bed. "You recall I told you of a wise woman who might bring you comfort?"

"No, I do not," I said peevishly. "I can't be expected to remember every nattering thing you speak to me, Wilson."

"As you wish, madam," Wilson murmured, but I noted, too, that she didn't leave me. "I've brought the woman to you here. Her name is Mistress Nan Quinn."

"Good day, Mistress Palmer," said a new voice I took to be this other creature, introduced into my presence without my permission. "If you please, madam, to answer a few questions, so I might—"

"You might not!" I tore the cloth from my eyes, squinting at the pair of them. This Nan Quinn looked to be much like Wilson herself, another square, squat personage past her first youth, who spoke as if the world would wish to hear her. "Wilson, why must you vex me like this? Asking me questions, bringing strangers to my very bedchamber! Can't you see how poorly I am, how being forced to address you now causes me infinite suffering?"

"But that's why I've come, madam," the other woman said, her voice low and soothing. "I can help you, madam, and answer your suffering."

"My suffering is my own doing," I said. "I know the cause is wine, and I know there's no cure beyond what I do."

"But there may indeed be ways to ease your pains and aches, madam," the woman countered. "I know many such cures."

"How?" I demanded skeptically. "You're neither surgeon nor physician or apothecary. Are you a witch, then, to make such promises?"

"No witch, madam, no," she said in that same soothing voice. "Only a friend who desires to help. Would your maid have trusted me so far if I couldn't do as I claim?"

That was logic enough, for one of the reasons I so trusted Wilson was that she shared my dislike of fools. Besides, I felt too sick to quarrel.

"Very well, then," I said, letting my head drop back on my pillow. "I shall answer your questions, if you'll bring me relief."

"Thank you, madam," Mistress Quinn said, respectful enough. "You claim your head aches and spins as if from strong drink?"

"It does, because strong drink was in fact the cause of it," I said, hoping her other questions would prove less obvious. "Drinking is commonplace in Whitehall."

"Yes, madam." She presumed to take my hand in hers, which I permitted, her fingers being cool and gentle. "Yet this distress eases as the day progresses?"

"Yes, yes," I said. "Surely Wilson's told you that much."

"She has, yes," Mistress Quinn said. "She's also told me that you've pain in your breasts when she tries to lace your stays."

I glared at Wilson for such a revelation, for I knew the cause of this condition, too. The king admired my breasts enormously, proclaiming them the most perfect he'd ever seen, or held. Yet on occasion during our amorous play, he would caress and handle them with such enthusiasm that the tender flesh would ache afterward. I didn't think to halt him, for at the time I found his forcefulness only served to heighten my own delight. But when Wilson would try to lace me too tightly—ah, then I'd yelp and squirm.

"Forgive me, madam, but such questions do have their purpose," she continued. "Do you find that your desire for your husband has recently increased?"

Behind her Wilson coughed. Too pointedly for her station, or my tastes, to be sure, and I glared at her anew.

Indeed, my ardor *had* increased, but because I'd finally a lover whose appetites matched my own. My husband had nothing to do with it.

"Very well, madam, I shall take the happy glow of your cheeks for a yes." The woman smiled kindly, and patted my hand with such understanding and encouragement as to make me wary.

"I've one final question for you, madam," she continued, "the last key to your little mystery. Do you recall the date of your last courses?"

My little mystery, indeed. As soon as she asked, I realized the sorry truth for myself, or rather, let myself realize what I'd denied for so long. In the excitement of these last months, I'd lost track of my flowers, and I'd not noticed that they'd not come. Since when, since when: not since the days before the king's return to London, on the twenty-ninth of May.

I was ill in the mornings, yet voracious the rest of the day and night. My breasts were tender, and swollen, too, though I'd not admitted it to myself. If Wilson were having difficulty with my stays, then it was because my waist was already beginning to thicken, and not from the rich food I consumed at the palace feasts, either.

My eyes filled with hot tears of emotion and dismay. My joyful summer had come at a costly price. I didn't need a midwife—for that, surely, must be this Nan Quinn's trade—to tell me that I was seven weeks gone with the king's bastard.

"What's this, Barbara?" Roger pushed the door open, looking with concern at Wilson, and Nan Quinn, and me lying in bed with tears on my cheeks. "I come home for a paper I'd forgotten in my study and find you abed. What has happened? Are you unwell?"

"Not at all, Roger." I didn't doubt for an instant what I'd do next. I'd no real choice. I sniffed back my tears and forced myself to smile as I held my hand out to him. "Only the happiest news. You are at last to be a father."

# Chapter Ten

I begged Roger to keep my pregnancy a secret, pleading that it was such early days that my condition might still prove false or premature. Even Mistress Quinn urged this reticence to him. There was no absolute certainty until I could feel the child quicken in my womb, some months from now.

In reality, I knew that above all things Charles must hear such news from me and no one else. The court and London in general was so ripe for gossip and scandal of any sort that if Roger were unable to control his burgeoning male pride, and tell but one of his colleagues or friends, then the tale would spread like fire in driest tinder, with no way to stop its blistering progress.

Yet how was I to tell the king? I knew what I meant to him: that I was so young as to make him feel younger, yet old enough not to be missish. I was a convenient amusement, a beautiful, witty ornament, an amorous adventurer with him in that great bed of his. Because I was another man's wife, I was his to enjoy without any responsibility.

In short, I was a Villiers, beautiful and fashioned for royal pleasure, to his charming, irresponsible Stuart.

Where would I be without my beauty? How could I amuse him if I were as swollen and heavy as Anne Hyde? What could I offer him like that, when the court was filled with other willing ladies without big bellies?

Worst of all, I'd played my hand every bit as badly as had Lucy

Walters, no matter how much I'd pitied or condescended toward her memory. For the sake of discretion, I'd agreed with him to keep our connection between us, and thus lost whatever power and influence I might have gained. I'd become so enamored of the man that I'd let the king slip free.

Bitterly I recalled what Charles had said to his brother James: this was a mistake of my own making, and now it was up to me to make it right as well. Yet how, truly, was I to do so?

It was Charles's habit to move freely among his people. Unlike his cousin, the French king Louis, Charles did not keep himself locked away in his palace but was often to be seen throughout London, whether at the theatre, at services, or on the river. Most famously, he walked through St. James's Park, the greenway behind the palace, and walking with him was as good a way as any to win his favor or simply his ear.

But those walks could likewise become a trap for the unwary: with his long legs and lean body, the king set a breakneck pace that left many of his courtiers huffing and puffing in his wake, and open to ridicule. While his small dogs had no problem trotting alongside him, older courtiers, or those who'd drunk too freely the night before, found the challenge not worth the gain.

Being young and long-limbed myself, I was one of the few ladies who'd dared to join the king and his brothers on these walks. Feeling ill, I'd not gone lately as often as before, but now, fortified by Mistress Quinn's potions, I decided there'd be no better way to reinforce my place at Charles's side.

Dressed in blue as bright as the summer sky, with a wide-brimmed plumed hat and a parasol to keep my fair skin from the sun, I bravely stepped up as he began from the palace on a warm August morning.

"Mistress Palmer, good day," he said, surprised, but obviously pleased as well. "How handsome you look this morning. It's been a long while since you've joined us, but how happy we are that you have."

Around him the others welcomed me, too, for it is the role of a courtier always to echo and agree with the king. I tipped my head winsomely to one side, twirling the handle of my parasol against my shoulder. "We are happy to be here, Your Majesty, indeed, *most* happy."

He smiled in return, a heavy-lidded smile that lingered so upon me that I knew he was thinking of last evening, when I'd gleefully played the wanton for his amusement. The trick now would be to make the world know it, too.

Yet though I'd sallied forth full of bravado, we'd not walked far before I began to wilt. A walk that earlier in the summer I'd completed with breezy ease was now making my heart quicken. I felt flushed and heated, and my smile seemed tacked upon my face. Though I willed my feet to keep pace with the others, the effort was becoming more and more difficult. Charles recognized my distress, too, for though at his elbow walked some gentleman droning earnestly about a scheme for saving the souls of the red savages in New England, he kept glancing to me.

"Mistress Palmer," he called at last, interrupting the droning gentleman. "Is the morning too warm for you?"

"Not at all, sir," I answered with grim determination. "I am well enough."

But I wasn't well enough for much, and as we climbed toward the crest of a small rise in the path, I seemed to hear naught but the rise and fall of my own blood within my veins, a roaring sound that clouded everything else before my eyes. I felt myself swaying unsteadily, my legs wobbling beneath me as if I were at sea, and before I could steady myself I began to topple, sinking down with my skirts puffing around me.

Strong arms caught me and guided me to a nearby bench in the shade of a small copse of trees.

"Put your head down low, my dear," Charles ordered. "Breathe as deep as you can."

Obediently I leaned forward, though in truth I doubted I could have done much else. My hat slid from my head to the grass, and I left it. The little dogs snuffled around my feet, excited by my fallen hat, until Charles shooed them away. I closed my eyes and tried to regain my composure. Around me I could hear others murmuring with a show of concern, like the fluttering wings of pigeons.

"Shall I call for a surgeon?" some gentleman asked, eager to appear helpful before the king.

"Should we send for the lady's husband?" asked another. "If she's ill, he should be informed."

"I know the lady's constitution," Charles said, "and she'll be set to rights soon enough. Likely it's only the heat. Clear away, now, so she might feel the breeze. We'll rejoin you when the lady's better."

I heard them dutifully withdraw. My head was clearing now, and I dared to sit upright, discovering the king on the bench beside me.

"Forgive me, sir," I whispered miserably. "I didn't mean to be so weak."

"Drink this, Barbara," he said kindly, handing me a tumbler of the cider sold by peddlers in the park. "You grew too warm, that was all."

I raised the cup to my lips. The oversweet scent of the pressed apples assailed my nose, and my stomach leapt in such swift rebellion that I lowered it at once, gulping for air. If there were anything worse than fainting before the king, then it would surely be to spew upon the grass at his feet, in full sight of all those idling, curious spectators.

"Perhaps not, eh?" Gently he took the cup back from my hand.

Tears of frustration stung my eyes, and I pressed my hand over my mouth to keep them from spilling out. Was this part of breeding, too, tears and fainting and behaving as poorly as the babe I was doomed to bear?

"So tell me, Barbara," he said quietly. "Is the child mine or your husband's?"

That was enough to make me sob, the tears now flowing unchecked. "How—how could you know?"

"You forget that I've been down this path before," he said wryly and handed me his own royal handkerchief. "Likely I knew before you did yourself."

"Oh, I am so shamed, sir," I cried softly, my voice breaking. "How could this have happened to me?"

"I should expect in the usual way," he said. "Given how often—

and how well—you've entertained me, madam, I'd be more surprised if I hadn't filled your belly. I suppose you'll swear that it *is* mine?"

"Of course it's yours," I said through my tears, stunned he'd even suggest otherwise. "I've been with Roger for over a year now with no result, yet with you—ah, I'm certain it's yours."

"As certain as any lady can be in such circumstances. Amazing how often ladies are always certain it's mine."

"But this one *is*," I cried, stunned he'd even suggest otherwise. "The night of the procession, sir, when you first returned to London, and to me—I'm sure it was then."

"That night?" He smiled with male pride at the memory. "I suppose I must believe it. Ah, well, a child will be a more lasting memento than all those bouquets tossed my way."

I bowed my head, wounded that he'd not understand more of how I was suffering. I forgot the curious bystanders, forgot my promises to be discreet.

"You—you won't want me any longer," I wailed. "I'll be fat and clumsy and—and *hideous,* and you'll—you'll put me aside, and forget me and—and our babe."

"Hush, now, Barbara, I'll do nothing of the sort," he said. "Hush, please, don't cry. Why should you believe I'd abandon you now?"

My snuffle was full of bitterness. "Why should I believe otherwise? What assurance have you given me of any lasting affection, or honorable proof that you would provide for me if such a misfortune as this befell me?"

"Ah." He looked down at the front of my bodice, as if imagining the tiny babe that must already be curled deep within me. "I haven't, have I?"

"No, sir, you have not." I blew my nose noisily, not caring if my nose or eyes were red. Likely it was too late for that, anyway, just as it was likely too late for the protests I was making now. "The only plum that's come my way was the lease upon the King Street house, and Roger must still pay the rent."

He nodded, though I doubted my words had left their mark. "Does Mr. Palmer know of the child?"

"He knows," I said. "He's strutting about like the biggest cockerel in the barnyard, too."

"So he believes it's his?"

"I told him it was," I said bluntly. "If he believed otherwise, then he would have turned me out of our house into the streets, and I could not have trusted in you to save me."

"Oh, Barbara, Barbara." He looked at me with genuine sadness, so much so that I knew my arrows had at last struck home. "You've become far too dear to me ever to scorn you like that."

I raised my chin to keep it from trembling. "Am I?"

"You are," he said with unquestionable conviction. "I won't fail you, Barbara, you or our child. You have my word."

This was far more than I'd dared to hope to gain. He was a careless Stuart, true, but now that he'd given his word I believed I could count on him to uphold it.

And if he didn't, why, I now knew I'd the right to demand that he did, the way any good Villiers would.

He reached down and plucked my hat from where it had fallen on the grass and settled it back on my head. A small gesture, but a tender one, and I understood how much it symbolized for us both. In return, I longed to kiss him, but instead contented myself with merely covering his hand with my own. There'd be time enough now for the world to speculate that this child was his.

"Thank you, sir," I said softly. "Thank you with all my heart."

"Yes." That was all, no more nor less. His black eyes glittered like jet in the sun. "Are you better now?"

I nodded, wondering if I'd only imagined that rare glimpse of vulnerability from him. Now when he smiled, the curve of his full lips was more suggestive than understanding.

"Are you well enough to return with me?" He glanced down again at my body, this time with more frank appraisal than wonder. "I'll like to watch you ripen, Barbara, and know it's my seed that's done it. Your breasts are already larger in my hands."

I smiled, too, such talk stirring my desires to match his. I did feel better now, but even if I hadn't, I knew I'd have to feign that I did, and if my swelling breasts ached when he fondled them, then I'd not complain. *That* would be my part of our bargain.

He threaded his fingers into my hair to hold my head steady, and kissed me then, hard and possessively, so that anyone who saw understood everything.

And may God forgive me, I kissed him back in exactly the same way.

The letter on the salver in Wilson's hand looked innocent enough. The paper was worn and stained from having traveled far to find me, but once I saw the familiar seal my heart jumped within my breast from well-trained habit.

"I thought it best to bring it directly to you, madam," Wilson said. "I was certain you'd want it kept from Mr. Palmer."

"Thank you, Wilson, thank you." I seized the letter and carried it off to my closet to read alone, so there'd be no witnesses to the power that Philip's words might still have over me. For the letter was in fact from my old lover the Earl of Chesterfield, writ from his exile in Paris. It had been many months since I'd last heard from him, let alone lain in his sweet embrace.

Yet though the hand on the page was achingly familiar, the opinions to be found in the words were new between us. He'd heard of the king's admiration for me, and even at a distance he'd understood our situation with a clarity that Roger did not possess. But while Philip had always thought nothing of keeping other mistresses besides me, he couldn't bear to extend the same favor to me.

Instead he claimed the unfamiliar role of a wounded lover. He congratulated me on my good fortune with the king, yes, but at the same time he lamented what he perceived as my unfaithfulness to him, and begged for me to send him a portrait of myself as a memento of past times: "For then I shall love something like you, yet unchangeable."

I laughed softly at this backhanded request, shaking my head to think of how no other gentleman I'd known could compose such a *billet-doux* quite like Philip. He even concluded his plea with a pretty couplet in French, exactly as he'd ended so many other missives to me:

> *Beautiful savage, you starve me of hope,*
> *And for all others extinguish desire.*

That made me sigh, for love lost and long done. He would always remain my sweetheart love, the one who'd introduced me to so many of life's greatest joys and pleasures.

But the last lines of Philip's letter were likewise a product of his character. He informed me that he was at last to wed Lady Elizabeth Butler, the daughter of the Marquess of Ormond, with a fixed dowry of six thousand pounds. As if by accident—though I knew every word was written with intent—he mentioned that this happy match had been contrived with the assistance of that dear gentleman Edward Hyde.

There was an unpleasant edge to this little message, as if to say, well, you might have His Majesty in your bed, but *I* will marry a titled heiress, and I'll do it with the aid of a man who loathes you.

I remembered Philip well enough to see both the gloating behind this and the malice as well. Neither sat well with me. All my earlier gentle feelings, my tender memories, toward him vanished, and my first impulse was to crumple this odious letter and hurl it into the fire, where its author deserved to be, too.

But as I raised my fist over the grate, I'd second thoughts. With his prize bride on his arm, Philip was sure now to be permitted to return to court. Such a letter might prove useful to me at a later date, perhaps to humiliate his new wife, or cause him some other shame or discomfort. I'd not let Philip hurt me again as he'd wounded me before.

Some would say that the life at court had hardened me since my girlish days. I saw it more as becoming stronger. I was no longer a sighing, lovesick lass, but a woman grown who'd taken her place in a difficult world and meant to keep it.

I smoothed the wrinkles from the crumpled sheet and tucked it into my pocket for safekeeping. The sages claim that revenge is a dish best served cold, and at that moment there was nothing more icy than my heart set against the Earl of Chesterfield.

In the end, the golden days of that first summer of Charles's reign could last no longer than any other season. The days grew shorter and my waist thickened, but there were other, larger events and signs of change to remark in London at that time as well.

The Duke of York did finally honor his vows to Anne Hyde, and though the new duchess soon after presented him with a son, there were many whispers about how the Stuarts had lowered themselves by such a marriage. Most vehement in her criticism was the Queen Mother herself, who vowed that if the slatternly Duchess of York dared enter the front gate of the palace, she would be sure to leave by the back, to avoid having to be civil to such a daughter-in-law. Charles attempted to calm this talk by making old Sir Edward a baron and thus improving the family enough that Anne was now a lady in her own right, but no one believed she was any better than she'd been born.

My mother the Countess of Anglesea died in September, after a long wasting condition of the lungs that served neither to sweeten her temperament nor increase her kindness toward me, her only child. She chose not to summon me to her deathbed, and I in turn did not grieve for her. But I did attend her funeral and burial at St. Martin-in-the-Fields. I knew what was proper, even if she never had.

In her will, she left me nothing.

Death was present in other ways, too. One of the most popular conditions of the Declaration of Breda had been the general pardon it offered to all those who'd supported Cromwell and the Commonwealth. Charles had shrewdly realized that people turned with political winds, and it would be both more providential and more popular to welcome the return of those who'd wandered from the Royalist cause for one reason or another. Though the sternest Royalists did not like to admit it, there were many aspects of the Commonwealth government that had run far more efficiently than under either of the two previous Stuart kings, and Charles needed the experience that these ministers and other officials could bring. Reconciliation was the only way to restore England as a whole, and in August, at Charles's urging, Parliament passed the Act of Indemnity and Oblivion to make official the pardon that the Declaration of Breda had promised.

Yet as encompassing as the pardon was, there was one group of individuals that Charles refused to include: the regicides, the fifty-nine men who'd signed his father's death warrant, as well as the officials of the High Court of Justice who'd served at the trial, and the army officers who'd overseen the execution.

On this Charles and his brothers were inflexible, and were determined on vengeance in their father's name. Already the surviving members of this shameful group had been arrested and brought to the Tower to stand trial, with the special court ready to convene in October. There was no doubt what verdict Charles expected the court to hand down, nor any doubt that they would do it, either. The sentence of death would be equally inflexible: to be hanged, drawn, and quartered at Tyburn, with the gruesome remains publicly displayed on pikes to rot and be picked clean by the crows. Those others, like Cromwell himself, who'd already escaped into death, would not be spared the punishment, for their bodies were to be exhumed and hanged in chains at Tyburn.

It was no more than what those heinous villains deserved, and there were few in London who disputed the king's right to so serve his father's memory. Yet the coming trials and executions darkened the city like a noxious black cloud, tainting the merriment and good humor of the Restoration and bringing back ugly memories that were, in many ways, better forgotten.

There was other unhappiness, too. The first giddiness over the king's return—the constant "feast days without fasts," as one wag phrased it—had passed. All the best rewards and places had finally been given out, and as was only natural, those who'd been neglected or denied began to grumble and complain and find empty fault with the king. It was still slight, to be sure, but it was there, a ruffle of uneasy discontent beneath the surface of content.

But worst of all came in the middle of September. The usual group of us was playing at cards at the palace; the wine and laughter were easy and the spirits high. Though Charles himself never drank to excess, and seldom made serious wagers, he liked for others to enjoy themselves however they pleased. Often he'd sit beside me at the gaming table, his arm draped casually over my shoulders as he offered wry comments about the play.

This night was no different, save that I was winning handsomely, nearly fifty guineas and the evening still young. This may not seem so vast a sum, I know, but in those days the captain of a ship of war earned but twenty pounds a year, and my own maidservant Wilson subsisted nicely on her four pounds for the same twelve-month.

Suddenly, after playing his hand, the Duke of Gloucester tossed down his cards, pushed his chair away from the table, and stood, holding to the back for support. This was not like him: he drank even less than his brother, and he was so fervent a gamester that he'd never willingly leave the table.

"What's amiss, Henry?" Charles asked cheerfully. "You can't leave with Mrs. Palmer winning like this. It's bad luck for the rest of us."

But Henry only shook his head, his color poor and his eyes dull. "Forgive me, sir, but I must withdraw," he said. "I'm not well."

"Then take to your bed, Henry," Charles said. "Go on, that's the best thing in the world for you, so long as you take your lady for companionship."

While the others laughed, Henry retreated, his current mistress darting after him as if fearing to disobey the king. She was a small gold-haired girl, very young, whose name I no longer recall, nor did it matter, considering what we all learned the next day.

The Duke of Gloucester was suffering from the smallpox.

Because I'd had this foul pox and could come to no further harm, Charles asked me to call with him upon his brother, thinking to cheer him. But with Henry the disease had moved with astonishing haste, and by the time I came with Charles the next afternoon, the physicians were already despairing of his recovery.

The room was stifling, the walls draped with red cloth and the fire blazing hot, as was the recommended practice to help draw out the pox's fever. Henry's handsome face was covered with sores, fever racked his body and slicked his hair with sweat, and he knew none of us gathered around his bed. At one side sat the Queen Mother, Henrietta Marie, small and wizened as a French monkey, along with James, and their sisters Mary, the Princess Royal from Holland, and Princess Henriette Anne. It was a melancholy family group, made more distraught by the squabbling between the Queen Mother's Roman priests and the Anglican bishops over which should administer the final rites. I saw at once I'd no place among them, and with a sad heart I murmured my farewell to the prince and left.

The next day, Henry was dead.

The stunned court was swathed in the deep purple mourning required for a royal prince. Grieving put a temporary halt to our parties and gaming, and the theatres that Henry had loved so well were ordered closed for six weeks. I'd never seen Charles so distraught with sorrow, nor seen him use his work for the new government as a way to ease his loss. Swallowed up in his grief, Charles could not bring himself to attend the funeral at Henry VII's chapel, and sent James in his place to act as the family's principal mourner.

Much of the court pretended to be scandalized by this imagined slight, but I knew better. Henry's death had left a tattered hole in our little circle that could never be mended or filled. But the question of another Stuart heir was a different matter entirely.

Whether I liked it or not, wished it or not, for the sake of England it was time for Charles to take a queen.

# Chapter Eleven

"A girl, mistress, a lovely girl!" exclaimed the midwife. "Well done, mistress, well done!"

"A girl?" I raised my exhausted head from the pillow to look. In her hands, the midwife was cradling a squirming, muck-covered creature, still bound to me by the snakelike cord.

"Yes, mistress, a girl, a beautiful, perfect girl." I heard the first mewling cry, and then the babe was deposited upon my poor ravaged belly. "Your daughter, mistress."

Without thinking, I reached down to steady the baby, not wanting her to topple off after so much toil and labor to bring her forth. She was sticky with my blood and twisting in my arms, and as the midwife tied off the cord, my new daughter began to wail as if her tiny heart would break.

"Hush, enough of that," I whispered, my eyes filling with tears. I'd no idea what to do with an infant, not even my own flesh and blood.

"Here now, madam, let me tidy her for you." Wilson swept the babe away while the midwife finished tending to me.

With dismay I surveyed the wreckage of my once-beautiful body, stretched and flaccid and worn beyond all recognition, and when I thought of how my pitiful seat of delight had been forced to stretch and tear to accommodate the babe, I wept anew. Once Charles had likened me to Venus herself, but now—what man, let alone a king, could ever find pleasure in me again after this?

"Will I ever be as I was?" I begged the midwife through my tears. "How, oh, how?"

But the midwife only chuckled, wiping me clean. "Oh, it's always the same with new mothers," she said. "You scarce finish birthing one child, and already you're planning how to entice your husband to give you another."

"Not at all," I whimpered, horrified. If I'd my way, I never wished to endure such a trial again. "I wish to be restored for myself."

Mistress Quinn clucked her tongue. I was certain she knew the truth, either from gossip or from Wilson. Even though I'd retired from the court and the palace before Christmas, when I'd grown too ungainly to pretend to grace, Charles had continued to attend to me with letters, small gifts, even visits to King Street when he could.

Yet I was not so foolish as to have demanded he remain faithful to me in my absence. I'd not heard of any other ladies having taken my place, but Charles was a man of such voracious appetites that for him to have abstained for so long would have been an unthinkable fast.

"You're a young woman, madam," the midwife said finally, propping a fresh pillow behind my head, "and in fine health. You did not grow overfat with the child, nor was your labor long. I should expect you to recover, yes, but with an added glow to your beauty that only motherhood can grant."

"How long?" I demanded. "I cannot lie here idle forever."

She shrugged with maddening imprecision. "Some women need a full year to heal, madam. But for a lady of your vigor, I'd venture three months, perhaps four."

"One," I said succinctly, and I meant it, too. I'd stayed away from court and from Charles for too long as it was to make my absence any longer than that. As soon as my lying-in was done, I would return.

"Here you are, madam," Wilson said, presenting me once again with the baby, now more agreeably swaddled in a soft woolen cloth, with a worked linen cap tied over her head. "Your beautiful daughter. She favors you, surely."

She set the bundled babe into the crook of my arm, and for the first time I gazed into her tiny wrinkled face. For her part, she stared back at me so boldly that I laughed through my tears.

"Mark that, the saucy little baggage," I said. "She's my daughter, no doubt of that."

"Yes, madam," said Wilson. "She has your mouth, and your lips, too."

"That fine black hair's from her father," Mistress Quinn said, as politic an observation as I'd ever heard, considering how both Charles and Roger had dark hair. "She'll break her share of hearts. Have you chosen a name for her?"

"Anne," I said softly, a name common among the Villiers. I knew most women—and their husbands—longed for sons, but I was glad for a girl. There'd be no difficult question of naming her after either Charles or Roger, and besides, I'd know what to do with a beautiful daughter. I touched my finger to her cheek, marveling at the softness of her skin. "Her name is Anne."

But abruptly her tiny face crumpled and her eyes squeezed shut, her toothless mouth springing open to wail again.

"What have I done?" I asked, startled and worried. "How have I hurt her?"

"She's not hurt, madam, but hungry," Mistress Quinn observed. "You must put her to suck."

"To suck?" I asked incredulously over the baby's growing cries. "But that is why I hired a wet nurse, to spare me that."

"The girl won't come from the country until tomorrow, madam," Wilson said firmly. "You won't wish Miss Anne to starve until then, will you?"

"She'll not stop crying until you feed her," Mistress Quinn advised, speaking plain. "You can suckle her for this day or the next, and not harm your breasts, if that is what worries you. There's plenty of time to bind them and dry your milk."

"Very well, then," I said, steeling myself. "If I must."

With trepidation I looked down at that small, demanding mouth. I knew a score of clever ways to suck a man's cock, but not one for suckling my own daughter.

"If you please, madam, like this." The midwife arranged the baby in my arms, and guided my nipple to her mouth. "She'll know what's proper."

The sensation of Anne latching on to my breast and drawing my milk was astonishing, pulling as it did clear to my womb, and, in a way, tugging at my heart as well. I smiled down at my new daughter, her eyes now closed with contentment as she fed. I'd do everything in my power to see that her father recognized her royal blood and made her a lady in her own right. I'd lavish whatever I could upon her—gowns and jewels, pretty toys and dolls—all the trinkets and amusements that had been absent from my own dismal childhood. I'd make certain that she'd a dowry fit for a princess, and a noble, titled husband worthy of her heritage.

A king for a father, and I for her mother: what babe could ever ask for a more splendid, more glorious birthright than that?

"Barbara, my dear wife!" Roger hurried to my bedside and kissed me on the forehead. "I came as soon as I received Wilson's summons. Oh, Barbara, who is this fine little person? Our son?"

"My *daughter*," I said defensively, holding her the more tightly. "I've called her Anne."

"Anne," he said, his expression soft with wonder. "A good name, a saint's name."

"My grandmother's name," I said, not wanting my Anne burdened with his saints. Roger's mother was a papist, and in the last months it had seemed to me that Roger himself had turned more and more toward the Roman church. His conversation had become peppered with Romish sayings, and he now numbered priests among his acquaintance. I even suspected that he ventured to Mass like the Duke of York, and without telling me, either. With the Declaration of Breda, Charles had vowed that Englishmen were now free to worship however they pleased, but I'd never guessed that freedom would extend to my own husband.

"Anne is a good English name," I continued. "An *Anglican* name."

"Of course, of course," he murmured, too enchanted with the babe to listen to me. "How beautiful she is! Oh, Barbara, I cannot wait to show our daughter to the world."

"Forgive me, sir," the midwife sternly interrupted. "But you must take care of a new babe's health. To parade her about before others and let her be passed from hand to hand, to haul her about amidst the uncleanliness of the city—that, sir, is to put her young life at gravest risk."

"I'd never do that," Roger said, chastised. "I only meant to take her with me to Dorney Court, for my mother's blessings."

I gasped, horrified, and hugged Anne more tightly in my arms. "What you truly mean by that, Roger, is that you plan to spirit my daughter away to your mother's chapel and have her baptized as a papist, delivering her soul into the hands of the priests."

"Hush, madam, hush, don't alarm yourself," cautioned Mistress Quinn. "Childbed is a most delicate state for a woman, and ill humors such as these are a hazard for your condition as well."

"Yes, yes, Barbara, please calm yourself," Roger said softly. "I've no wish to harm you or our child. Nothing will be done in the matter of baptism without consulting you. How could I ever treat my Anne's mother with so little regard?"

"I do not know," I said, still on my guard. "But I will tell you this: *I'd* never dare make such a grave decision without consulting her father, and I'd hope you'd do the same with regards to me."

He smiled again, though I doubted he understood the depth of the truth, or the threat, behind my words. Instead he leaned forward to first kiss Anne's cheek, then mine.

"Whatever you wish, Barbara," he said softly. "I know better than to cross you, even on this day when you've made me the happiest of men. Whatever you wish, I shall abide by it."

Charles was overjoyed at the news of Anne's arrival, and promised to call upon us as soon as I was permitted to sit up, and the rigors of my lying-in were lessened. In the meantime, he wrote to me the prettiest letter imaginable, full of tenderness and promises for my future and for our daughter's, which I carefully saved for her to read when she was older, as proof of her father's devotion. He also sent as a token to her a handsome rattle truly fit for a princess, a large coral set within a silver handle with numerous bells and much fine engraving. For me came a pair of large, exquisitely matched pearl drops for my ears, all the more memorable for being my first pearls.

I still did not trust Roger in the matter of Anne's christening. Instead, three days after she was born, I arranged for the Anglican minister of our parish to come to King Street and baptize Anne in the proper faith. It was done with as little fanfare as can be imagined, with her godparents left to be named later. But at least now I could rest easily, knowing her little soul was preserved as a Protestant, and that whatever Romish tomfoolery Roger might attempt would be of no effect.

At this same time, my stepfather, the Earl of Anglesea, perished of smallpox. He was buried beside my mother in the churchyard of St. Martin-in-the-Fields, where I hoped they'd plague one another for all eternity. Like my mother, he left me nothing, his entire estate passing to his decrepit sister, the Countess of Sussex, who never would deign to receive me. I would remember her later, I promised myself, and in a way, too, that would show her who was above, and who was beneath.

But for most of that February and into March, I concentrated on regaining my strength and my form. I'd missed Charles while I'd been away, missed him mightily, missed his wit and his charm, his affection and his lusty skills as my lover. I could but hope he'd missed me as much. Like a warrior who readies himself for battle, I planned my return to court, determined to defy those like Hyde who'd try to keep me away from the king.

April would at last mark the celebration for his coronation on St. George's Day, nearly a year after his return, and the pageantry and show would be rare indeed. The first uncertain days of his realm were done, the shabbiness of exile forgotten. It was not just Charles who'd been restored to power, but the palaces and churches, the markets and shops and theatres—the life of the entire city had returned with him. Soon guests and dignitaries would begin arriving, adding even more luster to the court.

I could not take part in the coronation itself, of course. Neither my beauty nor the king's affection for me could accomplish that. Just as in the procession that had marked his return to England, nearly all of the participants would be men, and the few women permitted to watch in Westminster Abbey would be ladies from the highest-ranking families of the peerage.

It vexed me mightily that I was not among them, just as it vexed me that for now my daughter was no more than lowly Miss Palmer. But I vowed that would change. As much as I longed to be again with Charles, I wasn't returning to court simply to enjoy myself. I was twenty now, and already I'd squandered too much of my youth on idleness. A gentleman can rely on his intelligence, education, and courage to advance himself, but while the surest weapons a lady has in her arsenal are far more potent, they are also far more fleeting. If I wished to make the most of my Villiers gifts, I must use my wit and beauty while I could to advance my station and secure my future. I owed it to my little Anne to settle for nothing less.

Thus when Roger insisted on taking my daughter to his mother at Dorney Court in March, I'd no choice but to agree. In the eyes of the world, he was her father, and had that right. It was better that way, too, I suppose, to have them both away from London now. Besides, the Palmers had even less wish to see me than I them, accepting my excuses so I could remain behind in town. I put aside the crystal cypher heart that Roger had given me at our betrothal, and instead hooked the pearl drops from Charles into my ears, ready for my triumphant return to court.

To court, to Charles, and to battle.

One of the first acts that Charles had ordered on his return was to re-open the theatres. Unlike Cromwell, he found no sin in plays or players, and unlike his father, he preferred to venture out and see the public performances among his people, rather than isolated command performances at the palace. Most startlingly of all, however, was how he'd ended the long-held ban of women upon the stage. Now instead of beardless men assuming roles meant for females, women actors in the style of the French theatres played the parts as surely Nature ever intended.

For me, whose life had coincided so completely with the parliamentary locking of the theatres, seeing plays for the first time was both a wonder and a treat, and my enthusiasm had delighted Charles as well. There was no finer entertainment to be had—excepting, of course, the one—than a night spent at the theatre, whether the King's Company in Vere Street or the Duke's Company in Lincoln's Inn Fields.

And I found pleasure not only in viewing but in being viewed. Attending plays was the finest way to increase my reputation as the king's favorite. Though I'd doubted the midwife's prediction when I'd first heard it, my *accouchement* had indeed added new richness to my beauty, a soft luxuriance that Charles had noticed at once with demonstrative approval. I was commonly called the most beautiful lady at the court; no other came close.

Now even the lowest clerks and apprentices who paid their two shillings to sit on the board benches in the pit recognized me by name, and I'd become better known than any of the high ladies at the court, or the most popular actresses on the stage. In turn Charles fair glowed with pride to have me so noticed, and to know that I was his.

On such a night, soon before the coronation, I'd gone with the king to see a new play by Beaumont and Fletcher called *The Humorous Lieutenant*. The king's entrance to the royal box was greeted with the usual cheers and huzzahs, and, alas, the usual lower salutes as well.

" 'Ere, Yer Majesty, 'ere!" The girl's flushed face was as round as the oranges in the willow basket on her hip as she grinned up at us from the theatre's pit. Every such chit in the place would come parade below the royal box, flaunting their overripe breasts like more oranges for sale in the hope that Charles would notice them—oh, yes, and the girl herself, too. "Fine, sweet oranges, oh, Yer Majesty!"

Charles could never resist such pleas, and leaned over the rail. "How sweet, lass?"

"Taste f' yerself, Yer Majesty!" The girl reached into her basket to choose the most luscious fruit, and gaily tossed it up toward the box.

The king reached out to catch it, but beside him I was the quicker, snatching the fruit like a golden ball from the air.

"The game's faster than that, sir," I said as I leaned back once again in my chair and began to peel my prize, digging my thumb hard into the thick skin to make the juice spurt free. "I wonder you didn't realize it, considering how quick you are in most other matters."

He laughed, his brother the Duke of York laughed on his other side, and the others in the surrounding boxes and in the pit below laughed, too, the way it always was with the king.

"It's only an orange, Barbara," he said, "not the Apple of Discord."

"It's mine now," I said, breaking free the fruit's first segment, "and that's what matters most to me. Here, sir, open."

Obediently he parted his lips, and I slid the crescent-shaped segment into his mouth, brushing my fingers lightly over his lips and mustache for good measure. That, I knew, would put the yearning orange-girl from his thoughts for good. For in the carriage from Whitehall to the theatre, I'd brought him to the crest of delirious pleasure with my mouth before he'd swept up my skirts and pulled me astride his glowing cock, and carried us both to rarest heights of satisfaction. I knew our mingled scents still clung to my fingers from where I'd dipped between our joined selves, and purposefully I mixed that musky scent with the juice of the orange beneath his nose.

He smiled and caught my wrist to hold my hand there while he ate the fruit.

"Which goddess of the three would you be, I wonder?" he asked, his gaze intent upon me. "Hera, Athena, or Aphrodite?"

I grinned slyly and eased my hand free of his grasp so I might slide a segment into my own mouth, lasciviously curling my tongue about it.

"The only proper judgment for King Paris should be that I am the sum of all three," I said. "That is, the proper judgment if he wishes to ride home again."

That made him laugh again, even as the overture's trumpets sounded to begin the play. As the audience's attention turned away from us and toward the stage, he leaned across and kissed me, his mustache sweet with the juice of the orange.

"You can't know how I missed you, Barbara," he said in a rough whisper.

"But I do know, sir," I said softly, "because I missed you the same."

"All the goddesses combined in one, and more besides," he said. "How could I ever wish to let you part from me again?"

The parting would come soon enough, and both the king and I and every other Englishman knew it, too. Yet when the first hint of it came, I was still unprepared for the force with which it would strike me.

It came later that summer, after the coronation, after Charles had been formally crowned and declared master of Britain. I had spent a pleasant day and evening with Charles and several others sailing on the river in the handsome yacht that the Dutch East India Company had given to him in honor of his coronation. We'd wearily climbed the river steps near Whitehall, and after a late supper repaired to Charles's rooms.

He'd stopped to disrobe in his closet while I waited in his bed-chamber. My skirts and stockings stank abominably from having been splashed and sprayed by the river's waters, and I was quick to shed them and the rest of my clothes, leaving them in a sodden pile for Charles's dogs to investigate with their usual eagerness before the ser-vants took them away. I wrapped myself in a coverlet from the bed and stood before the fire, unpinning my hair and tossing it between my fingers to take the damp from it as well. I turned my back to the fireplace, shaking my hair over my shoulders, and for the first time saw the portrait, propped on a table against the wall.

It was a small painting, dark and poorly limned and framed clumsily in black, in the oppressive Iberian manner. The subject was a woman with heavy, dark features, and fearful eyes ringed with shad-ows. It was impossible to guess at her body, for she was encased in a black gown so rigid as to be hammered from iron and extending far over her hips in an old-fashioned farthingale. These skirts were so wide that her flat-palmed hands hung over the front, dangling like a scarecrow's. A wide swath of lace wrapped over her shoulders and breasts like a bandage, and her hair was forced into a style as unyield-ing as her dress, with stiffened black curls at her cheeks and another clump of hair flattened strangely over her forehead.

It was monstrous attire, on a plain, pinched, swarthy woman. Yet even without a plaque or label, I knew who she was: the Portuguese infanta Catherine of Braganza, soon to be Charles's bride.

Clutching the coverlet around me, I stared down at the small, ugly portrait. I knew the reasons for such a union, and the compli-cated terms of the marriage settlement that made it so desired by both countries. They were hardly secret, not with Sir Edward—now raised to Lord Chancellor Clarendon—boasting to all about how much he'd achieved by arranging the match. I knew that the union would give Portugal a strong ally against Spain and secure the Braganza throne. I knew it would deliver both Tangiers and Bombay into English hands as new possessions of the crown, as well as trading rights throughout the Mediterranean.

I knew the other reasons, too, the ones based less on politics and diplomacy. I knew Charles needed a wife to get his heirs, just as I knew the infanta had been reserved for him since they'd both been children. And perhaps most important of all, I knew the Portuguese were will-ing to send nearly half a million pounds to England, hard money that the country desperately needed.

I knew all of that, yes. But when I looked at that portrait, my only thought was how this woman would take my place in the king's bed. She would be the one he'd make cry with pleasure now, and the one who'd be revered at his side. She'd take his seed and bear his sons, this short, dark, ugly virgin who was three years older than I.

"Ah," Charles said, coming to stand behind me, his gold brocade dressing gown fluttering around us both. "Were you admiring my bride?"

I swung around to face him. In my fury, I raised my hand to strike him, but he caught my wrist to stop me, holding my hand impotently over my head.

"Mind your temper, Barbara," he warned mildly. "Smite the King of England and you go straight to the Tower."

I tore my hand free of his grasp and stepped backward, rubbing my wrist where his fingers had gripped me. "She is an ugly Iberian dwarf. I don't know how you can bear to have her hideous picture in your chamber."

"I decided I should grow accustomed to her visage now, before the lady herself arrives early next year." He sighed wearily. "I am sorry, my dear, but you know I have no choice in this marriage. Kings are not like other men."

"No, they are not," I said furiously. "Kings are infinitely more cruel."

"What is cruel is that I must wed her at all." He sighed again, looking at the portrait. "Clarendon swears she's a sweet-tempered nature."

"Oh, yes, which is to say that I have not." I rushed to the picture and snapped the frame facedown on the table. "There. What a considerable improvement."

He folded his arms over his chest, the deep-cuffed sleeves of the dressing gown giving him wings like an avenging angel. "Don't test me in this, Barbara, because you will not win."

"How can you say that, sir, when I have lost already?" I burst into tears, my hands twisting miserably in the coverlet. "She—she will have you, and I—I shall be left with nothing."

"Hush, hush, it's not like that." He drew me into his arms, into the enveloping folds of gold-colored silk. "The country expects me to take a wife, and I must obey."

I rested my cheek familiarly against his shoulder, letting my bitter tears fall where they might. "What if the country likewise expects you to honor your vows to her?"

"The country expects me to sire an heir or two. That's the extent of the country's expectations."

"You don't know that, sir," I said unhappily. "The country might very well expect you to be faithful to her, and cast me away."

"Hah," he said. "They already wish me to do that, and I haven't heeded them, have I? Why, there's parsons speaking sermons against you from their pulpits, warning me of the perils of adultery before I've even seen my bride."

"They do hate me for that." I sighed against his shoulder. "The priggish bastards."

He grunted, too thoughtful to be amused. "I do believe my father was entirely faithful to my mother."

I'd not expected that, and I pushed back to search his face. "And I am frequently unfaithful to my husband. What of it?"

"*You* are not my mother, Barbara." He paused just long enough. "Thank God."

I slipped my hand inside the silk to find his bare chest. "You will not forget me then, sir?"

"We've been through far too much for that, Barbara, haven't we?" He settled his hands at the narrowest place on my waist. "I don't know if I could give you up even if I wished it."

"I would never want you to try," I said, unable to keep the sadness from my voice. "Never."

"No." He began to tug on the coverlet, pulling it relentlessly lower across my breasts. "What can I offer you as a pledge, eh?"

I looked up at him through the haze of tears still beaded on my lashes. "You've been generous from your own pocket, sir, but if I were to have a title, and an income of my own, why, then I would have full reason to be at court, no matter what your queen might say."

"A wise notion." He nodded, even as he continued toying with the coverlet. "I'll have Clarendon prepare the warrant, and arrange with Southampton in the Treasury for an income to support it."

I caught the coverlet in my hand, keeping it in place to stop his progress. "Clarendon won't do it, and neither will Southampton, not for me."

"They will if I order it," he said firmly, and now I'd more hope that it would be done. We weren't finished with this topic, to be sure, nor was the pain caused to me by his coming marriage any lessened, but for now I was content with the ground we'd made tonight.

"Thank you," I said softly, beginning to loosen my grip on the coverlet. "For me, and for our daughter. You are kindness itself, sir. But there is one more matter I must share with you."

"*I* know what you must share, madam," he said, his gaze dark with wanting as he began to unwrap the coverlet in earnest. "Come, to the bed with me."

"I'm late," I said bluntly, for there was no other way to say it. "My flowers."

He sucked in his breath. "How late?"

"Enough."

"Enough," he repeated, considering. "When?"

"Next spring. I should guess at the time of your wedding."

He groaned. "Yet because it is you, Barbara, I am glad."

"As am I." I raised my arms to loop around his neck, letting the coverlet drop between us as I kissed him. "Because, sir, it *is* you."

"Rest your head upon your hand, madam," Master Lely said, studying me critically from behind his easel. This would be an important picture for him, one that could bring him much credit and fame. "Turn your head a fraction, if you please, so the light from the windows can catch the sapphire color of your eyes. There! That is the pose exactly."

I held still then, as frozen as December ice, while the painter's long brush began to fly across the canvas, sketching in the beginnings of the picture. It had been one of Charles's first acts as king to name the Dutchman Peter Lely as his Principal Painter, with a pension of two hundred pounds a year to go with it. As his father before him had employed Master Van Dyck to record the major personages of the old court, so now Charles had Master Lely. This artist was not a young man, having passed sixty years, and like so many of us, he had survived, even prospered, with a variety of patrons. Charles could recall being painted by him as a child with his brothers and sisters, while during the Commonwealth Lely had painted the Lord Protectorate himself. And now, at Charles's suggestion, he was to paint me as well.

I'd had my miniature limned twice before by Mr. Cooper, but this was the first time I'd sat for a full portrait. While most ladies had pictures that showed only their heads and shoulders, or perhaps to their waists, Charles had requested Master Lely paint me in my entirety. The resultant canvas was very large, and on its stretchers alone, without a frame, it must have stood taller than Charles himself—the perfect size for a wall at the palace, and I imagined with amusement what the new queen would make of being confronted each day by this large copy of me.

"Do not smile so broadly, madam," the painter scolded, the long-ago remnants of his Dutch accent still clotting his words. "You are to look sweetly melancholy, not as if you're laughing at a dancing bear at the fair. There is no such creature as a jolly Magdalene."

Contritely I recomposed my features. I'd worked too hard with the painter deciding the intricate symbols of this painting to ruin it now. The best fashionable portraits were not simply representations of features and form, but held deeper meanings and undercurrents, and this one would be no exception. I wore the rich undress favored by Master Lely, more of a bed-gown of heavy white satin, clasped together with a sapphire broach, with a kind of satin cloak of my favorite blue draped to fall over one shoulder. Much of the cream-colored skin of my breasts and shoulders was finely displayed in this attire, especially with the bed-gown slipping carelessly off one shoulder. I wore no extra petticoats beneath my skirts, so that the white satin draped and clung brazenly to my well-shaped legs. The first pearl drops that Charles had given me at Anne's birth hung from my ears, now joined by his latest gift, a necklace of more costly fat pearls around my throat. All that had been chosen to reflect my worldliness, while the pose itself was to be more spiritual.

I would be shown seated on a velvet-covered rock in a wilderness, to be added later, with my hair long and unbound to my waist like a true penitent. My head was supported by my hand, a romantic pose suggesting melancholy and reflection. But what most viewers of this picture would see and understand was how it harkened to the penitent Saint Mary Magdalene, a wicked woman saved by the grace of Our Lord Jesus Christ. If I were viewed as the Magdalene and Charles then as Our Lord, why, the irony of the painting would be clear as day.

When I'd described what Master Lely and I had planned to Charles, he'd laughed aloud at the scandalous double meanings. I was sure the pious new queen would recognize them, too, just as she'd understand how I'd been portrayed as a Protestant saint, without all the tawdry trappings of the Romish church to which she'd such devotion. And how I wished I'd be able to see her shock when she noticed that first gentle swelling of Charles's babe beneath my painted white satin!

"Madam, your smile!" the painter said again with exasperation.

"Forgive me, Master Lely, forgive me," I said dutifully. But it was so hard not to smile, really. Master Lely had told me that engravers were already clamoring for a portrait of me to copy and sell to the world. That sorry picture of the infanta that I'd seen in Charles's bedchamber—and had since banished—had likewise been copied, with engravings of it springing up everywhere like toadstools after rain. She might be queen, but my portrait was bound to outshine hers, just as my beauty would, and it delighted me to consider how many more people would appreciate Master Lely's rare talent than the heavy-handed work of the anonymous Portuguese daub who'd painted the new queen's portrait.

"Madam, please!"

"Oh, Master Lely, I'm sorry!" I exclaimed. "I vow it will not happen again."

Once again I forced myself to look sad. But oh, how vastly hard it was to appear penitent when in my heart I believed I'd done nothing—*nothing*—that needed forgiving.

# *Chapter Twelve*

As the year had progressed, I'd spent less and less time in my husband's company, and he did not appear to wish to spend any more time with me than I did with him. He often returned to Dorney Court, to his mother and the country tedium that pleased him so. He busied himself with both his parliamentary and legal responsibilities, and likely a good many other affairs that I'd no interest to hear.

He also was devoted to my daughter, Anne, my lovely, innocent cuckoo in the Palmer nest, and he continued to believe that he was her sire. This was well enough with me, for never did a child suffer from too much love. Besides, my own days—and nights—were so full that I'd little time to spare myself on her welfare. I didn't fault myself, for I knew that my role at the palace was far more important to Anne's future security than hiding myself away in the nursery at King Street to warm her caudle and change her soiled clouts.

Yet even the most pliant willow has its point when it will bend no more, and snap in two, and so toward Christmas Roger's long-bowed complacency finally broke.

I was sitting at my looking-glass while Wilson brushed my hair when Roger burst into my chamber. His face was flushed and livid, and clutched tight in his hand was a letter.

"Good day, Roger," I said cheerfully, hoping to dispel this storm cloud before it burst and spoiled my day. "Not ill news, I trust?"

But he was far too deeply into his rage to be coaxed from it. "Leave us, Wilson," he ordered curtly. "Leave us at once."

Silently Wilson curtseyed to Roger, granting me a quick glance of sympathy before she fled.

I waited until the door closed after her before I spoke. "What is it, Roger? What is so grievous that you send my servant away?"

"What is?" he demanded. "What isn't!"

He flung the letter on the dressing table so hard that it immediately fluttered to the floor. I bent as if to read it, but instead he grabbed my shoulder so I'd no choice but to face him.

"You already know what that says, Barbara," he said, giving me a small shove as he let me go. "Likely you even composed the words yourself."

"You make no sense, Roger." I frowned, more at being disturbed than by whatever irked him, and shook my hair out over my shoulders to show my disdain. "How can I possibly know what is written in that letter without seeing it for myself?"

"Then I shall tell you, madam, as a reminder," he said. "His Majesty has requested a warrant for my ennoblement. I am to be made an Irish earl, for some godforsaken bog of a village called Castlemaine, in County Kerry, with a barony in Limerick."

"Why, yes," I said. If he would be angry, then I was determined to remain calm and keep my temper in check. "The king asked me my preference, and that was what I chose."

He stared at me with disbelief. "Do you truly think I *care*?"

"You should, I suppose," I said defensively. "It's been the very devil to have that warrant put through. Every such request must pass through that meddlesome old goat Clarendon as lord chancellor, else it cannot be registered as an effective act. Because Clarendon hates me as much as I hate him, he tried to block it, until the king was forced to order him to do it."

"The king could have saved his trouble, Barbara," he said curtly, "for I care nothing for such a shameful act as this."

"But you should, Roger, you should," I insisted, wanting to explain why this particular title was so important to me. "You see, my father was Viscount Grandison of Limerick, but on his death his title went to my uncle. This way, you see, it will return to me, with my son to be known as Lord Limerick."

"To you, Barbara, yes, always to you," he said, breathing heavily. "That's how you want everything, isn't it? Then you know the wording of this warrant, too, that the succession of this title is to be restricted to the children gotten upon Barbara Palmer, my wife. My *wife*."

I flushed at that, for though the wording had made perfect sense when the king had proposed it, designed as it was to protect his children with me, to hear the clause read now by Roger did give it an especially humiliating sound.

"So you still possess the decency to blush, madam," he said, his voice rising. "I didn't believe a mare in rut would care to whom she presented her rump. Or perhaps she does choose which will cover her, and prefers a stallion with a royal pedigree to his prick."

"Roger, please," I said, my flush deepening. I'd not expected such passion from him, and it frightened me. "Consider the servants!"

"Why should I consider anyone for your sake," he demanded, "considering how little regard you've shown for me?"

"I'll not listen any longer, not when you're like this." Swiftly I rose from the bench, but Roger grabbed my arm.

"You will stay, madam, and you will listen, and answer," he ordered. "You're with child again, aren't you?"

"It's early days, Roger, and I don't—"

"Answer me, Barbara. Are you with child?"

His fingers tightened on my arm.

"I am," I said at last. I could scarce deny it to him, not when it was already the talk of the court. "I *am*."

"The king's get, then, not mine," he snarled. "My father warned me that you'd make a whore, not a wife, and by God, how I wish now that I'd listened to him."

I tried to twist free, my long hair tangling around us. "Please, Roger, you're hurting me!"

"No jury in England would convict me if I throttled you now, Barbara," he said. "Now tell me: is Anne my daughter or the king's?"

"I do not know, Roger," I said, and that in nearly perfect honesty. "I do not know, nor ever shall. I swear it, please, I swear it."

"Why do you need to be a countess when you've already title enough as the king's whore?" He shoved me free, sending me stumbling backward.

Yet when he turned to leave, I gathered up the warrant letter and ran after him. "Wait, Roger, please! You must accept the title, else I cannot have it, either."

He stared at me, his contempt so deep it made me shiver. "So there you are, Barbara. An empty title you've earned by spreading your legs is worth more to you than I could ever be."

I caught at his sleeve. "Roger, that's not—"

"You've said enough, Barbara," he answered sharply, shaking me away. "I'll have my things taken from this house tomorrow. It's yours. You earned it, too."

"Roger, please, I don't wish—"

"No more, wife, not for either of us." He looked back for one final time, not at me but over my head at the room. "I wish you luck on your course, Barbara, because by God, you will need it."

And like that, with as little fanfare and bother, my marriage to Roger was done.

I would be remiss without adding a last word regarding my title—for, as Roger felt so sadly compelled to state aloud, it was in fact my title, and not his. But a title cannot be granted to a wife alone, and the fact that Roger peevishly delayed accepting his half of it was especially humiliating to me, nor did he ever take his seat in the Irish Parliament as he was entitled to do.

Worse still were the ways that Clarendon had struggled to keep me back. Charles had purposefully chosen an Irish peerage instead of an English one, which the lord chancellor had the power to block. Yet even when the king insisted on the warrant, Clarendon had one more trick left to play. One of his dearest cronies was the Earl of Southampton, who served as lord treasurer, and together they resolved that no documents favoring me would pass through their care. Thus that pompous, self-serving pair risked treason to counter Charles's gener-ous will, and made certain I received no grants drawn on the treasury. Instead I was entirely dependent on gifts from Charles's privy purse, and from the financial enticements offered by others in return for us-ing my influence with the king.

Charles advised me to ignore Roger's petulance regarding the earldom, and led others in calling me Lady Castlemaine. I was not so confident, and though I held my head high whenever I was an-nounced at court, for the first months I took care to keep the warrant, signed by the king, within my pocket in case I was challenged.

But the truth was that I was now a lady and a countess. My en-emies might quibble, but they couldn't take the title away from me or my children. Charles had been my champion as well as my lover in this, as he had in everything else, and no one could take that from me, either. Those who'd no knowledge of the depth of our friendship saw only the weakness of my position as the king's wedding drew closer, and looked at my swelling belly as a sign that the lure of my beauty was fading.

There were factions that tried to promote new ladies at court to take my place, among them Lady Frances Stuart, a fresh fourteen-year-old Catholic beauty—oh, to be fourteen again, now that I was advanced to twenty-one!—who, though no true kin to Charles or the other royal Stuarts, had served as a maid of honor to the king's sister in France.

Others, like my older cousin Mary Villiers, Duchess of Richmond and sister to the Duke of Buckingham, simply set to defaming me for their own jealous purposes; Mary might be my own kin, yes, but she loudly likened me to Jane Shore, the unfortunate mistress of King Ed-ward IV, who was said to have died in disgrace on a dunghill.

But I knew that Charles had sworn to care for me despite his mar-riage, just as I alone knew that in a way he loved me more, not less, when my body was filled with his child. Just to set these tongues to wagging further, I put out the rumor that I meant to have my lying-in at the palace at Hampton Court, at the same time as the king would be there with his ugly new bride.

Why shouldn't I let those tongues wag? I'd already set my sights on my next title, and the court post that went with it. Worthy of my new rank as Countess of Castlemaine, this post would bring me a salary and pension, influence, and prestige, as well as a good deal of amusement. I could justify having lodgings within the palace. My very presence would irritate and vex the queen, especially with duties that would have me participating in her most intimate daily rituals, in her private rooms. Best of all, it was one of the few high court posts that were granted to ladies alone and not bound in any way to their husbands, so I wouldn't need to consult with Roger.

I wished to be named Lady of the Bedchamber to the new queen.

"I am huge, sir," I announced, leaning back in my armchair, the better to display my belly to the king. We were sharing supper in my bedchamber, our table set before the open window. "I am enormous, a giantess, nay, a veritable mountain!"

The king raised his goblet to me. "And I say, my dear Barbara, that you have never been more beautiful."

"Bah," I said with disgust at my own girth. It was May, and I was wallowing through the last weeks of my second pregnancy. "They say the Alps of France are beautiful, too."

Charles laughed, not unkindly, but with his customary generosity of spirit toward me. Not only were these my last weeks before I'd be brought to childbed, but his last days free of his own ordeal, for word had come yesterday that the infanta Catherine of Braganza had finally begun her journey here to England for her wedding to Charles. Dutifully Charles had insisted that Parliament work late into the night to conclude this session's business before he must leave London to play the ardent bridegroom, but he still made time each night to come to me in King Street.

"You're cruel to yourself, Barbara," he said easily. "You're not half so vast as you claim."

I narrowed my eyes at him, likely the only part of me left that could be called narrow. I'd received him in undress, all that was comfortable, a loose gown of blue silk with a deep neckline, graced with my pearls. "I thought we'd settled that last night with the scales."

"Oh, those infernal scales!" he exclaimed and laughed. "Only you would do that."

"Only to prove my point, sir." I'd vowed that I'd grown so large with this child of his that I outweighed him. Charles had not believed it, not until I'd ordered my servants to fetch a set of scales from the market to my parlor, and had each of us weighed, king and countess. I'd won, or perhaps I'd lost, for in fact I did weigh a fraction more than did my great, strapping lord. It had amused us both no end, but Wilson, scandalized, had reported that the men who'd brought the scales had tattled widely, and by nightfall all of London had heard the story.

Not, of course, that I cared a fig. "I'm as big as any of your French mountains, and I defy you to say otherwise."

"*Le Mont de Barbara?*" he asked, teasing.

"More likely Mount Barbara," I said, "which is I fear what you must do these days if you wish the challenge of coupling with me."

With a sigh I pushed myself from the chair and went to stand at the open window, my palm pressed to the side of my belly. I was sure this child was a boy, for only a boy would be so restless as this one was, always leaping and tumbling within me to disturb my ease. The night was clear and warm, but what I saw was not the stars and new moon overhead, but the bonfires dancing before most houses and on street corners as far as I could see.

"Look," I said, not bothering to hide my glumness at such a sight. "They've all obeyed the lord mayor's order and lit fires in honor of your bride's arrival in Portsmouth."

"Not all," he said, coming to stand behind me. "I don't see one before your house."

"Why, sir, I must have forgotten." Of course I'd purposefully not done so; what reason had I for such a celebration? It was my neighbor Admiral Lord Sandwich who'd been charged with bringing her to London, and how I wished he'd misread the winds or waves, and sailed with his dour little passenger to India instead.

Now I rested my arms on the window's sill, watching the fires light the night sky, picking out the chimneys and the square towers of St. Paul's. The mayor's order had included the ringing of every church bell as well, and while most had stopped by this hour, a few too-zealous bell ringers continued. "However will Her Majesty ever forgive me?"

"Oh, she'll forgive you that," he said. "I'm not sure I will. People notice such things, just as they've taken notice of my presence here. Why do you delight in making such trouble for me, Barbara?"

"Because you delight in tormenting me," I said. "How can you expect me to waste my firewood on welcoming your ugly little queen to your bed?"

"Be gracious, Barbara," he chided gently. "How many times have I told you that though she'll be my queen and my wife, she won't change my friendship for you. From what Clarendon tells me, she's little more than a child. She'll do as I tell her."

I sniffed. "She's far older than I. She's no child."

"In years, no, but in innocence, she's worse than a child. They say she's not been permitted to leave her father's palace in years."

"That's ignorance, not innocence," I said bluntly. "What shall she make of you on your wedding night?"

Charles groaned. "It's more what I'll make of her. Tomorrow night I'll ride to Guilford, then to Portsmouth, where we'll be wed, and then—"

"Then you must do your best to get your heir upon an ugly, ignorant child," I said. "I wish you joy of *that* task, sir."

"God only knows what they've told her to expect," he said with gloomy resignation. "Likely she knows nothing whatsoever of men. The Iberians are strange about such matters."

I shrugged, with little sympathy for his misery. "As you say, you must perform your duty. Close your eyes and plant your little prince, and pray Her Majesty doesn't cry too loudly when you do."

"Don't jest, Barbara. It could well be that way." He slipped his hands around my belly, over our unborn child. "Ah, someone's dancing tonight."

"Someone is always dancing," I said wryly. "I vow this is your son, sir, to plague me so."

"No trouble siring children with you, Barbara," he said, his breath warm against my ear. Because I was as tall for a woman as he was for a man, we'd always fit together well, and as he pulled me closer, I could feel his cock hard against my bottom. "No duty there."

"Don't neglect me when you're at Hampton Court with her," I said softly, stretching myself languorously against him. I would miss him; I always did when he was away from me. "You don't wish me to be lonely."

"Why do I suspect you're never lonely for long, Barbara?" he asked, filling his hands with my milk-swollen breasts. "I'll come to you as often as I can get away."

"You're the king," I reminded him, even as I reminded him of other pleasures as well. "You decide when you wish to come back to London to me. Though if I were a Lady of the Bedchamber, I'd always be at court, and waiting for you. I'd never have to leave. I'd always be . . . there."

"I've told you, Barbara, you are on the list of names for the queen to approve," he said. "Once we're wed, she'll be shown the list, and then the posts will be granted. It's a formality, no more."

I pressed myself more wantonly against him. "She will agree?"

"She'll do as I tell her," he said. "You know me as well as anyone. I'll not let myself be ruled by any woman."

"Oh, no, sir, not you." I was thankful my face was turned away and he so preoccupied, so he'd not see how I smiled at that. I arched my back, and he grunted with the anticipation of pleasure. "But now I believe it's time to scale Mount Barbara."

To Charles's credit, he wed the infanta as he'd promised, despite the appalling show she made of her landing in Portsmouth. Though Clarendon and others in her party had urged her to adopt English dress, she and her party had insisted on clinging to the ancient fashions of her father's court, with stiff, heavy fabrics, outlandish hairstyles that needed hidden wires for support, and wide farthingales that caught the breezes from the sea and threatened to sweep the new queen and her ladies clear back to Lisbon.

At the sight of this black-clad party, the king's comment to the friends who stood with him on the wharf was so amusingly frank as to be instantly, and often, repeated—"I thought they'd brought me a bat, instead of a woman"—and pleased me enormously. And while he was as determined to behave with honor and bravery toward his bride as any other man upon the scaffold, he could scarce contain his relief when the marriage's consummation was briefly postponed. Not only was Charles exhausted from his long ride and the bride still feeling the effects of seasickness, but, as he wrote to me in a jovial note, he'd also had his nose shut in the door by the unexpected arrival of "Monsieur le Cardinal." That made me laugh aloud, and clap my hands as well: to think that Clarendon's great plans were undone by an inadvertent dribble of monthly blood on the queen's smock!

Yet somehow the deed was finally done, with hearty sighs of relief all around. The king was observed as being extraordinarily courteous and gallant to the queen, who was said to have fallen at once into moonstruck love. I was not surprised that she'd been dazzled, for the king was by nature a supremely gifted lover, and a tall, handsome one, too.

But the reports I preferred to heed were the ones that spoke of her sallow complexion and deep-set eyes, her shyness, her unappealing frailness, and how her upper teeth thrust so far outward against her lips that she lisped. She'd trouble with English, so even the choicest particles of wit escaped her comprehension. She wore the English clothing given to her without grace, and she shuffled along with an ungainly fear in the kind of high heels that I'd worn as long as I could recall. She was exceptionally pious and kept a trail of priests constantly by her.

Yet even the priests were said to be preferable to her ladies, deemed elderly, ill-humored, and ill-favored, yet so proud that they'd scarce acknowledge their English hosts. They were also said to be oppressively concerned with their virtue, however little tested it might be, and refused to rest their bodies on any bed that had previously been slept upon by a man. Worst—or most amusing—of all was their horror at the habits of Englishmen, who were accustomed to relieving themselves wherever they pleased. This shocked the sensibilities of the Portuguese ladies no end, making them protest that everywhere they looked, even about the palace, they were confronted by the rude sight of outsized English pricks.

My old lover Chesterfield, once again returned both to England and to favor through his wife's family's connections with Clarendon—which was of course another black strike against the old man in my mind—had been made chamberlain to the queen, and was much in her company. Yet though Philip knew it was to his good that the queen prosper, he couldn't help but note in the hearing of others that there was nothing about the new queen that could make the king forget his devotions toward the Countess of Castlemaine. While I recognized this to be in part cunning flattery of the kind so inherent to Philip's very soul, I also was confident that it was largely true. For how, really, could a plain, priggish creature like the queen ever hope to rival me?

While Charles was thus occupied in Portsmouth and then at Hampton Court, I made sure to show my unwieldy self about London as best I could. I couldn't afford to retreat the way I had before Anne was born. For my confidence I needed to be observed and remarked, for my beauty to be noted and marveled at, and for word to be carried back to the court that I was neither dejected nor sorrowful that the king had wed.

On the very day of the royal wedding, I had my laundresses wash all my Holland smocks and under-petticoats and hang them to dry on the mulberry bushes behind Whitehall. By so doing, I gave all London a long look at my finest privy linen, bordered deep with lace and point, which was usually seen only by the king. All London noticed, and were so vastly titillated that they forgot the queen.

I'd only one small setback at that time, and I chose to think of it as a temporary inconvenience rather than a lasting wrong. I'd requested a post in the queen's household as Lady of the Bedchamber, and

Charles had agreed that it would be a place both fit and convenient for me to have. He'd added my name to the list presented to the queen for her consideration, and was sure that, in her untutored ignorance of the English court, she'd pass it through among the others without any comment.

But Charles had underestimated his foes in this. The queen might be little more than a stubborn, prattling simpleton, but her mother the Queen Regent of Portugal in Lisbon had excellent spies to advise her, and she'd made the infanta promise never to accept me in either her presence or her court. The queen had at once recognized my name on the candidates' list and scratched it out as unacceptable to her. Just as surely, Charles had added my name back, and there the impasse stood.

Only the First Lady of the Bedchamber had been chosen, a lady whose other appointments included Mistress of the Robes and Keeper of the Queen's Privy Purse. By no small coincidence, this lady was my late father's sister Barbara and my namesake, now fashioned Countess of Suffolk. More given to gentleness than I, she appealed to me to withdraw my name for the sake of Her Majesty's peace, which I of course saw no reason to do.

Because of me, no further appointments were made to the queen's household, though many gentlemen and ladies were hovering with hope and trepidation, and everything was made to wait until I relented, which was not likely to happen, or Queen Catherine agreed to humble herself and accept my presence.

And though only a dozen miles or so stood between my house in Westminster and the king and queen at Hampton Court, in these ways I kept my place as surely as if I'd been there among them.

Early in June, I was brought to bed of the son I'd been expecting all along: a fine, strong, lusty boy, with dark curling hair. My labor was not so hard as I'd remembered from the first time, and I was delivered just as the sun was rising, as fair a portent as I could wish. The boy favored his father, especially in his size and in the length of those same limbs with which he'd been kicking me so vigorously.

I named him Charles, and sent word to the king of his arrival.

The king came to me at once, with gratifying haste and without telling his wife, which was more gratifying still. He kissed me with great fondness and delight, and thanked God for my safe deliverance. He delighted in his new son, holding him close in his arms with no regard for what an infant might do to his finery, or with any of the fearfulness that most men demonstrate toward their children. Instead he cooed and sang and kissed the tiny boy, and then sighed and wept with sadness when the time came for him to return to Hampton Court. I could not imagine a prettier scene than to see Charles with our son, nor one more full of love and regard.

I heard from others that that night he could not have praised the child more if he'd been brought to earth on angels' wings. His pride was fair to overflowing, it seemed, and his courtiers remarked that they'd never seen the king more joyful or content.

The queen, however, did not share his joy, and after the pair had retired, the sounds of their heated argument were clear throughout the palace.

Was it any wonder that I slept more peacefully than I had in months?

"My lady, oh, my lady!" Wilson rushed into my bedchamber, her round face contorted with shock and fear. "Oh, my lady, what has happened!"

"What is it, Wilson?" I demanded, sitting upright in my bed. Though it was midday, I was still enjoying my lying-in seven days after my son's birth, or so I had been until I'd seen Wilson's face. "Is it fire? Tell me, Wilson, tell me at once!"

"It's Lord Castlemaine, my lady!" she cried. "He's taking the babe!"

At once my heart leapt in my breast with fear for my little son. I clambered from the bed and ran through the door to the hall, my smock and my hair flying every which way. I could hear Roger's steps on the staircase, my baby wailing with fear, and servants shouting. Though my legs trembled with disuse and with fear, I ran barefoot down the stairs after him, fair hurling myself after my child.

Roger was already at the doorway, little Charles wrapped like a hasty bundle in his arms.

"Roger, stop, oh, please, you must stop!" I shouted with growing desperation. "He's mine, Roger, he's mine, not yours!"

Roger stopped, his face taut with anger, his mouth an implacable slash of displeasure as he paused in the open door.

"He's mine, Barbara," he said curtly. "At least so long as I am wed to you, any child of your flesh is mine by law."

"No!" I cried, catching at his arm. "You know as well as I that this babe is the king's, not yours! You said so yourself! Now please, please, return him to me!"

"And I say he's mine, Barbara." Roger lifted the child higher from my reach, while tiny Charles wailed as if his heart would break at such ill use, his fists waving impotently at this terrible cruel man who'd seized him from his cradle. "Every judge and law in the country would agree with me. And as I recall, you told me yourself you'd never be sure it was otherwise."

"Every law except that of a mother's heart and love!" I cried, anguish and fear wringing tears from my depths as I struggled to reach my son. "Where are you taking him, Roger? What would you do with him?"

"I'm doing what is right for his mortal soul, Barbara," Roger said. "I'm taking him to be properly baptized in the one true faith of the Roman Catholic church."

I gasped with horror and shock. "You cannot do that, Roger! The king would not wish it, not for his son!"

"*My* son, Barbara," he said. "I will do what is right for *my* son, in *my* faith."

He turned away and passed through the door to the carriage waiting outside. I tried to follow, stumbling on the steps as the carriage pulled away. Broken with grief and loss and exhaustion, I sank to the paving stones, not caring who saw or heard my plight. My face was wet with tears, my smock soaked with the mother's milk that my poor bound breasts had given down at the sound of my babe's distress.

"Come, my lady, please," Wilson said, hurrying to wrap me in a wide shawl. "You must come inside and away from the street."

"But what can I do?" I sobbed. "He took my babe, my son, my own dear little Charles! What can I do? What can I do?"

Wilson's jaw was firm with resolution. "We must do the only thing possible, my lady. Lord Castlemaine cannot be permitted to follow this course. We must summon His Majesty."

# Chapter Thirteen

"He's a handsome lad, isn't he?" Charles smiled at his son, sleeping in the nursemaid's arms as we rode together in the royal carriage. "A fine cross between the two of us."

"More you than me, sir," I said, and it was true, too. Little Charles was barely a fortnight old, and already there was something eerily like the king about his face. "You must have looked the same when you were small."

"Hah, as if I ever was," he said, chuckling. He drew off his glove and touched his fingers lightly to the baby's downy cheek. "You know I've never been able to be at the christenings of any of my other sons. To see this one now, like this—ah, Barbara, you cannot know what it means to me."

I'd never seen such tenderness in Charles's face before, a kind of awe as he gazed down at his son. I was glad that he felt this way for my son, and though it was a wicked thought that ran counter to the good of England, I selfishly hoped that Queen Catherine would never give him a royal prince, so that my little Charles would always have this love undiminished from his royal father.

Now he shifted in his sleep, making a sweet little coo of a sigh that made Charles chuckle.

"He seems to be a peaceful lad," he said. "Quiet, too, as the best babes are."

"Not always," I warned. "He can be the very devil when he's crossed."

"This little fellow?" Charles's black brows rose with his skepticism. "I cannot believe he'd have anything at all to be cross about."

"Oh, I believe Lord Castlemaine would qualify." Less than a week had passed since Roger had dared kidnap my son and take him against my will to be baptized by a Romish priest. He'd returned the baby unharmed by nightfall, saying that he'd only done what I'd done to my daughter, Anne. He claimed that if he were to be expected to give these children his name, then he'd a right to determine how they'd be raised in Christ. "You've no notion of the heartache he caused me by stealing my son from his very cradle."

"He's safe now," Charles said. "And we'll put the other matter to rights this day."

" 'The other matter'!" I exclaimed. "You make it sound as nothing. To steal away the son of the Protestant King of England and give his soul to Rome—"

"Hush, Barbara. Please, don't worry yourself," he said, resting his hand on my knee to calm me. "We're putting it all to rights now."

"Thank you, sir," I said softly and sighed. "Now if the queen will only relent and take me among her ladies—"

"I'm tending to that as well, Barbara," he said without looking away from his sleeping son. "Her Majesty will be made to understand. She should be grateful I'm not like my grandfather and asking her to accept my entire Turk's harem of lovers into her fold."

"Your grandfather might not have been a Turk, sir, but he was French." I'd heard this argument from him, and from his brother James, a good many times when the two of them were in their cups and longing for the unabashed indulgences of Henri IV's court. "You'd shock a good many Englishmen along with the queen if you tried that."

"But you're not some French slattern, Barbara," he said almost wistfully. "You're English, and a peeress. We made certain of that earlier exactly so there'd be no trouble now."

I rested my hand over his in a sweet show of understanding. "There is no trouble, sir," I said. "Not with me."

"Nor will there be with the queen, dearest," he said, turning his hand so our fingers were intertwined. "I expect everything to be re-solved as soon as you're ready to rejoin us at court."

"You please me, sir," I said, in a voice that made him look away from my son to me. "I miss you."

His smile was full of warmth. "I miss you as well, Barbara. I al-ways do."

"Will you be returning with us to King Street later?"

He looked puzzled, yet intrigued. "Are you certain, Barbara? You've only just risen from childbed."

I smiled wickedly, heedless of the nursemaid. "Oh, sir," I teased. "You're not such a greenhorn as that. There are so, so many other ways for us to amuse ourselves."

"And you know them all, my dear." He grinned, his hand sliding from my knee along my thigh. "I suppose I could stop for a short while before I go back to Hampton Court."

Our ride was not far, the carriage stopping at the porch of St. Margaret's, Westminster. Drawn by the sight of the royal coach, a small crowd gathered to cheer the king, and he waved back to them with joy and good humor, unashamed of the errand that had brought him here. At his side, I proudly held his son, the costly embroidery of his long gown spilling over my arm. This was the first time I'd ven-tured out since his birth, and I'd taken care that both I and the babe looked as fine as possible to honor the king.

Inside the church, we were met by two friends who had come down from Hampton Court with Charles: my namesake, Aunt Barbara, Countess of Suffolk, my closest relation and the one who would stand as godmother, and another old friend, Aubrey de Vere, Earl of Oxford, for my son's godfather. Together this little party gathered around the stone font with the church's minister, and witnessed my son being baptized into the Anglican church, with Charles himself responding as his father. His new son slept through it all, only wrinkling his nose when the holy water touched his face, and my heart swelled to watch them together.

Afterward, the ceremony was duly marked into the church's reg-istry: Charles Palmer, Lord Limerick, son to ye right honorable Roger, Earl of Castlemaine, by Barbara his wife.

That was what was written, in the cleric's spidery hand. But now everyone in London knew the truth.

"I cannot believe that you would do such a thing, Barbara!" Roger struck his fist on the tea table between us. "To countermand my wish, my desire—"

"I can scarcely be blamed, Roger, if you've gone to the incense and priests." At the door, he'd pushed past the footmen to find me here in my parlor, giving me little choice but to receive him. "You're a grown man. That was your decision to make. But I've no reason to see my children traipse after you to Rome."

"Yet you see nothing wrong with humiliating me by giving them my name!"

I looked at him as levelly as I could. "You are my husband."

"But not the father of your son?"

I glanced back down at my cup. "I never said you were, Roger, or that you weren't."

"But you'd tell *him*!" With his arm he swept my tea table clean, sending the pot, the creamer, the sugar bowl, and my cup crashing to the floor.

"Blast you, Roger." I rose swiftly, the spilled tea splashing my silk skirts and staining my petticoats as I kicked aside the shattered porcelain. "*He* is His Majesty the king!"

"Oh, aye, to the rest of England, but to you *he's* only another willing stiff cock!"

My temper growing, I used both my hands to shove hard at his chest. "What do you know of cocks willing or stiff? I can't recall the last time I've seen either from you!"

He grabbed my shoulders and pushed me back. "Why should any decent gentleman wish to go to that poisonous cunt of yours?"

"You *wish* you could have me!" I shouted. "Ha, you wish you could raise a cockstand long enough to please me, or any other woman!"

"No man can ever please a whore with a gaping maw like yours, nor would he risk the pox to try."

"Go!" I shouted furiously. "I don't need to hear such vile slanders from you. Leave my house at once."

"*Your* house, madam?" he snarled. "You forget that this is *my* house by law, just as those children upstairs are *my* children, and you, may God protect me, remain *my* wife."

"My lady?" My two largest footmen stood in the doorway, summoned by Wilson, who stood behind them. "My lady, do you need—"

"My Lady Whore needs nothing," Roger said bitterly. "Not from you, or me, or even the king himself."

He shoved his way past the servants. I stood surrounded by shards of flower-painted porcelain and puddled tea, so angry I was shaking from it. I listened to his boots on the stairs and how he slammed the door as he left the house.

*My* house, yes, but still his by English law.

And my mind was set. "Wilson, have my belongings packed. All my clothes, my jewels, my plate, my china, and my paintings. And pray have the servants and the children readied for a journey."

Wilson's eyes widened, and the two footmen exchanged startled glances. "A journey, my lady?"

"To my uncle Lord Grandison's house in Richmond," I said. "I'll not stay another night of *my* life here beneath Lord Castlemaine's roof."

There are those who believed my retreat to Richmond was no more than a calculation to place myself and my children closer to the king, who continued on his newlywed stay with Queen Catherine at the palace at Hampton Court. Considering how often the king had left his new wife to come to me in King Street, I found these whispers ridiculous, with little basis in fact. I was far more secure in my friendship with Charles than that, and besides, I'd gone to Richmond largely to escape Roger. But I will grant that the proximity of my uncle Lord Grandison's house did make Charles's visits to me and my children less arduous and more frequent, and likely more vexing to the queen as well.

Besides, I could not fathom why the king had chosen Hampton

Court for his bride's idyll. True, it was a lovely place in the summer, with long walks through fine gardens full of flowers. But the palace itself would, I think, hold many grievous memories for him. When Charles I had been removed from his throne by Parliament, he'd been imprisoned at Hampton Court before his last attempt at escape, the one that had led to his execution. Then Cromwell himself had chosen the place for his personal palace, home to the Lord Protectorate. Though it had come back to royal hands with Charles's restoration, I'd heard from other courtiers that many of the smaller chambers had fallen into sad disrepair, and that the glorious days of the reign of King Henry VIII were unlikely to be repeated amidst such broken-down remnants of lost splendor.

Though perhaps in truth Hampton Court *was* an appropriate place to begin this unfortunate marriage twixt English king and Portuguese queen. For wasn't it full of the old ghosts of King Henry's doomed queens, condemned to their deaths for never bearing him the son and heir every king needed?

Certainly that summer Charles was reminded often enough of how the womb of his new queen remained empty, despite his dutiful efforts to fill it. Clearly the trouble didn't lie with the royal seed, either. For irrefutable proof, he'd only to look at my brave, lusty babies, tumbling across a coverlet on the grass in the sunshine whenever he visited me at Richmond. Though he was too gallant a bridegroom to confide overmuch to me, he did confess his near-constant quarrels with his new queen. He even sorrowfully complained of how often she tried to resist him, in ways that ranged from her insistence on maintaining her discordant Portuguese musicians to her continuing refusal to accept and include me in her household.

I never learned exactly what she'd done to goad the king into final, furious action on my behalf, but during one of his visits he abruptly told me to come with him, that it was past time for the madness to stop.

He was taking me to Hampton Court to meet the queen.

I dressed quickly, thankful that by now I had recovered enough of my shape to wear a certain dark blue open gown of silk velvet, dressed with furbelows of pale yellow silk, that I knew was vastly becoming. I added a splendid leghorn hat, for we were in the country, with a curling ostrich plume, and with my pearl earrings and necklace that had been earlier gifts from the king, I added the sapphire necklace that he'd sent in honor of little Charles's birth. I dared anyone to guess I was only six weeks removed from the ordeal of childbed, or say that I'd not regained every drop of the beauty I'd possessed before my pregnancy, and perhaps even more with the joy of bearing the king's natural son.

As soon as we entered the palace, I was made aware that Charles had brought me here on impulse, without any forethought or plan. Of course I was recognized by everyone, from the lowest maidservant sweeping ashes from a grate to the highest dukes waiting in attendance on the king. But though they all bowed and curtseyed to the king and nodded in acknowledgment to me, none of them could keep their true emotions from their faces: surprise, shock, outrage, or bemusement.

We found Her Majesty in a far parlor, stitching at some sort of grimy handwork in wools on linen. She was framed by two diamond-paned windows, the sunlight that streamed around her full of dancing dust and motes. Other members of the court stood about the room, amusing themselves and one another. From the corner of my eyes I glimpsed my old friend the Earl of Chesterfield, and Sir Edward, now made Earl of Clarendon, his fat face mottled with fury at what the king was doing.

As Charles and I came closer to the queen, I could see that she was every bit as plain as her portrait, a sallow small creature with hollowed eyes and teeth protruding so far that I marveled Charles could kiss her without having his lips nipped. Her ladies clustered around her on low stools, each one more sour and unpleasant-looking than the other, their peculiar farthingale skirts thrust out around them like barriers thrown up to protect their queen.

On a stool to one side sat my aunt, the lone English lady in this party of harridans, her pink gown like a flower growing cheerfully in a heap of cinders. She looked up first and saw me before the others, her cheeks flushing with dismay at the scene she knew would come next.

"Catherine," the king said, pleasantly enough to draw his wife's attention, "I've a lady I'd like to present to you."

She gazed up at him with childish eagerness. It was clear enough that she loved him, loved him deeply. I could see it written large across her plain, round face. Though I was confident I was the one he preferred, this open joy from my rival at seeing her husband cut me as surely as a blade, and likewise cut away any guilt or remorse I might have felt for what happened next.

"I am honored, Your Majesty," I murmured, kneeling gracefully before her, my velvet skirts crushing gently around my legs. I was so much taller than she that I felt as if I were worshipping a child, not a queen, and a small, dark, unappealing, foreign child at that. She held out her small, stubby hand with too many rings for me to kiss in loyalty. I did, noting how she'd bitten her nails to the quick like an anxious schoolboy.

Around us in the parlor, every conversation stopped and every head turned toward us. This was better than anything a playwright could have crafted, more entertaining than anything shown on the stage.

"You are a very beautiful English lady," the queen said to me in a thick Iberian accent. "You are welcome. What is her name, Charles?"

Charles smiled. "My Lady Castlemaine."

At once Catherine realized who I was. I was the adulteress, the unclean interloper, the great whore who'd corrupted her husband, the calculating demon-bitch who'd taken his seed and born the bastard children that should have been hers, and God only knew what other rubbish her mother and advisors had told her of me.

I smiled too. I'd nothing to fear.

She wailed, a loud, keening howl torn from deep within her tiny body. Her head jerked back as if pulled by an unseen cord, and tears of ostentatious shame seemed to explode from her eyes. Blood began to stream from her nose and across her chin, falling and staining her bodice. She swayed in her chair, her one hand clawing at the other that I'd kissed, and abruptly she toppled to the floor at my feet in a dead faint.

At once her attendants came to life, crying out strange exclamations in Portuguese as they rushed to her aid like a flock of chattering crows. Charles took my arm and pulled me back. He kept his hand there, too, linking us together, and making it abundantly clear to everyone which lady he'd champion. His face was taut with fury, the corners of his mouth pale from the force with which he compressed his lips.

The attendants gathered up their fallen queen and carried her from the room to another chamber, leaving behind fallen stools, forgotten prayer books, a broken strand of jet rosary beads, and Her Majesty's handwork, the threaded needle jutting from the tight-stretched cloth.

The silence in the room was almost unbearable, with everyone waiting to measure their own response to the king's.

His fingers tightened around my arm, his anger glowing not at me but at her.

"You must forgive the queen, my lady," he said to me, raising his voice so that those who remained wouldn't miss it. "She is obstinate, and ill-mannered."

He turned to lead me back to the door and my carriage. Not one person we passed would meet that stony gaze, and our footsteps echoed together in the too-silent hallways.

"I'm sorry, sir," I said on the steps, though of course I wasn't. "I'm sorry."

"It's she who should apologize, Barbara, not you." He kissed me a fierce kiss born of his anger toward his wife. "She has publicly defied me for the last time. I am her husband, and her governor, and I refuse to tolerate such from her again."

I reached up and kissed his cheek, thankful he could not see my smile. Not a single person at court could now doubt that I'd be made Lady of the Bedchamber. The only question was how soon it could be done.

For many weeks, Charles and his queen had argued over my being Lady of the Bedchamber, a quarrel that had been unpleasant, even on occasion noisy, but at heart without any real violence or consequences. Because of the newness of their marriage, the king had been inclined to be gentle with his bride, and not so stern perhaps as her petulance deserved. At heart he was a kind man, even a gallant one. But even the most gentle of gentlemen can be pushed too far, and so at last Charles showed his true mettle, and taught the queen the consequences of her stubbornness.

One more time the king submitted the list with my name attached, and one more time the queen struck me from it, further demanding that he break with me and send me from the court entirely.

In turn Charles announced that he'd had enough of her enormous retinue of sour-faced, arrogant attendants, and he was packing nearly all of them back to Portugal. He'd precedent on his side; his father had done exactly the same thing with his mother's French attendants soon after their marriage, and things had improved greatly after that. Catherine was permitted to keep a few priests, a handful of kitchen maids to prepare her appalling Iberian food, her musicians, and one ancient crone who'd been with her since birth, the Countess of Penalva, with the extra warning that the countess would be next on the ship back to Lisbon if the queen did not comply.

The queen shrieked and railed and likely tried that clever trick of a fainting nosebleed again. When that had no effect, she threatened to leave the king and return to her mother—a threat that truly infuriated Charles, for women never left him. It disturbed her mother far more, and, as the ambassador respectfully hastened to relay to Catherine, such a retreat was impossible for reasons of state. Part of her marriage settlement had included English troops to help Portugal face Spain, and the Portuguese Queen Mother was loath to give back that military support for the sake of her daughter's tantrums.

The king held fast.

To my delight, Clarendon now stepped into the fray. He'd arranged this unfortunate marriage, and besides, he would always take anyone's side against me. But the queen refused to heed him, either, turning shrill against her strongest ally, and the king vented his frustration on the chancellor. It was also at this time that Clarendon began to refer to me among his cronies only as the lady, refusing to speak my name outright. In a way this was an odd kind of compliment, and demonstrated how much he both hated me yet feared my power with the king.

The king failed to see it as anything but the basest insult, just as he was also angered by the chancellor's attempts to have me removed from his company and banished from the court. The chancellor had been Charles's constant supporter since he'd been a child, one who'd stayed by his side through the darkest days of exile, and Charles had always been faithful and respectful toward him in return. But in attempting to cross me in the guise of protecting the queen, the old man had gone too far. Charles turned on him most viciously, telling him that any enemy of mine was likewise an enemy of his—a killing rebuke that they say made Clarendon weep in bitter fury at my growing power. Though I thanked Charles profusely for being my champion, I was wise enough to keep my glee private.

Left with few supporters who spoke her language, the queen turned next to a young priest at court named Father Talbot, who could speak, and listen, to her in Spanish. This foolish young fellow urged her to stand firm against both her husband and me, branding me an "enchantress." This made me laugh when I heard it, for in English such a title would hardly be an insult.

Yet in Spain and Portugal, an enchantress was close kin to a witch, using her seductive powers in consort with the Devil himself. This infuriated the king, as did the fact that both the queen and Father Talbot made the fatal mistake of repeating these conversations between them. Father Talbot, too, was sent away, and further, the few friends that the queen had made at court grew distant, fearful that she'd betray their conversations as she had Father Talbot's.

Through her own foolishness, the queen now found herself deprived of her husband's regard, her friends, her supporters, her priests, even servants who spoke her tongue. She was isolated and ignored in the public chambers at Hampton Court, and likely the private ones, too. Charles made no secret that he preferred my company to hers. Worst of all for a queen in her position, she'd still yet to demonstrate any signs of conception.

And at last she gave way.

The warrant was submitted for me to be named a Lady of the Bedchamber to the queen. My influence with the king was perceived as the strongest it had ever been, and I was flattered and courted wherever I went. His joy and delight in me was boundless.

For now, I'd won.

The twenty-third of August was set aside as the date that Charles would return to London with his new queen. Beyond the court, few knew of the troubles that had attended this still-new marriage, and most of Charles's subjects were eager to welcome their queen and catch a glimpse of her. Instead of entering the city by carriage and horseback, Charles decided on a water-bound procession on the Thames, from Hampton Court through the countryside and city to the palace steps at Whitehall. He and Catherine would ride on an elegant open barge so all could see them, while the rest of the court would travel in decorated boats.

I decided to come back to London with my children early, to open and freshen my house in King Street. I'd learned through letters that when Roger had returned to the near-empty house after I'd fled to Richmond, he, like the queen, had finally conceded. He agreed with me that the house was mine and announced his plans to leave not only London but England entirely. He planned to remove himself to Paris or Venice, where he'd been offered a post in the doge's navy. So far from London, no one would know his shame, and he could practice his faith freely.

I thought this was an unnecessarily overwrought gesture, especially when he coupled it with a bond of ten thousand pounds through the Earl of Suffolk, wed to my namesake, Aunt Barbara, and my uncle Lord Grandison, to indemnify himself against any debts, contracts, or pledges I might incur. *That* was unkind, and spiteful, too, considering how my fortunes were already soaring higher than his ever had. But if such an action helped soothe Roger's pride, so be it. I'd so much else to consider in my life at that time that I'd not fuss with him over so paltry a question as that.

My neighbor Admiral Lord Sandwich had also come back to town early, leaving his lady to follow. As two bachelors by circumstance, we joined together at my house to sup and play cards. He was an agreeable older gentleman with a bluff sailor's manner, and despite his wife's attempts to tame him, he'd a sailor's randiness, too. It was well known that he kept a mistress in Chelsea, and when in sport I proposed we play for more entertaining stakes, he was quick to agree. He gallantly lost fifty pounds to me at our little table, and when his pocket was empty, I claimed his kisses for a night or two, a settlement that pleased us both mightily.

The day of the procession on the river was warm and sunny, as fine a late summer day as can be had in England. I awakened early, as much from excitement as from the sounds of the hammering carpenters making final adjustments to the pavilions and scaffoldings along the river. As was always the case with any form of celebration in London, boys, and men who'd still the amusements of boys, were setting off firecrackers and unloaded guns for sport. By ten in the morning it was clear from the off-key singing and bellowing that a great many Londoners had decided to welcome their new queen with a cheerful bout of heavy drink.

Though I'd no formal part to play in the day, I still would be seen on the walkway that ran between the river and Whitehall and overlooked the palace's steps down to the water. This viewing spot was reserved for favored courtiers and the highest guests of the king and queen, and was shaded beneath a sailcloth awning rigged to shield us from the harshest sun. I wished to be dressed with splendor and gaiety not only fitting to my rank and the day, but also so as to be easily spied by Charles when he looked for me among the crowds—as I was most confident he would do. I chose a bright sateen gown of my usual blue, bound in cherry red, and a gold striped silk shawl that I hoped would catch Charles's eye and act like a beckoning flag around my shoulders.

The royal barge was expected to arrive early in the afternoon. Because my house was only a short distance from the river, I walked to the steps to join the others. I took my two babes with me, to amuse them, with their nursemaid and Wilson to carry and hold them high to watch. And if the queen should happen to glance my way and see them, the proof of the king's devotion to me—ah, well, I could not concern myself with that, either.

The river was already thick with boats and skiffs of every kind, most of them decorated in some fashion with ribbons or wreaths of flowers. From the windows of every house hung banners or pennants, and as the crowds had done for Charles's coronation, his subjects had worn their most festive clothes in honor of the new queen. Children clustered on the bridges and along the wharves with bunches of flowers, waiting excitedly until the moment that the royal barge would pass and the flowers could be tossed toward the king and queen.

Slowly I made my way to the walkway, pausing here and there to greet friends and acquaintances. Master Lely's portrait of me had proved to be one of his most engaging, and most popular. Engraved by Faithorne, the prints had been selling so briskly from Lely's studio that he was already begging me to sit for him again and calling me his muse. Because of these engravings, and my new appointment, I was now more freely recognized and acknowledged than before. Even on this day that belonged to the queen, I was aware of people in the crowds below us pointing and gazing up at me, of apprentices climbing the scaffolding to ogle me and my two beautiful children—Anne was a toddling year and a half, while Charles was two months—so clearly sired by the king.

Yet as I made my way along this walkway, I realized too late that Roger was heading toward me from the opposite direction. I'd come too far to turn around, nor truly was there anything to be accomplished now by avoiding him. Instead, as we passed he raised his hat to me and murmured some polite nonsense, while I in turn nodded genteelly and said much the same. We were well past anything more, though I did wonder what manner of bemused fate had brought us here together at the same place and time.

A few minutes later, I realized he'd paused before the nursemaid and had gently taken my son into his arms. I joined them, not because I feared for little Charles—I trusted Roger with so many others around us—but because I was a proud mother, eager to display my charmer.

"How well the boy looks, Barbara," Roger said, smiling down at the child in his arms. "He's grown so much, I'd scarce know him. You've a gift for motherhood."

"I'm fortunate in my children, that is all." He'd aged markedly in the months since I'd seen him last, his dark hair now flecked with white at the temples and a generally melancholy air about his person; the trials, I suppose, of being wedded to me.

"More fortunate than in your husband," he said, still concentrating on the baby. "I will be leaving for Paris as soon as my affairs here are in order."

"I wish you well, Roger," I said softly, not wanting the ready ears around us to overhear. "Perhaps there you'll find a lady worthy of you."

"No, I don't believe I will." He shook his head, and little Charles reached up to try to catch the swaying locks of his hair, his bright black eyes rapt with fascination. "After you, Barbara, I don't think I could ever love again."

"Hah," I said wryly. "Either that is a very fine compliment for me, Roger, or very much the opposite."

"You may decide that for yourself." He kissed the baby's forehead, and with obvious reluctance handed him back to the waiting nurse-maid. "*Bonne chance*, Barbara, and may God keep you well."

He bowed, and I curtseyed. Then swiftly, before he could stop me, I kissed him, my lips scarce brushing over his. I had a strong and awful premonition that I'd never again speak with him in this life, and despite the sorrows we'd each brought one another, I wished to part with amity.

Without smiling or offering me any other salute, he bowed one final time, his sweep as gallant as could be. He knelt to kiss my daughter Anne on each cheek, the daughter he still chose to believe was his. Then he turned away from me and our past, and toward France.

# Chapter Fourteen

"A touching family scene, that, my lady."

I'd scarcely had time to bid Roger farewell there before the palace when I realized Henry Bennet, Lord Arlington, had come to stand so close behind me. But that was the gentleman's manner, creeping about the wainscoting to gather up whatever crumbs might fall his way.

And because those same crumbs might be useful to me as well, I now turned toward Arlington with the pleasantest face imaginable. "Good day to you, sir," I said. "I'd not known you'd be here among us this afternoon."

"What, miss such a splendid display of support for His Sacred Majesty?" He extended one hand toward the boat-crowded river and smiled at me. "You underestimate me, my lady."

He gave a smile, or at least what passed for a smile on his disfigured face. A member of an ancient Middlesex Catholic family and newly made a baron, Arlington had served valiantly among the Royalists during the wars, and for his bravery had earned a gruesome scar that almost sliced his nose in two across the bridge. To mask the scar—and, I'd heard, to keep the lower half of his nose from drooping over his mouth—he wore a black plaster across the bridge.

I smiled in return, but with purpose, too. "I should never underestimate you, Arlington. Only a fool would do that."

He laughed. "Even a fool only makes that mistake once."

"Only once, because they'd learned not to trust you?" I countered. "Or only once, because they'd thus met their ruination at your hands?"

"Ah, my lady, you know me too well." He wagged a knowing finger at me. "Such beauty is so seldom coupled with such wit. I must take care around you."

"Indeed you must," I said playfully, "just as I guard myself around you."

We laughed together, as if this was a jest, but both of us knew it wasn't. Arlington and I had the healthiest of regards for one another, and for our mutual ambitions. Staring at that plaster on Arlington's nose, it was too easy to forget how he was one of the most clever and accomplished gentlemen in Charles's circle, one who spoke several languages with ease, and one so skilled with flattering words and diplomacy that he could persuade others to his will without them realizing it. As Keeper of the King's Privy Purse, he held one of the most lucrative posts at court, and one of the most important to me, too, for any moneys that Charles wished to give me came through Arlington. He also shared my hatred of Clarendon, and wished his ruin as much as I did myself. Was it any marvel, then, that we'd lately become allies?

"You will join us this night, Arlington?" I asked. "I'm sure Her Majesty will be weary after the ceremony of the procession, and the palace will be a dull place. But in King Street, I promise you that won't be the case."

"The court is often dull, my lady," he said, "while the company that fills your home in King Street is always amusing. You may count on me to join you."

"I'm glad," I said, and I was. As soon as I'd returned to London, I'd begun to invite certain others to my house in the evening, gentlemen like the king's raucous old friends Harry Jermyn and Tom Killigrew, who would amuse Charles away from the regimen of the palace. I made certain that the wine flowed freely, and that my cook was the best that could be found. I wanted my table to be among the best in London. I myself looked after the company, and the conversation, to keep those at the highest and most entertaining level as well.

Those first gatherings had become informal collections of politically like-minded gentlemen, too, gentlemen like Arlington: Lord Ashley, Sir Charles Berkeley, and Sir Thomas Clifford, as well as my wily cousins, Lord Edward and Lord Ralph Montagu, and the more infamous Duke of Buckingham, and even my King Street neighbor Lord Sandwich. Such diverse gentlemen were unified by a dislike of the chancellor and a fear that he would push Parliament and the country toward a more conservative point of view that was not so very far removed from the old days of the intolerant Commonwealth.

Charles had promised religious tolerance in the Declaration of Breda and this year in the Declaration of Indulgence. But Clarendon was at his chilly heart more of a Puritan than an Anglican, I think, and encouraged the fearfulness and suspicion inherent in Englishmen of anyone not of the Anglican faith. Whether Friends or Scottish Presbyterians or members of a score of other lesser sects, they were all lumped together as dissenters, while often papists were tossed into this same stew as well. Clarendon had already pushed through one statute excluding dissenters from town governments, and another that limited the livings of their ministers. Neither was well intentioned, and both were at odds with the king's best intentions for his people.

So while these gentlemen enjoyed the hospitality I granted them, we also shared as our goal the downfall of the lord chancellor. I listened to what they said, and if I then carried what I heard and learned to the ear of the king that night in his bed, why, everyone was pleased. While Charles himself was often in attendance on these evenings, he also asked me to relay what I'd heard, especially about Clarendon, whom he increasingly distrusted.

It was a heady responsibility, but a role that pleased me in many ways. Now that the court was back in London, I saw my influence only growing as the king grew to depend more upon my opinions as well as my friendship. He often spent the night with me at my house, leaving at dawn on foot to cut through the palace's Privy Garden back to his rooms with so little ceremony or regard for his own safety that both the chancellor and the sergeant of the Life Guards scolded him for it. Yet his nonchalance amused me—to think that the King of England went whistling down my back stairs like any other skulking lover!

If I accepted a garnish here and there to promote a special notion or individual to the king's attention, such rewards seemed fair enough. *This* was how the game was played, not by the long toil that poor Roger had so espoused, and no one was more eager to throw the dice than I.

No one understood this so well as Arlington. "Are you expecting the usual gentlemen this evening, my lady?"

I nodded, glancing past him toward the river. The royal barge must have come into sight around the Westminster bend of the river: the crowd had grown even louder, more ecstatic in their cheers, and the trumpeters waiting on the palace wharf had begun to play the heralding fanfares. Three rows of temporary benches had been thrown up on the embankment below the walkway to hold a group of young girls, waiting in their white gowns and ribbon'd caps to toss small bouquets of pinks before the queen. Now they were hopping up and down on the benches like so many pretty little chicks on their perches, fair bursting with giggling excitement.

"What of His Majesty?" Arlington persisted, shifting closer so his voice could be heard over the rising din. "Do you expect His Majesty in King Street tonight as well?"

I shrugged, the silk shawl sliding from my shoulders in the breeze. As much as I wished to please gentlemen like Arlington, I still didn't like to reveal too much of the king's doings. To do so would be to betray my private life with Charles, yes, and that I'd no desire to do. But to show too much to others would also be like drawing the curtain on the man whose hands make Punch and Judy strike one another, spoiling the secrets and the mystery.

"I cannot say for certain if His Majesty will be joining us," I said. "I expect his attendance will depend upon the wishes of the queen."

"The *queen*," he said, scoffing. "The little Portuguese poppet may wear the crown, my lady, but everyone knows who has the surest hold on the king's affections and interests."

"Don't be disloyal, my lord," I warned, tapping his arm lightly with my fingers. "His Majesty won't care for that."

"No, my lady," he said shrewdly, "but it's no wonder he does like you. You're the greatest beauty of the court, true enough, but anyone who believes that is all you are is grievously mistaken."

Playfully I parted my lips a fraction and turned my head to one side to look back at him. "Like Lord Clarendon?"

"Like Lord Clarendon," he agreed. "The Chancellor will learn that—"

But before he could finish, his words were lost in a great crashing of timber below us and screams of pain and horror. One of the raised benches holding the small girls had given way beneath their excitement, and the shattered plank had cast a dozen of the poor creatures into the muddy embankment. The fall was not so great that any of the girls was badly hurt, but still they wailed and wept with bloodied knees and battered chins and muddy stains upon their once-snowy gowns. Terrified mothers rushed to find their daughters, scooping them into their arms to ease their tears with the balm of kind words and tenderness.

Yet one little mite remained unclaimed, sprawled on the sodden ground with her cap missing and rivulets of her tears streaking through the mud on her cheeks. With a thought to how I'd hate to see my own Anne suffer so, I ducked beneath the railing and hurried down to her, giving no care to my fine clothes or how others might judge my impulse.

"Here now, duck, don't cry, don't cry," I said gently, bending beside her. I fished my lace-bordered handkerchief from my pocket and used it to blot the tears from her eyes, and set her back on her sturdy small legs. "You don't want to weep before the queen and make her sad, too, do you?"

The child sniffed and rubbed her fists into her eyes, trying to stop her tears.

"There now, be brave," I said, pulling a yellow silk ribbon from my gown. "A girl so fair as you should never have reason to cry, you know. Let's see how this ribbon will look in your hair, shall we?"

Letting the child solemnly hold my handkerchief, I tied the length of yellow silk into her auburn hair and into a bow that left the ends dancing over her plump shoulders.

"There now, that's very pretty," I said, nodding at my handiwork as I held up my small round pocket-glass for her to see her reflection. "Are you pleased, madam?"

Finally the girl smiled, as enchanted as every female is by the sight of her own face.

"Mary!" A distraught red-faced woman in a green apron rushed forward to clasp her arms around the girl, who immediately buried her face in the woman's plump, comfortable shoulder. "Oh, daughter, thank th' merciful God that you be safe."

"Safe as can be," I said, standing upright.

The woman looked up at me over her daughter's head, recognition flashing through her eyes. The shift of emotions across her face was so bold that she might have spoken them aloud: savior, lady, Lady Castlemaine, His Majesty's whore. Abruptly she let her daughter go, shoving her down into a curtsey to match her own self-conscious effort.

"Oh, my lady, forgive me, I did not know," she said, her face even more red with embarrassment and a certain secondhand shame. "Mary, make your thanks t' Her Ladyship, what saved your life."

"No thanks, mistress, no thanks," I said, smiling at their reunion. Mutely little Mary held up my grimy handkerchief, and I shook my head. "It's yours now, duck. You keep it, and remember the day you saw the king."

"An' Her Majesty th' Queen, my lady," the mother said, as much a rebuke to me as she'd dare make, given how much higher in station I was than she. "What's wed t' His Majesty."

"And the queen," I said, and smiled wryly as they left me to hurry back to the others. Ah, yes, wedded virtue must triumph again. The queen, the queen: however had I forgotten *her*?

I stood by myself near one of the pillars that held the awning, apart from the other courtiers from the palace, yet not among the group of toppled girls and their mothers, either. I linked my fingers together and held my hands across my brow to shield my eyes from the brightness of the sun as I watched the scene before me.

The royal barge was drawing close to the end of the wharf, and the fiddles and drums were sounding now, too, along with the trumpets. The boatmen on the wharf were leaning out across the water with their boat hooks, intent on catching the barge to draw it into shore. The rowers shipped their long oars in elegant synchronism, the drops of water raining down from the flat blades like scattered diamonds in the sun.

I could recognize the barge's passengers now. My eye was first drawn to Charles, of course, as it ever was, seated on a thronelike armchair. He looked blissfully happy, the way he always was on such occasions, as if he'd never tire of the acclaim of his people, a soothing balm to that unhealed sore of his father's martyrdom.

Behind him the queen was set apart under a golden canopy, the supporting pillars wrapped with garlands of flowers. Having Catherine sit separately like this was intended to display her like a precious gem to her new subjects, alone in her royal bridal splendor. But to me, who knew the truth, I saw only how distant she was from the others in reality as well as in spirit. She was dressed in white and cloth of gold, her hands clutching tightly to her own armchair, as if she feared she'd be swept over the side by this enormous wave of English goodwill.

There were others on board, too, of course, a jumble of courtiers. Beside Charles sat his eldest natural son, James, by Lucy Walters, newly retrieved from the French court, and also newly fashioned Duke of Monmouth. He was a comely black-haired boy of thirteen—in age I was curiously between father and son, with James eight years my junior and Charles eleven my senior—tall and well made, and already striving to continue the amorous career he'd boasted of beginning in Paris.

But another passenger of the same youth wanted nothing to do with love, no matter how much she was pursued. Frances Stuart, a maid of honor to the queen, continued to cling to her overvalued virtue despite the pursuit of the Duke of York and several others. I found her too simple to be truly beautiful, almost childish. Yet I couldn't help but notice the intensity with which Charles himself was watching her now as she sat at the feet of the queen.

I took one step forward, into the sunlight, like the leading actress will step to the front of the stage to say her piece. I raised my arms and held my shawl out on either side of me so it caught the breeze from the water, dancing out around me like a strip of gold. At once Charles's head turned toward me, and he smiled, as if I were the only woman that counted among so many thousands of others around him.

My returning smile was as radiant as my golden shawl. As it should be, I thought happily, and with endless relief.

As it *must* be.

By the end of 1662, there was much in my life to please me. I suspected I might once again be with child by the king, a circumstance that pleased him mightily, for he was a doting father and found enormous contentment in our children.

The queen, however, still showed no signs of conception, a subject that was much studied and discussed among the Ladies of the Bedchamber. Anticipation grew each month, yet each month hopes were dashed again by the unwelcome advent of her flowers, whether showing on her smock or sheets. Though she'd been sent to Tunbridge Wells to take the waters, a sure cure in most cases, nothing changed. The whispers were already growing that she was barren, and more, that Clarendon had somehow known this yet had nonetheless urged the match because he'd greedily wanted claim to Tangier and Bombay, territories that seemed of little value to most Englishmen.

My house in King Street remained a center for important gatherings, and we'd successes to claim, too. When the office of secretary of state came open, it was filled not by one of Clarendon's cronies, as he'd expected, but by Arlington. He'd had to give up the privy purse, of course, and that post was handed to Sir Charles Berkeley, another friend of my King Street suppers. The king was well pleased with the new appointments, for these gentlemen were more agreeable in their persons and beliefs to him than Clarendon ever could be.

Encouraged by these gentlemen, Charles had also agreed to a

Declaration of Indulgences to be introduced into Parliament for consideration. If this declaration succeeded, it would serve to nullify the more intolerant restrictions of Clarendon's Act of Uniformity, aimed at hobbling Protestant nonconformists and Catholics in their worship. What pleased me most, however, was how it would also serve to blacken Clarendon's eye again.

While the warrant for my new place as Lady of the Bedchamber had yet to be confirmed—with Clarendon again delaying the process, just as he had with my title—Charles proceeded with granting me lodgings within the palace, my first rooms at Whitehall. I was given the apartments above the Holbein Gate, recently vacated when the Duke of Ormonde gave up the court for Ireland. There were few lodgings more convenient in the palace, nor more pleasantly situated, than these: through one set of windows I'd a splendid view of the garden and river and the balmy breezes that rose from them, whilst on the other side I could look down on the guards on sentry duty and see exactly who was entering or leaving the palace.

With Sir Charles holding the privy purse—and now opening it wide to me at the king's request—I was able to refurbish everything to a nicety. I took special care not only with my bedchamber but with the nursery as well. Charles came often to play with our children, tossing them high into the air and letting them pull on his hair and mustache.

Roger kept to his word, and kept to Paris, and to Venice, and did not trouble me again.

It had been a good year, yes, and I'd precious little cause for complaint or remorse. Yet like every confirmed gambler, I could take no lasting pleasure in my good fortune, but must always look ahead to the next hand, the next trick, the highest stakes that might bring the greatest reward of all.

Although winter was slow in arriving, by Christmas the winds had turned wickedly cold and the snow lay thick upon the ground. The fires in the palace weren't banked for the night, but kept tended and burning until dawn, and even so the vast rooms never shed their chill.

Spoken words froze in the air, and even the most fashionable gave up their silk and cotton thread stockings for the warmth of wool. Gentlemen and ladies alike slung enormous fur muffs around their necks to warm their hands while conversing. The water in the washstand pitcher froze solid each night, and I was forced to keep my ink on the chimney piece to keep it from freezing, too.

The Thames froze thick enough to hold a Frost Fair, with peddlers selling hot chestnuts and chocolate and toys and trinkets to those who wished the novelty of strolling across the river and beneath the arches of the bridges. The gallants had their horses shod with studded shoes and raced one another across the ice, their cloaks billowing after them, while the less adventurous bundled themselves in rich furs from New England and rode along the river in open sleighs strung with tiny brass bells. Each morning beggars were found dead in doorways or on church steps, frozen where they'd tried to sleep.

However fierce, no mere cold could keep Charles from his daily walks through St. James's Park. Though fewer courtiers chose to join him, preferring to stay within beside their fires, I refused to be left behind. I needed half a shopkeeper's stores to fortify myself: a fur-lined cloak, stout leather lady's boots, a quilted petticoat interlaid with sheep's wool, a muff, gloves, gossamer-fine scarves, and a black velvet hood lined in thick beaver on my head.

"There's nothing like a fair winter morning to clear the head," Charles declared, his face ruddy in the icy air beneath the wide brim of his black beaver hat. The walk itself was easy, for servants had come out from the palace before dawn to shovel and sweep the paths clear of new snow for the king's walk. Only a half dozen or so other gentlemen had joined us, and they kept respectfully at a distance behind us. "I don't know why you're the only lady to brave it."

I grinned. "Why should that surprise you, sir? Am I not often the only lady who'll dare things in your company?"

He laughed. "That is true. Outdoors, indoors, in beds and in carriages, under trees and in ponds, by day and by night, against walls and on floors and—"

"I don't much care for the floors," I said, wrinkling my nose at the hard memory. "I know it was the convenience of the moment, but it's difficult being on the bottom."

"I wonder what it would be like in the snow?" he asked with a philosopher's thoughtfulness. "Have you ever tried that, Barbara?"

I shook my head. "Perhaps if one were well protected with furs or coverlets, then—"

"No, I meant in the snow itself," he said with relish. "Hot flesh smoking in the snow."

"Hot flesh becoming very cold as the snow melted around it, and a catarrh and a putrid throat to follow," I scoffed. "I'm not so adventurous as that, sir."

The truth was that while I still felt as strong an attachment to the king as ever, and I knew he loved me more than any other woman, time had in fact worn and softened the excitement of our passion. At least it had for me, though I'd never be so foolish as to confess it.

Oh, most times between us were just as exuberant, just as pleasure-bound, as they'd been those first nights in Brussels, or maybe even more so. Yet there were others where I'd catch myself with closed eyes, imagining a man other than the king to be swiving me, or tasting and tickling another man's cock for the sake of variety. It was not that I loved Charles the less. Only that even the most succulent dish devoured at every repast loses its power over time to delight, and I longed for a fresh sprinkle of spice to restore the tempting quality.

"Ah, well, perhaps not dallying in the snow," he agreed, amused. "But surely that must be the first suggestion I've made to you in that vein that you've refused."

"Wisdom does on occasion prevail," I said coyly, "even with us."

He chuckled, the warmth making a cloudy puff in the chill air. "Not often, my dear Barbara," he said, "and thanks to the heavens it doesn't."

He smiled with such fondness and fervor that I felt shamed by my discontent. But then as king he'd never had to make do with a single dish, not when the entire groaning board of womanhood lay spread for his enjoyment. I knew that even after a dutiful bout with the queen was followed by a delicious night with me, he'd still in the earliest hours engage in a quick ramble with an actress or brothel favorite.

These encounters meant nothing more to him than a fast spend in a willing cunt, and as such I felt no jealousy toward these faceless women. How could I, when I'd dabbled in this way myself, a quick tumble with a handsome footman or stable boy, another with an actor in a darkened theatre when we'd both too much to drink, even once, in the heady days of Philip, with a swarthy sailor who'd caught my letch, my petticoats rucked up in the shadows of London Bridge?

But I *was* envious of the opportunities Charles had that I didn't, of more enticing adventures than a lady at court—particularly a lady who regularly shared the bed of the king—would ever so easily find. It was considered scandalous enough that I had at once an absent husband and a king for a lover, more men by one than most ladies could claim in their lifetimes. A gentleman who'd dare explore many partners was a libertine, but a lady was damned as a greedy whore.

I say that it was unfair, yes, but I must also admit that at this time I'd begun a dalliance with Harry Jermyn, one of my friends from the gatherings at my King Street house, and a boon companion of Charles's as well. With his turnip-shaped nose, Harry had always made me laugh, being the sort of man who, being unfavored by nature in regards to his face and form, was never too proud to turn his droll wit toward himself as well as toward others. He was a smallish gentleman, given overmuch to dueling like my first love, Philip, but as I'd soon discovered, he compensated for his slight stature by being most excellently skilled in the French manner of love, with the most cunningly adept tongue. I enjoyed his attentions, much as he enjoyed knowing that he was going where the king had preceded him, but neither of us were so foolish as to mistake our occasional meetings together for anything more than they were.

Of course I kept these assignations with Harry to myself, as I did so many other things, locked tight within me where they belonged. Now I only smiled at Charles's words, as if in perfect agreement, and turned back to the snowy landscape of the park before us.

"Oh, sir, look," I exclaimed. "See all the skaters and sliders this morning."

Last summer Charles had ordered a long canal dug and filled across the lawn that ran between St. James's Palace and Whitehall. It was supposed to provide the same watery imagery as the canals of Venice, a cool respite in the heat of summer, but Charles had discovered that once the water froze, the canal proved the ideal spot for the Dutch sport of ice-skating. He'd imported a small troop of the most accomplished from the Hague to demonstrate and teach their skills and to provide a pretty scene on the canal.

"They're almost like acrobats, balancing on their blades like that," Charles marveled as we paused to watch. "Mark how they fly across the ice."

I stood close before him, sharing our warmth. "Should you like to try?"

He slipped his arms around me and drew me closer, tucking his hands inside my muff. "I'd like to try, yes, or rather I should have liked to have tried," he said with regret. "But I fear that's too fast a sport to try afresh at my age."

"Your age," I scoffed. "You're not so old and bent as that, sir. Thirty-two is not old, not by anyone's lights. You might recall that you still ride and swim and hunt and bowl and play tennis, thrashing gentlemen ten years your junior."

"I do at that," he said cheerfully. "But I still believe it's best to leave this ice-skating to younger men and put aside the spectacle of an aging monarch tumbling on his ass on an ice-covered canal."

"You've scarce aged at all," I protested, twisting around to look up at him. It was unthinking flattery, I know, the kind all women must pay to men, and I gladly offered it up to him. But the truth was otherwise: the trials of his earlier life had done much to age him beyond his mortal years. Oh, Charles remained virile and strong as ever, his body muscled and lean, but there was so much gray in his hair now that he kept threatening to crop it short and wear a periwig instead. The long lines that ran from beneath his nose to the corners of his mouth were carved more deeply now, and the shadows seemed to linger more often beneath his dark eyes. "You're still the very image of a gentleman in his prime."

"You're kindness itself, Barbara," he said wryly, though still pleased I'd spoken in his defense. "You can be the wickedest and most lascivious of fair creatures, but the world never sees the other side of you that I do."

I laughed softly, but without humor. "What, the side that the world is certain is shrewish and cold and avaricious?" I said, thinking of all the slander that was both written and said of me. "The side that damns me as Lady Barbary for introducing you to pleasures that no sturdy English monarch should ever wish to explore? Or perhaps the side of me that seeks to wrest control of the very country away from you, and corrupt you with my charms?"

"Oh, sweet," he said sadly. "Pray don't pay any heed to that rubbish."

"I don't," I said, because I didn't.

"I do only so far as to remember the speaker's name," he said firmly. "Any enemy of yours, Barbara, becomes an enemy of mine as well."

Pleased, I wriggled more closely against him, though as thickly dressed as we were, such motions were affectionate symbols and little else. "Now which of us is kindness itself?"

"I am serious, Barbara," he said with far more solemnity that I'd expected from him so early in the day. "No one else but I seems to understand how tender your dear heart can be."

"Pray don't tell the world, sir," I said blithely, "else the world will cease paying me any particular regard."

He grunted with displeasure, as close to an oath as he ever went. "The world can go hang itself for all I care."

"It most likely will," I said, "whether I am a saint before God or a whore in your bed. But lah, how did we lapse into this grim philosophizing?"

"Lah, indeed," he said. "All I meant to do was ask a favor of you for tonight."

"Tonight, sir?" I turned in his arms to look up at him mischievously beneath my lashes. "Why wait until tonight?"

"Not that, you sly creature," he said. "I meant for the ball this night. Will you open the dancing on Monmouth's arm?"

"I?" My eyes widened with surprise. We were in the heart of Christmas season now, with a ball planned for nearly every night until Twelfth Night. Tonight's was set for the Banqueting House, already bedecked with holly and other boughs of greenery brought down from Windsor. The first dance of any ball was by custom begun by the couple of highest rank in attendance. At Whitehall, that generally meant the king and queen, even if they never danced together again for the remainder of the evening, but now he was suggesting I claim that honor with his son. "If you're not going, then I won't—"

"Oh, I'll be there," he said. "Never a fear of that. But I thought it would be a pretty honor for Jamie to go in my stead, considering this will be his first ball in the Banqueting House."

I tipped my head to one side, curious. "A pretty honor, indeed," I said. "But why not with the queen as his partner? I know she has a rare fondness for His Grace."

This was in fact so. Though no one could quite determine why, the queen had taken a special liking to her husband's eldest bastard and had made something of a pet of the boy since he'd first come to court in the summer, saving special sweets for him at table and having him sit beside her in drawing rooms. Perhaps he was lonely for his grandmother the Queen Mother, his guardian for so much of his unsettled childhood. Perhaps Queen Catherine, being small, dark-haired, and foreign, as well as another Catholic outsider, reminded him of her. Or perhaps Catherine thought that by being kind to the son she'd win more affection from the father.

"The queen could let Jamie lead her, I suppose," he said, musing, "but she feels uneasy with so much attention on her. It strikes me as unfair to the boy to make him responsible for supporting her."

I studied him shrewdly. "Why do I guess, sir, that that's but half of your reasoning?"

"The half." He scowled, and shook his head. "You know I've found him a fine little Scottish bride. Countess of Buccleuch in her own right, and with a sufficient fortune to keep even him happy. I want them wed this spring, to save them both from mischief. The girl's only twelve, you know, so—"

"Twelve?" I asked, raising one brow with mild surprise. "Isn't that dipping a bit deep into the cradle, even for a Scottish peeress?"

"Mind that he's only thirteen, Barbara," he said, "so they should get on famously. But he needs some seasoning before he's a husband, a chance to shine here at court, and I'd—"

"Oh, pish, sir," I said. "That's not the half, either, but a tiny scrap of the truth, isn't it?"

He sighed with resignation, for he never was good at keeping such things from me.

"Very well, then, Barbara," he said, "but you must swear not to tell a soul. The boy complained to me in confidence that the queen is not so skilled a dancer as you, and he'd much prefer to make his opening with you than with her."

"He did?" My mouth curved with amusement. With my natural grace and long legs, I *was* a far better dancer than the squat little queen would ever be, but I hadn't expected the thirteen-year-old duke to recognize it, too. "What excellent taste your fair Monmouth displays for his youth. Like the father, so the son."

"There now, that's exactly why I didn't tell you," he said peevishly. "You'll give the poor young fellow the same teasing trouble as you do me, and then—"

"Oh, no, sir, I won't," I said softly, resting my gloved hand on his sleeve. "At ease, at ease. I'll be as gentle as can be with him, elderly Aunt Castlemaine."

"Don't be too gentle," he warned. "The boy's wretchedly spoiled already."

"Exactly like his father," I murmured and raised my mouth to kiss him, my tongue darting warm between his chilled lips. "Exactly, exactly so."

"I'm honored you're my partner tonight, my lady."

The Duke of Monmouth bowed before me, too deeply to be appropriate, really, and betraying his eagerness. He wore a flamboyant jacket and petticoat breeches of pale blue satin after the fashion of France—where, I'd heard, a gentleman's suit of clothes required at least two hundred yards of silk ribbon to be worn in the presence of King Louis!—with so many points and furbelows and ribbons dangling from the waist and slashed sleeves that it seemed to be sprouting pink silk. He was dark complected like his father, but his features were more delicate, like those of his mother, the ill-fated Lucy Walters, they said. He was already taller than I, but with the gangliness of youth, his feet and hands seeming too large for the rest of him. He was trying with difficulty to grow a mustache like his father's, a sparse sprinkle of hairs on his upper lip, and his voice refused to keep to a manly register, but squeaked upward at the most humiliating moments.

Monmouth was, in short, the most charming young gentleman imaginable, and if he were a sweetmeat dusted with powdered sugar served to me on a silver salver, I would have devoured him in a single bite.

"You know the first dance tonight will be a *sarabande*, Your Grace?" I asked. The *sarabande* was an elegant, dignified dance with steps in triple time, much favored by the Iberians and thus by the queen. It was often danced to begin the evening, because the intricate steps displayed the ladies and gentlemen to advantage, and because the dance's complexity was better undertaken before too much wine had been drunk by the participants—the opposite reasoning behind saving raucous country dances for after midnight. I wished His Grace to be aware of the *sarabande*'s challenges, and withdraw now if he'd any doubts.

"It's a difficult dance to execute well, Your Grace," I continued, "particularly before so large a crowd, and I would be perfectly happy to be your partner later in the evening if—"

"No!" he exclaimed plaintively, then realized how rude that must have sounded. "That is, Lady Castlemaine, nothing could make me abandon the pleasure of being your partner. Besides, I've been practicing the *sarabande* specially with my dancing master, to be ready."

"I am honored, Your Grace, and impressed," I said, delighted by his unwitting guilelessness. "Most gentlemen would not take that effort."

He pressed his hand over his heart, a courtly gesture undermined by fingernails gnawed to their quick.

"My lady," he said solemnly, "I am not most gentlemen."

"How very true." I smiled warmly at him, then glanced over his shoulder toward the gallery. The musicians were taking their seats, settling themselves and their instruments with a final tuning. As the first couple, we could take our places at any time.

"Your Grace," I said, offering him my hand. "Whenever you please."

He did not so much take my hand as seize it as his prize, as if ready to urge me onto a steeplechase instead of a *sarabande*. Gently I reined him back to a more reasonable pace as we entered the room and went to the center. As other couples fell in behind us, I could hear the startled murmurs rippling through the crowd. There was no place like this court for understanding all the delicacies of order and precedent, and having one of the great Christmas balls opened by the king's mistress and the king's bastard was a sight ripe for endless remark.

I'd taken care to dress for my role, too. I wore a gown of red velvet, embroidered overall with twisting vines of silver threads that caught the candlelight, and around my throat I wore my lover-king's new Christmas gift to me, a large Venetian cross set with cabochon rubies and hung from a strand of pearls as thick around as my little finger. As was his custom, Charles had let me choose among the treasures that had been given to him by various other rulers and lords seeking favor, a system that offered me the finest jewels in Europe.

Now I sought, and found, Charles in elegant black and sitting in his tall-backed armchair, his expression indulgently bemused by the small, scandalous spectacle he'd created. I touched my fingers to the ruby-studded cross so he'd be sure to see I'd worn it, and he nodded, pleased to see me gratified. I'd wear it later with nothing else, to please him more.

Beside him, the queen was stony-faced and glowering at my having usurped both her place in the first dance, and with her husband's son. Near Charles's chair stood a genial Arlington, while beside the queen was Lord Clarendon, supported by a walking stick to ease the pain of his gouty foot and the equal agony of his disapproval—for even in the midst of the court's yuletide festivities we were incapable of setting aside our politics.

"You know that every eye in the room is on us, Your Grace," I said softly, giving his hand a small squeeze of reassurance. "Yet I care not, because you are my partner."

His cheeks colored, the dear. "That's what *I'm* supposed to say, my lady, not you."

But then the music began and he was saved from having to make more conversation. We stepped, and spun, and paused and turned and stepped again, my skirts fanning out against his legs. I was impressed by how well he did, keeping every movement across the sanded floor with surprising grace. He truly *had* been toiling with his dancing master to do so well, though his fixed smile betrayed how carefully he was counting the measures so not to blunder. By the time the dance was done, his face was flushed from his exertions, but he was also close to crowing with pride, the happy young cockerel.

I curtseyed my thanks to him as applause rippled through the hall. At once the musicians began the introduction to the next dance, and another set of couples began to assemble themselves on the floor behind us.

"I thank you for that honor, Your Grace," I said with a smile, and began to turn away to take my place with his father.

But Monmouth seized my hand again, unwilling to give me up so soon. "A word before you go, my lady?" he begged urgently, tossing his black hair back from his eyes. "In private?"

"Very well, then," I agreed, though I couldn't begin to guess what that word might be. "A moment."

Before I'd finished agreeing he was pulling me through the others and into the narrow hallway that led to the long path to the kitchens. His hand was endearingly moist with nervousness. Around us servants were hurrying great covered platters of food into the hall, but

Monmouth cared only for me, drawing me to a halt as soon as we were out of sight of the other guests.

"Forgive me, Your Grace, but I cannot stay away from your father His Majesty for long," I said, although I was entertained by his desire for such privacy. "Pray, what is this single word you so wished me to hear?"

"Only this, my lady," he said, and boldly grabbing me about the waist, he kissed me, kissed me with considerable enthusiasm and not a hint of skill or finesse. Startled, I flailed with equal clumsiness in his arms, shoving against his stripling chest, yet still he clasped me tight. He was stronger than I expected, his youthful body already honed by the same manly sports that so pleased his father, making him as difficult to push aside as his sire. He ground his mouth against mine to thrust his greedy tongue within, and my single thought was of being violated thus by a large, unruly young dog. And oh, how he'd terrify that poor twelve-year-old bride!

Yet at the same time the untrammeled intensity of his assault was vastly flattering to a lady such as I, twenty-two and more than eight years his senior. It was . . . *exhilarating*. What he lacked in experience he'd traded for eagerness, and I also could not put from my thoughts the titillating realization that he was Charles's son.

"More care, Your Grace, more care," I whispered as I finally managed to turn my face away from his lips. "*Amour* is not a race to be won with breakneck haste. A lady appreciates being coaxed, and wooed."

His face was flushed and his eyes were dark with longing, and I could feel his young heart thudding in his chest as if in fact he'd already finished half that race. I was wise to slow his pace, else he would shame himself in his breeches, or worse, on my petticoat.

"Like this, sweet," I said, brushing my lips lightly over his before I gently increased the pressure. "And like this."

At once his kiss was checked, the improvement immediate. The thought that I was teacher to so apt a pupil delighted me, and with more daring I took one of his hands from my waist and placed it lightly over my breast. Instinctively his fingers curved over the swelling flesh that my tight-laced bodice raised high for adulation, and instantly he forgot everything I'd taught him, lapsing back to the sloppy impetuosity of before.

But now I was roused by this impulsive lark, too, and answered his passion in kind, slipping my arms around the back of his neck to steady myself as I arched wantonly against him. He pushed me back against the wall, the wood panels pressed into the small of my back. His prick was hard in his breeches, a goodly size and ready for play. I wondered if he'd yet had any woman of flesh and blood, or only the ones that tumbled through his dreams as he slept.

"Oh, my lady," he groaned into my mouth, his voice taking that unfortunate moment to squeak upward. "My lady, I—"

"James," the king said sharply, "what is this?"

The boy jerked away from me, breathing hard and standing uncertainly to one side as he waited for his father's reproach.

"Father," he began. "Forgive me, Father, but—"

"Go," Charles said. "Leave us."

His head hanging more with relief than shame, Monmouth hurried away, leaving me alone with the king. Here in the shadows of the staircase, he was silhouetted with the light behind him, and I could not see his expression to judge his humor. How long had he been standing there? I wondered. How much had he seen of me and his son, or had he been watching, rather than seeing?

"Sir," I said softly, still pressed against the wall. I tipped my head back, my lips parted in invitation, and shifted my legs restlessly against one another.

Without a word he was on me, hoisting my skirts high and entering me without any prelude. I was already ripe with wanting, and the edge of his anger made him take me so fast and hard against the wall that he lifted my feet from the floor, there within hearing of the sounds of the dancing and the servants and the laughter of his courtiers. He shuddered when he spent, his pleasure so great it racked his body, while I bit his shoulder in my passion, my teeth leaving a half ring of bruises on his skin through the heavy broacaille of his coat.

"How was he?" he asked afterward as he fastened his breeches.

"Not you." I smiled as I let my skirts fall, relishing the sensation of his royal seed on my thighs, no matter with whom I danced this night.

"As it should be, Barbara," he said, and offered me his arm. "Now take care not to forget it."

# Chapter Fifteen

"You are pleased with the painting, Master Lely?" I asked, my excitement growing as the artist led his assistants into my rooms. "You like it?"

The two assistants carried the picture between them with great care, taking it to stand before the tall windows that overlooked King Street, where the light would be best. Framed and ready to be presented to the king as my gift to him for his thirty-third birthday at the end of the month, the painting was still covered for transporting, its face wrapped in a protective cloth like a bride with her beauty hidden behind a veil.

"My lady, I cannot recall being more content with any picture," the artist said proudly. "But then, how could it not be a masterpiece, with such a beautiful subject as yourself? My Lady Castlemaine, my muse?"

"Oh, pish, Master Lely, we both know that's idle nonsense," I declared, coming to stand before the two assistants. "The real proof's in the picture itself. Enough waiting, if you please! Show it to me properly, before I come pull that wretched cloth away myself."

The artist nodded cheerfully, by now accustomed to my ways after so many sittings together. We understood one another well: he claimed to be so inspired by my beauty that he'd begun putting my famously languid eyes on the face of every other woman's portrait he painted. For my part, I favored him like no other artist with my custom, seeking to have my likeness preserved by his paintings and the engravings he printed and sold from them. But this portrait—ah, this portrait had been a true collaboration, and would do far more than that for us both.

"As you wish, my lady," he said, unfastening the cords that held the wrapping in place himself. "If you do not agree that this is a most rare and wondrous painting, my lady, then I'll throw down my brushes in despair."

"Show me, then," I ordered. "Show me."

He smiled, and bowed, and threw back the cloth like a curtain being drawn from a stage. I gasped and pressed my hands over my mouth in amazement. It *was* rare and wondrous, a work of beauty and of genius, too.

It was a dual portrait, of me supporting my little son Charles beside me, and so tenderly drawn that it brought tears to my eyes. At Master Lely's suggestion, we'd agreed to copy the same composition of mother and child that had been so prevalent among the old Italian painters like Raphael, with me seated and turned to hold my son—a pose only used to show the Madonna with the infant Christ. Likewise I'd purposefully left off my jewels and rich silks, and dressed myself more simply in a loose red robe to signify the Virgin Mother's passion, draped with a blue cloak to show her role as Queen of Heaven. My head was demurely covered, my hair parted simply in the middle of my forehead; there was no mistaking that I was again with child, too, the eternal Mother. Even my son was painted in the tradition of the young Savior, naked save a white cloth around his loins, and his downy cheek pressed lovingly to my forehead.

It was a beautiful painting, yes, but also a scandalous one. To show me as the Virgin and Charles's bastard son as the infant Jesus would surely shock a good many persons. And yet as full of irony as it was, in a way the allegory made perfect sense. Wasn't Charles the leader of the Anglican church, God's own representative here on earth? And wasn't I wed to another man who'd never fathered any children of his own with me, much as Mary had been with Joseph?

I was sure that Charles would see all this, and more as well. He'd

see the picture of me with our first son and great with our next as testimony not only to my devotion to him but to his own potency. Our
son was the perfect image of him, with his dark eyes and black curling
hair, undeniable proof that no matter if the queen proved barren, his
progeny would continue on this earth. It was also a composition in
the Romish tradition, for no Anglican worshipped the Holy Mother
as feverishly as the papists.

I'd noted well that the one thing about the queen that continued to impress Charles was her self-conscious piety; she attended
to her services and prayer as many as three or four times a day—
as good a way as any for passing her time, I suppose, considering how little the king spent with her. His mother was a fervid
French Catholic as well, and had tried hard to woo her children
to the faith, with the result that I knew Charles continued to have
well-hidden leanings in that direction. As it was, he encouraged
the most Romish side of the Anglican church, with music, singing,
and art within the churches, and he stunned many of his subjects
by kneeling to take the Sacrament. Therefore to intrigue and please
him the more, I'd begun taking private instruction from a noted
Jesuit whom Arlington had recommended to me, with the hope of
eventual conversion. This painting was meant as a sign to Charles
of the seriousness of my intention, another way of signifying how
closely we two were bound.

"You *are* pleased, my lady?" the artist asked with a touch of anxi-
ety as he misread my silent appreciation of the picture. "You still believe it will make a suitable gift for His Majesty?"

I smiled and clapped my jewel-covered hands in appreciation. "I
am more pleased, Master Lely," I said, "more delighted, more overjoyed by this picture than you can ever, ever know. His Majesty will
appreciate it as no other gift."

He bowed again with clear relief, and I looked back once again
at the painting. It was an excellent likeness, a gift only I could offer to
Charles, a tribute to him as king, to me as his mistress and mother of
his children, and to Master Lely's talent. But most of all, it would set
all of London talking in horrified, scandalized whispers.

My smile widened, for I was pleased and content. For what more, really, could I ever hope to ask?

In June, after a year of Clarendon's shilly-shallying, I was finally granted a warrant as Lady of the Bedchamber to the queen. I was permitted a higher status within the court and granted the negligible income that came with the position. Most important, I was formally allowed to have lodgings in the palace—which, of course, I'd already had for some time, thanks to the king's insistence.

There was never really any question of me performing many actual services for the queen. The primary role of a Lady of the Bedchamber was to keep company with the queen, and, in theory if not practice, to be ready to guard her honor. While I took my appointed turns— divided among a dozen or so of us, all peeresses—accompanying her to her chapel, meals, and other events within the palace, the queen had no more wish for me to be in her intimate company than I did desire to be there. She neither acknowledged my position with her husband, nor took note of the fact that I was great with his child. Nor did I taunt her with it, or mention Charles's name in any but the most general way. In every way that mattered, I'd won. I could be gracious. Thus I held the title with little of the responsibility: a solution, I believe, that satisfied us both.

But this triumph for me was swallowed up by a much larger misfortune at the same time. Charles had labored long on persuading Parliament to pass his Declaration of Indulgence, softening Clarendon's restrictions against religious dissenters and keeping his own promises made through the Declaration of Breda. Yet to Charles's irritation, Clarendon had fought back, marshaling support against the declaration. Clarendon encouraged the malcontents within Parliament who felt that Charles was a spendthrift king, squandering too much of the country's resources on his own pleasures.

It was obvious to all that Clarendon meant such charges as a direct attack at me, and to a lesser extent at the gentlemen like Arlington, Bristol, and Buckingham who shared the same views of tolerance. I was painted worse than the Great Whore of Babylon, leading the king by his cock to his doom and the country with him. I was portrayed by my rivals and in the newssheets as avaricious and grasping and a cross-tempered shrew, and though these slanders infuriated the king, there was little he could do to counter them.

Worst of all, Clarendon's supporters in Parliament made the passage of the declaration contingent upon the king's funds voted for maintaining the court. By doing so, they effectively refused to give him money on which to live unless he withdrew the declaration. The days of an English king being free to rule as he chose and not be choked and tripped by the mean-spirited, small men in Parliament had died with Charles's father. Humiliated, Charles was forced to agree to their terms and withdraw the declaration.

Such a disaster made for a black, ill-tempered June, turned worse when Lord Bristol foolishly attempted to remove Clarendon from office. The articles of impeachment against the chancellor were too hastily drawn up and filled with illogical holes, so that the judges dismissed the case as having no merit or cause of treason, and further stated that Bristol had overstepped, for one peer could not legally impeach another. Bristol was banished for his behavior, and not only did this ugly scandal show the king and my political friends in an unfortunate light, but it also served to make Clarendon's position stronger than ever.

Quite naturally, such unpleasantness put the king in the foulest of humors, his customary good nature turning dark and disgruntled. The pleasure he'd had in his birthday celebration—and in the picture I'd given him—was soon forgotten. He resented Parliament's refusal, and he rankled at how Clarendon continued to treat him like an overbearing governor treats an obstreperous pupil. Not even I could coax him from his unhappiness, and the summer stretched before us as long indeed.

Worse was to come, as it always seems to do. My Wilson, that most excellent spy, was the first to alert me of the whispers around the court. A group of gentlemen, led by my own duplicitous cousin Buckingham, had decided upon a plan to cheer the king and likewise promote their own causes. They'd plotted to replace me in the king's bed with a more malleable candidate of their own, the luscious Frances Stuart.

As can be imagined, I railed soundly against the ungrateful scoundrels who'd schemed against me in such a fashion. I could scarce believe that these gentlemen whose acquaintance I'd fostered would toss me over with such ease, or that they believed the king would show so little loyalty or regard toward me, especially now that I was once again swollen with his child.

But soon my temper cooled, and I began to plan my defense. I'd no intention of stepping quietly aside and relinquishing my power to another. Instead I would show the court my resolve as well as my cunning as I dealt with this sponsored rival, and prove I'd still a place not only in Charles's bed but in his life, and his heart.

It was a gamble, yes, but in this game I knew I held all the winning cards.

I watched the house of cards grow and grow, each layer of the triangular tower built at the risk of toppling all those beneath it to the floor of my parlor.

"If you add another, my dear," I said, "then it's sure to fall beneath its own weight."

"No, no, it won't," said Frances Stuart in a breathless whisper, afraid to scatter her precious tower by a breath of her own wind. "I've done this endless times, my lady, and I know just how to place the cards."

"Indeed," I murmured, thoroughly bored. I'd cultivated Frances all this summer, and the girl was so simpleminded that it had been easy enough to win her trust. Several times I'd even had her company in my bed—a not uncommon diversion among those of us at court who occasionally wearied of gentlemen—where she'd shown a placid aptitude for such games.

The real trial for me was determining how to survive the tedium of Frances's confidence once it was mine. Even I had to admit that she was as pretty a girl as had ever come to court, with her golden blond hair, straight dark brows, and tiny bud of a mouth, and having been raised at the French court, she had a rare gift for dressing herself handsomely.

But in her manner she was more like a child of ten than a maid of honor of fifteen. Her attempts at conversation were full of pointless exclamations and other foolishness, and she delighted in conjurers' tricks and card houses like this one. It was most telling that the gentleman whose company she best enjoyed was Monmouth, simply because he could walk on his hands like a juggler to amuse her.

Yet there was no doubt that Charles was infatuated with her empty-headed self. He would treat her like a doll, feeding her sweetmeats and kissing her with great fondness in full sight of everyone else. She accepted his attentions as docile as a sheep, until he tried to press home his advantage. Surely this was the most foolish part of her entire foolish self: she clung to her virginity like it was made of purest gold, and refused outright every offer Charles made to her. I was certain that if she'd finally granted him the last favor, he would have been done with her within a week. But because she kept him dandling like this, he continued his fascination with what was forbidden.

Not, of course, that I'd encourage her to let him take her. I hadn't tolerated her all this time to turn him over to my rival so easily as that.

"There now, my lady," she said, placing another pair of cards with the utmost care. "There, there, see how it stands!"

"Yes, I see," I said, and didn't bother to cover my yawn of indifference. I slumped down lower on the cushions of my daybed, striving to find a more comfortable position. I was in the dwindling weeks of this pregnancy, and on warm days such as this one it was more and more difficult to remain awake late in the afternoon, even if I didn't have Frances's company as a soporific. "How marvelous."

But my little daughter, Anne, was not so jaded, toddling over to stand closer to watch the tower grow with shining eyes.

"More?" she asked with real hope. "More?"

Frances pressed her finger across her lips to silence Anne, and slowly added another row to the tower.

"There, Lady Anne," she exclaimed in a proud whisper. "*There* is more."

But my delighted daughter failed to comprehend the impermanence of towers made from playing cards, and without a thought for the consequences clapped her pudgy hands together with applause. That was all the breeze that was necessary to destroy the delicate structure, and the whole careful tower collapsed in a shuffle of cards across the tea table and the floor.

Anne's face crumpled with horror. "Oh, no!" she wailed. "All gone!"

"We can build another, Lady Anne," Frances said, dropping to her hands and knees to crawl beneath the table to retrieve the scattered cards. "I promise. I'll make one that's even taller."

But Anne was inconsolable, her eyes squeezed shut and her arms held out from her sides as her wailing increased so quickly that I put my hands over my ears and called for the nursery maid to take her away.

"You didn't have to send her off," Frances said sadly as Anne was carried back to the nursery, her indignant cries still echoing in my parlor. "She would have stopped once I'd begun another house."

"I'm not sure I would have survived so long as that," I said wearily. "Besides, she needed tending."

"Yes, my lady," Frances said, methodically turning the cards in her hand so they all faced the same direction. "As you wish."

"As I do," I said idly, glancing down at the cards in her hands. "Have you ever noticed how much the kings on pasteboard cards look like His Majesty?"

Almost guiltily, she stared down at the cards as if seeing them for the first time. The printed kings in red and black ink did in fact strongly resemble Charles, complete with the curling dark mustache; I'd remarked it from the first time I'd met him.

"How—how *curious*," she said. "I did not notice."

Silly, empty-headed goose! "Then perhaps you haven't noticed, either, how much your beauty pleases the king."

She blushed furiously. "I wouldn't know, my lady, not as you."

"Well, you *should*," I said. "He kisses you and fondles you before us all often enough."

"Yes, my lady." She drew in her small pink mouth even more tightly. "He says he likes it."

"Do you?"

Her eyes widened. "Oh, yes, my lady."

"Yes." I smiled and tipped my head back, my eyes heavy-lidded as I studied her, the skittery innocent. It amused me to speak so plainly to her like this. Ah, what mischief I'd already tasted with Lord Chesterfield when I'd been her age!

"You are wise to guard yourself further, Miss Stuart," I said softly, crossing my ankles in white satin mules with high red heels. "As pleasant as it is to kiss His Majesty, it's a hundred times better to lie with him. A *thousand* times. And once you begin, you will never, *ever* wish to stop."

"My resolve is never to lie with him and risk shame and ruin. I've pledged my honor before God." She swallowed, a single convulsive clutching of her slender white throat. "You are kind to warn me, my lady."

"Oh, yes, I'm *most* kind," I said, laughing softly at that. "At least I am to those I like."

She smiled uncertainly and glanced back toward the door. "I do believe I hear Lady Anne weeping still, my lady. If you wish, I could go to her, and calm her, and see if—oh, Your Majesty!"

She dropped into a deep curtsey as Charles joined us, several of his small dogs trotting along with him. He often came by my rooms at this time of day, after he'd played tennis and before he returned to his more formal duties at the council table, to visit both me and the babes. If he'd heard that Frances was here as well, then I suspected he'd have made an even greater effort to come a-calling. Perhaps he had; he certainly didn't seem surprised to see her with me. He smiled down at her, his desire almost laughably apparent, then remembered to come to me first where I lay on the daybed, bending to kiss me while the long curls of his periwig fell on either side of my face.

"How good of you to come see *me,* sir," I said, and laughed softly to show I understood him all too well. Two of his dogs had begun sniffing and licking the third one's bottom, the plumed tails wagging happily on all three: as proper a metaphor for this little scene as ever could be imagined. "You've just missed Lady Anne."

"I was making card castles for her, sir," Frances said eagerly, as if to explain her own reasons for being in my rooms. "But they fell—they always do—and then she would not stop weeping, and Her Ladyship had to send her away with her maid."

"Poor little duck," Charles said with genuine fondness for our daughter. "She doesn't yet understand that whatever is raised to giddy height must in time inevitably fall."

"A woeful, sorry truth indeed for all young ladies to learn, sir," I murmured with the exact degree of melancholy. At once Charles caught my meaning, and laughed, while Frances, unsurprisingly, did not.

"It's in the set of the cards, my lady," she said earnestly. "If I don't set them properly, then they will always collapse beneath any stress or force."

"Ah, so that's the secret," I said. "To lavish the greatest care on the *erection* of the tower, or risk suffering the devastation of an untoward collapse."

That made the king laugh even harder, while Frances only stared wide-eyed and unaware.

"Yes, my lady," she said uneasily, for my words had made only the most obvious sense to her. "If you wish, my lady, I could go to the nursery, and if Lady Anne is recovered, I could bring her back to us."

"You needn't go, my dear," Charles protested. "We like your company."

"Oh, let her flee if she wishes," I said with a languid wave of my hand. "She's built enough towers for one day. Come, Frances, a kiss before you leave."

It was common for ladies at court to kiss one another's cheeks in parting, and my friendship with Frances was sufficient that she thought nothing of my request for such a salute. Dutifully she came forward and bent over me, her lips pursed. I slipped my hand into her hair to cradle the back of her head, and guided her lips not to my cheek but to my own mouth. I kissed her, coaxing those tight little lips to soften and relax and part for me, and dipped my tongue within to touch hers, fleeting gentle, before I drew back. Her eyes were startled, but not alarmed. Her breathing quickened, and lightly I patted her cheek to calm her.

"Watch yourself, my dear, and come back to me tomorrow whenever you are free," I said. She'd been sweet to kiss and obligingly docile; no wonder the gentlemen all fought for the privilege. "Now go, we won't keep you longer."

"What of my kiss, eh?" Charles demanded, and I heard the roughness in his voice that showed he'd enjoyed my little indulgence exactly as I'd hoped. "I won't let you go until you grant one to me."

Without hesitation, Frances stepped forward to where he was sitting and let him kiss her, too. She might claim to enjoy his attention, but she stood still and stiff as a piece of wooden figure while he did his best to rouse her to a passion. At last he broke away, and she curtseyed.

"Good day, sir," she said. "Good day, my lady."

She backed from the room as was exactly proper, neither hurrying nor lingering as she closed the door after herself, and her steps in the hall were equally measured, and remarkable for it. It was not that she was so cold, I think, but stupidly innocent, or rather innocently stupid.

"Are you in the habit of doing that?" Charles asked, scarce waiting until the door was shut.

"Doing what, sir?" I asked, my arm languidly over my head as I lay back against the daybed's cushions.

"Kissing her," he said, the two words crackling between us.

"Oh, that." I yawned, feigning indifference. "She's quite sweet that way. But then, you should know, yes?"

"For God's sake, Barbara, have you any notion of what that does to me, watching you with her like that?"

I smiled wickedly. "Tell me, sir. I'd like to hear."

He leaned forward in his chair, his elbows on his knees. "Have you dallied further with her? Is that her trick—that she prefers Sapphic love to men?"

"Oh, I shouldn't tell," I teased. "Lovers' secrets."

"Barbara," he said impatiently. "You know I don't care where you venture, so long as you don't shout it about the town."

"Hah," I said, my eyes narrowed at that bit of nonsense. Only recently poor Harry Jermyn had been temporarily banished from Whitehall on some trumpery that I was certain had more to do with his attentions toward me than any real sin. "Then pray tell why you've sent gentlemen from court simply because they dared to speak to me?"

"Only if they've crossed me in other ways, or have slandered you," he countered, his gaze falling lower, to my breasts. "You well know I have no boundaries to my loyalty to you, just as you do mine. Have you taken the girl into your bed?"

I crossed my ankles anew, letting my smock slip higher over my bare legs. Because it was warm, and I'd grown so large, I wore only the lightest lawn bed-gown over my smock. I wasn't shy about the great swell of my belly through the linen, or how the nipples of my heavy breasts jutted forward, already dark and ripe for the greedy lips of my coming child. I knew from my earlier babes that Charles was fascinated by the fertile luxuriance of my changed body, undeniable proof of his own potent virility.

"You'll never have her," I said softly, arching my back restlessly against the pillows. "She's a papist, you know, and she's pledged God to remain chaste as a nun in a convent until she weds. All of Buckingham's schemes won't change that."

"A pox on Buckingham's ambition." He made a small scoffing sound of disgust. "I'd rather the girl were old and fat and willing."

I laughed. "To her, you're only one more unclean adulterer, doomed to burn in hell for your many sins."

He rose, coming to stand over me. "So are you."

"So I am," I admitted, "but she trusts me because I'm not equipped to prick her saintly maidenhead."

I reached out and touched the pleated front of his breeches, finding his cock as hard as I'd expected it to be.

"So which heated you more, sir?" I sat upright on the daybed, leaning toward him. I stroked his cock gently, the way he liked, and I looked up at him from beneath my lashes. "Kissing the girl yourself, or watching me kiss her?"

He groaned, pressing his cock into my palm as he filled his hands with my breasts. "You know me too well, Barbara."

"We know one another that way," I said, raising my face to him so he could kiss me.

But he was done with kissing. "Turn around," he said, breathing hard. "Now."

I smiled with lustful anticipation as I did as I was bid. We'd used the daybed like this before, and though the midwife had urged me to cease such play so close to my time, I was too heated for caution. He caught me by the hips, and I sighed with joy as he entered me.

"No other woman can replace you, Barbara," he muttered fiercely into the back of my hair as he moved over me. "*None.*"

I set my tea-dish down hard with a clatter of porcelain on the table. "You are certain of this, Aunt?"

"I would not tell you if it were otherwise, Barbara." My namesake, Aunt Barbara, Countess of Suffolk, reached out herself to blot her napkin on the tea I'd spilled. "Take a care of my table, if you please."

"What I'll take a care of, madam, is our wretched cousin Buckingham." I pushed myself from my chair and began to pace the length of my aunt's parlor. "When is his infernal entertainment?"

"A fortnight from yesterday, at Wallingford House," she said. "Barbara, for the sake of your child, I beg you to calm yourself, and—"

"To think that he would dare invite the king *and* the queen *and* that simpleminded Frances without me," I railed furiously. "He should have included me because we are kin, *and* because of my place with the king, *and* because I'm a Lady of the Bedchamber! Any of those reasons would have been enough, and yet he has seen fit to ignore them all, and ignore me."

"Perhaps he is mindful of your state," she suggested. "More so than you are yourself, it would seem. You couldn't attend even if he had invited you. You're perilously close to your time."

"I should go and drop the babe in the middle of Buckingham's drawing room floor," I said, shaking my fist in the general direction of my cousin George's house. "*That* would make the king forget his precious little Stuart."

"Barbara, please, sit," my aunt begged. "*Sit.*"

I stopped, my hands on my hips, as determined as ever that Buckingham and his party would not succeed.

"Well, much good their entertainment will do them," I declared. "For all that, I'll be more merry than they."

And I *was*. On the same night as Buckingham's entertainment, I ordered a great dinner to be readied at my King Street house and let Charles know I'd be waiting. Before the evening at Wallingford House had progressed very far, Charles abandoned his queen, Buckingham, Miss Stuart, and the rest of the tedious company, and came to me in King Street with Lord Sandwich, where he stayed all the night long.

No one that night was more merry than we.

But though Buckingham fumed and stewed at my audacity, while Miss Stuart continued to be oblivious, it was the queen who proved most vindictive, though I do not believe her actions served to place her in a better light with the king.

In late September of that year of 1663, shortly before my twenty-third birthday, I was brought to bed of another fine son, my second boy and my third child with the king. I named him Henry, to honor Charles's much-lamented youngest brother, the Duke of Gloucester. Those of mean intent crowed that it was the name of the babe's true father, Harry Jermyn, which was laughable indeed; I did enjoy Harry's company, but given his modest constitution, I doubt very much his seed could ever have muscled aside that of the king's in planting a child. Charles knew that Henry was his, and anyone who saw the babe at once remarked on his likeness.

He wrote to congratulate me immediately, and promised to come to me in London as soon as he could. As was his habit, he was away with a select group of courtiers on his summer progress through the countryside, traveling through Badminton, Cirencester, Cornbury— the country home of Clarendon, who'd invited the progress as his guests, the wily old rascal—and finally Oxford, where the king was meeting with the various scholars and students. Ordinarily I would have been with Charles on this progress, but he'd forbidden it this year for the sake of my safety and the coming babe's.

Of course the queen had refused to acknowledge that I'd been with child even as I'd attended her, let alone that I'd given birth to an-other lusty, bawling son by the king. I'd laughed over her willful, stub-born ignorance with the other Ladies of the Bedchamber, wondering aloud how she could overlook my enormous girth, as in the last days I'd had to squeeze myself sideways into the pew of her chapel.

Yet two days after I'd given birth, I was forced to realize the depth of the queen's Iberian cruelty. Her order came to me while I still lay abed. She wished to journey to Oxford that day to join the king, and she wished me to attend her. Because the weather was still so mild, she would ride not in a carriage but on horseback. She expected all her ladies—including me—to do likewise. Were I to refuse her order, I could consider myself dismissed from her household.

I knew she planned to be rid of me this way. I refused to give her that satisfaction. Against the protests of Wilson and my midwife, I rose and had myself laced in tight enough to wear a riding habit, and joined the queen's party as I'd been ordered. She was stunned to see me, her small, dark face sour with displeasure at once again being so outplayed by me.

The ride was an agony far worse than little Henry's birth had been, and there were times when I feared I'd fall from my horse, from dizziness and weakness and pain. But my determination and resolve to confound the queen gave me strength, and I was able to ride the entire distance, joining the rest of the royal party in Oxford.

When Charles learned of what his queen had ordered, he was fu-rious with her for treating me so. He came at once to my bed, and stayed with me instead of his wife. As compensation for my suffering, as well as in honor of the new babe, he gave me a splendid set of pearl cuffs.

The unhappy queen was sent back to Tunbridge Wells, in the ever-dwindling hope that the waters there would assist her in conceiving a child.

With the king at my side, I returned with great cheer to London.

"You've done it, then, Barbara?" Sir Charles Berkeley, newly made Viscount Fitzhardinge by the king, lowered his voice to a careful whisper as if he suspected spies in my own bedchamber. "This is no teasing jest, but truth?"

"I'd not jest of such a matter," I said, critically considering my reflection in the glass on my dressing table. On the tip of my finger was poised a tiny black taffeta patch in the shape of a crescent moon, ready with a dot of sticking gum to apply wherever I chose on my face. "I'd thought you'd wish to hear it from me first."

"Thank God for that," he said, swirling the sweet canary in his glass. "Have you told His Majesty?"

"Of course." I puffed out my cheeks to smooth my skin and placed the little moon to the left corner of my lips: a witty small accent, I thought. Perhaps another—a sun, a diamond, or a heart—beside my eye?

"Well, then, what did he say?" he prompted. "You can't drop such a declaration upon me without any explanation!"

"Oh, my lord, don't turn tedious." In truth, he already was, and I was beginning to question why I'd asked him here in the first place. Lord Fitzhardinge was escorting me to tonight's ball, one of many for the Christmas season, and if he'd come here to King Street earlier than was necessary, what of it? We'd been friends long enough for that, and he was a friend of the king's since the dark days in Brussels. He'd always supported me against Clarendon, and indulged me considerably as the Keeper of the King's Privy Purse. Besides, I'd always judged him a handsome gentleman with a sharp, appealing cleverness to him, and we'd found a convenient way to pass the idle hour, drinking canary, plotting politics, and swiving in the genial way of old acquaintances.

"I'm not being tedious, Barbara, only practical," he said. "I cannot fathom what His Majesty said when you told him you'd converted to the papists."

"Oh, yes, you can," I said, turning in my chair to look at him more squarely. "He said I should do whatever pleased me. He said he didn't care what I did with my soul, so long as he could still have sway over my body."

I thought Fitzhardinge would laugh, but he didn't. "That is all?" he asked earnestly. "Not a word for the consequences?"

"Not a breath," I said. "Though he has already promised me a small oratory of my own, decorated as I please, for my reflections and worship. Should I add another patch?"

"No, no, you're perfectly lovely as you are," he said, not wanting to be distracted. "Don't you realize how much talk this will cause? The queen will believe you're mocking her own piety, Clarendon will fear you'll win His Majesty over to the pope, and the whole of Parliament will heartily wish you away from London and to Rome."

"I think a tiny patch, a heart, beside my eye." I turned back to the glass, sorting through the little box of patches before me. "I chose to convert because I knew it would please the king, and his is the only opinion that matters to me."

"But you just said he didn't—"

"Oh, he cares," I said with great confidence, for I'd considered this well. I knew Charles, perhaps better than anyone else. "He cares very much. He just can't say so, not as head of the Anglicans. He's not about to toss over his crown just to be able to hear a Latin Mass, the way the Duke of York has done. Why else do you think he was so pleased that I'd had myself painted as the Virgin Mother last summer?"

"I believed it simply to be another way you sought attention," he said, "just as in this."

"Cynic," I said mildly. The portrait of me in the virginal pose with my son had caused an enormous outcry that had been most gratifying. "But you'll see. When the king is on his deathbed, he'll take last rites from a Romish priest, and I mean to go to heaven with him."

"More likely Romish hell," he scoffed, emptying his glass.

"Perhaps," I said, carefully placing the second patch. "But at least he'll know I'll be with him. And if with one simple act I can please the king and anger Clarendon, why, what is better than that?"

I shrugged out of the short bed-gown I'd used to protect my gold silk gown while I'd finished painting my face, and as I rose, I tossed it onto the rumpled bed behind me. "Shall we go, my lord?"

Swiftly he came to stand behind me, one hand at my waist while with the other he drew aside my carefully arranged curls to kiss the side of my throat.

"What's your haste, Barbara?" he whispered eagerly, striving to pull me close. "We could tarry here another hour or so, and none would be the wiser."

"None but I," I said, easing free. I'd been right before: he *had* grown tedious. "Now come. I don't like to keep His Majesty waiting any longer than I must."

My conversion to the Roman Catholic faith did in fact cause much talk and more consternation among the court, and the country, through Christmas and Twelfth Night and well beyond. The queen and her priests were shocked, even appalled. The French and Spanish ambassadors began to woo me in earnest, considering me more sympathetic to their countries, and willing to use my influence with the king on their behalf. Clarendon despised me even more. Charles judged it all to be a most amusing fuss, and brushed away earnest requests for him to persuade me to return to the Anglican fold. Yet it was the honest response of Bishop Stillingfleet that made me laugh outright: that if the Church of Rome had got by me no more than the Church of England had lost, then the matter was not much.

In perfect honesty, I would have to agree with him—something I seldom do with any cleric. But considering other things I'd done or said, this seemed to me a mild matter that should most interest me, and Charles, and few others. I refused to regret my choice, or wish it undone. That was not how I'd lived my life. But when later I saw the consequences of it, I did wonder, and couldn't help but think of how the cards would have fallen if I'd not chosen to wager that particular stake.

# *Chapter Sixteen*

When spring rains first begin to fall, most Englishmen will turn their heads to the skies and thank their maker for these gentle, warm drops that will nurture new crops and flowers and soften the frost-hardened earth for summer's bounty. But when those same gentle drops are magnified a millionfold, when they fail to cease, but continue day after day after day, swelling rivers and creeks and washing aside boats and houses in a torrential flood of cruel reality, why, then that same rain that was once considered so nurturing and restorative is cursed as a damaging evil, without merit or kindness.

So it was with Charles's monarchy. When first he returned to his throne, Englishmen welcomed him with cheers and flowers strewn in his path, sure that all the evils of the world would now be solved. They expected all the wrongs of the Protectorate to be righted, and further that they'd magically be granted reparation and rewards simply for agreeing to have their rightful king restored to them. They were worse than children, imagining the very streets of London would be paved with golden coins as soon as Charles returned.

Alas, such hopes were grounded not in genuine possibility but in fantastical, idle dreams that paid no heed to how matters *were*. No king could ever oblige such enormous expectations with a happy result, not even if he had the greatest treasury in the world at his disposal. My Charles was a good man, an honorable king who listened and was touched by his people's woes.

But he was also a very poor king as kings went, his throne supported by a wobbly assortment of loans from other rulers and debts he could never hope to repay, balanced atop a country that had been ravaged by civil war for an entire generation. Anyone who was dissatisfied with what they'd received, whether a farmer who'd lost his rooster to a parliamentary cavalryman or a Royalist grandee who'd sacrificed many thousands of pounds in support of the king, now grumbled at the iniquity of Charles's reign, and at him. Parliament was full of such disgruntled gentlemen, blocking his every effort to rule for the good of all. Nor could I help but see Clarendon at work, lurking and lobbying on his gout-ridden feet to pry Charles's hand from England's rudder, and steer it to his own intolerant course.

And unlike most other rulers, Charles was forced to struggle with the untidy balance of religion among his people. No matter that overbearing religious zealots had torn the country asunder before; there were plenty of others of every faith who'd learned nothing from that, except that they wished to promote their particular God to the oppression of all others.

Most frustrating to me, of course, was how the people wished the spectacle of a king and court but were loath to support the cost. They wanted England to be superior in every way to France or Spain, yet compared to the grandeur of King Louis's Versailles, Whitehall was a poor, crumbling excuse for a palace bereft of ceremony or delights. Charles could ill afford any of the outward displays of royalty, so necessary to maintain his stature with foreign countries, whether by supporting composers or artists, hosting banquets, masques, and other celebrations, maintaining a sufficient stable of blood-horses, or even by making sure that I was splendidly dressed at his side, reflecting his glory in the jewels on my person. Instead Charles was forced to grovel and beg for every farthing from Clarendon, with no relief from a tightfisted Parliament, who encouraged the people in calling their king an idle spendthrift.

They would even deny him the pleasures and comforts he found with me and our children together, and call out for him to restrict himself to the bed of the barren queen, a woman he'd wed from duty to England, not from desire or love. I gave no care to the evil slanders said or published of me—my skin was too tough for such barbs to penetrate—but I resented the sorrow it brought to Charles on my behalf and the spleen he felt toward those who'd call me whore, traitor, or even evil incarnate.

All of which is to say that by the spring of 1664, the sweet optimism that had greeted Charles at his return four years before had soured and grown darker. And though by my nature I would never turn away from a risk or a hazard, the growing discontent of the country was an uneasy burden for all of us at court and a rising challenge for my king, my lover, and me.

"Oh, come, Miss Stuart, it will be but a frolic." I took the girl's hands, intent on leading her back to my rooms. "You've been party to weddings before, and the beddings afterward. You know what sport it can be."

"I cannot say, my lady," she said with her usual prim reluctance, hanging back on my hands. "This does not seem right, to make sport of a sacrament."

"Oh, it's right, it's right," Lord Fitzhardinge said heartily, his arm around the waist of some pretty maid or other. "It's only a passing amusement, like a masque. It signifies nothing more than that."

The others in the room agreed with him and loudly echoed his urging. What had begun as a simple gathering of Charles's friends in the royal privy chamber was rapidly growing into something more. I'd concocted this pretty whimsy in the moment, something sure to entertain and distract the king on a chill night in late spring. A mock marriage between two ladies, with Frances as the chaste bride and I to play the gallant bridegroom: could there be anything more amusing?

"I do not know, my lady," Frances said, more crossly this time, as if the notion taxed her brains more than her virtue. "To play such a part—"

"Please me, Miss Stuart," Charles interrupted, his expression deceptively mild. "Do what Lady Castlemaine asks. Surely you know the peril of disappointing her."

She turned and smiled at him, all bright sunshine for his sake, the crafty little minx. "If *you* wish it, sir."

"I'll play the minister to wed this happy couple," my cousin Buckingham declared. He stepped forward, taking Frances's hand away from me, adopting a waggish, scolding manner. "Not before you're properly married, young blade."

The others around us roared with laughter, so much that I had to raise my voice to be heard.

"My bride is properly garbed, yes, but I've no suit of wedding clothes," I said, turning in the center of them with my arms outstretched. "Who'll grant me their breeches, so I might tend my fair bride as she deserves?"

A half dozen gentlemen called out offers to share their clothes with me, with several at once beginning to unbutton their breeches to display their accommodating eagerness.

"I'll share my wardrobe with you, young sir," Charles called. "I wouldn't want you to shame yourself before your lady. Come, I'll lead you there myself, to best advise your choices, while we leave the bride to her handmaidens."

That made everyone laugh anew, for in that merry group Frances was likely the only one still a maiden of any sort. As the other women gathered gaily around Frances, I let the king lead me back through his chambers to his wardrobe, the other gentlemen trooping after us. As can be imagined, the king's closet was a vast chamber toward the end of his rooms, with a multitude of cupboards, shelves, and chests to hold his clothes, from the rich, embroidered robes, trimmed in ermine, that were reserved for ceremonial occasions such as opening Parliament, to the simple linen shirts and dark breeches he wore for bowling on the lawn or playing tennis. Such lavish excess made me recall the days when we'd first met in Brussels, when he'd but a single sad, worn suit of clothes to his name. How much our fortunes had changed since then!

With his manservants hovering anxiously, Charles himself threw open a chest.

"Here now, greenhorn, we'll see you outfitted," he said, tossing a shirt to me. "Large for a stripling like you, but it will suffice for now."

I caught the shirt. "When can I ever hope to match your measure of manhood, sir?"

"Never, if I've anything to say about it." The others laughed, and Charles grinned roguishly. "Now you fellows leave the poor lad here with me to dress. He's shy enough without your catcalls to wither his courage."

Disappointed, the gentlemen left me alone with the king.

"Here now, sir, unlace me," I said, turning my back to him. "I know you can do that faster than any lady's maid."

"I can." Deftly Charles picked apart the bowed knot at the top of my gown's lacing and tugged it through the eyelets, then did the same for my stays.

"Experience does breed confidence, sir," I said breathlessly as I shrugged myself free of my bodice and my stays after that. I was rather touched by his insistence that they not see me undress, considering how we both realized a good number of those same gentlemen had known me far more intimately than that. "And in our case, a good many children as well."

He laughed as I pulled my smock over my head and stepped free of my gown and petticoats, standing before him in only my stockings, garters, and high-heeled shoes. My waist was thickening and my breasts full, for I was once again with child. This would be my fourth child, with little Henry scarce six months old. But considering how the king himself was the reason that I was more often in this condition than not, I remained confident in my beauty regardless.

"My shirt, if you please," I said, smiling wickedly as I held out my hand.

"In a moment," he said softly, his heavy-lidded gaze studying me with relish. "How far do you mean to take this with Frances?"

"As far as she'll let me." I laughed, in truth as excited by the prospect as he. "Isn't that what most bridegrooms do?"

His eyes glittered with both desire and amusement. "Do you mean to succeed with her where I've failed?"

"I mean to try," I said. "But I expect you'll want to witness our consummation, won't you?"

"How else will it be considered a proper union?"

I laughed again, my head tipped back. "You can't know how weary I am of her simpering empty virtue."

"So am I." He reached for me, and I stepped backward, away from his hand.

"I should save myself for my bride," I said coyly. "I wouldn't wish to disappoint her."

"Don't disappoint me first."

"Hah," I said, backing farther away. "You, sir, should know the advantages of patience."

"You're a fine one to lecture me," he said, chuckling as he followed me. "As long as I've known you, Barbara, you've never demonstrated a thimbleful of patience. I'd wager fifty guineas that if I touch you now, you're already flowing dew."

"I'd not take such a vulgar wager from you, sir." I'd reached the end of my escape, bumping against the door of a tall cupboard behind me.

"And why not?" he asked, coming to stand over me. "Are you afraid you'd lose your stake?"

"No, sir," I said, looping my arms around his shoulders to kiss him. "I'm certain of it."

He took me then with pleasurable leisure, standing against the cupboard, or rather I took him, for it amounted to the same. I'd no doubt that the others in the privy chamber knew what we'd been about, too, for when we finally returned, they greeted us with calls and cheers that seemed even more raucous and untoward than earlier.

Now, and at last, I was dressed in a shirt, doublet, hat, and breeches that belonged to Charles, everything comically oversized and drooping around me. Somehow Frances had been persuaded to shed all but her smock as well, her golden curls unpinned to fall down her back. They'd even tied white ribbons into the lace that edged her smock, as a true bride would have.

With what I hoped was true swaggering male bravado, I took my place at her side while Buckingham solemnly opened a prayer book before us. In honor of the Roman faith that Frances and I now incongruously shared, my cousin had gotten a priest's cassock and an oversized crucifix from somewhere, and the sight of his most Anglican face pretending to Rome was riotously blasphemous. In the gutter of the book—held upside down, I noted—he'd even placed a pair of pinchbeck rings for us to be blessed as he intoned who knew what in reverent Latin. He was an excellent mimic and could capture anyone's voice that it pleased him to mock, and now as he imitated one of the queen's most pompous priests, there was not a person in the room who was not laughing, tears sliding down our faces.

When he'd finished, I slipped one ring on Frances's finger and she did the same to me. Her cheeks were flushed with far more excitement than I'd expected, and though she giggled like the foolish goose she was, when I leaned forward to kiss her, she kissed me back.

After that we were swept into the king's own bedchamber, a place I'd visited so many times that it felt like my own. Frances's blue eyes were round as the moon, and I wondered what manner of nonsense she'd heard did occur there—certainly much more scandalous than what was happening this night.

"Time to cut your maiden ribbons, sweetheart," Buckingham declared, now having shed his priestly role for his more usual one as Frances's pimp. "Best to do everything we can to ease that maidenhead of yours."

With a pair of oversized shears, he snipped every bow and lace on her smock, even cutting the drawstring at the neckline so she was forced to clutch the linen to her breasts to keep from displaying herself to the company. I, however, had no such qualms, cheerfully doffing my doublet, hat, and breeches, my secrets boldly apparent through the fine Holland of Charles's shirt. While the others began to sing bawdy songs, I hopped into the enormous bed beside Frances, who'd pulled the coverlet demurely up under her chin as she sat against the bolsters. Her face was so flushed, her smile so fixed, that I suspected they'd already given her strong liquor to drink for courage.

The sheets smelled familiarly of the king, and of me.

"Here's your wedding posset," Buckingham announced, thrusting a two-handled tankard into my hand. "Drink up, you two, and fortify yourselves."

I drank first of the sugary sack, then passed it to my bride, who, to my amusement, gulped it down as if it were mother's milk. If she weren't in her cups now, she would be soon after that.

"You must toss your stocking now, pet," I said kindly, slipping my arm around her shoulder. She was trembling, the little goose, whether from the posset, fear, or excitement, I couldn't say. "Whoever catches it will be next to wed, you know."

She reached under the sheets to pull off her stocking, wadding it into a ball that she hurled into the crowd. Fitzhardinge caught it, unrolling it to press the toe to his nose, then his lips, finally waving it over his head like a trophy.

"Hah, you'll not have Elizabeth Mallet," I called gleefully, naming a twelve-year-old heiress that I knew Fitzhardinge was clamoring to woo. "I've already claimed her for my cousin Rochester."

"The devil you have, my lady!" Fitzhardinge draped the stocking round his neck. "Your cousin's only seventeen. Mistress Mallet will need more from a husband than that."

That earned a chorus of scornful hoots and laughter that, of course, I couldn't help but answer.

"My cousin's an earl, Fitzhardinge, and a gentleman, which makes him already thrice the man you are," I crowed. "And at my special request, His Majesty has already given his approval of the match."

"Quiet now, both of you!" the king ordered, his voice rising so strong that all others fell silent, chastised. "We're here to see these two fairly wed, not bicker over some distant pimply children. Now kiss your bride, fair young sir."

"I'll kiss her once for you to view," I vowed, "but I'll not attempt the rest until the curtains are drawn, from fear of unmanning myself before so many virile witnesses."

The king laughed. "Fair enough," he said. "I'll draw them myself, once you seal your troth with a kiss."

I tucked my hair behind my ears so my face could plainly be seen, and gently turned Frances's face toward mine to kiss. So it was fear she felt: I could taste it on her tongue along with the posset, and I touched my palm gently to her jaw to calm her. She slid down the pillow-bier as if she were made of wax and melting, and I pursued her, leaning half over her to kiss her, much to the delight of the others. My eyes shut, I heard the scrape of the curtain rings along the metal rod, and the howling, disappointed protests of those who'd wished for more of a show.

"We'll leave them for now," the king was saying, all jovial teasing. "With such youngsters, it's best to let them fumble their way without an audience."

"Are they gone, my lady?" Frances whispered when we'd both heard the chamber door closed. With the bed-curtains drawn around us, we were snug in the shadowy bed, as if in a second room within the larger.

"For now," I said, my elbow cocked so I could rest my head on my hand beside her. "You've no reason to be frightened, you goose, not of them."

She looked a most delectable little creature, there in the shadows with her fair hair spilled out across the pillows. I understood entirely why Charles was so beguiled with her. Yet surely I'd been born a squalling infant with more wit than she showed now at sixteen, and more sense of the world as well.

"You will not . . . *consummate* me?" she asked anxiously. "I will still be a virgin, my lady?"

Delectable, yes, but her empty-headed foolishness irritated me and had no place at this court.

"With what exactly shall I do the odious deed, Frances?" I asked. "This was a mock wedding, and I your mock bridegroom with only a very mock cock to take your very real maidenhead."

"Then you will not harm me?"

"No," I said, the truth, and slipped my hand beneath the sheet to find her. "I'll only grant you the same sweet pleasures we've shared before."

She smiled then, and wriggled closer beside me. "Very well, my lady. Should I please you, too?"

But though by pleasing her I pleased myself, she fell fast asleep before she could return the favor she'd promised, her breath sweet and cloying from the surfeit of sherry. Not that I cared overmuch, for I knew what else lay ahead. I tossed back the coverlet, eased the bed-curtains apart, and padded quickly across the floor in my stocking feet and billowing man's shirt to the small door that led to the king's infamous back stairs.

This passage was ordinarily overseen by Will Chiffinch, the Page of the Bedchamber, who used it to squire in every manner of secret visitor, from actresses to couriers from King Louis. Now I'd hoped to employ Chiffinch myself to find Charles without being seen by the others still carousing in the privy chamber.

Yet as I reached for the latch, Charles himself stepped from the shadows and caught my wrist. I gasped, my heart racing from being so surprised.

"Oh, sir, how you startled me when—"

At once he pressed his hand over my lips to silence me. Drawing me with him, he went to the bed to gaze upon the sleeping girl. Her gown was rumpled and still pulled high from our earlier play, with most of her lovely young limbs and body arranged unwittingly for our full admiration, like the most wanton of antique nymphs. She was sixteen, her body unmarked by childbirth or usage, and I could not help but compare it unhappily to my own. I would be twenty-four in the autumn, a vast age for a lady in my position, and this girl before me only served to remind me of how much I'd sadly changed.

"Temptation incarnate," whispered Charles hoarsely. "She is will-ing, then?"

I looked down at Frances, my thoughts as tumbled and disor-dered as her smock. This *was* temptation, the kind of temptation of the flesh that I seldom resisted, nor wished to. The girl was the worst kind of fool to have let herself be drawn into this court, let alone this bed, and fiercely I told myself that she deserved whatever now came her way. There was also an unsavory small part of me, fed by venge-ful jealousy and regret, that did wish somehow to punish her for her unthinking sin of being younger and fresher than I was myself.

And yet, though few would believe it, I was not so hardened as that. I would not condone a rape. The little goose had trusted me, and besides, she built endless card castles for my children to topple.

"No," I whispered. "She remains intent on preserving her cursed maidenhead."

"You are certain?" he said, lust making his voice sharp. "You cannot persuade her?"

I shook my head. "She is a fool, yes, but that's not reason enough to ravish her against her will."

Roused by our whispers, Frances stirred and woke. It took but an instant for her to realize her situation, and with a small cry she started upright, frantically grabbing for the coverlet to hide her nakedness.

"Hush, Frances, be calm," I said swiftly. "You're safe, and unharmed."

"That's true, my dear," the king said with undisguised regret. He reached out to stroke her cheek, and instinctively she turned toward his caress. He had that power with women; I'd seen it far too often. "Though I warrant you're wondrous fair to look upon."

"Yes, sir," she said, her tremulous smile proof again that flattery is the surest path to a woman's ruin. "That is, thank you, sir."

I sat on the edge of the bed beside her and took her hand in mine, the way I'd done scores of times before.

"Your beauty is rare, Frances," I said, my voice coaxing velvet as I gently stroked little circles into her palm with the tips of my fingers. "So rare that you tempt the king, just as you've tempted me."

"But I cannot—"

"Hush, hush, we know of your vow," I said, soothing, coaxing, wooing her to follow my lead. "But just as you and I have discovered ways to . . . amuse one another, so it could be with His Majesty, too, the three of us together."

Now she was the one who was tempted, drawn by the same wicked novelty of it. I caught her glancing toward the king, standing there with his arms folded over his chest, so very great and manly, and I knew she'd agree.

"That is all, my lady?" she asked, her fingers twining restlessly into mine. "The same . . . amusements?"

"The same, dear Frances," I whispered, smoothing her tangled hair back from her face, her shoulders, her breasts. "Except with two of us, the pleasure will be twice as great."

Twice as great, aye, twice as great. The next morning the court spoke of nothing else but how the king had awakened between his two favorite beauties, and that the young maid of honor was a maid no more. By the next nightfall, every tavern and coffeehouse in London was full of the king's prowess, and my lubricity. By the end of the week, the French ambassadors had made sure to report the shocking tale of our latest debauchery to Louis, and the French court as well.

Yet only we three knew the truth: That though Frances Stuart left the king's bedchamber with both her vow and her maidenhead still intact, her innocence had been reduced to a tattered memory. While I would not condone him lying with her, I did it not from respect for her sacred pledge but from knowing I could never watch him love another woman in my presence. And, finally, that though I could not bear to watch him with her, I'd no such qualms about her watching me with him.

Let them talk, I thought, and with my usual brave insolence I walked beside the king through St. James's Park the next day. I wore the jewels he'd given me for all to see, a curling plume in the crown of my hat, as he kept my hand tucked fondly in the crook of his arm. Let them talk, for it would matter not to me.

But to my bitter sorrow, how soon—too soon!—I'd learn that even talk could come with a price, and a steep one at that.

By strange coincidence, that summer of 1664 the three of us ladies— the queen, Frances Stuart, and I—each sat for our portraits.

Her Majesty chose as her painter the Dutchman Jacob Huysmans, a favorite of the queen's dour Catholic circle, and with little patronage among us courtiers who aspired to a likeness with fashion and wit. As he did with so many of his ladies' portraits, Master Huysmans decided to depict the queen as a shepherdess dressed preposterously in pink-

and-white satin whilst guarding her flock: a most insipid depiction, dark and ill drawn, much like the queen herself.

Frances likewise sat for Master Huysmans, but instead of a simpering shepherdess—which would, in truth, be much to her character—she chose to dress herself as a gallant gentleman gone riding. Her fair hair was loose and fluffed like a periwig, and her woman's form covered completely by a buff leather waistcoat and breeches. One hand rested on the hilt of a sword, while the other held a military baton.

No one knew what to make of this strange ambiguity, nor did either the artist or the sitter offer any explanation for its conceit. When I first saw it, I wondered myself if it meant in some way to refer to our mock "wedding." Suffice to say that it did not serve Miss Stuart's beauty in any way, nor did even the king wish to add such a picture to his collection, which was, perhaps, given her continued reluctance with him, exactly what she'd planned all along.

As for me, I returned once again to the studio of Master Lely. I know he often protested that he could never capture my beauty, no matter how he labored, yet still I found his brush the most flattering of any, and surely the number of prints that the master's studio sold of me afterward was testimony to his talents.

This time I decided not to hide behind any role but to be shown as myself. Though I was close to my time for my fourth child, I asked Master Lely to narrow my waist for this picture as if I'd already given birth. My gaze was confident, my smile slight, as if pondering a rare secret. I wore gold silk satin, and all my favorite pearls, gifts from Charles. It was Master Lely's notion to have my hair arranged in the style of Venetian ladies of a hundred years before, in their portraits by the Italians Titian and Tintoretto. My hair was drawn up on the back of my head in a kind of coronet, then cascaded loosely down my back, and was threaded throughout with more of my pearls. I looked more regal than any queen, more an elegant consort than a concubine.

Yet most who saw this picture first noticed not my hair but the jewel at my breast: a heavy gold cross set with cabochon stones such as was worn only by French ladies and Roman Catholics.

·  ·  ·

In early September, I was brought to bed of another daughter, a pretty babe with a profusion of black curly hair like her father's. For her father, too, I named her Charlotte. She was styled with the surname Fitzroy, the traditional heraldic way of signifying her sire. (My sons Charles and Henry were likewise Fitzroys, with only my first daughter called Lady Anne Palmer, after my husband.) The birth was an easy one, and within two weeks I was entertaining once again at King Street, staging a supper for the French ambassador and his wife. Though it was my house, Charles sat at the head of my table and played the host, a distinction that was much noted.

One evening soon after that, I went to call upon the Duchess of York and her ladies at St. James's Palace. Though I'd had little use for Her Grace when she'd been lowly Anne Hyde, now that she'd been raised to Duchess of York, I'd found her more to my liking, and we'd become friends, swiving the royal brothers as we did. We'd played basset and whist for small wagers—perhaps because she was Clarendon's daughter, the duchess was tight with her funds and refused ever to play deep. Over our cards, we exchanged our share of gossip and talk of children, the way all women will do. But my lying-in with Charlotte was still sufficiently recent that I tired early, and I made my farewells before midnight.

St. James's Palace, the home of the Duke of York, lies diagonally across the park from Whitehall Palace. The way between the two is clear and pleasant, with walks and a scattering of trees for shade and beauty, as well as the new canal. Because the night was still warm as summer and the distance so short, I decided not to bother sending for my carriage, but to walk and clear my head in the evening air. For company I had Wilson, and as our linkboy my page Pompey, a young African boy whom I dressed amusingly in a jeweled satin turban to match his saffron livery.

"So tell me what you heard below, Wilson," I said as we walked, eager as always to learn how differently the servants spoke from their mistresses of the same events or persons. "What news from the House of York?"

"Little that is new, my lady," Wilson said, her regret as deep as my own that she'd been unable to gather any fresh snippets of scandal in St. James's servants' quarters. "For all that Her Grace the duchess tries to bring His Grace to heel, his nose is still up the petticoats of her newest maid of honor, the sweet-faced Miss Arabella Churchill."

"Arabella Churchill," I repeated to make sure I'd remember the name so I could in turn tell it to Charles, to amuse him with his brother's misdeeds. "Hah, the duchess could sooner rein the moon from the sky than stop her husband's cock from wandering."

"Yes, my lady," Wilson said, reaching forward to thump my page with her knuckles between his narrow shoulders. "Take care with the light there, Pompey. If Her Ladyship stumbles, you'll be the one must answer to His Majesty, you impudent rascal."

The boy turned to face us with the lantern in his hand, walking backward simply because he could, making the candlelight dance crazily across the lawns on either side of us.

"If His Majesty asks such of me," he taunted Wilson, "I'll tell him 'twas you that tripped her, you clumsy old slattern."

I laughed, no matter that it was wrong to encourage the boy's sauciness. "Enough of your wicked tongue, you little monkey," I said. "I'll thrash you properly, as you deserve, if you don't change your—"

"My Lady Castlemaine," a man's voice said curtly behind me. "A word."

I turned and found not one man but three. All were dressed in dark clothing to blur the lines between them and the night, their hats pulled low across their brows and black scarves tied across their mouths and noses to further hide their faces to me. Even thus disguised, I knew them as gentlemen: the quality of their boots and the cut of their dark clothes, combined with their costly periwigs and overall demeanor, meant that they were likely gentlemen of my acquaintance.

Nonetheless, I was not reassured.

"Pompey," I said. "The lantern, if you please."

For once obedient, the boy stepped forward, heels together as he held the lantern high. His bright turban and livery looked sadly gaudy against so much somber black, and vulnerable, too. The gentlemen did not back away from the lantern's glow; on the contrary, they crowded closer, blocking our path to either palace.

"Pray state your business, sirs," I said, making my voice as severe as I dared. I felt Wilson shrink behind me, too terrified to be of any use. "I'm expected at the palace. If I do not return soon, I'll be missed."

"No one misses a worn-out whore," the second man snarled. "Except to toss her poxed carcass on the dunghill."

The first man nodded vigorously. "Aye, with the likes of Jane Shore and other filthy offal."

"I've no reason to listen to you," I said, my heart thundering in my breast. "Stand aside, I say, and let me and my servants pass."

I tried to push my way clear of them, but they came together to stop me, jeering cruelly at my effort.

"You will stand and listen to us, you reeking papist whore," another ordered. "You've bewitched His Majesty long enough. You've bled this country for your gaming and your bastards, and you've sold English interests to Rome, and to France. You've few friends left at court, lady, and fewer still who don't damn you as the greedy, grasping *whore* that you are."

"Shall we use her as she deserves?" said the other. Without waiting for an answer, he reached out and tore the front of my cloak open, the velvet rending and the seam cutting into the back of my neck so hard I yelped with surprise and pain.

"Let me pass, I say." My voice quivered with fear as I stumbled backward, clutching together the edges of my torn cloak. "Let me *go!*"

"We decide that, not you," the first man answered. "We speak for many, lady. We want you gone, you and your litter of bastards. Leave our country and our king, else next time we won't be so kind, to you or your brats."

He stepped aside, leaving a gap for me to make my escape. I grabbed Pompey by the arm and hoped Wilson would follow, and hurried toward Whitehall as fast as I could go. I didn't dare look back from fear the men would be coming after us, for I'd no notion of what I'd do if they were.

"Go—go to the king," I told Pompey as soon as we were safely inside the palace. "Tell him what happened, and to—to come to me at once."

"His Majesty will have their heads, my lady," Wilson said, her voice returned now that we were inside. "His Majesty will see those three rogues in the stocks for frighting you, see if he doesn't."

But I'd no mind of revenge then. All I wanted was to see my children and to know that they were safe. With my tattered cloak fluttering behind me, I ran as fast as I could through the palace halls, speaking to no one and stopping for nothing until at last I reached my rooms over the hither-gate and the nursery beside them.

The room was dark, of course, the nursemaid dozing in her chair near the chimney corner and the embers glowing softly in the grate. The nursemaid rose sleepily as soon as I entered, but I waved her away.

I went to each of the two small beds in turn: Anne, as eldest, slept alone, curled on her side with one hand beneath her cheek, while Charles and Henry lay snug together like two round-bellied puppies, their lips parted for their soft baby sighs and their thick black lashes feathered over their cheeks.

Last I went to the cradle with tiny Charlotte. As I bent over her, she sensed my presence and stirred. Her eyes fluttered open, not awake, yet not asleep. I swept her from her cradle into my arms and held her tight, swaying to calm her and myself, while she made the sweet snuffling sounds that new babes make to settle themselves. At last her breathing grew calm and she relaxed back into sleep, and gently, so gently, I laid her back in her cradle, tucking her coverlet around her. I patted her tiny rounded back one last time, my eyes filling with tears, and finally returned to my own rooms.

I stood before the tall window while Wilson fussed about me, taking away the torn cloak, begging me to sit. I was shaking now, so hard I could not stop, and once the tears had begun I let them course down my cheeks unchecked. I'd known I was hated and reviled, and I could bear that, but the thought that my darling children could be made to suffer for my sake was beyond bearing. I would have to do better for them. I would have to think less of my own pleasures and more of their futures.

"Barbara!" Charles rushed toward me, his expression an odd mix of relief and anger. "Thank God you are safe."

I turned toward him and fainted in his arms.

# Chapter Seventeen

I'd never seen the Banqueting House so full of candles, nor so crowded with brilliant company, but then there'd been no such grand masque at court as this one in my lifetime, not since the old king's time thirty-five years before. The masque was in celebration of Candlemas, a holy day commemorating the purification of the Virgin Mary and the first presentation of the infant Jesus Christ to the elders in the temple, a feast said to be much favored by Her Majesty.

There were many whispers as to why exactly a barren queen should so enjoy a feast in honor of the Virgin Mother's purification after giving birth, an event that Her Majesty herself seemed doomed never to experience, but that was only the second mystery of the day. The first one was how a celebration of a joyful birth and delivery had somehow been transformed into a bellicose glorification in favor of a war with the Dutch.

The theme of the masque was to show how the various enemies of England and her king would be vanquished. As most such allegorical entertainments were, this masque was an astounding confluence of specially composed music and dances, dubious classical references, elaborate costumes and settings, and theatrical devices like small explosions and otherworldly messengers made to "fly" on ropes overhead. The spectacle of the entertainment mattered far more than its making any sense, and no one in the audience expected more.

Like every other fair lady at the court, I took part in the masque.

I was granted the prominent role as Venus (who else could I have played, I ask you?), determined to urge my lover Mars to glory on the field of battle. My costume was described as "antique," though in style it looked back only so far as the masques designed long ago for the Queen Mother and the king's father. It featured a low, tight bodice and full sleeves sewn over with sparkling sequins, a tall feathered helmet, and short breeches beneath a shorter skirt, the better to display my legs in golden stockings. Once it was known that I would wear breeches in my costume, all the other ladies had clamored for the same, eager for this excuse to show their own limbs to advantage. First among them was Frances Stuart: a year older at seventeen, negligibly wiser and markedly taller, but still no more willing to let the king have what he most wished. Not that I cared overmuch for their squabbling. The king had already declared I'd the most elegant legs of any lady at court, and I welcomed the chance to shame any rival, even the ever-foolish Frances.

I did, too, before an audience filled with courtiers, ambassadors, and other visitors from abroad. The Banqueting House, where such masques had always been held, back to the time of the old king, was close with such a crowd, the scores of candles necessary to light our production giving off more heat as well, but I didn't care. The crowd admired me, and the candles made my jewels sparkle all the more. As the music swelled one final time, I held my hands gracefully out from my sides, turned twice with surpassing grace, and sank into my final bow. Applause burst around us in a wave, and the king himself came to raise me up.

"Handsomely done, Barbara, well done indeed," he said, handing me a glass of wine to refresh myself. Once the scenery and extra candles of the masque's makeshift stage were cleared away, he'd have to open the night's ball by dancing with the queen, but for these few moments he chose to be with me. "If that didn't persuade the last malcontents to challenge the Dutch, then nothing shall."

I laughed and kissed him. "I doubt that idle trumpery persuaded anyone to so much as rise from bed, let alone go to war."

"Now you sound like Clarendon himself," Charles said and took my arm. "Walk with me, my dear."

I curled my fingers into his and let him lead me into one of the hallways, the curled plume on my helmet bobbing as I walked. No one would follow or join us; they knew to respect the king's privacy when he was with me. In the past, I would have expected him to find us some shadowed corner, press me against a convenient wall, and press home a satisfying advantage. But now his mind was full of other, more weighty matters, and he was as likely to use me as an excuse to escape the rest of the court to talk as for a quick jig beneath my skirts.

"You've no right to put me in with Clarendon, sir," I protested as we walked. "It's not that I believe the Dutch to be right, but that I cannot see how any war can be of benefit to England now. The country's scarce recovered from Cromwell's foolishnesses."

"But this is different, Barbara," Charles said confidently. "This will only help England."

"'Only help,'" I repeated, unconvinced. For months it seemed that the gentlemen would speak of nothing else but the glories to be gained by war, boasting and strutting about and rattling their swords in a most tedious fashion. Even the gentlemen who met regularly at King Street—Arlington, Fitzhardinge, Coventry, Admiral Lord Sandwich, of course, and the others—spoke of little but which members they'd persuaded over to the cause of war, or who had promised to vote funds for another new warship. "Is there anything more costly to a country than a war?"

"But this war would be fought at sea, not on English soil," Charles protested, warming to his argument. "Our navy is unrivaled, Barbara. Parliament has always supported the navy without question, granting them all the funds they've required for ships and sailors. You should hear my brother speak of what they've accomplished at Portsmouth this last year, or better yet, go down there with me to see for yourself. Then you'd be convinced."

"Oh, yes, smelly boats and noisy cannons," I said dryly. "How fascinating. Though I suppose the handsome sailor boys scampering up and down the rigging would be a fair sight to see. Until you must tell their mamas and sweethearts that they've died so you could feel superior to the Prince of Orange."

He stopped beside a window, gazing out across the snow-covered park and London beyond, the moon and the stars bright in the night sky over the sleeping city. It was hard to imagine a more peaceful scene, or one more at odds with the kind of carnage and destruction he was proposing.

"I'd never start a war for so idle a reason, my dear," he said softly. "I'd not do that to my people. But the Dutch can't be allowed to go on like they have, attacking English merchant ships as they please and plundering our colonies and forts in Africa, the Indies, America—that kind of impunity must be stopped, Barbara, before they sail their ships up the very Thames."

"That *would* be wrong." I sighed and slipped my hands inside his doublet. Beneath my palm I felt his heartbeat, strong and sure, and yet a reminder, too, of how tenuous and fragile life could be. "But I cannot help but think of how we both lost our fathers to war, and how close you, too, came to being killed, again and again, before you'd a chance to reach your prime. What if you'd perished before I'd met you? What would my life have been without you in it?"

He smiled. "Mine wouldn't have been much without you, either, and considerably shorter as well."

"I'm not jesting, sir," I said softly, drawing him closer. "Life is full of peril. For women, it's childbirth, but for men, it's war. I know as king you'll not face the guns yourself, but when I think of our little sons—"

"My dear, they're still in the nursery," he said fondly. "They're in no danger."

"Not now, no," I admitted. "But their world, their lives, are so uncertain."

"But this will help make their lives more certain," he insisted. "Not only will England be stronger for standing up to the Dutch, but their country will feel happier for it. You'll see. A few victories and London will feel like the old days."

By the "old days," I knew he now no longer meant his father's reign but those first glorious months when he was new returned from exile, and it seemed his people could not lavish enough love and regard upon him. It had only been five years since he'd returned to London, yet already it seemed further in the past. That kind of boundless joy hadn't been the temper of the country for a long time now; I'd only to think of the hatred that washed around me to understand that. Since I'd been attacked in the park by the disguised gentlemen—who of course had never been identified or punished—I'd become more cautious of my own safety and no longer went abroad unattended. If challenging the Dutch at sea could change that ill will for the better, then I could scarce find fault.

"What of France and Spain?" I asked, though I must admit that this question was one of strictest curiosity. The careful balance between our four great countries—England, France, Holland, and Spain—was something that endlessly concerned a great many wise heads in Europe. If the English went to war with the Dutch, then the French and the Spanish worried over whose side they should take, or more perplexing, whose side the other would choose as well.

Because of such concerns, both the Spanish and the French ambassadors in London pursued me, hoping in return I'd offer some hint of Charles's inclinations, or better yet that I'd persuade him in their individual favor. I made sure to receive my garnish for these, my "incense." The ambassadors lavished me with costly gifts, held suppers and entertainments in my honor, and best of all made subtle payments of moneys to my accounts. My old friend Fitzhardinge, newly made Earl of Falmouth, still held the privy purse, which meant that any gifts or allowances from the king came to me discreetly through that quarter, without anyone else being the wiser.

Wilson kept careful tallies for me, as she did with all the little favors and rewards it was in my power to dispense. It was all part of the game of "courtship," and one practiced by nearly every person, great and small, within the palace's walls.

And one, of course, that Charles understood better than anyone else, for what else did a king do but bargain with Parliament and foreign powers?

"You know perfectly well how an English war would affect France and Spain, my dear," he said now with a single cocked brow. "Likely you've heard all the advantages for each side more thoroughly than I have myself."

I smiled up at him. "I won't pretend otherwise. All of the gentlemen can be most persuasive regarding their respective causes."

"I trust the incense they offer you is sufficient to keep your interest?"

I tipped my head back, ready to be kissed if he so wished it. "Ah, sir, you know me so very well."

"As you know me." He sighed, his hands settling familiarly around my waist. "I can't fault you for picking their pockets, if they're going to dangle them before you so you hear the coins jingle. God knows I'm as generous as I can be with you, Barbara, but even with Falmouth at the privy purse, I have my limits."

"If I ask for more, it's for the sakes of the children," I protested. "Their welfare must come first. They are your flesh and blood, sir, and as such must be raised with certain expectations."

He grunted. "Am I to believe that little Charlotte is the one wearing that last diamond ring, the one that Master Leroy's bill valued at two thousand pounds?"

"You told me I could choose something to cheer myself after those men came upon me in the park last autumn." I shrugged winningly, and looked up at him from beneath my lashes. The ring was most handsome, and sure to hold its value over time to pass along to my daughters. "Besides, if I'm to be at your side, sir, I must keep up appearances."

"You *appear* lovely enough to me without all the baubles." He sighed again, his hands sliding more purposefully from my waist over my hips and back again. "That's another thing about this war, you know. Prize money from the sale of any fat Dutch merchantmen we capture. Nothing an army can do in the field will rival that. Most of the funds will go to the navy treasury, of course, but a nice part of the pie comes to me, to do with as I please."

"As you please, sir?" I chuckled and leaned into him, pressing my breasts against his chest as I slipped my hands into the back of his breeches. "Or as I please you?"

Yet he didn't smile the way I'd expected, not at all.

"I know what you are to me, Barbara," he said instead with care. "You needn't try to put a price on it. But if you wish to have your lodgings at Hampton Court refurbished again, and a new coach in the spring, as well as more diamonds for, ah, Charlotte and Anne, then you'd do well to cheer as loudly as anyone else for the victories and glories of this little war."

My smile turned more wistful. "You sound very confident, sir."

"I'm the king," he said, and there was no mistaking the melancholy that showed on his face. "I must be confident, or we will all perish."

To no one's surprise, England declared war on the Dutch on the fourth of March. War fever filled London, and Charles's optimism about the ease and swiftness of victory was a giddy fever in the streets. From Cheapside to Portsmouth, in every tavern and rum shop, sailors were toasted and told to drink their fill before they sailed off with the pride of England beneath their flying banners. Only Clarendon remained as a kind of potbellied Cassandra, predicting a long, ruinous war and disaster to the fleet.

Nor was the Queen Mother happy when her second son assumed his naval command and set sail with the rest of the fleet in late May. Charles ignored her pleas to stop James; it was good for the royal family to have a representative in such a highly visible place of authority, and at the same time to be seen sharing the same risks and dangers as the common sailors. Also on board and eager for glory were the king's cousin, Prince Rupert, and our friend Charles Berkeley, the Earl of Falmouth.

Fitzhardinge—or, rather, Falmouth—had recently wed Mary Bagot, one of my favorites among the other Ladies of the Bedchamber, and together the new countess and I waved as he left, and wept in each other's arms when he disappeared from sight. We were both of us with child, too, though this was her first babe with her husband, and my fifth with the king.

Thus we were not only bound together by our affection for Falmouth but also by our condition. When it came time for the queen to make her annual fruitless visit to the waters of Tunbridge Wells that summer, like convicted murderesses in Newgate we could plead our bellies and be spared the particular dull punishment of accompanying Her Majesty.

Yet because of that circumstance, we were together at supper on June second, in my lodgings with the king and several others, when Mr. Pepys, secretary to Admiral Lord Sandwich, was brought to us to deliver momentous news fresh arrived. The English fleet had sailed from Sole Bay and sighted the Dutch almost at once. A battle between the two forces was imminent; it might even be happening as we nibbled at our roast pigeons.

By dawn we could hear the sounds of the great guns firing clear in London, echoing and ominous in the distance, perhaps thirty miles away. The next three days were long, it being June, and extraordinarily hot and still, which likely made the sounds of the gunfire travel so, like a thunderstorm that never arrived. We went for walks, attended chapel, bowled on the lawn, and fed the tame ducks on the canal in the park. Everyone tried to go about their lives as if the sounds meant nothing.

Everyone failed.

Rumors raced through the countryside, along the river, the city, and the palace. Not even Charles knew anything for certain. The Dutch had been routed; they'd retreated; they'd disappeared in a great bank of fog. The stories changed by the hour, with little substance or reason. The Duchess of York locked herself away in the dark of her closet at St. James's Palace and prayed fervently for her husband's safe return. The Queen Mother did likewise, setting her ladies and priests to lighting candles and keeping a vigil for her son's deliverance.

Once so insistent, the echo of the great guns faded, then stopped.

Finally disjointed scraps of news came straggling through, confirming that the Dutch had in fact fled in disarray. Bonfires were lit, church bells rang, and people laughed and danced and drank in the streets, with relief and joy. Of course this must mean victory: we were the English, and we'd expected nothing less.

But later reports were more revealing, and far less delightsome. The Dutch ships had in fact fallen back in confusion, but instead of pressing their advantage, the English captains had also withdrawn. Even their enemies at the Hague wondered and remarked it incredulously. Instead of capitalizing and winning a monumental victory that would have ended the war with a single battle, they appeared to have behaved with a cowardly lack of resolve. Oh, these same captains and masters bragged and boasted and paraded their prisoners and smallish captures as if they'd won, but gradually the sorry truth came limping to light with the sorry procession of English wounded and their damaged vessels.

And the horror of war, not the glory, was soon to come crashing into our lives.

The unbearable heat had continued, as dry and constant as if all of London had been set within a monstrous grate, with glowing coals to roast the city to a well-browned turn. In any other summer, the court would already have retreated to one of the cooler palaces in the country, but because of the war, Charles had decided it best to remain in town. Every window in Whitehall was thrown open in hopes of capturing a breeze. Gentlemen left off their periwigs and ladies their stays, and both alike were excused from full dress. Like nocturnal creatures, many kept to their rooms throughout the worst heat of the day, emerging only in the relative cool of evening to learn the freshest advices from the war.

One afternoon I'd joined the king and several other gentlemen and ladies in his rooms overlooking the river. We'd begun a desultory game of basset, when of a sudden we heard a great commotion and raised voices in the hall. At the door, the guards started in readiness, but instead of any intruder, James, Charles's younger brother the Duke of York, himself came striding into the chamber, newly returned from the fleet.

He looked bluff and hearty from his time at sea, and burned

brown as a farmer after harvest. Though we'd already known the duke was safe, Charles cried out with joy when he saw him and clasped him in his arms as if they'd been parted for years, not weeks, while his dogs leapt and yipped about his feet with excitement.

"Let me look at you, James!" Charles exclaimed, laughing and thumping his brother on the shoulders with genuine pride while we all clapped and cheered for him as our returning hero. "How the sea agrees with you, you rascally dog! Come, here, sit with me, and tell me all."

But the duke's smile vanished from his newly browned face, and his bright eyes clouded. "Forgive me, brother, but I must tell you sad tidings before the happy. Is Lady Falmouth here?"

"Lady Falmouth is in her rooms resting, Your Grace," I said, already feeling the first sick dread of what would come. Not Falmouth, not that fine, handsome gentleman! "Should I fetch her?"

"Falmouth?" Charles asked slowly, that same dread now showing in his face. No one else in the room dared speak, for they'd felt it, too, while the foolish small spaniels continued their cheerful barking. "Quiet, dogs, be still. Quiet! What has happened, James? Tell me. What has happened?"

The duke took a deep breath. "Lord Falmouth was standing by my side on the quarterdeck in the fiercest heat of the battle. One moment he was there, and the next he—he was gone, taken by a cannon's shot. He'd no time to suffer or regret, may God rest his soul with the angels. He died a hero of England."

"*Dead.*" Charles's shoulders bowed and his head fell forward as if he'd been struck, and if he'd not still held fast to his brother, I felt sure he'd have dropped to the floor. As it was, the tears spilled from his eyes and down his cheeks, tears I'd never seen him shed before, no matter how many other sorrows had cursed him: tears for Falmouth, for the past they'd shared for so many years, tears for England's disgrace, and also, I should guess, for his own endless optimism turned so sorrowfully wrong.

But while we at court grieved mightily for Falmouth, snatched from us so cruelly in his prime, Death was intent on cutting a far

wider swath through London that summer. The heat continued un-
abated, and with it came the usual cases of illness and summer fevers,
especially among those nearest the river and docks.

Yet soon another kind of sickness had appeared, one that began
with chills and trembling, then swiftly progressed to boils on the neck
or groin, unbearable headaches, delirium, and an inevitable, painful
death. The plague was nothing new to us at that time—it ran its course
through the poor every decade or so—but this particular year it seemed
to strike with more virulence than any of us could remember.

The first cases in the late spring had hardly been noted, but by the
end of that same awful June, plague was already claiming hundreds
of Londoners each week. The gravediggers could not keep pace with
the demand, and from the roof of the palace the wavering light from
nighttime burials could be seen across the city like earthbound stars.
The houses where the plague struck were marked with red crosses to
warn others away, with an extra scrawled warning or prayer on the
door for God to be merciful to those remaining inside. By the end of
the summer, the deaths would be too great for proper burials in con-
secrated ground, with corpses dumped willy-nilly into open pits.

From fear of contamination, the court barricaded ourselves fear-
fully in the palace, and no others were permitted inside. The markets
and shops were shut and the streets were empty, save the occasional
nameless corpse abandoned to bloat and decay in the summer heat.
Grass grew high in the middle of King Street and in the other streets
surrounding the palace. Even the river was empty, devoid of the boats
and watermen that usually plied their courses and trades across the
shining water.

Terrified for my children as well as the babe within my womb, I
pleaded to Charles for us to leave the town. By early July, he agreed,
and the court joined the thousands of others fleeing the sickness.
Highborn or low, no one wished to remain in such an unhealthy
place—even, it was said, the very president of the Royal College of
Physicians.

Like restless gypsies, we followed Charles from Whitehall to
Hampton Court, to Salisbury and Portsmouth, and finally to familiar

Oxford. It was almost as if he believed that by never settling too long in one place he would outpace his kingdom's woes; for in addition to the plague, the war continued to founder without purpose, while prices for all crops and goods were driven beyond bearing.

Likewise, to avoid the plague, Parliament assembled in Oxford, with Charles nearby, but the members had lost the pleasing good humor they'd shown earlier in the year. They questioned his requests for more money for the war and the navy. They challenged the incompetence of the war's leaders, looking for scapegoats for their own impulsiveness. My old friend and neighbor Lord Sandwich was dismissed from his admiralty post, and retreated in disgust to a distant embassy in Spain.

Worst of all, Charles himself was openly, and unfairly, faulted for spending too much time on his own pleasures and not enough care on affairs of state. I found myself blamed again for corrupting the king and cursed as a grasping, avaricious strumpet. The wit and cleverness for which I'd once been praised was now transformed into sharp-tongued shrewishness, and I a scold who bedeviled the king. When the pulpits of Anglican ministers in London had been emptied by the plague, nonconformist preachers had appeared to claim the leaderless congregations with the most evil of messages: that the plague had been sent by God to punish the debauchery and corruption of the king and his court.

Mindful of the earlier warning I'd received from the disguised gentlemen in the park, I no longer went into the street alone, but only when attended by a pair of brawny guards with pistols as part of their livery. There were more guards near the nursery, too, for folks as evilly righteous as these might not pause at wreaking their vengeance on me through my little innocents.

Nor were risks to my person the only attacks I feared. One night when I returned to my Oxford lodgings after supping with the king, I discovered a hand-drawn note attached to my door:

*The reason why she is not duck'd?*
*Because by Caesar she is fuck'd.*

Stunned, I tore the note down at once. To suggest that I deserved a session in the ducking chair, a barbaric and watery punishment reserved for the worst scolds in backward country villages, and that only my place with Charles protected me—oh, it was not to be believed.

I called once again for my carriage and raced back to the king's lodgings in Merton College. I found him in his dressing room, preparing himself for a visit to the queen's bedchamber down the hall.

"Barbara," he said, his smile puzzled. His Gentlemen of the Bedchamber had already been dismissed for the night, and one of his two manservants had just taken away his periwig to place on its block for combing and curling. Though he was but thirty-five, his short, cropped hair was mostly gray now, as was the curling hair on his chest that showed at the opening of his scarlet silk dressing gown. "I'd not expected to see you again so soon, my dear."

Impatiently I waved away his servants, waiting for them to leave us alone before I spoke. Yet the man with the periwig still hovered, smoothing the carefully arranged curls back into place, wanting more to finish his task than to heed me.

"You, there," I said, glowering, for I'd no notion of his name. I pointed at the door. "Leave us at once. At *once.*"

The man glanced at the king first for confirmation, unwise in my present humor, then finally, as I raised my fist to strike him, he scurried from the room, the periwig still in his hand like the trophy scalp of an Indian savage in the wilderness.

"You're shaking," Charles said. "Are you that angry with me, or another?"

I thrust the scurrilous note into his hand. "Read that," I ordered, "and tell me I've not reason to be angry."

He read it, and let out his breath in a long sigh. "Where was this?"

"On the door to my rooms, for all of Oxford to see," I said, not bothering to hide my bitterness. "Likely the rest of this dreadful country town was already party to the jest."

"And likely the work of students who fancy themselves wits," he said, understanding my anger. "They've no right to write such libel about any lady, least of all you."

"Fah." I snatched up the sheet again, crumpled it into a tight ball, and hurled it into the grate to burn as it deserved. "*That* is what I think of them! Now what shall you do about it, my fine Caesar?"

That made him wince, though I was too furious to care. "A thousand pounds reward for the name of the author. That should work with impoverished students."

"What should work better is a good dose of the plague," I said. "They'll never be caught, any more than those men in the park. They'll all preserve the names of their confederates among themselves, no matter the reward you offer."

Restlessly I went to stand before the grate, watching the flames lick through the crumpled, curling paper. A small looking-glass hung over the fireplace, and as I looked up from the flames I was confronted with my own face, angry and weary and wounded, too, all at the same time.

"Look at me," I said miserably, unable to turn away. "Perhaps they are right. Perhaps I *am* so old and cross that I truly do deserve to be ducked."

He came to stand behind me, his reflected face beside mine in the glass. "You'll never deserve that, Barbara. You're as fair today as you were when I first met you."

"You're full of ash and straw if you believe that," I said forlornly, rebuffing his gallantry. "I'm twenty-five, sir, and by Twelfth Night I will have born you five children in as many years. Is there any wonder I look as I do?"

"Beautiful," he said softly, pushing aside my curls to kiss the nape of my neck. "That is how you look to me."

"I don't know if I can bear it much longer," I said, the weighty discomfort of the child within me making me pity myself. "The insults, the faultfinding. It's worn on me, sir, and I can't tell you the times it's frightened me, too."

"It does do that, yes," he said. "You've only to recall what it did to my father in the end."

"I didn't mean—"

"I know what you meant, Barbara," he said, more firmly this time, and far more firmly than I expected. "And the way that I see it is this. You have two choices. You can stay at the court, and turn a blind eye and a deaf ear to your critics. Or you can retreat to the country, and live there for the rest of your days. Within six months' time, none will recall who you are, or were, or call you any name other than 'my lady.' And *that* is your choice."

That was what he said, but what he was telling me in truth was altogether different. I'd no right to complain or whine or be fearful. I received plenty in return to compensate me for such trials. More important, it was not my choice whether I remained at court, but his, and I'd do well to remember the difference.

A year ago, he would never have spoken so plainly to me, and I thought uneasily of my future, and my children's.

Was it any wonder, then, that I turned swiftly to face him, my voice full of sweet protest. "But I do not wish to leave you, sir."

"Then stay," he said, more royal order than suggestion as he lowered his mouth to mine. "Bear it bravely, Barbara, the way I do, but stay with me, and do not go."

"Yes, sir," I whispered just before he kissed me. "*Yes.*"

# Chapter Eighteen

I began the new year as happily as any woman can, standing at a baptismal font with a new babe in my arms and his loving father standing proudly at my side. George Fitzroy (a king's name if ever there was one!) had been born at Christmas, a healthy, squalling lad like his older brothers. In a time when most women sorrowfully buried half the number of children that they bore, with likewise half of all husbands losing their wives in childbed, I was in this regard supremely blessed by God and good fortune. Every one of my children lived to embrace their majority, graced with the same robust strength and health that Charles and I each enjoyed throughout our lives.

But as I kissed the tiny boy in my arms on that cold January day, neither Charles nor I could have known that George was to be the last of his sons born to me.

While most of the court had finally returned to London, I'd remained at Oxford, awaiting George's birth, and to the queen's chagrin, the king had stayed with me. He'd been in no hurry to go back to his blighted city, and really, why should he have been? He could as easily rule from Oxford as from London, and enjoy the healthier air to be found here, as well as hunt and ride as much as he pleased. And, of course, he'd be with me.

As I'd predicted, no one had come forward to claim the reward offered in regards to the libelous note against me. And as I'd likewise expected, the entire town had known of it and its contents. I paid them no heed, or tried not to, and concentrated instead on keeping my place with the king. It was in a way an idyllic time for us, away from the press of London. He'd more time than usual to play with our children, and our suppers together were less centered on the intrigues of the court than on events of the nursery: one-year-old Charlotte sprouting her first tooth, or two-year-old Henry laughing as he toddled after the dogs, or little Charles, now three, delighted by sitting between his father's arms as he rode on horseback.

But just as all bad times must pass, so must the good, and with considerable reluctance we returned to London in February. With the winter frosts, the plague had finally run its course and the constant tolling of church bells had ceased. People were once again to be seen in the streets and on the river, going about the business of their lives, but there was no doubt that the city had been changed by such a sweeping scourge. By kindest estimates, at least a quarter of London's people had perished, and though most had been among the poorer sort, their absence was still noticeable. There were fewer crowds to be seen in the markets, theatres, churches, and other public places, while certain shops remained forever shut and boarded, their owners dead.

And though the plague itself may have subsided, the gloom and pessimisms that so much death had brought to the town could not be so easily dissipated. The war with the Dutch continued to drag onward, accomplishing nothing, and was widely viewed as an outlandish waste of both money and men. Yet sentiment against the French was also growing, until it seemed that war with them, too, would be inevitable, leaving Spain as England's only ally. The Spanish ambassador spent so much time striving to influence me and thereby the king that I might have well given him a room in my lodgings if he'd been more handsome and his breath less foul.

But I was glad for the bribes he was willing to offer. Thanks to Parliament, the king's generosity could only go so far. My establishment and my habits were costly ones to maintain, my expenses high. I was also an avid gamester, like much of the court, and I enjoyed the excitement of laying sizeable wagers to give teeth to my play. On a night when Fortune smiled my way, I could win as much as ten thousand pounds at the table, yet of course my detractors were quick to report only my losses to the same tune. Though I'd taken care to forge a sound acquaintance with Baptist—called Bab—May, the gentleman who'd newly replaced Falmouth as Keeper of the King's Privy Purse, even that source had its limits.

But I'd found others. To anyone outside of court, the notion that every place and bit of influence has its price may seem a curious practice, but I assure you, that is how much of the court, and the world, continued onward. A title, an officer's appointment, even a cleric's living: all of these were in my power to favor, and to sell. My beauty had come from my Villiers blood, true, but I'd come to appreciate the shrewdness I'd inherited from my Bayning ancestors with their roots in trade and the City. I could guess the value of most everything, both intrinsically and for how dearly another would pay for possession.

Thus I could set the price of securing, say, an Irish peerage at one thousand pounds but the place as a maid of honor to Her Grace the Duchess of York at only a third of that. I understood that a goldsmith would charge one sum for a set of finely wrought rings, but that the value of the same pieces would drop substantially if the owner were forced to offer them in exchange for a debt of honor. Conversely, if those rings had at one time slipped over His Majesty's finger, then they'd absorbed the glow of his royal self, and for that their value doubled, or even tripled.

Yet even such petty amusements could bring little light to that grim spring and the summer after it. Once again the sun was bright and distressingly hot, as it had been last summer, and once again, in early June, we heard the thunderous sound of the great guns firing in the distance, the sign of another momentous battle at sea. And once again, the battle fought off Sheerness lasted for four days, with grievous loss to lives and ships, and seemingly nothing to show for it.

The news from the fleet seemed to bring back Charles's grief over the death of his old friend Falmouth. He was subdued and quiet, his thoughts his own, and while some like Clarendon approved this change as a favorable sign of suitable sobriety and dignity in a monarch, I knew him better than that. Yet when I tried to cheer him from his doldrums as any dear friend would, he snapped at me like an intemperate dog, making my own hackles rise in return. We couldn't continue for long with so much hostility bubbling unaddressed between us, and we didn't.

It came late one July afternoon. I was sitting with the queen and her other ladies in the long parlor that overlooked the park. The room was too warm for comfort, a last tedious hour in company to be endured before we could retreat to our own rooms and prepare for supper. At least then we'd have the amusing company of the gentlemen, and not just the queen's sad-faced priests. I sat on my cushioned stool near the windows, too bored for anything else, while Pompey stood nearby and fanned me.

"Lady Castlemaine," the queen called suddenly, in her peculiar lisping English. "You will show that regard to me, will you not?"

"Your Majesty." I'd been too lost in my own lassitude to be paying much heed to her conversation, and now realized belatedly she'd been addressing me. "You know I always hold you in the highest regard."

"That was not my question, Lady Castlemaine." She looked at me smugly, pleased with herself for catching me out. Though she'd never acknowledged either my pregnancies or the five children that had resulted, she'd noticed now that for the first summer since the king's restoration I wasn't with child; she'd read far more into this than there was to read. These empty assumptions had made her bold with me, addressing me like this with more directness than she'd previously dared.

Not that I cared overmuch for her opinions one way or the other. Melancholy or not, the king still came to me, and if I hadn't conceived another child with him as soon as I'd delivered the last, as I had the past five years, then that was a blessing to me, not a disgrace. The king still had plenty of other arrows in his quiver.

"Forgive me, madam," I said now, making a show of suppressing a drowsy yawn. "I did not hear your query."

The queen raised her chin in puppy-dog defiance, her words snagging on her jutting front teeth. "I did not ask any query of you, my lady. You were only to agree."

I leaned forward on my stool, and smiled slowly while Pompey's fan continued to blow gently over me.

"Forgive me, madam," I said. "But I never agree idly."

Behind the queen one of the other ladies tittered nervously, and the queen's sallow cheeks flushed. "The king has a cold."

"An annoyance, madam, but of no lasting danger." I touched my fingers lightly to my cheek to remind her of the size and value of my pearl earrings, an admiring gift from her husband. "His Majesty is a strong and vigorous gentleman in his prime. *Most* vigorous."

"The king's health is always important to me, Lady Castlemaine," the queen insisted. "I believe that he contracted his cold from coming home so late from your house through the Privy Garden."

"But he never stays late at my house, madam," I protested softly. "Not at all."

"Not unless four in the morning is early, and not late," whispered one of the younger maids of honor to another beside her, who promptly hushed her.

"Then where is the king, my lady, if not at your house?" the queen demanded peevishly. "Where else would he be at that time of the night?"

"Where, madam?" I stretched my arms luxuriantly, enjoying myself. "Ah, I wonder that, as his wife, you do not know."

The queen's little fingers clutched the arms of her chair. "Tell me, my lady. Tell me!"

"As you wish, madam," I said easily. "You see, by the time His Majesty leaves my house, madam, I am *so* thoroughly tired, *so* weary and spent, that all I can consider is the peace of sleep. But as after even the richest banquet, a plate of common cheese or fruit is a final nicety, so the king will often choose to end his night in a certain Southwark brothel, where—"

"Silence!" Of a sudden, the king came striding into the room, his expression black as thunder. In unison we all rose and made our curtseys, not daring more. I wasn't sure how much he'd overheard of my little speech, but clearly what he'd heard had been enough.

"Your Majesty," the queen murmured, unsure of whether she was to enjoy a rare triumph or not. "How good to have you join us."

But Charles saw only me. "You're a bold, impertinent woman, my lady, to speak so to Her Majesty."

I stared at him, stunned he'd address me with so little regard before the others, and I felt my face glow with my anger. I felt all the little tensions and squabbles that had been simmering between us these last months gather and swell in my chest, filling me with an anger to rival his.

"Your Majesty," I began, my voice clipped and taut at such grievous use. "Her Majesty had asked me a question, and I did but answer in—"

"No more, Lady Castlemaine, no more," he shouted at me, his face livid with fury. "I won't have such foul talk at this court before my wife."

"You've had a great deal more than talk of me, sir, and I—"

"Silence!" he roared. "You will leave my court at once, my lady, and you will *not* return until it is my pleasure for you to so do."

"As you wish, sir." I curtseyed, but I did not bow my head, refusing to give him the satisfaction of breaking my gaze with his. "As you *wish*."

With my fury making my spine as rigid as iron, I began to back away from his presence, the wide-eyed Pompey at my side. The room around us was as silent as the grave, with every eye intent upon us. If I'd any sense, I should have left then, and said not a word more. But sense had never been a strength with me, and besides, I was far too angry to hold back what must be said, even though it would be before such an audience, and at the doorway, I paused.

"I will leave your wretched court, sir," I said, "and I will be gone before nightfall. But mark you, if you slander me further in this way, I swear I will publish every letter of love and promise that you have written for the entire world to read."

Then borne on my fury, I turned on my heel and fled.

"The papers, my lady." Wilson set the silver tray with the stack of the latest newspapers and sheets on the bed. "That was all the footman could collect."

Wearily I opened my eyes a fraction, my head still back against the piled bolsters. A perfumed cloth lay across my forehead, which ached abominably: no surprise, really, after the trials of these last four days. To remove myself, my household, and my children and their nursemaids from the palace with no notice at all, to bring them all to these hastily found lodgings here in Pall Mall, and to do it all while enduring the displeasure of the king—who could fault me for suffering after that?

I closed my eyes again. "What do the vile tattlers say of me, Wilson?"

"You do not wish to read the papers, my lady?"

"Would I have asked you if I did?" I sighed mightily. "Go ahead, tell me. I know you and all the others have likely read them for yourselves, so don't pretend you haven't."

"Very well, my lady," Wilson said, unperturbed. "They say you're an evil, avaricious slattern, Lady Barbary, the Great Whore of Babylon—"

"Oh, lud, they've been using that one for years."

"Yes, my lady," Wilson said. "They also say it was high time His Majesty served you as you deserve. They say he should have gone further and had you arrested for high treason against his person and taken to the Tower. They say there are preachers cursing you back to hell and the devil. And they say it is most fervently to be hoped that you never return to sully Whitehall or the king with your presence."

"Hah," I scoffed. "That's not so very bad. What of the queen?"

Wilson hesitated, choosing her words with endearing care. "They champion Her Majesty against you, my lady."

"You mean to say they treat me as a wicked, whoring, sharp-tongued shrew, come between a man and his honorable, virtuous wife." I sighed dramatically. I'd plenty of friends—Arlington, Jermyn, Killigrew, even Bab May—who had come to me at my new lodgings already and reported much the same thing. "Her Majesty must be in heavenly Portuguese raptures, imagining she's rid of me. Hah! If she knew her own husband as well as I, then she'd realize he meant nothing by this. Has he sent any word to me yet?"

"Not here, my lady," Wilson said. "But they say he did call last night at King Street."

"Did he indeed?" I smiled, more relieved than I wished even Wilson to know. I'd suspected that Charles would relent once his temper had cooled, but I'd no wish to make a reconciliation too easy for him. That was why I'd retreated here to Pall Mall, and not to King Street, to make him have to hunt a bit harder for me and the children. "So I am in his thoughts. That is good."

"Yes, my lady," Wilson said. "But you know he couldn't forget you for long."

"No, he could not." Yet I knew I was playing a most dangerous game with Charles, one with much higher risks than any mere hand of cards. As stakes I wagered the friendship and attachment and yes, the passion, that he and I had shared for these last years, counting on the hope that he could not turn me out from his life. Against that I set our children, and whatever security I could earn for them and myself before, finally, Charles and I parted for good.

But not this time, not today. Today I still was safe, and beneath the perfumed cloth across my forehead, I smiled. I'd still a few more hands to play.

"Bring me pen and paper, Wilson," I said softly, my resolve sure. "If I'm truly to be banished from court, then I must claim my things, yes? I vow it must be time to ask His Majesty for his permission to remove my possessions from the palace."

The letter was written not by Charles but by his secretary, yet his hand was all over it. Knowing him as I did, I suspected its intention was more to teach me a lesson than actually to banish me from court, but still I knew I'd be wise to take its content seriously. In it, I was given a specific time to return to my lodgings over the hither-gate only long enough to make arrangements to have the rest of my belongings removed from the rooms.

I took special care with my dress for this appointment, for I knew the odds were very much higher for me to be met by Charles himself than by one of the palace porters that the letter had promised would greet me. I wore a gown of pale blue silk so light that it floated and shimmered about me when I walked, as if it had been plucked from the sky itself. I wore the pearl drops in my ears, but no other jewels, and beneath a wide-brimmed lace hat I had my hair dressed in a simple knot, with a few loose tendrils. I wanted to look as fresh and inviting as a summer morn, and I wanted to look young, to remind the king of earlier, happier days for us both.

I greeted the palace guards by name at their posts as I entered through the main door with Wilson as my attendant, and I took the main hallways and staircases, cheerfully calling to all I passed, as if I'd every right to be back. To a courtier, their surprise and bewilderment was so complete that I realized Charles had kept my return a secret. Did he fear I'd refuse to come back, or had he wished to keep it a secret until it was made real?

But as soon as I unlocked the door to my lodgings, I knew he'd tipped his hand to me: the windows I'd left closed and locked were now thrown open wide to let in the summer breezes, and there was a huge porcelain bowl of cut roses, white and red, on the table.

At my side, Wilson understood it all, too.

"If you please, my lady, you won't be needing me," she said with a philosophical sniff. "I'll be waiting with the coachman below."

"Don't be impertinent, Wilson," I said mildly as I chose one of the white roses from the bowl. "I'll send for you when I'm done here."

I raised the flower to my nose, inhaling its rich fragrance before I snapped the stem short and tucked it into my bodice. I recognized the flowers from the garden at Hampton Court; he must have had them brought up this morning by boat.

"Good day, Lady Castlemaine," he said at the door behind me.

I finished arranging the flower in the valley between my breasts before I turned toward him and curtseyed. I made my smile beatific. "Good day, Your Majesty."

Gently he closed the door after him. "You are looking well, madam."

"As are you, sir." It had only been six days since he'd banished me from court; strange to realize it was the longest we'd ever been parted since his return to the throne. In an odd way, I felt as if I were seeing his handsome self for the first time again, as I had so long ago in Brussels, and I was . . . *charmed*.

Automatically he came to raise me up, then hesitated, a last doubt, I suppose.

I stood on my own, giving my petticoats an extra little shake as if I'd intended that all along. "You're not here to have me tossed out for disobeying your orders, are you? I was asked to come now, you see, to discuss arrangements with your porter for having my lodgings emptied of my personal effects. Your secretary sent me a letter, setting this time. Rather like a royal dispensation."

"You won't need that," he said, "because you won't be removing so much as a single chamber pot from these rooms."

I looked up at him sideways, peeking slyly beneath the lace brim of my hat. "Are you taking custody of all my belongings, then, sir? Are you so vastly cruel that you would send me into the streets with only the clothes upon my back?"

"When you left last week, I'm told it took six wagons to carry off your wardrobe alone, Barbara," he said, coming to stand directly before me. "If those are the clothes you mean, then you are supplied for the rest of your mortal days. You can have it all hauled back tomorrow."

"You're very sure I'll return, sir," I said, touching the rose at my bosom. "To have filled the empty rooms of a banished lady with flowers— that's bold confidence, indeed."

"I'm king," he said, as if that explained everything. "Now pray tell me why you chose to dress to meet my porter in my favorite shading of blue silk."

"Bold confidence, sir," I said, "nothing more, nor less."

He chuckled, and plucked the rose from my bodice. "Do you recall the first night I returned, when you waited for me after the procession? You had flowers at your breasts that night, too."

"Primroses," I said, for of course I would not forget that night, either. "Now we've only roses, with none of the prim."

That made him laugh outright. "How can I send you from court, eh?" he asked, teasing the flower's petals lightly over the swell of my breasts. "This week's been damnably hard without you here."

"You took the queen's side against me," I said. "*That* was damnably hard for me."

"She is my queen, Barbara, and my wife," he said, and there was warning enough unspoken that I knew I'd not win that point. "I owe her that loyalty."

"Indeed," I said softly, arching my back so my breasts rose higher above my stays and toward the flower in his hand. "I've known you longer."

"That is true," he said, letting his fingers slide over the mounded flesh I was offering to him. "How are the children?"

"They miss their father." I took the rose from him, running it lightly down the front of his waistcoat and along the front of his breeches. "*I* miss their father."

He reached out and caught my wrist, stopping my hand and the rose's progress. "Have you truly kept all my letters?"

"Oh, yes," I said, and smiled up at him. I'd wondered if we'd come round to my threat. "Ah, such ardent love letters! I would keep those always."

"Where are they, Barbara?"

"Where they are safe." Deftly I slipped my wrist free of his hand. "Not with me."

"Keep them from harm's way," he said, curling his arm around my waist to draw me close against him. "Because if you ever do as you threatened, then you would suffer far worse than I."

"Oh, sir," I said, lifting my lips toward his. "You, above all others, must know that I'd never do it."

He shoved the lace hat from my head, the better to kiss me without knocking into the brim. "If I believed that, Barbara, then I'd be the greatest fool in Christendom."

"You're not a fool," I said breathlessly, twining my arms around him as he shoved aside my petticoats. "You're the king."

"Remember it," he said, lifting me onto the edge of the table so I could wantonly wrap my legs around his waist. "Remember, my lady, and forget it at your own peril."

He took me there, sweet and languid, yet desperate, too, for after so many days apart we were like drunkards shaking in the desert without strong drink. Our lusty cries echoed from the windows, over

the guardhouse and the courtyard and the street below. Before supper, everyone in the palace knew we'd reconciled, and my banishment
from court was done.

And later, much later, I heard that on that same night the queen
had cried herself to sleep.

One night in early September, when the air was still warm with summer, I was wakened in Charles's bed to the creaking of hinges as he
swung the casement open more widely. At the end of the bed, one of
the dogs shifted in his sleep and whimpered without waking. I rolled
over and squinted at Charles, trying in my drowsiness to find sense in
his actions.

"What are you doing, dear?" I asked sleepily. "What are you
about?"

"There's a fire to the east, beyond London Bridge," he said, leaning from the window. "I can see the glow against the sky."

"There are fires almost every night," I said, pulling the sheet over
my bare shoulder. "Come back to bed, where you belong."

"This must be a large one." In the square of the open window,
his cropped head was cast in profile against the night sky. "I heard the
watch call it."

"Just because the watchman calls for help from God and king
doesn't mean you must do so," I said irritably. "It's only a saying. No
one expects you to trot over there to help in your dressing gown with
a bucket in hand."

"I suppose not," he said, still watching from the window. "Go
back to sleep. I'll be there shortly."

The next morning, a Sunday, I sat in the palace chapel with the ladies
of the Duchess of York, the queen being on one of her fruitless pil-
grimages to Tunbridge Wells. I'd forgotten entirely about the fire in the
night, and no one else around me mentioned it, either. Though I was
a Catholic (as was also Her Grace and her husband the duke, though
both in secret), I was still expected to attend the Anglican services as
a member of the court. For all that we usually had a bishop presiding

over us, these services were far closer to Rome than Canterbury, full of music and Latin at the king's request. Even Charles himself followed the Continental traditions, and knelt at the altar rail to take Communion, a simple act that caused much worry in stricter circles.

Yet on this particular morning, the most noteworthy event was the interruption of the service by a messenger. I recognized the man as Lord Sandwich's old secretary Pepys, but he came to us now on his own accord, intent on informing us of a great fire spreading through the city. It was the same fire that Charles had spied last night, grown larger and more deadly with the push of the wind. No one was really surprised: London's narrow streets and ancient wooden buildings, dried by two summers' worth of unseasonable heat, had turned the city into so much tinder. Though London was in fact often plagued by fires, this one was already proving to be far more ominous, and nearly unstoppable.

Charles and his brother James flew to action. First Charles led his own guards to assist in the firefighting efforts, while he and his brother were rowed down the river to view the fire directly. No one could remember a fire such as this, jumping from the roofs of one neighborhood to the next and consuming all in its path.

Unlike the plague, which had concentrated its fury among the poorest Londoners, this fire ravaged rich and poor alike. Nothing was spared, from the most humble of houses to the square towers of St. Paul's, where Roger and I had wed. The neighborhood where I'd lived with my mother when I'd first come to town was gone by the first day, and her house with it. Waterman's Hall, the Royal Exchange, Blackfriars, the wharves along the Fleet River bank all met the same fate, as well as scores of houses, shops, taverns, and churches.

For more than forty miles around the fire the air was full of smoke and drifting ash, of scraps of burning paper and scorched canvas and silk. The bells of surviving churches tolled incessant alarms, and over the crackle and roar of the flames came the howling cries and laments of those who struggled to save a few precious belongings as well as themselves from the fire's relentless path.

Many of the courtiers fled from the palace, some to their own estates at a distance from the city, some attending the Queen Mother, and others escaping by the Thames to the sanctuary of Hampton Court. I stayed behind, refusing to believe the fire would dare strike the palace. Yet for safety's sake, portions of the palace closest to the fire's path, near Scotland Yard, were torn down to make an empty break that flames could not cross.

Striving to be brave for the sake of the children and servants, hearing nothing but wildest rumor and fearing worse than that, it was only much later, when the fire finally was spent, that I learned how courageously Charles and his brother had labored to help save the city. While others around them had panicked or simply collapsed beneath the unimaginable burden, the two Stuart brothers, as well as the seventeen-year-old Duke of Monmouth, had led with tireless efficiency and little regard for their own safety.

From that first Sunday morning, Charles had directed his troops in fighting the fire, ordering burning buildings torn down to save others in the fire's path. Whether on horseback shouting orders or standing deep in mud and water as he wielded a bucket or spade like any other Londoner, his bravery and leadership were a revelation to many of his people. Some said he'd spent thirty hours straight in the saddle, and I believed it.

After four days and nights, the fire had finally burned itself out, followed by a heavy, drenching rain that flooded the steaming ruins. Yet Charles continued to work for his people's welfare, ordering food and fresh water to be distributed from the navy's stores to the now-homeless crowds who'd gathered in Moorfields. With almost no attendants he walked and rode among them, offering comfort and cheer and displaying a rare empathy for the suffering among even his poorest subjects that put most of his self-centered courtiers to shame. He showed himself to all as the rarest of gentlemen, full of natural courage, resolution, and honor.

But not even Charles could change the fire's awful aftermath. An enormous part of London had vanished, an area of over a mile and a half long and half a mile in width. Not only buildings had been destroyed, but the businesses, homes, and congregations that had been housed inside were now gone, too. There were no certain figures for the loss of life; it was simply too vast and overwhelming to calculate.

While Charles was promising that London would rebuild like a Phoenix from the ashes, a splendid new city of wide streets and buildings of brick and stone to resist any future fires, other, darker forces sought to undermine the goodwill he'd earned from his courage during the fire. The special investigative group formed by the Privy Council could not have been more clear in naming the fire's cause: "Nothing had been found to argue the Fire in London to have been caused by other than the hand of God, a great wind, and a very dry season."

A reasonable explanation, and one that Charles repeated again and again. But in the face of such a disaster, reason becomes less appealing. There were plenty of Londoners who believed the Hand of God might have been a Catholic one. Even as Charles sought to calm one rumor, ten more sprang up besides, like heads of the Hydra. French spies had set the fire, or nefarious Dutchmen had crept into the city to destroy it. Later, when the city authorities—who should have known better—would put up a monument to the fire and its victims, the plaque would unkindly attribute the disaster to "the treachery and malice of the popish faction."

Grievous, too, were the sermons offered by meddlesome preachers as well as certain strident Anglican bishops and clerics. Using vague quotes from scripture to make their cases, such hateful men claimed that God had shown his displeasure with the debauchery at Charles's court by striving to destroy it by both the plague and the fire. They pointed at the very year—1666—saying that those three sixes within the date were the mark of the Devil himself.

And worst of all to me was how often I figured in these tales of woe and damnation. Somehow I'd personally caused this disaster for London and its king by being a Catholic woman with power, a known and flagrant adulteress, and the most evil and debauched influence possible upon England's king.

I knew these tales were empty lies that meant nothing, yet still I felt the impossible burden of so much suffering. How could I not?

That autumn, I'd little taste for the gaiety of the court. Instead I kept to myself, with my children and with Charles, when he came to me. While some gentlemen and ladies rode out with him to survey the damaged neighborhoods and offer encouragement to those who'd lost the most, for me the risk to my person was too great to consider accompanying him.

But the finger-pointing and blame didn't end in the pulpit. Parliament, too, wanted a scapegoat for the disastrous war with the Dutch, as well as for the Great Fire. My cousin Buckingham, who had been pushed aside and denied his chance at glory in the first enthusiasm for the war, now turned his earlier exclusion to his advantage. He alone in Parliament stood free of fault and recrimination, and began to be seen as a serious leader, drawing supporters to him and away from once-strong men like Arlington.

There was a sense that the order was shifting in the court as well. Just as Buckingham had emerged in Parliament, so, too, was his old protégé Frances Stuart once again being promoted and paraded for the king's consideration. She was eighteen, more beautiful than ever, and still, miraculously, a virgin. Charles was still fascinated by this one woman who'd never succumbed to his desires, and everyone whispered that at last she was about to give way. Buckingham was said to have gleefully predicted that by the new year Frances would replace me entirely in the king's affections.

I refused to believe it. Yes, I'd just passed my twenty-sixth birthday, an unthinkably great age for a woman in my place. And yes, these last months I had kept myself away from many of the festivities as well as the fiercest politics of the court, needing time by myself. But didn't the king still profess the greatest affection for me? Hadn't he fair begged me to return to court after the foolishness of my banishment?

Then came news that shook my confidence more soberly than idle whispers ever could. It was Bab May, Keeper of the Privy Purse, who told me, not Charles himself, and directly before the first of the Christmas balls, too. The king had asked for a review of all my debts, with an eye to settling them for me once and for all. May said by his first reckonings he'd discovered I owed close to thirty thousand pounds for gambling and to assorted merchants. For the king to pay such a sum when he was having trouble paying the sailors in his navy was exceeding generous, yes, but May and I both understood the real significance of this gesture: that Charles was considering formally breaking with me.

I watched as the king led Frances Stuart in the dancing. She was dressed all in black and white, with diamonds at her throat and in her ears that made her glitter like the moonlight on new snow.

I'd kept away long enough.

# Chapter Nineteen

"You are certain of this, Wilson?" I asked, though I knew she never erred. "You can trust your source?"

"Yes, my lady," Wilson said, twirling the rod in the chocolate mill as she blended my morning brew. "It was one of the lady's maids to the queen's maids of honor. She was asked by Miss Stuart to dress her hair, and then while she did Miss Stuart spoke most freely to her, confessing her great attachment to His Grace the Duke of Richmond and Lennox."

"Richmond," I said thoughtfully, hugging my knees as I sat in the bed. "I've never seen them together."

"That is because his second wife only just died a few months past," Wilson helpfully supplied. "But Miss Stuart told my acquaintance that His Grace was exactly the sort of man she'd always hoped to wed, handsome and dashing, and with a grand title, too."

"He's also in debt to the skies," I said, for this was common enough knowledge. I'd never had much use for the gentleman; he seemed dull-witted and unimportant, outside my circle of acquaintance, though he was held to be handsome enough. "And Richmond is so given to strong drink that he falls into bed every night dead to the world. With him she could well be a virgin the rest of her days."

Wilson gave a small eloquent shrug to her shoulders as she poured my chocolate. "She may have already made the sacrifice, my lady. It's

305 SUSAN HOLLOWAY SCOTT

said she entertains His Grace in private, and considers herself 'rapturously in love' with him. Those were her words, my lady: 'rapturously in love.'"

"Frances has always been a fool." I laughed softly as I took the tiny cup of chocolate, cradling its warmth between my palms. "'Rapturously in love'! There are few things that lead to more indiscretions than that, my dear Wilson. The only trick will be how to use it to our own rapturous benefit."

If I had seen what happened that night on the stage of a playhouse, I would have laughed uproariously, but I would have also scoffed at any possibility of it being a real occurrence. Yet it was, and all the more enjoyable to me for being such a common farce.

From Wilson, and in turn her confederate, I knew that Frances would be expecting her "rapturous" duke in her quarters at nine that evening. I also knew that Charles was in the habit of visiting her earlier in the evening, to talk and amuse himself with the few favors she would agree to share with him. That done, and in a usual state of high frustration and complaint, he would come to me in his bedchamber, or my own, where his welcome would be infinitely more warm and passionate. That was the setting of our little play; the extra characters in our cast included Bab May, Will Chiffinch, the king's Page of the Bedchamber, and, of course, me.

There was always a small crowd lingering in the queen's drawing room after supper in Whitehall, down the hallway from her bedchamber and the lodgings of her various ladies and maids of honor. It was easy enough for me to join this gathering, for I did by rights belong among the ladies, though I took care to stand a little to the back of the room where I could see without being at once noticed. From this vantage I could see when the king entered Frances's chamber and closed the door after him.

At once I was off. In addition to the main hallways that linked Whitehall's different quarters together, there were numerous secret passages and forgotten staircases. Chiffinch knew them all, of course, for they were most useful to him in his trade, and I in turn had made sure that the old man had shown them to me, as a useful bit of knowledge to posses.

Now I ran along these secret ways without being seen, through Chiffinch's own quarters and up the last private staircase to Charles's bedchamber. I kicked off my shoes and hopped onto the bed with a book in my hand, and settled myself to appear as if I'd been waiting there all the night long. I'd scarce done so before Charles reappeared, throwing open the door so hard that it cracked against the wall.

"Good evening, sir," I said mildly, turning the book over like a little tent on my belly. "You seem grievously disturbed."

"It's Frances," he said crossly. "At supper she seemed well enough, all pretty smiles and laughter, but when I called on her just now, she sighed and groaned and made her excuses in her nightcap, pleading some little ailment or another. And quick as that, she sent me on my way."

"She did?" I asked, feigning great surprise. "An ailment?"

"Yes, an ailment." Charles paused and scowled suspiciously. "What do you know of this, Barbara?"

I sighed and turned back to the pages of my book. "Why should I know anything of anything, sir?"

"Because there is nothing in this entire palace that escapes your notice," he said with exasperation. "You know more than—who is it?"

He swung around to face the door and the polite tapping that had interrupted him. Cautiously the door swung open, and Bab May peeked his doleful face with the high forehead inside.

"Forgive me, Your Majesty," he began, "but if you wished to review the papers with those figures—"

"Not now, you rascal, not now," Charles exclaimed. "Cannot you see I'm engaged with this lady?"

As quick as a crab back into the sand, May scuttled away in retreat. But he'd done his part as we'd arranged between us, for his interruption was the sign that rapturous Richmond was now with Frances.

The king turned back to me on the bed. I crossed my legs in their bright green stockings, letting my lace-trimmed petticoats slip high enough over my knees to show my flowered garters and to draw his gaze. He couldn't help from looking; he never could.

"Tell me, Barbara," he said. "What is Frances about? What is the true nature of this ailment of hers?"

I ran my fingertip back and forth along the top of the book, my head tipped quizzically to one side.

"If I tell you the truth, sir," I said, "you'll vow I'm being spiteful, and not believe me, and then where shall I be?"

"Barbara, please."

"You will promise not to fault me," I said sweetly, "or slay me like the unfortunate messenger in that old tale?"

He took a step toward me, his face so black that I didn't dare prolong his fury, especially since it would soon be aimed instead at my pretty, foolish rival. Besides, I wished only for Charles to break with Frances, not suffer an apoplexy.

I sighed mightily, as if he'd won me over only with great reluctance. "Very well, then. If you return to Miss Stuart's bedchamber, you'll see with your own eyes that the lady's 'little ailment' takes the form of His Grace the Duke of Richmond."

"Richmond?" cried Charles, his voice strangled. "*Richmond?*"

I sighed again. "There, I knew you wouldn't believe me," I said, turning back to my book. "But before you doubt me further, go to her room. By now His Grace is likely in her bed."

That was exactly where poor Charles found them. The perfect virgin was shown to have feet of very ordinary clay; I'd never seen anyone fall so fast and so hard from favor at court. In his fury, Charles ordered that her name never again be mentioned in his presence. Exhausted by the furor and shamed by the disgrace, Frances eloped soon after with her "rapturous" duke, to become his boring, honest, rapturous duchess.

I consoled Charles, and pleased him well in the manner that I knew better than any other woman. The ominous significance of settling my debts was forgotten—except, of course, that my accounts had been nicely paid off to the sum of thirty thousand pounds. With Frances gone, the French ambassadors turned all their flattery and incense to me. My parlor at King Street was crowded to overflowing; even the new style in which I dressed my hair was praised and copied.

And the field again was mine to rule.

"The sword in one hand and a palm frond in the other, and a broken wheel beneath your disdainful elbow," mused Harry Jermyn as he studied all the emblems in the new painting on Master Lely's easel. "Oh, I say, my lady, you're not truly having yourself done as St. Catherine?"

"I am," I said as I walked from behind the changing screen, still tugging my gold satin robe into place beneath the flowing blue cloak. Master Lely liked to make a goodly show of drapery in his pictures, but while so much extra cloth was good for artistic virtuosity, it was the very devil to haul about in any sort of garment. "St. Catherine is a perfectly respectable saint. Where's the harm in it?"

"The harm's in your intention, darling, not in the pious old girl herself," Harry said, settling his short legs on a stone bench supported by twin satyrs that the artist kept among his props. "I can guess why you've done it, as will Charles and everyone else."

"Then let them guess," I said as I took my pose against the truncated plaster column. I'd sat often enough for Master Lely to know how he hated to be kept waiting, and I wished to be ready as soon as he joined us. "There'll be those who will speculate and invent tales whether I fuss about it or not."

"It's Her Majesty that will fuss, and with good reason, too," Harry continued, leaning gallantly on his elbow. He remained one of my circle at court, an old friend of Charles's and a casual lover of mine, whenever I felt the need of an entertaining, uncomplicated fuck. He'd also been banished once or twice by Charles for making his wit a shade too sharp, so we'd that in common, too.

"You've usurped the queen's very own saint for your own purposes, you know," he continued, "just as you've claimed her husband."

"I was the Blessed Virgin, too, and *she* didn't complain," I said. "Besides, I've already been St. Barbara, and Master Lely wished to paint me in this gold color. Mind you, Harry, I brought you along here to amuse me, not to be a critic."

"But it's by being a critic that I'll amuse you best," he said, twisting his fingers idly around the beribboned lovelock he'd tied into the front of his periwig. "Ah, my dear, your necklace has slipped. Shall I come adjust it for you?"

"You damned well may not," I said, laughing at his impertinence. The long strand of pearls was supposed to represent some sort of sword belt, for it had been the painter's idea to sling it crossways over one shoulder and between my breasts with most unsaintly emphasis. I narrowed my eyes in a menacing fashion, and aimed my palm frond at him. "Behave yourself properly, now, else I'll have to put you out before Master Lely returns."

"*I* am behaving," he said, glancing back at the unfinished canvas. "It's you that isn't. With this painting, you're taking on a sizeable challenge. By making yourself Catherine, one might argue that you're setting yourself up as the queen's equal, even her replacement. That won't sit well with our Charles. He's remarkably without humor when it comes to his doughy little queen."

"I might as well have taken her place," I said brashly. "I've born the king three sturdy sons. That's three reasons why I succeeded where she failed."

He sighed. "And you're a Villiers, full of daring and dash and not the common sense God granted a flea. What does that prove, I ask you?"

"It proves I'm willing to fight," I said, thumping my oversized prop sword against the plaster column. "I'm a well-seasoned warrior of the battles of court, Harry, and I always play to win. Charles knows that of me, and respects it. You'll see. He'll fancy this picture as much as any of the others that Lely's painted of me."

But Harry didn't laugh, or join in my bright declaration the way I'd expected. Instead his lumpen features turned serious and grave, his popping eyes full of uncharacteristic concern.

"Give a care to yourself, Barbara," he said softly. "The court is changing, and things aren't what they seem. Even, I fear, for a warrior queen like you."

As I'd hoped, the new painting was done in time for Charles's thirty-seventh birthday at the end of May. He celebrated it not with the queen but in my lodgings, with Irish fiddlers, French wine, and a very late night. It was close to dawn when I finally took him alone to see the painting that was his gift.

"For your collection of Lelys, dearest sir," I said, clinging to his arm both from fondness and for support, for I'd had my share of the wine as well. "To remind you of how much I love you."

He studied the painting, going very still.

"You don't like it, sir?" I asked, my voice rising upward to fill the silence. "You don't think it's—it's a fair likeness?"

"Oh, it's like enough," he said. "Master Lely seldom disappoints. But I doubt that the choice of St. Catherine was his notion, was it?"

I frowned, my pleasure in the gift gone, and too late I thought of Jermyn's warning.

"I thought you'd like it, sir," I said. "I thought you'd think it amusing."

"It's a beautiful picture, yes," he said curtly. "But it does not amuse me."

He shook me from his arm, and left, and came not to my bed that night, or the next eight beyond it.

In the same week, Dutch ships attacked the Medway. The English were caught completely unawares, and put up no fight. Led by two traitorous English pilots, the Dutch bombarded the fort at Sheerness, sailed boldly up the river Thames to Gravesend and then to Chatham. People fled from London into the countryside in terror, convinced the Dutch and French were invading and meant to take the city itself. But the Dutch were content with burning the four English ships they found at Gravesend, and towing away as a prize the *Royal Charles*, the flagship of the English fleet.

To plague, fire, and flood we now added humiliation, cowardice, and despair: a "Black Day," as the poets called it. The country was in a panic, the navy in toothless confusion, London in ruins, and Charles's reign a crumbling, ignominious disaster.

And no one gave another thought to my portrait as St. Catherine.

With neither money nor ships left to support the war, England had no choice but to agree to a disreputable and shoddy peace with the Dutch. Though Charles would have preferred to continue the war to a more honorable result, Clarendon insisted that peace was the only way to salvage the country. By the end of July, the Peace of Breda was signed. The war that was supposed to have refilled the country's coffers had only emptied them further, and created nothing but ill feelings at home and abroad.

As part of the treaty, the Dutch received colonies in West Africa, Pulo Run, and Surinam in the Caribbean. England received even less, the pitiful holdings in the new world of New York, New Jersey, and New Delaware.

The bonfires that marked the end of the war in London were scattered and few, the celebrations subdued. When a medal was cast to mark the peace, I was chagrined to learn that the profile of the still-disgraced Frances, Duchess of Richmond, had been used as a model for Britannia.

I demanded angrily to know why I'd not been honored instead. "My dear Barbara," Charles had told me wearily, "the medal is to honor peace, not more war."

But that disgruntled summer was still far from done, as much as I could wish it so.

My cycles had always been as regular as the moon, and as easy to predict. Their regularity had helped make me certain that Charles was the father of each of my children. Thus, when by the end of July I was three weeks late, I sensed I'd gladsome news to announce to the king. He'd always been such a happy, indulgent father with our little dark-haired brood that I couldn't imagine a better surprise to offer him now when so many other things were sadly askew.

A small company of us were still at table after supper one night, and the conversation had turned to the Duchess of York's latest pregnancy, and whether or not after two daughters and several stillbirths she'd manage this time to grant the duke a live son. Given how by now all hope had been abandoned for an heir by the queen, the duchess's fecundity was of obvious interest. Listening to this discussion, I finally could contain my own news no longer.

"Likely you'll have another son yourself this winter, sir," I said proudly, resting my hand on his shoulder. "At least I've every expectation of it."

Yet to my shock, Charles said nothing, and did nothing, in marked contrast to the well-pleased delight with which he'd received all my other, earlier announcements of this nature.

"Indeed, my lady," he said evenly, far more interested in shelling the walnuts before him than in my news. "And when precisely do you believe this event will come due?"

"By April of the spring," I said. "I know it's early days, yet still I—"

"Then I fear you are mistaken, my lady," he said, still not raising his gaze to mine. "If you are indeed with child, you must lay your brat at some other gentleman's door."

All other conversation around us had ceased, with every ear now listening with horrified fascination.

I took my hand from his shoulder, deliberately setting both my hands flat upon the table's edge, so no one could later say they'd seen them shake. "Forgive me, sir, but I am right in my calculations. I swear to it. Any child I carry now is yours."

At last he raised his gaze to mine, his eyes as hard as jet. "Lady Castlemaine," he said, "no matter how violently you swear, that child isn't mine, for I can't recall a single day or night in the month of June when I did lie with you."

At the far end of the table a gentleman sniggered. I don't know who it was, nor did it matter, not really. He represented everyone who'd ever question the parentage of any of my children, or laugh at them behind their hands for my not being wed to their father. In my mind's eye, I saw their small, trusting faces, and I knew I'd do all in my power to keep that trust, no matter who might laugh or jeer at them.

Even, so help me, if it was their own father.

I rose swiftly to my feet, my hands knotted in tight fists at my side. "That's a lie, sir, as you know full well."

"Perhaps," he said with maddening calm. "Perhaps not. Who knows which of us lies, eh?"

"God damn me, sir, but you *shall* own this child!" Anger filled my head like a storm cloud, obliterating all else. With my forearm, I swept my place clear of tableware and porcelain, sending it all crashing to the floor with a noisy clatter. "It is yours, sir, and you will own it!"

Charles stood, intending to overwhelm me by his size alone, the way he did with most other persons. "Barbara, please."

"Please what, sir?" I demanded hotly. "Tell me that! Because if you do not have this child baptized in the Royal Chapel at Whitehall, if you are not standing as its rightful father as you have for the others, then I shall carry it myself into the palace and dash its brains out against the gallery wall before your very eyes, and for all the world to see, and know what kind of father you *are*."

I shoved my chair backward and stalked from the room, too angry now to bother any further with Charles or the formality his presence should have required of me. I called for my carriage and left the palace, and at that moment I didn't care whether I returned or not.

There are those cynical enough to believe that whenever I wished something from the king I would pick a battle with him, and then retreat and hide until he felt sufficiently contrite to grant whatever I pleased. Such a tidy notion fits conveniently with the image of me as a calculating and avaricious harpy, and thus I suppose is a convenient interpretation. Yet, if any of those same cynics could ever see me after I'd quarreled with Charles, how the force of strong words and stronger emotions tore at me until I was often sickened by it, then I'd hope they changed their opinion. For though it might seem that I was no more than a careless wanton where Charles was concerned, in fact my heart felt enormous tenderness for him, and when we fought, I often felt afterward that I'd been stabbed again and again with the sharpest stiletto. We were so much alike, the king and I, that we knew exactly what words would cause the keenest wounds to the other. Like a lioness injured defending her cubs, my suffering had no cure but solitude, away from him who had caused me such pain.

After I left the palace on the night that Charles disavowed my nascent babe, I retreated not to my King Street house but to the house of a friend, Lady Harvey, in Covent Garden. Though not beautiful, Lady Harvey was quick-witted and clever, exactly the sort of company I needed after such a heated exchange with the king. She was a member of the Montagu family, a clan as ambitious as the Villiers were, and since I'd also had a brief intrigue long ago with her brother Edward, we were all tangled together in friendship—and now with my latest sorry quarrel with the king.

Lady Harvey was perfectly willing to send back Charles's letters to me unread, as I'd requested, and she also was clever enough to deflect the equally clever Bab May when he came to try to orchestrate a reconciliation. But when after two weeks of this dance Charles himself appeared at her door for me, she and I both agreed the time had finally come for me to meet with him.

I sat waiting in Lady Harvey's small garden, a pleasant, private place tucked behind her house. Pear trees had been pegged to grow flat against the tall garden walls, plump rounded fruit and glossy green leaves against the rosy red brick, and benches and tables were arranged beneath the single spreading elm.

"Your Majesty," I murmured when Lady Harvey herself showed him into the garden and, with a wise understanding of how Charles and I ordinarily reconciled, promptly left us alone. "Good day to you, sir."

Determined to begin better than I'd left off, I made him a graceful curtsey on the sun-dappled grass, then offered him one of the garden chairs.

Yet still he kept back, standing at the edge of the grass and restlessly jabbing his tall walking stick into the soil. Though dressed in his customary somber black, he wore the new Eastern, or Russian, style of gentlemen's dress that he'd introduced to the court: a long, loose open coat over an equally long waistcoat, lined with dark red silk and pinked along the edges. It was a fashion that suited his height and frame well, and I wondered how many other shorter, stouter gentlemen would remain wedded instead to the French fashion of short doublets and cloaks that they'd worn all their lives.

"I've come to ask after your health, Lady Castlemaine," he said with excruciating politeness. "Last time we spoke, I showed less than proper concern for your welfare, and I regret that."

"Not at all, sir," I demurred. "My health is excellent, and I thank you kindly for your inquiry."

"Yes." He glanced about the garden before finally coming to stand directly before me. "You are well, then?"

He glanced so pointedly at my belly that I colored. "I am, sir."

He sighed, and shook his head. "Of course I'll own the child is mine, Barbara," he said. "With you—with us—I'd never do otherwise. Though how I'm to support another when Parliament won't give me two farthings to strike together is beyond me."

"I knew you would, sir, and I thank you for it," I said softly, and sadly, too. "Your first refusal did not seem like you at all."

"You surprised me before the others," he said bluntly. "A man doesn't like to learn that sort of news before an audience."

"You hurt me," I said, just as blunt. "Me, and our other children."

"You offered to hurt them a good deal more," he said. "I don't like threats like that, Barbara."

I bowed my head contritely. As with even the most humble of men, I needed to take care to let Charles believe he ruled supreme in all things. "I was distraught, sir."

"You were fit for Bedlam," he said, more pointedly. "You know that you're being likened to Medea now."

I winced, for what mother wishes to be compared to that horrifying example? "You know I'd never harm any of our children."

"Love is a curious thing, isn't it?" For the first time he smiled at me, and I realized again how sorely I'd missed him. "The palace is far too dull without you."

I laid my hand on his chest, over his heart, with our old familiarity. "I was wrong in my reckoning, or perhaps I miscarried. I cannot say, so early. But there is no babe."

I'd expected him to be relieved, but instead found only sadness in his face. Of course: he'd heard that same message from the queen so many times, it couldn't help but bring him sorrow.

He cupped his hand around my jaw, turning my face up toward his. "Come back, Barbara. Don't stay away from me any longer."

"I won't," I said, brushing my lips over his. "I can't, or survive without you."

As was our custom after separations, he had me then, in the garden. Yet there was an unusual tenderness to our coupling, and as I sat astride him on the bench, my petticoats fluttered around us like the petals of some late-summer bloom.

And when he returned to Whitehall, I went with him: where he wanted me, and where, for now, I still belonged.

There were many advantages to being back in my lodgings at the palace. I was once again near my children, the king, my friends, and the general excitement and intrigue that life at court could bring. But the best that could be said of being in the palace in late August of 1667 was that I was in residence to see the end of Lord Clarendon.

Although the old chancellor had been against the Dutch war from the beginning, and had been the first to desire to sue for peace, he was ironically the one of Charles's ministers who would be made to take the blame for the war's miserable failure. There was more to it, of course: how Clarendon had continued to try to control Charles as if he were still a schoolboy instead of a man and king well grown; how he struggled to impose his intolerant will of how England should be; and his contemptuous hatred of me as a sinful, selfish, expensive influence upon the king.

I do not have to say which reason meant most to me. Suffice to say that I could scarcely wait for the morning when Charles called Clarendon to him to ask for his resignation. Being kind, Charles phrased his request as being for the old man's own good by placing him outside the reach of the vengeful Parliament before they began the postwar inquests. But even Clarendon himself knew the queasy truth. The only way for Charles to appease the still-angry Parliament was to send Clarendon away in disgrace.

"My lady, wake, if you please!" Wilson shook my shoulder to rouse me. "It is done, and His Lord Chancellor is leaving Whitehall."

"Now? What hour is it?" I asked, shoving my hair back from my face. "How?"

"Nearly noon, my lady," Wilson said, her words tumbling over one another in her haste to spit them out. "Lord Clarendon has met all this morning with the king and Lord Arlington and the rest in the king's offices, and they say he has resigned, and is leaving, and if you wish to watch him depart in disgrace, as you've said, you must rise at once."

But I was already out of the bed, ignoring my slippers and the dressing gown that Wilson held out for me. I did not wish to miss this glorious sight, and in my smock I ran from my rooms into the gallery that overlooked the Privy Garden. If Clarendon had met with the king in his rooms, then he must cross the garden on his way from the palace to the street. To see better, I hurried through the aviary that faced the gardens, scattering the bright-feathered rare birds, gaudy parrots and macaws, sending them chattering and scolding to their perches.

Pulling my smock back over my bare shoulder, I peered down through the aviary bars just in time to see Clarendon. He'd always refused to follow the fashion for periwigs, and from where I stood above I could see his balding pate gleaming through his wispy hair in the noonday sun. His shoulders were bent with age and discouragement, his gait shuffling as he crossed the white-stone garden path. Most of all I noticed how his gnarled hands were empty now, without the purse and mace that had been the symbols of his office. So he had resigned; he was done, and I couldn't help but clap my hands with glee. Vexing, confounding old man: he might have been a true friend to my father, but he'd done nothing but judge and cross me from the first moment we'd met.

"Your dressing gown, my lady, please!" Wilson said, trying to cover my near nakedness, but I shrugged her away, not wanting to be distracted from this glorious moment of an enemy in defeated retreat.

"Enjoy life in the country, my lord!" I called out to him in my triumph, unable to keep still. "Remember in the end who has won, and who has lost!"

He heard me, and to my surprise he stopped, and gazed balefully up to where I stood in the aviary. "My lady," he called back, "pray remember that, if you live, you too will grow old."

I laughed. I was only twenty-six, rich in my beauty and power. I had won, and he had lost, and that was all that mattered.

"My Lady Castlemaine! Here, my lady, here!"

I shifted my gaze away from Clarendon to where a group of young gallants had gathered to loll in the garden after playing a game of tennis on the palace courts nearby. In charming undress of white open shirts with the sleeves rolled high and plain black breeches, they glowed with ruddy health and vigor as they grinned up at me.

Most likely that same shining sun that had illuminated Clarendon's disgrace was now revealing all my charms to them through the fine linen of my smock, explaining the sauciness of their salutes to me. But it was too late to be falsely modest, and so I did no more than toss my long unbound hair over my shoulders and wave in cheerful acknowledgment.

Squinting into the sun, the ringleader clasped his hands over his heart, much to the jeering delight of his compatriots.

"Ah, my lady, my lady," he called up to me. "Surely to see you there is to view the beauty of the true bird of paradise."

"A pretty speech, that, my proud young hawk," I called back through the bars, laughing merrily, and glanced back for a final, rewarding glimpse of Clarendon's disgrace.

But by now the old man was gone, from the walk and the palace and from my life forever, and gaily I turned back to the young bucks preening at my feet below.

# Chapter Twenty

Wisely Charles did not name a replacement for Clarendon at once, leaving the chancellorship vacant while he made a careful decision. Like a stone tossed in a pond, this single momentous event sent repercussions rippling outward throughout the court and beyond, and in ways no one could have predicted.

With Clarendon gone, the tension that had been growing between Charles and his brother the Duke of York—and Clarendon's son-in-law—now vanished. This pleased Charles no end; having endured a childhood where his siblings were scattered by war and misfortune, as a man he treasured all the more his surviving brother and sisters. Because it was becoming increasingly likely that either James or a son of his would be the next king, childless Charles became more interested and involved with his brother's growing family.

Less commonly known but another link newly reinforced between the brothers was their involvement in the Catholic faith. Charles was delighted to have Clarendon's overweening Anglican influence removed from his life. Though the nominal leader of the Anglicans, the king was drawn seductively toward beckoning Rome: among his closest family and circle, his mother, brother, wife, and I were all Catholics, as were many of his closest friends. Though he would never dare be seen attending a Roman mass or service, with James he could discuss and compare the merits of the two faiths with a freedom he'd never have elsewhere.

As a Catholic myself, one committed to the true church as founded by Our Savior, I took special note of this. I resolved to pay more court to the Yorks with an eye to my own future, and that of my children.

Unaware, or more likely choosing to be so, Arlington negotiated an agreement among the Protestant powers of Europe, united against the Catholic states. The Triple Alliance joined England to Holland and Sweden; what would their leaders say, I wondered, if they'd seen the private chapel for Catholic Mass that I visited with the Stuart brothers in St. James's Palace?

Likewise Clarendon's fall sent the other ministers and members scrambling to make what they could of it, reaching for fresh favors and places. In a way I was no different, for though as a woman I'd never have any actual effect in Parliament, through my favor with Charles I was perceived as having secured the chancellor's resignation. With Frances Stuart gone now, too, the French ambassador lavished many more bribes and blandishments on me, and called me the true English queen.

Of course the jackass who brayed the loudest was my cousin Buckingham, who tried to claim he'd unseated the chancellor entirely by himself. But while no one could doubt Buckingham's persuasive abilities, or how readily he could gather a collection of supporters by the sheer force of his personality and good looks—ah, how blessed we Villiers are in that regard!—he often had no notion of what to do with the power he amassed, and as surely as he gathered new followers, others would drop away, disillusioned. Though Charles valued his long-standing friendship and delighted in his amusing company, in the king's eyes Buckingham was now repeatedly tripped by his own foolishness, and thence proved himself untrustworthy.

With his protégé Frances Stuart gone, Buckingham had returned to his old plan to replace the queen with a more fertile Protestant princess. Again and again he proposed a royal divorce, which inflamed the ever-loyal, if not faithful, king. His harebrained plots even included kidnapping the queen and sending her to some distant wilderness in New England, in the hopes of establishing abandonment as grounds for a divorce.

Nor did Buckingham's private life encourage trust or support. It was known to all that the king hated the tragic waste of dueling, and always had. Yet still Buckingham indulged himself in this practice over every slight against his honor, imagined or otherwise. When in January he was prominent again in a sordid duel over his mistress the Countess of Shrewsbury, which ended in the death not only of that lady's husband but his second as well, the king had had enough. Though I persuaded Charles to pardon Buckingham—rascal or not, he was my kin, and from my long-ago days with Chesterfield I'd not the same hatred of dueling—the king withdrew his trust, and Buckingham's political star began to dim and fade.

There was, however, one place where Buckingham was of peculiar use to Charles, and, in a way, to me as well. From the instant that Charles had reopened the theatres after his return to London, Buckingham had been thick in the world of actors and playhouses. He knew all the playwrights, managers, and players and all the titillating scandals backstage, and he was quite willing to act as a liaison between the stage and the palace.

Charles had always enjoyed the theatre, largely for all the pretty women on display in the audience and on the stage—he'd always had such a lickerish eye for beauty, he'd journey to a Welsh pigsty if he'd heard of a pretty woman there—but he'd previously been content until now to have the occasional actress or orange-girl brought to him by way of Chiffinch's back stairs. But now Buckingham was opening the entire box of jewels for his choosing, and God preserve him, Charles could not refuse.

Nor, to my own delight, could I.

Eagerly Charles leaned over the edge of the box, watching the girl who danced and sang on the stage before him. She was supposed to be some fairy or another—I'd long ago lost track of the muddled, foolish plot—but Buckingham had told us that this girl was the reason that every seat in the playhouse was taken. Seeing the grace and lightness with which she danced and how much of her nimble body was shown as she spun on her toes in her gossamer fairy costume, I could well believe it.

"What a sweet little sprite," Charles whispered to Buckingham, sitting on his other side. "Her name is Moll, you say?"

"Moll Davies," Buckingham whispered back. "She's either the bastard daughter of Colonel James Howard or of a Wiltshire blacksmith employed near the Howard lands. You can choose whatever story pleases you, I suppose."

"She's what pleases me," Charles said. "Mark her voice in this song! What a joy it is to hear a voice like that."

"Huh," I said, unimpressed as I sipped my wine. We were all three of us a little drunk by then, the best way, really, to enjoy the playhouse. "She'll sound the same as any other lowbred woman in the cold light of dawn. All screech and scold, and guard your purse."

"Don't be so harsh, Barbara," Charles chided. "Ah, now that's a line to bring tears to any tender heart: 'My lodging it is on the cold, cold ground.' I'd take her from the cold ground and into a warm bed, if she's a mind to it."

"Of course she's a mind to it, sir," I said succinctly. "You're the king, and she's a whore."

Buckingham laughed. "Mind where you toss that particular turd, cousin, lest it fall across your own skirts."

"If it does, Your Grace," I replied graciously, "I'll be sure to catch it first, and hurl the stinking thing back to you as the rightful owner."

Now Charles laughed, too. "You can't play games like that with Barbara, Buckingham, she'll always win," he said. "So what of Mistress Davies? Can I meet her after this is done?"

"Meet her, sir, and anything else you'd like, I'd vow," Buckingham said with his usual expansive generosity, so necessary to pimps of any degree. "I'll take you to the tiring rooms myself. Will you join us, Barbara, or will the company of so many fair rivals put you to spleen?"

I smiled at him, serene in my confidence. "I promise no spleenishness, Your Grace, for I don't consider such tawdry baggage as any rival to me. I'll join you, yes. I've a mind to inquire after that handsome Mr. Hart myself."

"Hart, is it?" Charles said curiously, glancing back at the stage to see if the actor still stood by while Moll Davies finished her song.

"Well, Barbara, I'll grant he's of a rank higher than your usual low rascals."

"A prince among players," Buckingham said, obviously quoting something, though I'd no notion exactly what. "Did you know he's reputed to be the great-grandson of that most venerable bard William Shakespeare?"

"I do not know, Your Grace, nor do I care," I said solemnly, refilling my goblet from the bottle I'd tucked in the basket beneath my seat. "All that will matter to me about Mr. Hart will be the caliber of his performance."

The performances on all accounts proved high indeed, or at least high enough for the dull days of February. Soon after, Moll Davies was flaunting a diamond ring given her by the king, the price of which—six hundred pounds—she vulgarly announced to all who'd listen. After that she boasted of being put in keeping by His Majesty, with a furnished house and a coach of her own. But as I'd predicted, her keeping was short-lived, and Charles was quite willing to drop her back to that "cold, cold ground" whence he'd found her.

I'd more satisfaction with Charles Hart. He was a man most splendidly made, tall and well muscled, and while others might call him a prince of players, I'd say he had the carriage of a king, and a cock to match, too. There was a certain rare dignity and nobility to him that many true gentlemen could never achieve by birth alone, and I did enjoy his company for a time. My special delight was for him to keep in costume and play that role for me as well, so that I might swive mighty Alexander one night, and the next a red Indian king.

And in this grim time of wars and plague and fires, I could not see the harm in diverting ourselves with such play-actors, or a bit of playacting ourselves.

Shortly before the solemn season of Lent, we highborn amateurs acted in a special production at Whitehall before the rest of the court. Corneille's *Horace* was stripped of its French taint through a new English translation by the clever lady scholar Katherine Philips, and extra dances were added between acts so every little new maid of honor could have her part. As was fit for my beauty and height, I was given the leading role of Camilla, and under—and over, on occasion—the private tutorage of Mr. Hart, I performed my role to perfection, and acclaim, completely outshining all other ladies.

If I were to be entirely honest, I should add that it wasn't entirely my talent alone that was busily outshining my fellows, but my costume and jewels. As a special favor to me and to show how high I still stood in his favor, Charles had borrowed pieces—diamonds, pearls, emeralds, sapphires—from the Crown Jewels in the Tower for me to wear, to add more splendor to my royal role. I'd heard the value of the whole array set at two hundred thousand pounds, a handsome, glittering figure indeed.

"You are most beautiful tonight, my lady." The Marquis de Ruvigny smiled beside me as we all waited for the supper to be announced. After that, there would be more dancing, and more opportunities for all of us in costume to preen and strut like the peacocks we were. "I've never seen Camilla acted with more fire."

"*Merci*, my lord." The marquis and I had a thorough understanding of one another, and an appreciation, too. I knew he was in London with another draft of a proposed alliance between our two countries, just as he knew that because I was Catholic I'd speak favorably of France to Charles. "Though I should think you must have seen your share of French actresses with more sympathy to your great playwright Corneille than I could ever have."

He shrugged, his shoulders eloquent like all Frenchmen's. "Sympathy is not everything, my lady. There is much to be said for possessing the necessary beauty for the role."

"Also the jewels." I held my hand out before him, waggling my third finger to show him the ring with the large pigeon's blood ruby. This was the single piece not from Charles but from his cousin King Louis, as a little reward to me for some piddling service or another, and I'd worn it on purpose tonight so that the ambassador might see it. "Pray be sure to convey my gratitude to His Majesty your king. He has most excellent taste in baubles."

The marquis bowed and covered the ring and my hand with his.

"His Majesty knows the value of both your pleasure, my lady, and of your knowledge. He delights in rewarding you thusly."

"*Monsieur le Marquis,*" Charles said, joining us. He glanced pointedly at the other man's hand on mine, and de Ruvigny immediately withdrew it. "I trust you've enjoyed yourself this evening?"

"Your Majesty," the marquis replied, making a most elegant bow over his bent leg. "The performance was beyond all my greatest expectations, as I was just telling Her Ladyship. How ravishing she looks this night."

"Yes, yes," the king said, and took my hand, or rather claimed it, more precisely. "You'll excuse me, my lord, but I've a matter of some urgency to discuss with Lady Castlemaine myself."

He hurried me off and through the crowd, courtiers melting from our path like the Red Sea before Moses. On Charles's arm, I smiled like the benevolent goddess I was supposed to be, while he waited until we were well away from the Frenchman before he spoke.

"So what was de Ruvigny babbling about tonight?" he asked as soon as we'd reached a hallway with a modicum of privacy.

"Babbling is a de Ruvigny specialty, sir," I said. "You know that as well as I. Mostly he wished me to grovel and thank him yet again for the ring."

"Ring?" Charles frowned. "What ring is that?"

"Here." I held my hand out for him to see. "It was part of the last round of gifts from Louis. In return I'm to sway you toward the latest wording of the alliance."

He bent over my hand, critically studying the ring. "I am endlessly amazed by the amounts my cousin Louis is willing to shower on you, and for what gain?"

"So that I might influence you, of course," I said. "Do you feel influenced, sir?"

He grunted with disgust. "He should know better. I'm not about to let an impudent jade like you lead me by the nose."

"Not the nose, perhaps," I said, letting my hand drift purposely to the front of his breeches. "Hah, mark where Louis's ring is now!"

He caught my wrist to still my hand. "Take care with de Ruvigny, Barbara. He plays the silly Frenchman, but he's much more clever than he seems. Take whatever baubles he offers, if it pleases you, but promise him nothing in return."

I smiled slyly. "Oh, sir, you of all men should know me better than that. It's little more than another game to me, sir, and you know full well how I like to play."

"I am serious, Barbara," he said, and to my surprise he was. "I don't want your name linked too closely with the French, not now with Parliament meeting over the new bill."

I understood. With Clarendon's restraining hand gone, the king had sought once again to ease the sanctions against Catholics and other dissenters by presenting a Bill for Comprehension and Indulgences to Parliament. It had met with instant and vehement opposition, with seemingly all members uniting against it. Fears of popish plots were never far from the minds of most Englishmen, and the rumors that French Catholics had started the Great Fire refused to go away. Not only was Parliament against any new indulgences; they wanted the old laws more strictly enforced. It was not going to be an easy battle for the king.

"Leave the dirtiest of those games to Arlington and Bristol," he urged me now. "You've already damned yourself by your conversion, Barbara, and if you tumble too deep into Louis's pockets, I may not be able to pull you back out."

"I swear to you by all that's holy," I said, "you won't have to rescue me."

"Would that *that* were always so." He sighed. "You haven't shared his bed, have you?"

I wrinkled my nose. "The man stinks like all Frenchmen do."

"I could wish you'd a better reason than that, but I suppose it must do." He freed my wrist, letting me continue what I'd started. "He was right about one matter, however. You *are* ravishing tonight."

I kissed him by way of thanks, leisurely, though he was already hard in my hand, his breathing quickening.

"Later, sweet," he said. "I must be here to open the dancing."

"I'll come to you then," I said, flicking my tongue against his by way of a promise.

"Wear the jewels, too, before I must send them back to the Tower."
He smiled with anticipation. "Wear all of them. And nothing more."

By March the king had lost his latest battle with Parliament over religious tolerance. Not only were the old fears of Catholic plots raised
again, but once again Buckingham demonstrated his innate ability to
say the most foolish thing possible, when he proposed that the crown
solve its constant money woes by appropriating funds from the well-
lined coffers of the Anglican church. That was more than enough to
sink the king's bill, and under more pressure he felt compelled to issue
a proclamation enforcing the limits of the Act of Uniformity, a rem-
nant of the hateful old Clarendon Code.

Yet even this concession failed to calm the restlessness in London. On Easter Monday, a day that should have passed in peaceable
reflection, bands of apprentices and other wild young men rioted and
turned upon the brothels of Moorfields, setting fire to some and pulling down others, and pelting the hapless inmates with filth when they
ran out to escape in scandalous undress. From fear that this mayhem
might signal something more ominous, alarms were sounded with
trumpet and drums, and armed soldiers poured into the streets to
quell the confusion.

This should have been no more than a passing wonder, a scrap
of inspiration for the libertine pen of my cousin Rochester, and soon
forgotten after that. But some other nameless author blew his fetid
breath onto the tale, and made it burst into fresh flame, and then
dragged my good name unbidden into the middle of the whole reeking mess.

An ill-printed pamphlet, *The Poor Whore's Petition,* appeared from
nowhere, like the ugliest of toadstools sprung up through the grass.
Though pretending to have been written by the women abused by the
rioting apprentices, it was clearly the work of a person familiar with me
and my habits. Calling me one of their fellows and appealing to me by
name with coarse flattery as the "most eminent, illustrious, serene, and
eminent lady of pleasure," this so-called petition sought my protection
in the name of Venus, "that Great Goddess whom we all adore."

In the manner of such vulgar publications, it was of course signed by no one, yet read by everyone. Charles and my other friends agreed that it was a most grievous, scurrilous piece of claptrap, but also advised me to let it pass unremarked, and beneath my notice.

But worse was to come, and that—*that!*—I could not bear.

"Have you seen this?" I slapped the new pamphlet on the king's desk. "I know you preach Christian tolerance and a blind eye, but this, sir, I cannot stomach."

"More of the same?" Cautiously Charles opened the pamphlet and began to read aloud. " 'The gracious answer of the most Illustrious Lady of Pleasure Countess of Castlemaine'—oh, hell."

"That's as good a description as any," I said, seething with rage. "It's supposed to be my answer to that last pamphlet. Read on, sir, read on! Clearly it's written by someone who knows me, for there's perfect descriptions of my gowns and my jewels, and my lodgings, too. Mark what they say of me, and the children—*our* children—too."

I came to stand behind him, pointing out the most offensive lines over his shoulder as I read more aloud. " 'We have *cum privilegio* always (without our husband) satisfied ourselves with the delights of Venus; and in our husband's absence have had numerous offspring (who are bountifully and nobly provided for).' Oh, sir, this cannot be tolerated It cannot be *borne*!!"

"But it's even worse here, Barbara," he said, and now I heard the anger in his voice, too. "It's a mockery of my Bill of Indulgences. It says you'll suppress the Protestant nonconformists, but harbor all Catholics because they believe that 'venereal pleasure, accompanied with looseness, debauchery, and prophaneness are not such heinous crimes and crying sins.' "

I jabbed my finger at the page. "It blames Catholics again for setting the fire, and it says that those same apprentices who tore down the brothels are really the first Catholic Frenchmen come to lead an invasion."

Abruptly he shoved the pamphlet away and rose from the desk, too agitated to remain still.

"This goes too far," he said, striding back and forth across the room with long, furious steps. "This shames not only you, Barbara, but the crown, and the government, and all churches, of every faith. And I refuse to be libeled and bullied by faceless cowards who hide behind a printing press to spew their venomous discontent upon this country!"

I watched him pace, feeling as if the worst heat of my anger had somehow transferred to him. Reading the pamphlet again in his presence, speaking the hateful words aloud, had troubled me in a new way.

"How many will believe that I am in fact the author?" I asked unhappily. "What if those same apprentices who destroyed the Moorfields brothels seek me as their next victim?"

"So long as you and the children stay here in the palace," he said, "you will be safe. I guarantee it."

"But what of my house in King Street?" I was not a cowardly woman, or one who frightened easily, yet I'd not forgotten the time in the park when I'd been accosted by the disguised gentlemen. As terrifying as that had been, it would be as nothing compared to a vengeful mob determined to treat me ill. "My palace lodgings aren't my home. What if the same—"

"You *will* be safe, Barbara," he said, coming to take me in his arms. "You shall never be made to suffer on account of me. You have my word."

In the next weeks, as many copies of the pamphlet that could be found were taken in and destroyed. The press that had printed it was closed and shuttered. The identity of the true author remained a mystery, but since he'd been frightened into not writing more in a similar vein, I suppose that the goal of his silence, too, had been accomplished.

And in a most public display of his regard for me, and to prove how little he cared for my Catholic beliefs, the king then settled a pension of nearly five thousand pounds on me, and purchased Berkshire House in my name: a handsome, spacious property of great size and elegance that backed on the park and overlooked St. James's Fields and Pall Mall. Its cost was more than four thousand pounds and according to Bab May the grant for its purchase had been squeezed from customs duties.

I didn't particularly care how Charles had arranged the finances. In a house so large, and directly across from St. James's Palace, I *would* be safe, as he had promised, and in May I moved into my new home with my three youngest children. I'd already sent the older two, Anne, seven, and Charles, five, to be schooled in Paris, where the quality of genteel education was thought to be better, and where they'd be removed from the distraction of having their schoolmates link them to me.

There were many at court who believed such a generous gift from the king was intended as a sure farewell, a sign that he was ending our connection and putting me aside. I knew otherwise; he continued to come to me each day, and lingered as long as he could, and I often still did frequent my lodgings in Whitehall. Though our passion did not burn with the same bright fire that it had in the past, our friendship had been tempered by the flames and made stronger over time, and I never doubted I'd a place in his heart.

But the most advantageous feature of Berkshire House lay in its proximity to St. James's Palace, the home of the Yorks. As the two brothers had grown closer, both in their family and their sympathy with the Roman faith, this would become the location where decisions were made and policies determined, much as my old house had been earlier.

I already knew from de Ruvigny that Charles was considering another, secret alliance with France, one that would, if revealed, undermine the Protestant Triple Alliance made earlier this year. And I also knew that in return for the funds and military support that Charles so desperately needed to keep England afloat, Louis would insist on a condition requiring Charles to convert to Catholicism himself and deliver England back to the Holy Mother Church.

In the plainest of language, Charles had decided to sell his soul, and if such a treaty ever became known to Anglican England, he would lose his throne faster than his father had.

Perhaps because I did know of such dangerous intrigues, I could step back from the court. Perhaps because I'd felt so threatened by the *Whore's Petition*; perhaps because, at twenty-seven, I'd learned more of the value of patience; perhaps because I simply understood how momentous this time could be for England, I was willing to withdraw for a while from the busiest scheming of Buckingham, Arlington, and the rest of the court. When pressed, I gave as my excuse the outfitting of my new house, and the education of my children, both good and valid reasons, and true as well.

The world was shifting, and once again I'd made sure I'd be at its core.

Pinning my hair back into place, I glanced from the window of Charles Hart's tiring room. A carriage had drawn to the back door: a common enough occurrence, given the number of gentlemen who delighted in recruiting their mistresses from the theatre's stage. But though this carriage was purposefully plain, I recognized it, just as I recognized the horses and the driver.

Noting my interest, Hart came to stand behind me as he pulled his shirt over his handsome head. "That's for Nell," he said disdainfully. "The third time this week, and she always goes to him."

"To the king, you mean." I'd known that when the polish had begun to wear dull on Moll Davies, the king had looked to another actress, one who specialized not in drama but in comedic roles. Nell Gwyn was beguiling rather than beautiful, small and round in her person with ringlets so tight they bounced when she walked. *When* she walked, indeed: mostly she pranced on her toes, like a small spirited pony. She was quick as blazes, always ready with a retort or clever rebuttal, which was, I knew, why Charles had taken such interest in her. What I hadn't realized was how much.

"She goes to the king that often?" I asked Hart, keeping my voice idle and slightly bored, as if it really was beneath my notice. "He sends the carriage every time?"

"Aye, my lady," Hart said, not bothering to hide his bitterness. "Sometimes four nights from five. He's welcome to her, too, same as are all the other lords. I took her from the pit and put a play-sheet in her hands instead of a basket of oranges, yet first she betrayed me with Buckhurst, and then with the king. She smiles and smiles for him now, but in time he'll taste her ingratitude, too. Is your carriage down there, too, my lady?"

"It is," I said, reaching for my hat. "They're waiting at the corner."

Hart tucked his shirt's tails into his breeches. "You could always ride together back to Whitehall, I suppose."

"We could," I said, not wishing so much as to imagine enduring such a ride. "We won't. Good day, Hart."

I kissed him quickly, my joy in the afternoon spoiled. I wished nothing more than to be home, and I hurried down the playhouse's twisting back stairs to the street, holding my skirts and cloak clear of the grimy steps.

Four nights from five was a great deal for a common-born woman and Charles. What did she do to fascinate the king so? And how had I not realized it myself?

"My lady!" She was there at the doorway just ahead of me, her round little face as impudently merry here as it was on the stage. "Forgive me, but I didn't see you, my lady."

I nodded, but didn't deign to reply as I swept past her to my own carriage.

Forgive her, indeed.

# Chapter Twenty-one

THE RIVER THAMES, NEAR GRAVESEND
*May 1670*

I stood at the prow of the royal yacht beside Charles. Though the day was sunny and full of warmth, a stiff breeze from the water had driven all the other ladies and most of the gentlemen below. But I'd always been a good sailor, and with a broad-brimmed hat and a veil tied over my head to protect my skin from the sun and a stout cloak against the spray, I was willing to brave the deck.

Green fields full of dappled cattle and quiet country villages slipped by on either side, and gulls danced in the cloudless skies overhead. The royal banner, gold threads glittering, flew from the masthead to signify that the king himself was on board, and extra pennants streamed merrily from the spars and jackstaff. Two fiddlers sat on the quarterdeck to supply an extra measure of gaiety to our cruise, and even the sailors themselves seemed in a festive mood, singing to the fiddlers' tunes. When children ran along the bank to wave at us, we both waved back, and I couldn't think of any place under heaven where I'd rather have been. Besides, here I could speak to Charles alone, without fear of being overheard.

"A splendid day, Barbara, yes?" The king squinted up into the sun like a seasoned old salt. He'd always liked the water, and like his brother, he felt entirely at home with it as an element, whether sailing, rowing, or swimming. Free of the limits of the palace, he'd openly relaxed, his happiness palpable. "I cannot wait to greet my sister again. It's been far too long since I last saw her."

"She should have come sooner," I said. Henrietta, known by the family as Minette and the world as Madame la Duchesse d'Orleans, or more simply Madame, was Charles's favorite among his sisters. By being fifteen years older, he'd stepped into a role that was as much father as older brother to her, and the two of them had exchanged daily letters without fail for as long as I'd known Charles. "France is not so very far away that she couldn't have come visit."

"In distance, perhaps, but there are other hindrances," he said, meaning, of course, Madame's difficult husband, the duc d'Orleans. Madame's marriage had been as cursed as Charles's, doubly so since her lack of a male heir had been caused by Monsieur's catamite ways, dressing as a woman in paint and patches, and preying on young boys. "I don't have to tell you how kings and queens seldom decide such matters for themselves. But it will be good to see her at last, very good."

While our party was a small one, consisting of only the Stuart families, a few friends such as me, and our servants, Madame was said to be making the journey from Paris to Dover with over two hundred attendants. The reunion would be the cause for much celebrating and levity, as such family events tend to be. Only those closest suspected the real reason for Madame's journey, and we kept our thoughts tightly to ourselves.

Now Charles took my hand, tucking it gallantly into the crook of his arm. "I'm glad you're here, Barbara. Not many ladies find much pleasure in sailing."

"Ah, sir," I said, laughing, "I needn't remind you that I'm not like many ladies."

He laughed, too, as much from his delight in the day as from the foolish jest. "Surely that must be the greatest truth ever spoken, and the most apt."

"Indeed, sir," I said, "because we both know that you, too, are not like many gentlemen."

"Which is why I've always been so eternally grateful to have had you in my life, Barbara," he said, and even in the bright sun there was no mistaking the genuine fondness in his eyes. "Old friends, eh? Nodding together in the chimney corner?"

"Not so very old, sir," I protested, then laughed again. It had been ten years now since we'd first met in Brussels, a frighteningly quick passage of time, even between friends. I was twenty-nine, and he was soon to be forty, and I couldn't begin to fathom how that had happened to either of us. I curled my fingers more closely into his arm. "Old friends, yes. Which is why I trust you'll now tell me the real reason for this journey."

He smiled benignly. "To see my sister, of course."

"Don't lie to me, dearest sir," I said, my smile equally benign. "We've never done that before, and I'll thank you not to begin now."

He patted my hand and looked out across the water. "Louis and I are going to make a small agreement, Barbara, a little trade of pledges and services between cousins. It's been done without ministers or ambassadors, with only my sister to act as our go-between."

I narrowed my eyes. "What services, sir? What pledges?"

"With France's assistance, England will once again be superior to the Hollanders at sea," he said. "Our merchant ships will be safe in their trading, and our colonies will prosper unmolested by Dutch raiders. If such assurance takes a war, why, then with France at our side, we will fight, and we will win."

"Money, troops, ships." I nodded, watching him sharply through my veils. "And in return, sir, what have you offered?"

He still looked across the water, avoiding my eye. "England's loyalty to France, her most natural friend and cousin."

"And?"

He let the single word hang between us, so long I knew I'd sorrowfully guessed his secret.

"And," he said at last, so softly I could scarce hear him over the rush of the water and wind, "and I will admit to being convinced of the truth of the Catholic religion, and promise to reconcile myself to it as soon as the welfare of England will permit it."

I said nothing more, but leaned my head against his shoulder in silent sympathy. No matter where his own conscience did lie in this—and I believed in his heart it was with the warmth of Rome, and not the chill asceticism of the Anglican church—the knowledge that for the good of his people he must betray the will of the majority of them was as harsh a burden as any sovereign should have to bear.

Within the week, the Secret Treaty of Dover, as it came to be known, was signed, with the Catholic Lords Clifford and Arlington adding their names as witnesses. No one else knew of it, and the secret was kept better than any other I'd ever shared.

The rest of our stay in Dover was thrown over to amusement and diversion, with celebration of Charles's birthday. Madame proved to be a tiny woman whose frailty shocked me, familiar as I was with her tall, robust brothers, and yet her spirit and energy were a boundless match for Charles's. She attended every one of the dances and plays and parties at sea and on land, suppers given and gifts exchanged.

Yet through all these merry days, it rained, hard and chill and gray, as if the skies themselves did weep and grieve to know what had happened here, and what would happen in the coming weeks.

On the last day before Madame must sail, she insisted that her brother take one of her jewels as a memento of her and of this brief joyful time together. She summoned one of her ladies to bring her casket of jewels for Charles to make his choice. The box was presented by a small, solemn girl of enormous beauty and almost doll-like perfection, no more than fifteen or sixteen years old, I should guess.

I knew at once that Charles would be enchanted by her, and he was. He chucked the girl beneath her plump chin and asked if instead of a jewel he might take this little French girl back to England as his token. All around us laughed, but both Madame and I knew he'd spoken only half in jest, and from the terrified expression on the girl's face and how the casket of jewels trembled in her hands, I knew she believed the tall English king meant to claim her, too. But Madame was not afraid to refuse her brother, and swiftly took the girl from his reach to return her to her parents.

It was the last time any of us laughed. The next day Madame returned to France and we to London, and the tears that were shed between brother and sister rivaled the rain that still fell.

A month later, when we'd all settled back into our old lives, an exhausted French messenger came racing directly to the king with the most tragic news imaginable. Madame was dead, a painful, agonized death that had so stunned the French court that already there were whispers she'd been poisoned. Her last words had been of her brother, her only regret in dying said to be that she was leaving him.

Charles collapsed with grief, the blow of his sister's sudden death all the more shocking for coming so soon after their reunion. For days he lay unmoving and alone on his bed, the door to the chamber locked from within. Even I, old friend that I was, could not help him through his pain.

When at last he emerged, he was changed. Others did not see it, but to me who knew him so thoroughly, the difference was great indeed. There had always been a kind of sweetness that ran as an undercurrent to his habitual charm, a gentleness that seemed so at odds with a man of his size and power: this was gone, lost forever. Whether it perished because of the treaty he'd signed or his sister's death, or whether he believed the one had somehow been punishing retribution for the other, I never knew, nor would I dare guess.

Even among the oldest of friends, there are certain questions that must remain both unasked and unanswered.

In honor of my devotion to the king, as well as my reticence and support throughout this dire time in his life, in July I was made Baroness Nonsuch, Countess of Southampton, and Duchess of Cleveland, and given the great house at Nonsuch and the parkland around it. The oft-heard tale that Charles made this conditional on my giving up Harry Jermyn forever was of course the silliest of fabrications. With the king's permission, I chose those particular titles for myself with purpose, to settle old scores. I claimed Southampton from Clarendon's late crony, the fourth Earl of Southampton, who as treasurer had worked so hard with the chancellor always to thwart me; and Cleveland from the long-dead Earl of Cleveland, who'd borrowed money from my father before I was born and never bothered to pay it back to my widowed mother. The warrant for these titles gave as reasons my "noble descent, her father's death in the service of the crown, and by reason of her own personal virtues."

There were many at court and beyond who scoffed and sniggered at what exactly those personal virtues might be, just as there were others still who were sure now this was a sign of the end of my place in the king's life. I ignored them as I always had, and looked again to the future.

Soon after our Madame's death, Nell Gwyn was brought to bed of the king's son, her first by him. She made a great improper fuss of how shamefully dark and unattractive the babe was, as if she needed to reinforce the fact that the king was his father. To be doubly sure the world knew, she named the child after him, and the godparents who stood at the christening were a telling little group as well: her old lover Lord Buckhurst, Buckingham, and his mistress Lady Shrewsbury.

After such a dark and portentous year, my exhausted soul yearned for simple diversion. If the king could find relief in the uncomplicated arms of an actress like Nell Gwyn, then I could seek such solace, too. I'd not far to look, either, for temptation lay—or rather hung like a ripened fruit—before my very eyes in the form of the ropedancer Jacob Hall.

Much like the theatre, music, and dancing, circus and acrobatic shows had been prohibited by the Puritans. With Charles's return, the country seemed to fair erupt in acrobats and ropedancers and others who could perform rare feats of balance and contortion. Every country market had its tawdry traveling acts, pretending to be Indian or Italian or other exotics, when in fact they'd more likely hailed from Liverpool or Bristol. But the true artists of the craft were wondrous to behold and gifted in ways that few men are.

Jacob Hall was one of these. Handsome in his face and manner, he was a magnificently proportioned male creature, with legs so strong they rivaled a stallion's. He danced and vaulted on ropes strung high in the air with more ease than most men could on the ground, and he could perform twirling somersaults as well as fly over outstretched rapiers and leap through fiery hoops. The king had named Hall his court acrobat, and had him sling his ropes across the ceiling of the Banqueting House.

The entire court had sat with upturned faces and gaping mouths as he'd leapt over our heads, and when I'd praised the brawniness of Hall's thighs as revealed by his tumbling costume, Charles had jocularly suggested him as a suitable replacement for himself in my bed, and surely more agreeable than the stunted likes of Jermyn. I'd laughed at the time, and pondered the possibilities of a man so strong yet flexible.

Opportunity did present itself that fall. Hall had set up a booth for his performances at Charing Cross, where he'd drawn an immense crowd of onlookers. Alas, he'd likewise drawn the constable, who'd noted he'd made his erection without obtaining the necessary permissions. To the catcalls of the crowd, the constable arrested Hall and put him in prison. I soon heard of this grievous misdeed and promptly had it righted. In his gratitude, Hall proved most pleasant and agreeable, and more than willing to demonstrate his appreciation for his rescue.

Alas, with two persons so well known to the public, the merry songs and satires began, I think, whilst the man was still in my bed, and became so prevalent that even the king entered the front hall of Berkshire House one day singing a stanza or two in praise of our combined agility. Yet it was exactly as I'd hoped, a diversion and an adventure, and if it diverted Charles as well, then all the better.

For soon after this affair, the second, public version of the Treaty of Dover—a *traite simule*—was signed, the one with no mention of the Catholic church or Charles's planned conversion. Yet even in its muted state, the treaty brought down a huge outcry on the king and his ministers, with many suspecting Arlington and Buckingham of somehow contriving to betray England to France. Dutifully it was signed by all the ministers, including Arlington and Clifford, who'd also signed the secret version. When I heard the heated words about this false treaty and the ever-rising hatred and suspicions of the Catholic faith, I shuddered to consider the response that would have greeted its original form, and the king who'd signed it.

The *traite simule* did come with an extra unexpected fillip, however. Louis had heard how Charles had admired his sister's young maid of honor in Dover. With Madame dead, the French king had easily pried her from her family, and now young Louise de Keroualle was sent as a gift from one cousin to another, and most likely an amenable spy in the very bed of the English king.

Charles was delighted with Louis's thoughtfulness and the girl, too, so young and shy and unsure of her English that she was no trouble to him at all. Virgins had never held much allure for him—as they had for my old lover Chesterfield—though he'd made an exception with the fair Louise. In trade for her maidenhead, he soon found her a place at court and fashioned her Duchess of Portsmouth.

Now, however, he found himself with not one but three royal mistresses, a crowd by the standards of any man. I kept my first place at his side, by my rank, beauty, and presence, but even so I'd the disagreeable sense of being only the choicest peahen in his covey, and so I told him, too.

There'd been a time when I would have happily shared his bed with such rivals, as I'd done with Frances Stuart, but that manner of sport had lost its luster to me. How could it not, when I'd be forced to present my aging—though still most beautiful—charms beside those of lithe young girls to invite unfortunate comparison?

But as ludicrous as the situation with Charles was becoming, I'd recently discovered something more pleasing on my plate. On the eve of my thirtieth birthday, I met the young officer who would not only irrevocably change the course of my life, but that of English history.

"Pray, Anne, who is that young gentleman?" I was sitting with the Duchess of York, all of us gathered in Whitehall's long gallery after supper. It was a jovial group, for no purpose but amusement in our own company, and the wine and cards had already begun. Yet though people freely came and went as the night progressed, I noticed none of them until this gentleman. Now I could scarce look away.

"The young ensign?" Anne asked, her gaze following my own. She'd last month given birth to another daughter instead of the much-desired son, and perhaps because of this she still had the worn look of women directly after their lying-in. "That's John Churchill, the newest member of the duke's household. Isn't he a lovely young rogue?"

"*That's* John Churchill?" I exclaimed in disbelief. "I'd a letter from his aunt advising me of his arrival—you see, he is a second cousin of mine—but I'd no notion he'd be so—so—"

"Delicious," Anne said, finishing for me. "Is everyone in England your cousin, Barbara?"

"Only the handsome folk," I said, watching Churchill as he entered the room. He was tall and lean in his scarlet ensign's uniform with the satin sash and knot across his shoulder, his skin browned and ruddy, his hair streaked with gold by the sun. He wore his own hair, not a periwig, nor did he need to, crowned with such a lion's glory. I guessed him to be in his early twenties, no more, yet unlike most courtiers his age he moved with the confidence born of hard-won male experience, not swaggering bravado: a man, not a callow boy. "What place will he have in your household?"

"He's a Page of Honor, as well as being an ensign in the duke's guards," she said. "He's new returned from a post fighting in Tangier, which explains the brownness of his complexion."

"Tangier," I repeated, intrigued, letting the exotic name roll seductively off my tongue. "Land of harems and wicked heathen practices?"

"I doubt he could afford any harems," Anne said. "He hasn't a farthing to his name, poor lad, but he's sure to prosper with a face like that. He will, I think, find life at court most agreeable."

There was a slight edge to her voice, a barely discernible tightening of her fingers on the blades of her fan, and suddenly I remembered why I knew the Churchill name. It wasn't the letter from the distant aunt, for I received so many like that, I wouldn't recall any in particular. No, it was Arabella Churchill I recalled, an equally beautiful young woman who had swiftly moved from her place as the maid of honor to the duchess to mistress of the duke, and had borne him at least one bastard, maybe more. So the young rascal had lechery in his blood: all the better.

"Yes, yes, Barbara, I can read it in your face," Anne said crossly. "Yes, that trollop Arabella is his sister, and I can only hope he will prove less troublesome than she has."

"He won't seek a place in His Grace's bed," I said. "At least I don't believe so."

She scowled. "That's not in the least amusing, Barbara."

"Oh, hush, if I cannot make such jests, then no one can," I said. "Look at how his coat fits his shoulders, and tell me you'd not break a commandment for him."

"That's you, Barbara," Anne answered primly. "Not I."

"Well, then, *I* would break all ten, and willingly, too, for a face as fine as that." I rose gracefully, smoothing my petticoats in the way I had that still would draw every male eye in the room. "He looks a little lost, don't you think? In need of a warm welcome to court?"

Anne groaned. "Don't devour him whole, Barbara," she pleaded. "Leave a few crumbs to do my husband's bidding."

But I was already crossing the room toward him. I'd only come halfway when he'd begun looking at me with unabashed approval, and desire, too. That others were watching us in turn like players on the stage only added to my pleasure. Let them look, I thought, and let them tell Charles. He might content himself with his milky-pale French chit, but I'd capture the greater prize by far.

"Your Grace," Churchill said, bowing low over his well-turned leg. Being a soldier, he was permitted to wear his sword in company, a pretty attraction. He'd know how to use it, too. "I'd heard much of your beauty, Your Grace, but nothing could truly prepare me."

Slowly I opened my fan. "You know me, then?"

"Who does not, Your Grace?" he said frankly. He'd lovely eyes, gray green and bright against his browned skin. "I should know you anywhere."

I smiled, delighted. "I assure you, sir, I only improve on acquaintance."

"Then I pray I'll have that honor." Belatedly he realized he'd forgotten to introduce himself, a slight flush coloring his cheeks as he bowed again. "Ensign John Churchill. Your obedient servant, Your Grace."

I offered him my arm, and he took it as if it already belonged to him.

"Then obey me, Ensign," I said, teasing. "Come with me, and we'll see if you can both give and take orders."

He laughed, nothing shy. "I can assure you, Your Grace, you'll not find me wanting in any area."

Nor did I. He shared my bed that first night, and I could not recall a more splendid coupling. He was eager and ardent, young and strong: he delighted in me as much as I did in him. Though no greenhorn, he was willing to be guided in the finer points of love and seduction, and I was glad to share the delights of my lusciously won experience. As well matched as I'd always been with Charles, it was all the more pleasing with John, because I was the leader.

Which is not to say I was overbearing or unwomanly. On the contrary, we met each other as complete equals in my bed, and delighted one another over and over. But I'd come to an age that no lady wishes. While the world still lauded my beauty, I could not look at my face in the glass in the morning without feeling pangs for what I'd lost, to never be again recovered. I *was* my beauty, and when my share of it would finally drain away, I'd no notion of what else would be left.

But with John Churchill, all this was forgotten. He was young and handsome, and when he called me beautiful, I believed him, and gloried in it. When I lay with him, I was young again, too.

But it did not last. God help me, it did not last.

"Your Grace, you must wake!"

I rolled over to face Wilson, standing there with her face moonishly lit by the candlestick in her hand. Surely it could not be time to rise yet: the room was still black with night, and it seemed I'd only just laid my head onto the pillow.

"Go away, Wilson, you impudent creature," I muttered, turning my face back into the pillow. "And don't come back until a respectable hour."

"Forgive me, Your Grace, but you must rise," she insisted. "The messenger from St. James's was most urgent. The Duchess of York is perilously ill, Your Grace, and if you wish to see her again in this life, you must go to her now, before she dies."

I dressed as quickly as I could and hurried the short distance from Berkshire House to St. James's Palace. There were enough lights from within and carriages drawn up before the door to show that something was amiss. The servants were weeping, the women having thrown up their aprons to wipe their eyes. I found Charles in the small parlor before the duchess's bedchamber, and sorrowfully he drew me aside. I knew he must be thinking of his sister's death, still so recent and as unexpected as this one, and I put my arms around him by way of comfort.

"She ate a hearty dinner," he explained in a grim whisper, "then rose from her chair, and collapsed in agony. She was brought back here and the physicians called at once, but they say there is no hope for recovery."

I glanced through the open door, where the duchess's bed was surrounded by the huddled figures of those closest to her. Surely she did appear beyond all mortal help, her face unnaturally swollen and ashen, her breath so faint she seemed already a corpse. Her husband the duke crouched beside her to stroke her forehead, while her two young princess daughters—the Lady Mary, nine, and the Lady Anne, only six—stood miserably to the other side, too unsure and frightened to weep.

"Have they ventured a cause?" I asked. The duchess had recently given birth to her eighth child, another daughter, though only this babe and the two older daughters had survived. "Surely it cannot be childbed fever, not after so many weeks."

"They say it's some blight that's consumed her from within," Charles said. "I fear she suffers greatly, poor lady."

"Poor lady, indeed," I murmured. For all that she was Clarendon's daughter, I'd come to like her much, especially once we'd both made our conversions to Rome. "Has she been granted last rites?"

Charles hesitated, just long enough that I knew this to be a difficult question. "Her husband has decided that, yes."

But what I learned later was that no decision was made at all, with the duke so fearful of public outcry against the duchess's sworn faith that he let his wife die without the comforts of either a cleric or the sacrament. The suffering of her body must have been as nothing compared to that of her soul, and to bear witness to such pain was to feel a measure of it.

Whether because of this or the duchess's last illness, her bloated body decayed so swiftly that it was considered impossible for her to lie in state or be given a proper burial that was by rights her due. The scandal about her conversion that the duke had hoped to avoid occurred anyway, with her own Anglican brother denouncing her for her religion. In Parliament, too, she was not mourned, but held up only as one more ominous warning sign of the papists' infiltration into the highest levels of the nobility. To my mind, the whole affair of the poor lady's death was handled with unseemly haste and a shocking lack of respect.

The duchess had been but thirty-five. With her death following so closely on the heels of Madame's at twenty-six, I was made to feel the uncertainty of my life and the frailty of all my worldly pleasures.

"What a handsome rascal you are," I said to John, lying atop him with his cock deep within me. "Surely peace between nations is a most admirable state, if it means I can keep my warrior here with me."

He kissed me lazily, for we'd not left my bed for the better part of the day, and we were so spent that lazy, indolent fucking was all we were good for.

"You'd be the prize of any soldier's dream, Barbara," he said fondly, his hands full of my flesh as he held me steady. "So long as the French generals can't make up their minds to attack the infernal Dutch, I'm mightily pleased to stay exactly where I am."

He gave an extra thrust of his hips to remind me of exactly where that location might be, and I groaned in satiate delight. "You must swear to surrender your sword only to me, Ensign, else I—hark, listen to that."

I lifted my head the better to hear, and my heart lurched within my breast. There were certain sounds I'd recognize anywhere, and one of them was Charles's footfall on the stairs of my house.

"By all that's holy, it's the king!" I cried in a frantic whisper. "Quick, quick, away!"

I rolled off him and from the bed, hunting in vain for my discarded smock while he, too, scrambled for his clothes. Still buttoning his breeches, he turned toward the door.

"There's no time for that," I said, grabbing him by the arm. The last thing I wanted was for my two lovers to meet on the stairs; though each knew of the other, I understood enough of male pride to see the peril of having them together in such a circumstance. To one side of my bedchamber stood a large cupboard where I kept biscuits, wine, and other refreshments as well as extra coverlets. I threw open the cupboard's door and shoved my amorous soldier within, even as he stole a final kiss. I latched the door and dropped the key into the cup on the windowsill, kicked John's remaining clothes far beneath my bed, and hopped back under the covers only seconds before Charles opened my door. It was as baldly done as any comic scene in a play, though with the potential for far more lasting consequences.

"Good day, sweetheart," he said, full of smiles as he sailed his flat-brimmed hat across the room to the chair, as was his habit. "The afternoon's so fine, I couldn't keep at my desk another moment. There's nothing like a brisk walk across the park to fire the blood, eh?"

"Indeed there's not, sir," I agreed, letting the coverlet slide lower over my breasts so he'd see I was already naked, a patent diversion, yes, but one that cheerfully works with men. "I wasn't expecting you until later this evening."

"I like surprises," he said, shrugging out of his coat. But though he still smiled, I saw the change in his expression that showed I hadn't fooled him. I should have known, of course. He'd been on the other end of such games often enough himself to recognize every sign and trick. After the afternoon that John and I had had, likely my bedchamber was as ripe as any den with our scent, and Charles had discovered the truth as soon as he'd opened the door. But still I'd carry my bluff, and see how long he'd go without calling it: for what other ruse did I have, really?

He tossed his coat over the back of the chair and glanced pointedly at the cupboard. Oh, he knew, he *knew*.

"I'll have a glass of canary, my dear, to restore me after that walk," he said. "Go on, madam, fetch it for me."

"I—I can't," I said. "The door is locked, and one of the maids misplaced the key. I'll order you a glass brought up, so—"

"Lost the key?" he said, going to stand before the cupboard. I could too well imagine John inside, listening and holding his breath. "I hope you thrashed the chit for her carelessness. But these locks are easy enough to pick. One of your hairpins, if you please, and we'll make short work of it."

"No!" I cried, slipping from the bed. I clutched the sheet around me as a makeshift dressing gown and hurried to join him, slipping my arm around his waist. "That is, why should we squander our time picking locks?"

He frowned sternly, toying with me now. "Open the door, sweetheart," he ordered, "else the poor fellow shall smother inside. I'll not be able to save you from the noose if you're charged with his death."

"Fetch the key, Barbara," a muffled John called from inside the cupboard, and I'd no choice then but to obey them both. Contrarily I unlocked the door, and John stepped out in only his breeches, blinking at the light as he bowed deeply to the king.

"Good day, Your Majesty," he murmured, a brave salute, I thought, considering how he must have realized that his entire career could be at risk. One cross word from the king and he could be sent away to any English holding in the world, to languish forever at some faraway posting.

"And a wretched day to you, Churchill," Charles said mildly. "But I'll forgive you, since I know you're here only to earn your keeping and your bread. Now go."

"Thank you, sir," he said, the only possible answer. He bowed again, and left the room without bothering to retrieve the rest of his clothes.

Still holding the sheet around me, I looked up at the king, sheepish, not seductive.

"How much money has that rascal taken from you?" he asked finally.

I shrugged, and the sheet slipped lower over my shoulders. I'd indulged John, yes, the way I did all my lovers, but he was poor, and I was rich, so where was the harm to it?

"More than a pittance," I admitted, "but less than you've squandered on Portsmouth."

"Then far, far less than I've given to you." He sighed, more amused than angry. "Madam, all I ask of you is that, for your own sake, you make the least noise that you can, and I care not where you love."

I let the sheet drop to the floor. "Shall you stay, sir?"

"You wicked jade," he said, taking me in his arms. "You know I will."

By the beginning of 1672, the effects of the Treaty of Dover were finally being felt. Against the will of Parliament, Charles pressed through a new Declaration of Indulgence. He regarded it as another attempt to guarantee the religious freedoms he'd promised so long ago at Breda; his Anglican subjects bristled, and saw it instead as granting more unnecessary favors to papists.

For the handful of us who knew the details of the secret treaty, the new declaration could only be one more step toward the day when Charles might make his conversion to the Catholic church.

I was again denounced as the evilest of influences on the king, because of my faith, and he was pressured to put me aside because of it. Nor did it help his cause to have as his second mistress another Catholic lady, and a Frenchwoman at that.

But other aspects of the main treaty were coming to flower, too. King Louis's France was already at war on the land with the Prince of Orange's Holland, with Charles's England soon to follow at sea. John Churchill was already in Flanders, commanding a regiment for the French general Turenne. In the strange way of coincidence in our world, he also served with the king's first natural son, the Duke of Monmouth, who was likewise making his name as a warrior.

In London I listened to reports of the war with constant fear for John's safety, dreading that I might hear his name among the lists of those known killed. Like every other woman who has ever had the misfortune to love a soldier, I tried to remain cheerful. Given my natural humor, I succeeded. Especially since, as the weeks passed, I realized to my chagrin that he'd left me with a lasting memento of his own, and filled my belly with a most unexpected child.

And for all Charles had said he didn't care, with this particular peccadillo he was not amused. He could count the days and weeks as well as I, and likewise knew how seldom he'd been to visit my bed, or I his. Oh, he didn't scold or rant—that wasn't his way—but he made sure I knew that he was spending more and more time with the French Louise. He still came daily to Berkshire House, but it was to visit the children, not me. He took no notice of my swelling belly, nor did he once enquire after my health in that regard. As far as he was concerned, this child that was not his did not exist.

I'd misstepped, misstepped badly. I was thirty-one years old, and for the sake of my other children, I knew I could ill afford to falter again.

# Chapter Twenty-two

"How handsome they look together," I said, my eyes hazy with tears of joy, like every mother at her child's wedding. "Aren't they a perfect couple, my lord?"

Beside me Lord Arlington sighed, and to my surprise I saw the tears in those steely eyes, too. "To see my little Isabella a bride—ah, Your Grace, it both swells my heart and breaks it."

I nodded, understanding entirely. I'd spent the most ungainly months of my confinement arranging suitable matches for my children, a most satisfying task. Being a natural child of the king was a considerable attribute, especially since Charles had always treated our children with love and regard. They'd each been granted titles and livings commensurate with their royal blood, too, and I'd had my pick of the noblest families eager to blend their bloodlines and their fortunes with the king's. The fact that my sons and daughters were still too young to be true brides or grooms—my oldest daughter, Anne, was only eleven—deterred no one. Royal families did these things differently, and once a marriage was blessed by the church and the lawyers, then the happy pair would be returned to their respective nurseries until they were old enough to consummate their unions.

Today Charles and I had come to Euston Hall to see our son Henry wed to Lord Arlington's daughter Isabella. Though mothers are not supposed to have favorites, Henry was mine, the most handsome and charming of my brood, and at eight a most precocious small nobleman, too. As part of his wedding present, Charles had made him Baron Sudbury, Viscount Ipswich, and Earl of Euston, with a promise of the Garter and a dukedom to come. His five-year-old bride was Arlington's sole child, and through the settlement my Henry would now become his heir, to inherit not only his estate but his titles with it. Our lives had already been interwoven through politics and power, and now the bonds of money and family had been braided into the mix, too. Was there any wonder I wept with joy?

"I congratulate you, Arlington," Charles said, joining us. It had been seven years since Monmouth's wedding, and he enjoyed playing the role of the jovial father of the groom to the hilt. This elegant new house at Euston Hall, full of paintings and fine furniture, with gardens in the latest French style, reflected all the prosperity that Arlington had been able to reap from the king's reign, so it was a fine thing for Charles to see some of that largesse come shining back his way. "We've done well with our sprouts, eh?"

"A splendid match, sir," Arlington said, repeating what we'd all been saying over and over again. With such a couple too young for love, there wasn't much else that could be said, truly. "I thought the archbishop maintained precisely the proper manner."

"He did," Charles said. "Considering how unpleasant the bishops have been of late, I trust they'll duly report that my son and your daughter were wed with the full blessings of the Anglican church."

"Oh, come, sir, none of that, not today," I said, taking his arm. "Walk with me, and I promise I'll sweeten your humor."

"You see how it is, Arlington," he said as he winked at me with the old spirit. "I'm helpless before her."

In companionable silence, we walked away from the house and the party, across the raked gravel paths of the garden toward the fields beyond. The day was summer in her fullest glory, and I prayed it was another augur for my son's happiness.

"You look well, Barbara," he said at last. "I'm thankful for your safe delivery."

I glanced up at him from beneath the curled brim of my hat, surprised he'd finally alluded to the birth of John Churchill's daughter.

She'd been late arriving, like all my other babes, so late that we'd had to delay this wedding a month to permit me more time to recover.

"So am I," I said, trying to decide how much information he really wished to learn. "The babe's name is Barbara, Barbara Palmer."

He nodded, though I'm sure he already knew the name, or more specifically that I hadn't tried to claim her as a Fitzroy. There wasn't any question of her being his, anyway; she was clearly the little cuckoo in my nest.

"It's high time you named one for yourself," he said. "You've seen to the labor of raising them. You might as well claim the credit."

I smiled wryly. "How vastly generous of you, sir."

"No, Barbara, I mean that," he said, stopping to look me full in the face, there beneath a stand of oak trees so that the sun and leafy shadows played in equal pattern across us. "Has Churchill owned little Barbara yet?"

I shrugged. "He is young," I said, excusing him when he'd no right to be excused. "He has other matters to concern him, nor has he the means to support a child."

"That's no excuse," he said gruffly. "She deserves a father. Call her Fitzroy if you please."

I caught my breath with surprise, for I'd not expected that.

"You've done well for my other children, Barbara," he said, watching my reaction closely. "What's one more, eh?"

My smile faded beneath his scrutiny. I do not know what he saw, or what he'd hoped to find. He was the king, and he needed no reasons.

"Have you ever imagined what our lives might have been like if we'd been born ordinary folk?" I asked softly. "If we'd been only Charles and Barbara, instead of Stuart and Villiers?"

"Ah, Barbara," he said sadly. "I long ago learned the peril of longing for what might have been."

I thought of all that that simple declaration could include: his father's execution, his own exile, the deaths of every one of his siblings but James, his barren wife and empty marriage, the endless promise of a reign that was never so glorious as it should have been.

And me.

As if he could hear my unspoken thoughts, he raised my hand to his lips to kiss, and smiled wearily.

"No, sweet, it's better, far better, to accept the fate we've been given, and content ourselves with that. Now, come, let's back to the others, and pray that those naughty children of ours have kept from mischief."

Like the last Dutch War, this new one did not go as quickly or as well as everyone had believed it should with the French as England's allies. By the spring of 1673, Charles was forced to ask Parliament for more money, else his fleet could not go back to sea against William of Orange. Parliament would agree only if Charles would withdraw his last Declaration of Indulgence, that act of great tolerance so long dear to him. He resisted as long as he could, until finally he'd no choice but to do it if he wished his sailors fed. In return for seventy thousand pounds a year, he withdrew his declaration with considerable anger and mortification.

But Parliament decided that the revocation hadn't gone far enough. The fact that the widowed Duke of York now planned to marry the Italian Maria Beatrice, the sister of the Duke of Modena, and, of course, a staunch Roman Catholic, did nothing to allay their fears. If the king insisted on consorting with papists among his friends, ministers, and mistresses, then it was left to the government to prove England was no place for the papist menace.

Thus the Commons passed a most odious Test Act, calculated to winnow us Catholics like so much chaff from any sort of power. All holders of public office, high and low, must be Anglican, and take public Holy Communion in the Church of England. There were also sundry oaths of allegiance that must be pledged that were calculated to be impossible for any Catholics sincere in their faith to make. If the officeholder refused, then they must resign their place immediately.

The effect of such a hateful, prejudicial act was felt immediately. No matter that the Duke of York had served both his country and his brother with loyalty and distinction in war and in peace: because he was not seen to take Communion at Easter, he was forced to resign as Lord High Admiral, and watched as other lesser officers through the ranks of the military were compelled to follow for the sin of not being Anglicans. From Lord Clifford resigning from his place as Lord Treasurer to the lowest of His Majesty's fiddlers, the purge was thorough.

I'd not tended the queen in any real capacity for several years, not since she'd pleaded ill health and retired from court to live in seclusion at Somerset House. I'd kept the post as Lady of the Bedchamber, however, with the honor and income that came with it, and no one had thought the worse of me for it. But because I refused to toss up my faith for public consideration, I was asked to relinquish my post, and nothing Charles could do or say would change it.

The entire court was changing, and not for the better. I felt as if I were standing on the edge of the ocean with the tide pulling the very sand from under my feet, and no matter how I chose to thrash and fight to save myself, I'd no hope, and would soon be lost forever beneath the waves.

"No one dances like you, Your Grace." John bowed to me at the end of the set and took my hand to lead me from the floor. "You honor me."

"It's not often I have a true hero as my partner," I said, smiling my favor. He'd returned from the war heaped with glory and honors, and for his valor he'd been promoted to captain. He'd become boon companions with Monmouth, too, who credited John with saving his life in battle, almost as certain a path to success at court as having me as his patroness.

To be sure, I had welcomed him back to my bed when he'd returned from the Continent, and marveled at the lurid new battle scars that crisscrossed his splendid body. They were nothing, he'd demurred, mere scratches, yet how proudly he'd paraded them around my bedchamber for me to admire!

He'd shown far less interest in his new daughter, even daring to question if in fact she was truly to be laid upon his doorstep. I realized that he was an ambitious young man, with his way to make in the world; still, I could not help but sadly compare his disinterest in his small baby with Charles's constant delight in his own natural children.

"Ah, there's Monmouth," John said, smiling as he caught sight of his friend and fellow soldier across the room. "I must be sure to pay my respects later."

"Go now, if you wish," I said, giving him a gentle prod with my furled fan. There was little use in keeping him chained to my side if he wished to be elsewhere, and besides, the Banqueting House was full of other acquaintances of mine. I could let the bounding puppy run free, knowing he'd come back to me later at Berkshire House, where he proved his real merit, anyway. "I know how Monmouth needs to be amused."

"You are certain, Your Grace?" he asked, all tender solicitude.

"I am," I said, doting in return. "Now go, away with you!"

He grinned, so like an eager boy it could make me melt, and bowed quickly, before he slipped into the crowd. I turned to the front of the room, where Charles was sitting. Behind him stood the Duchess of Mazarin, a wild, black-haired Italian creature who had arrived at court dressed in men's clothes with a menagerie of wild animals and African servants. Rumor said that Charles was infatuated with her, though knowing his tastes, I could hardly credit it.

But it was Louise, the Duchess of Portsmouth, who was perched on a low stool beside his chair to rest her head against his arm like one of his infernal spaniels, and with as much wit in her round, empty head. Absently he stroked his hand up and down her back; he looked worn and weary to me, and disinterested, too. There'd been a time when he'd desired a woman to have the gift for raillery as well as rare beauty, and to me this insipid young creature was more a dull sheep than a fit mistress to such a king. It made me sad to see, and so instead I looked back across the room to spy someone else of interest less disheartening.

I found John again, standing with Monmouth as he'd promised. But there was another with him, too, one of the newest maids of honor. A pert, lively girl named Sarah Jennings, she had golden hair and bright blue eyes, and was said to be very clever. She wore no paint or jewels, nor did she need them. When she laughed at something he'd said, she touched her fingers lightly to his forearm, and I could see by the happy glow in his eyes that he was completely enchanted.

He'd never once looked at me like that.

Unable to turn away, I watched as he bent to whisper in her ear. She laughed again and took his hand, and let him lead her away from the room and into the hall.

I knew what they would do in those shadowy halls and staircases at Whitehall. This girl was fifteen, less than half my thirty-two years, yet the same age I'd been when I'd first dallied with the Earl of Chesterfield.

God in heaven, where had those years gone?

The day the letter came, I was sitting in the parlor at Cleveland House, the newer, smaller home overlooking the park that I'd bought when I'd sold Berkshire House for a great profit soon after Barbara had been born the summer before. I was listening to my daughter Charlotte plunk away at her practice on the virginals, and when they announced Bab May I smiled with pleasure for the past times.

"Let me send for tea, or something stronger," I said, my hand on the bell. "You can tell me all the news straightway."

But he shook his head, his unhappiness ripe upon his long face. "Thank you, no, not today. I've only come to bring you this letter, and no more."

"A letter?" I asked, surprised, as I took it from his hand.

"I could not send it through the ordinary messengers, Your Grace," he said heavily. "It didn't seem right to do that to you."

My uneasiness building, I swiftly cracked the letter's seal and read the contents for myself. The message was simple enough, signed and endorsed by some Whitehall functionary whose name I didn't recognize. Because I'd refused to abide by the Test Act, I'd lost my place as Lady of the Bedchamber. And because I'd lost my place at court, I was asked to vacate my lodgings in the palace as soon as such removal could be arranged.

"It's because of Parliament, Your Grace," May said, his insistence hollow to my ears. "It's their doing entirely."

Evenly I met his gaze, creasing fresh folds into the letter with my fingers. "So you would tell me that His Majesty knows nothing of this? That he does not wish my rooms for the Duchess of Portsmouth, or some other favorite?"

He shrugged his shoulders, all I needed to see. "I'm sorry, Your Grace," he said. "I'm sorry."

"Ah, sir," I said softly, tossing the letter into the fire. "You'll never be more sorry than the king himself."

For the final time, I walked across my bedchamber in the front of Cleveland House, to the tall window overlooking the park, and the canal, and Whitehall itself beyond that. It was a gray, chill February day, with the few people on the pathways moving swiftly with their heads down and shoulders hunched, and a skim of dull ice across the surface of the canal. Nothing to see, I thought. Nothing at all, and I closed and latched the window's shutters.

My footsteps echoed through the empty rooms. The grates were cold and swept clean, the curtains drawn and the windows shuttered, the furnishings shrouded with ghostly cloths and the paintings and looking-glasses draped against dust and damp. It was my decision to leave England now, and it would be my decision when, if ever, I returned.

Everything that was coming with us had been long ago packed and sent ahead. We required two coaches and as many wagons to carry me, my four youngest children, our servants, and our trunks and chests to Dover. From there we'd make the crossing to Calais, into France, and then to Paris. At least the sky was clear if muffled, so I'd dare hope the roads would be, too.

I'd spent the last fortnight settling my affairs. I'd made sure the incomes from my manors, six in all, pensions, revenues, and other sources would be forwarded to me. I'd let the house in King Street, now grandly known as Villiers House. I'd proven to have my share of Bayning blood from the counting house after all, and had husbanded my investments and properties so well that there was more than enough for me, my family, and my family's families into the future to live with great ease and comfort.

I'd already changed into my traveling clothes, a quilted petticoat and a fur-lined cloak, and stout shoes fit for cold weather. Safe in my pocket were the instructions written by the French ambassador for the customs house, excusing our party from tariffs and delays as we journeyed through France.

I'd taken much care and deliberation with these preparations, risking nothing to chance. I wanted no one to say I'd gone in haste, or been forced from London. I was leaving of my own choice, in my own manner, and I'd go with my head high. I'd made sure there'd be no place for me on poor Jane Shore's dunghill.

Yet there was only one task remaining for me before we left, and as I walked across the park this last time, I knew it would be the most difficult one of all.

I found Charles in his chambers, as I knew he'd be at this time of day, drinking his coffee and reading the newssheet, wigless, in his red silk dressing gown. In this he was like any other gentleman, and it was like this that I wanted last to see him before I left, without any pomp or spectacle or others around us to gawk and comment.

"Barbara," he said, his face lighting with pleasure and surprise as I walked across the black-and-white marble floor. He rose and came forward to take my hands in his. "Here, sit with me, and we'll break our fast together like old times."

My hands were cold inside my gloves, his so warm and familiar around them. Yet I did not turn my face to kiss him, or to be kissed, for that wasn't why I'd come.

"I cannot, Your Majesty," I said, determined to be steadfast. "I'm here to say farewell, and that is all."

"Farewell?" he repeated, his smile turning crooked and his voice too hearty. "How can you say farewell, eh?"

"I can say it, sir, because it's true." Without thinking I curled my fingers into his, the old fondness. Of course he knew I was leaving. I'd made no secret of it, and by now I doubted there was a single person left in London who wasn't aware that the Duchess of Cleveland was sailing for France. "Farewell, sir."

"No," he said. "No."

That made me smile. "But, sir, you know I always say yes."

"Then I'll say no," he said firmly, "and force you to stay."

I shook my head. I couldn't weaken, not now. In countless ways, large and small, he'd let me know I'd lost the power I'd once had over him and the rest of the court. At heart Charles was too kind to break entirely with me, but it wasn't in my nature to fade away as a graceful shade of the past. Better to end it like this, now.

"Even the worst gamester realizes when it's time to leave the table, sir," I said softly, "and I'm far from the worst. It's time I was gone, and you know it as well as I."

I reached up to kiss him for the last time, quickly, so I wouldn't falter and change my mind.

"Farewell, sir," I whispered, "and may God keep you always."

Then before he could try to stop me again, I slipped free, and away, and did not look back.

*Author's Note*

The end of Barbara's reign as Charles's mistress had been predicted for so long that when she finally left for France in 1676, most people at court believed she'd be back within a few weeks. To their surprise, she stayed abroad for the next three years, and when she did at last return to England in 1679, it was for the second wedding of her son Henry, Duke of Grafton (now sixteen) to Lady Isabella Bennet (twelve), now considered suitably of age for a "real" marriage. Though Barbara and Charles sat side by side at the wedding supper at Whitehall (the diarist John Evelyn, never a fan of Barbara's, cruelly described her as "the incontinent Duchess," as opposed to Isabella, "the sweet Duchess the bride"), Barbara afterward kept clear of the court and the king.

The rest of her life was markedly less flamboyant than her glory days. In Paris she reconciled with her husband, Roger Palmer, and their relationship seems to have been surprisingly cordial and centered around Barbara's children. Those same children also kept Charles in touch with Barbara. There were many letters back and forth between them that sound like those of any other parents concerned with their children's welfare.

Barbara left the court an extremely wealthy woman, and was able to lead the rest of her life without the penury that often plagues former mistresses. Yet she did have her share of money woes. Constant gambling for high stakes ate away at her fortune (one night of legendary bad luck was said to have cost her twenty thousand pounds in money and jewels), and while the Duke of York continued to pay her allowances and pensions after he became James II, his successor, William of Orange, ended all payments to her and the rest of his late uncle's mistresses as soon as he came to the throne.

After Roger's death in 1704, she made an unfortunate second marriage to a notorious womanizer named Beau Fielding, who spent a good deal of her money before she discovered he already had another wife, and charged him with bigamy in a much-publicized trial. Her children, now grown, were there at her side in support. She spent her last days living with her favorite grandson. She died in 1709 at sixty-eight, of complications from dropsy, that old-fashioned word for edema. Modern medical historians suspect it was only a symptom of long-standing venereal disease.

Charles II lived until 1685, dying of complications from a stroke at fifty-five. On his deathbed, he was granted last rites by a Catholic priest invited by Louise de Keroualle and his brother; no one is certain whether it was Charles's final wish to convert to Catholicism, or theirs. While his legacy includes the restoration of the English monarchy as well as parliamentary reform, he is today best remembered for ruling at the time of momentous events like the plague and the Great Fire, and for earning the label of "the merry monarch" on account of his lighthearted, immoral court—a reputation that Barbara certainly helped him to build.

He was succeeded by his brother the Duke of York, who became James II. With no regard for the doctrines of tolerance that were so dear to Charles, James's three-year reign was oppressive, disastrous, and mercifully short. He was overthrown in the Glorious Revolution of 1688, a bloodless coup led in part by John Churchill and his wife, Sarah. He lived the rest of his life in exile in France, while William of Orange and his wife, James's older daughter Mary, assumed the English throne as William and Mary.

Though Charles is credited with siring at least fifteen children, none of them were legitimate. The most famous of these was the first, James, Duke of Monmouth. Though handsome and charming, Monmouth was easily led by others, and ended up as the figurehead of a rebellion against his uncle James. He tried to claim the crown for himself as Charles's true Protestant heir, maintaining (fancifully) that Charles had in fact wed his mother, Lucy Walter. Instead the rebellion failed, and Monmouth was bloodily beheaded; among those who helped capture him were his old friend John Churchill, and Barbara's son, Henry, Duke of Grafton.

Barbara's first known lover, Philip, Earl of Chesterfield, was also a fixture of the Restoration court, but more for the immoral antics of his second wife than his own. In a wry twist of fate, she was reputed to have had so many lovers, including the Duke of York, that Philip finally had to banish her to his remote country estate to keep her from mischief. When she died early in their brief marriage, he was rumored to have poisoned her in desperation. His third wife proved to be the charm, and with her he retreated to a quiet life in the country.

Barbara's children turned out much better than many with more traditional upbringings. They all survived to adulthood, and all but one were married in the matches that Barbara arranged for them, with surprising success. None of them had the celebrity or charisma of either of their famous parents, but they were quietly happy, which is probably worth more in the long run.

The first, Anne Palmer, though recognized by Roger and his family as his daughter and heir, was nonetheless given away by Charles in a splendid wedding at Hampton Court, and like her sister, granted a dowry of twenty thousand pounds. (Her title of Countess of Sussex was another example of Barbara's long memory for slights; it had been carefully chosen by Barbara to spite her stepfather, who'd left his entire estate not to her but to his sister, an earlier Countess of Sussex.)

Her son Charles, the least promising of Barbara's children, inherited her titles at her death and became the Duke of Cleveland. Despite Barbara's own money woes later in life, she'd scrupulously provided and invested well for her children; by the middle of the eighteenth century, her grandson's annual income from interest alone was over one hundred thousand pounds.

Charles's favorite among the children, Charlotte, Countess of Litchfield, was a model of the virtuous English lady, happily wed for forty-two years, and even more happily the mother to twenty children of her own. Only Barbara's last daughter, Barbara Fitzroy, was truly scandalous: she had a brief, intense affair that resulted in an illegitimate child of her own, and then promptly retreated for the rest of her life to a French convent.

In the small world of the seventeenth century, Barbara's favorite son, Henry, Duke of Grafton, rose through the ranks of the navy, taking part in the Glorious Revolution and serving with John Churchill in James II's campaigns. He died at twenty-six of wounds sustained while fighting alongside Churchill at the Siege of Cork in 1689.

Her third son, George, Duke of Northumberland, was the child who most physically resembled the king. Even the ever-critical diarist John Evelyn praised George as "civil, well-bred, and modest" (adjectives he'd never use with Barbara), and the "most accomplished and worth the owning" of all of Charles's children.

John Churchill married Sarah Jennings. With money given to him by Barbara rumored to be as much as one hundred thousand pounds, he embarked on a political and military career that made him one of the greatest generals in English history, his wife the most powerful woman at the court of Queen Anne, and the two of them together the Duke and Duchess of Marlborough, and the wealthiest couple in Europe.

More than three hundred years after her death, Barbara Villiers continues to be one of the more reviled women in English history. A glance through the Internet message boards on the many sites devoted to the Restoration proves that whenever her name appears, the controversy does, too. The standard openings to such posts seem to be: "The Duchess of Cleveland was an ugly, greedy, stupid whore." And that's only the beginning.

Barbara has consistently been painted through history in the darkest colors imaginable. She is always the villainess, the evil woman of horrifying appetites, even, in the words of John Evelyn, "the curse of the nation." Because she was regarded as a genuine threat to the king and to England's stability during her own lifetime, a great deal was written about her, much of it patently false in the glorious tradition of tabloid celebrity bashing. Yet many modern historians who should know better accept these stories and perpetuate them to the point that, over the centuries, it's hard to tell fact from slander.

It's also impossible to feel the power of her much-lauded beauty. Tastes have changed, and modern eyes look at her famous portraits by Sir Peter Lely and wonder what the fuss was about. Beauty and sexual attractiveness are among the most transient and fleeting of qualities, yet even Barbara's harshest critics admitted she was the most stunningly beautiful woman of her day. Wherever she went, crowds would gather for a glimpse of her.

When I began to write this book, I'd no intention of becoming Barbara Villiers's apologist. It's impossible to gloss over some of her less appealing attributes—she *was* self-centered, vain, and avaricious. But she was also witty, passionate, and generous to those she loved, and to me she was clearly the one woman among all of Charles's mistresses who was his equal in every way except royal blood. If theirs was not one of the great traditional love stories of history, then it was certainly a great friendship between two people in complete sympathy.

Firsthand accounts of Charles's reign are surprisingly plentiful. Living as we do today in a security-conscious society, it's hard to imagine how freely Charles and Barbara moved through London. Together they walked with his dogs in the park, fed the ducks on the canal, and attended the same churches and theatres that his subjects did. They also didn't mind fighting (and reconciling) before an audience, either. Unlike his autocratic father, Charles believed in being accessible to his people, high and low, and his personal involvement in fighting the Great Fire is a testament to his rare empathy with his fellow Londoners. Everyone in the city recognized Charles, and they recognized Barbara with him.

James II, Lord Clarendon, and Bishop Burnet each wrote personal histories of the times, heavily based on their own experiences. The memoirs of the French Comte de Grammont, a visitor to the English court, make wonderfully gossipy reading. Two of the greatest English diarists of all time—John Evelyn and Samuel Pepys—were witnesses to much of Charles's daily life, and dutifully noted the details. While Evelyn despised Barbara (to him she was "that great Imperial Whore") and the hedonistic lifestyle she represented, Pepys was unabashedly obsessed with her, buying engravings of her portraits and carefully noting each time he saw her. He had many opportunities, too; in his position in the Admiralty Office, he was often at Whitehall on business or at the house of Lord Sandwich, which happened to be next door to Barbara's house in King Street.

For example, this entry in Pepys's diary for July 13, 1660, inspired the scene of Barbara's musical party for the king and his two brothers:

> Great doings of music at the next house, which was
> Whally's; the King and Dukes there with Madame Palmer, a pretty woman that they have a fancy to, to make her
> husband a cuckold. Here at the old door that did go into
> his lodgings, my Lord [Sandwich], I, and W. Howe did
> stand listening a great while to the music.

I've tried hard to keep to historical fact, and when historical fact was wanting, to the spirit of the times and people. I'm not a historian; I'm a novelist. Yet as challenging as Barbara could be, I've enjoyed the time I've spent in her company. I hope she'd approve of the result.

*Susan Holloway Scott*
*December 2006*

# Acknowledgments

No book comes into being without a slew of beneficent fairy godmothers (and a few godfathers, too) to guide it on its way. Heartfelt thanks are in order to those whose patience, wisdom, and combined senses of humor helped keep *Royal Harlot* on track.

First, of course, is my editor, Claire Zion, for her constant support and enthusiasm for these books, and for understanding that a final delivery day can sometimes be as ever-changing and elusive as the morning mists.

Next in line is Meg Ruley, the unquestionable Queen of Agents; Annelise Robey, surely the Princess; and everyone else at the Jane Rotrosen palace. Long may you reign!

For giving me a long-neglected presence on the Internet, and dragging me from the seventeenth century into the twenty-first, special appreciation must go to my webmistress, Mollie Smith, and to her mother (and my good friend), Jenny Crusie, for pushing me there, too, when I needed pushing.

I'd also like to thank my fellow blogging-wenches at www.Word-Wenches.com: Jo Beverly, Loretta Chase, Susan King, Edith Layton, Mary Jo Putney, and Patricia Rice. There's none better at understanding both the joys and the challenges of writing.

It's impossible to write historical fiction without research, and equally impossible to conduct research without libraries. I've been most fortunate to have had access to some of the best. Many thanks to the following libraries, and their staffs: the Mariam Coffin Canaday Library, Bryn Mawr College; the John D. Rockefeller Jr. Library, Colonial Williamsburg; the Earl Gregg Swem Library, College of William & Mary; and the Pattee Library, Pennsylvania State University, University Park.

**Susan Holloway Scott** is the author of more than thirty historical novels. A graduate of Brown University, she lives with her family in Pennsylvania. Visit her Web site at www.susanhollowayscott.com.

# Royal Harlot

## A NOVEL OF THE COUNTESS OF CASTLEMAINE AND KING CHARLES II

## SUSAN HOLLOWAY SCOTT

# QUESTIONS
# FOR DISCUSSION

1. By telling Barbara's story, the author also tells the story of Charles II's return to the throne. How would this story have been different if Charles had been the narrator?

2. Lord Clarendon, Barbara's enemy at court, called her a "woman of appetites." What do you think he meant by that?

3. Though the future of the English succession depended on Charles fathering a male heir, he refused to "put aside" his barren wife, Catherine of Braganza, in favor of a more fertile queen, as his ancestor Henry VIII repeatedly did. Why do you think he refused?

4. The rootless generation of young Royalists who came of age between the 1650s and 1670s were in many ways similar to the post–World War I generation that fueled the excesses and social changes of the 1920s. How are they alike? How are they different?

5. Do you think Barbara would have played a role in the politics of the Restoration court if she'd been born a Villiers man, like her cousin the Duke of Buckingham, instead of a woman?

6. One of the criticisms leveled at Barbara by her enemies was that she was an "unnatural" mother. What do you think was meant by this?

7. At the French court, the King's Mistress was an accepted, official post—the "titled mistress"—yet in England, Charles encountered great resistance and outrage to the amount of favoritism he showed Barbara and his other mistresses. Why do you think this was? Why would the cultures of the French and English courts have been so different?

8. Barbara was always conscious of her appearance, saying, "I *was* my beauty, and when my share of it would finally drain away, I'd no notion of what else would be left" (p. 342). How did she use her beauty?

9. If Barbara had been married to Charles instead of Roger Palmer, do you think she would have been a more faithful wife?

10. Seventeenth-century England was largely an Anglican nation, with only about 20 percent of the population worshipping as Roman Catholics. Yet because a much higher percentage of the noble families at court were Catholic, anti-Catholic hysteria was a real factor of the times. Do you think these fears were reasonable?

11. The promiscuous gentlemen of Charles's court were called libertines, while the equally promiscuous Barbara was called a whore. Discuss this double standard.

12. Throughout history, Barbara has been regarded as an evil, immoral woman who purposefully set out to bewitch the king for

her own gain. How much of her immorality was a product of her times, and how much do you think was a part of her character?

13. The artist Sir Peter Lely painted numerous portraits of Barbara, regarding her as not only his muse but the most perfect representation of feminine beauty. It also made good business sense for him to be so closely linked to the king's favorite. In an era before photography and television, how could painted portraits like those of Barbara influence public opinion?

Read on for a preview of
Susan Holloway Scott's next novel of Restoration England

## The King's Favorite

### A NOVEL OF NELL GWYN AND KING CHARLES II

Coming from New American Library in 2008

---

I never claimed to be a lady.

Why should I? In truth I'm proud of who I am, and what I made myself to be, and that is worth a score of the highborn idle dissemblers that chatter like magpies about Whitehall Palace. I am content to be Nellie Gwyn, no more, no less. That is enough for me, and for my great love the king as well.

To be sure, my life has been a merry path, full of cunning turns and twists. Anything seemed possible in those first early days, when Cromwell's sour-faced Puritans had at last been turned out and King Charles new returned to the throne. Even as I toiled away my nights at Madam Ross's, I wasn't afraid to dream beyond my station, or to vow to do whatever I must to make those dreams become golden truth.

Madam Ross's house stood off Drury Lane, a slanting, slatternly place whose slipshod front was a match for what went on upstairs. The front room was thick with smoke and grime that never faded, the low beams overhead blackened with it. There were round tables at the back for gaming at cards or dice, and benches at another long table for those who wished victuals with their drink.

But most men who came through the narrow door sought nourishment of a different sort, the saucy company of a willing slut that half a crown would buy. With the one-eyed fiddler to play the jigs, it was a jolly enough house for men. Ale and brandy-water swelled them fat with roaring good humor and boastfulness, as if they were the greatest cocksmen the mortal world had ever seen. With a smile and a sly wink, we women let them believe it, too, and in return neatly emptied their pockets when their backs were turned: the same trade practiced by females of every rank, low and high, and where, I ask, is the sin in it?

Now despite what has been said against me by those who delight in slander, I will vow upon the Scriptures that I never went up those twisting stairs with any man. Unlike most bawds in the town, Madam Ross didn't believe in breaking a girl to the trade by force, and was content to let me keep below, singing songs and ferrying pots of beer and ale to the tables all the night whilst I teased and danced free of groping hands. Hard work, aye, but far better than my last line of crying herrings barefoot in the street, fresh, fresh herrings, six for a groat. My mother and my sister, Rose, were not so nice, and jeered at how I'd earn so much less than they did upon their backs.

I didn't listen, or take any heed of them. What did I care for a few more coins in my pocket? Why should I, when I was so sure of the brilliant future Fate meant for me to have?

"Here now, Nell, along wit' you." Glowering, Madam Ross switched her clay pipe from one side of her mouth to the other, and gave me a sharp pinch on my arm to inspire me to haste. "The young scholars t' the back are asking for brandy an' a song, an' they wants it from you."

I nodded, standing on my toes to peer over the others to where she was pointing with the stem of her pipe. For certain they were young gentlemen, down from university for a bit of sport. Because I'd been born among the colleges in Oxford, I could always spot the ones we called "scholars," and a troublesome lot they often were. With a sigh, I began to go toward them, but Madam Ross pulled me back.

"Mark the dark-haired one—his fellows call him 'my lord,'" she cautioned. "An earl, for all he's such a pup. Kindness, Nell. Show him kindness."

I nodded. We often had noblemen visit us, playing at taking their pleasure like a common Jack; they were good for custom, and to be encouraged. I smoothed the front of my rough wool bodice as I made my way toward the table, and raked my fingers through my auburn curls to make them fall more sweetly over my shoulders.

"Good eve, my handsome lads," I said with my cheeriest smile. "What's your pleasure this night?"

The three on the far side of the table grinned at me like the happy young sots that they were, their downy, pimpled cheeks ruddy and their eyes fuddled. The one that Madam Ross had marked as an earl turned in his seat to face me, and lah! How different he was from the others! He was splendidly favored, with even features and a mouth ripe with amusement, his dark, thick hair tumbling down his back. There were gold rings on his fingers, and soft fur on the green velvet cloak that he wore tossed over one shoulder, the very picture, I thought, of a young lordling.

Not that I trusted him the more for it. Young I was, aye, but not so foolish as that.

"Your name is Nell?" he asked, as if this were some new drollery.

"Aye, my lord." I bobbed a quick curtsey, taking care to keep my back straight and my rump low, the safest posture amongst a crowd of rampant, rascally men. I was the shortest of all the women, yet prettily curved with the sweetness of youth, and I stood before this young buck proudly, with my arms akimbo, the better to display the neatness of my waist. "Nell, or Eleanor, or Nellie, I'll answer to them all, and a good deal more besides."

"Oh, I'll grant you will, Nell," he said slyly, looking me up and down with unabashed interest. "They say your voice puts the very lark to shame."

"They say true, my lord." I smiled, tipping my head coyly to one side. In return for a song, I likely could cull him for a whole shilling, maybe two. "I sing like a bird, and dance like a sprite."

"I'll wager a crown that you swive like a stoat, too," called one of the other young gentlemen at the table, to the roaring approval of his friends. "Like a wild stoat in heat!"

"Then I'll answer your wager, sir," I called, easily raising my voice to be heard over their din, a skill I'd practiced even then. "I'll wager that *you* bray your wit like a wild ass."

"Hah, Brinton, pay up, pay up, for you are most decidedly an ass." The young earl patted his hand on the table, his gold rings glinting by the light of the fire. "Come now, pay up. Don't keep this admirably clever lass waiting."

Grudgingly Brinton took the coin from his pocket, standing to push it across the table toward me. "It's a damned sorry day when you take a whore's side against me, Rochester," he said, wounded. "A damned sorry day."

Swiftly I claimed the coin before they changed their minds. "It's night, not day, sir," I said, "and I'm no whore."

"If you're no whore, madam," Brinton said with a drunkard's certainty, "then truly I *am* an ass. Rochester, we'll leave you to your *lady*."

Unsteadily he and the others reeled off into the crowd, and the earl looked back to me.

"How can you be in this place, dearling," he asked, "and not be a whore?"

I drummed my fingers lightly against my waist. "How can you be in this place, my lord, yet be a peer?"

"How?" With a single forefinger, he reached out to trace the angle of my bent elbow, so light and featherlike a touch that I shivered. "Because wherever I am, low or high, I will remain the Earl of Rochester."

"Just as I'm Nellie Gwyn, at Madam Ross's or anywhere else," I said firmly, drawing myself away from his wicked, teasing touch. "'Tis said the fairest blossom grows on the dunghill, you know."

He laughed again, settling back in his chair. "But unless that blossom's plucked at the height of its glory, then the stink of the dunghill will in time spoil even its sweet petals. What is needed is a wise gardener, to guide you through the seasons of love."

Love, hah. I knew full well what kind of offer this was, just as I knew I'd be a fool to accept it.

"My blossom's done well enough without some meddlesome gardener, my lord," I said, tossing my hair over my shoulder to show my disdain, "and even if I were crying for one in the market, why, I'd—"

"It's the king!" exclaimed a man behind us. "His Majesty's here!"

At once the words were picked up like a chorus all around us. Everything else was forgotten; every head craning toward the door to see if it were true. Unsure of what was proper to do, some men bowed low and women curtseyed, while others simply gawked to find the king so suddenly in our midst. Without a thought I hopped onto a nearby bench, desperate to see for myself over the crowd of heads.

"The king is here?" asked Rochester with disbelief as he, too, rose to gape. "In *this* place?"

But there was never a chance of mistaking Charles Stuart for anyone else, he was that much taller than the three gentlemen attendants who'd come with him, and every other man in the room. And that was not all: he was dark, almost swarthy, with long, curling black hair that set him apart from ordinary Englishmen, and even from across the room, I could feel the force of his personality, his regal power, and his genial charm, too.

*His Majesty! His Majesty!* I'd glimpsed him from afar like this many times since he'd returned to his throne two years before: when he strolled with his courtiers outside Whitehall Palace, or sailed in the royal yacht on the river, or rode on horseback through St. James's Park. With each sighting he'd bewitched and inspired me further, until I was fair lovesick with him, a man who'd no notion I lived and breathed within his very realm.

"He's come here to this house before, my lord," I now whispered with awe. "We're not supposed to recognize him, dressed so plain like that, but of course we all do. He'll take two or three girls upstairs at a time, and lah, they do swear he is the first gentleman of the kingdom in every way!"

"So it *is* him," Rochester said, his whisper a match for my own. "But why would he come to Drury Lane when he'd so fine a lady as Barbara Palmer waiting in his bed at Whitehall?"

"Oh, Mrs. Palmer," I scoffed. I'd often seen the king and his reigning mistress together. I'd grant that she was as fair as everyone said, dressed and bejeweled as richly as any true queen, but she'd also seemed to me to be haughty and shrewish, and unworthy of so glorious a king. "I've heard the king's lost all interest in her since she's swelled with his bastard."

"Mrs. Palmer's my cousin," Rochester said, "and I assure you, her grasp of the king's royal cods has never been tighter."

I made a small snort of dismissal. The king was laughing with Madam Ross now, while the house's three prettiest girls were blushing before him, as giddy as if they were rank virgins still. "His Majesty deserves better. Besides, Mrs. Palmer's old."

"She's only twenty-one," he said beside me, "and she's still the most beautiful woman in London, as well as the most wanton. Anyone with a mind to see the king does well to see my cousin Barbara first. Faith help me, he's looking this way!"

The earl dropped back down behind the others and into his chair, and to my surprise grabbed me with him. He pulled me onto his lap, his arm tight around my waist.

"What in blazes are you doing?" I demanded, shoving hard against his chest. Earl or no, I'd box his ears for him for his trouble, and he wouldn't be the first, nor the last. "Let me go!"

"Stay, stay, I beg you, for a moment," he said, drawing me closer. "I'm supposed to be at Oxford, and the king will have my head if he finds me here. Come now, lass, help me hide in plain sight!"

Before I could answer, he'd pushed me back into the crook of his arm and was kissing me hard, and no amount of scuffling would make him stop. I'll grant he kissed better than most whelps his age, but I was in no humor for it, and the first moment I felt him relax, I jerked my mouth free of his.

"You base rogue!" I gasped, pulling my hand free to strike him. "I told you I'm no whore!"

He grabbed my hand and held it, while other men around us laughed and called encouragement to him. His face was flushed, I suppose from kissing me, but his gaze seemed strangely old for his age, as if he'd already seen too much of the world.

"I did not kiss you as a whore, pet," he said, "but as a friend. You saved me before the king, and I thank you for it."

"Bah, why should the king care what you do?" I said, and spat on the floor, to show both my contempt for him, and to cast away any remainder of his kiss from my lips. "What could you be to him?"

"My father was his last guide from England," he said softly, "and at the peril of his own freedom and life, led Charles from Cromwell's men to exile. When my father died, Charles declared himself my guardian, rather like a favorite uncle."

The earl's sudden solemnity intrigued me, making me forget my rage, even as I still sat perched upon his thighs. I didn't doubt his story was true. My own father had likewise been killed in the old king's service, and besides, Rochester had no reason to lie to me. "If you are so dear to him, then why do you avoid his company?"

"Because I've no wish to disappoint him, or risk losing his favor," he said, and smiled wryly. "I cannot give him any excuse not to call me to court. *That's* where my future will lie, in the brightest eye of the world, and not among dry old dons and pederasts. For the king to see me here, tending to my pleasures instead of my studies—that would not do. That wouldn't do at all."

"I wish he'd seen *me*, my lord!"

He frowned, turning his head a fraction to look at me askance. "What? You wish you'd been one of those giggling jades he hauled up the stairs?"

I shook my head, determined to make him understand. "My fate will be grander than that. You'll see. I won't be here forever. I'll have a future for myself that's every bit as bright as yours."

His smile was indulgent, yet skeptical. "A miss with ambition!"

"Aye, and where's the sin in that?" I demanded. "I can sing and dance and recite by rote any piece you please. And everyone says I'm more than passing fair."

"That you are," he said, and as if to prove my words, his hand slid from my waist to cover the sweet, round swell of my breast.

Impatiently I shoved his hand away. "I told you, I'll not be a common whore, rucking up my skirts against a wall in Covent Garden."

He laughed, as if he'd been expecting me to rebuff him anyway. "There's no use saving yourself for His Majesty," he said, not unkindly. "He's no taste for virgin flesh, you know."

"Did ever I say I was?" I asked, though of course that very desire had long been in my heart. "I mean to make all London speak of me, and rise as high as I can in this world. Then the king will seek my company, and the rest of the court besides."

The earl leaned his face closer to mine, so close his long curls did mingle with my own. "Then let me confide the first lesson of the court, my sweet Nell. If you truly wish to rise to such heights, you must take care to please and favor those who hold the rungs steady beneath your feet as you climb."

I narrowed my eyes, and lightly tapped my forefinger twice across his lips. "I am sorry, my lord, but I must disobey your lesson, just as you have disobeyed your tutors. For I mean to continue as I've already begun, and please only myself—me, Nellie Gwyn!—and not give so much as a kiss your hand for the rest."

"Kiss your hand, you say." He gave an odd little smile, one I'd come to know better in time. "Ah, Nell, in truth then there's little left for me to teach you. You've already learned the hardest lesson, haven't you? If you can but please yourself as you say, then Fame shall always be your willing subject, and the court your servant."

"And so long as *you* make pretty speeches like that one, my lord," I said, kissing his cheek, "then I vow you'll find fat success at court, too."

He laughed at that, and I with him, a careless scrap of wit between us. Why should it be any more? We were much alike, despite the difference in our rank and place, and of the age for such foolishness. The Earl of Rochester was but fifteen, and I scarce more than twelve. Yet before the year was done, we'd each of us learn that fame came always linked to peril and bright fortune twined with danger, and as for the true cost of being a favorite of the King of England—ahh, we learned that lesson soon enough, too.

And so, my friend, shall you. . . .